# TIMELINE

Michael Crichton was born in Chicago in 1942. His novels include *The Andromeda Strain*, *The Great Train Robbery*, *Congo*, *Jurassic Park*, and *Disclosure*. He is also the creator of the televison series *ER*.

For more information on *Timeline* and other books by Michael Crichton, please visit www.crichton-official.com

*Timeline* is also available from Random House Audiobooks

## ALSO BY MICHAEL CRICHTON

*Fiction*

The Andromeda Strain
The Terminal Man
The Great Train Robbery
Eaters of the Dead
Congo
Sphere
Jurassic Park
Rising Sun
Disclosure
The Lost World
Airframe

*Nonfiction*

Five Patients
Jasper Johns
Electronic Life
Travels

# TIMELINE

## Michael Crichton

arrow books

Published by Arrow Books in 2003

1 3 5 7 9 10 8 6 4 2

Copyright © Michael Crichton 1999

Michael Crichton has asserted his right under the Copyright, Designs and
Patents Act, 1988 to be identified as the author of this work.

This novel is a work of fiction. Names and characters are the product of the
author's imagination and any resemblance to actual persons, living or dead,
is entirely coincidental

This book is sold subject to the condition that it shall not, by way of trade or
otherwise, be lent, resold, hired out, or otherwise circulated without the pub-
lisher's prior consent in any form of binding or cover other than that in
which it is published and without a similar condition including this condition being imposed on the subsequent purchaser

First published in the United Kingdom in 1999 by Century

Arrow Books Limited
The Random House Group Ltd
20 Vauxhall Bridge Road, London, SW1V2SA

Random House Australia (Pty) Limited
20 Alfred Street, Milsons Point, Sydney,
New South Wales 2061, Australia

Random House New Zealand Limited
18 Poland Road, Glenfield
Auckland 10, New Zealand

Random House (Pty) Limited
Endulini, 5a Jubilee Road, Parktown 2193, South Africa

The Random House Group Limited Reg. No. 954009
www.randomhouse.co.uk

A CIP catalogue record for this book
is available from the British Library

Papers used by Random House are natural, recyclable products made from
wood grown in sustainable forests. The manufacturing processes conform to
the environmental regulations of the country of origin.

ISBN 0 09 945792 X

Printed and bound in Australia
by Griffin Press

*For Taylor*

"All the great empires of the future will be empires of the mind."

WINSTON CHURCHILL, 1953

"If you don't know history, you don't know anything."

EDWARD JOHNSTON, 1990

"I'm not interested in the future. I'm interested in the future of the future."

ROBERT DONIGER, 1996

# INTRODUCTION

*Science at the End of the Century*

A hundred years ago, as the nineteenth century drew to a close, scientists around the world were satisfied that they had arrived at an accurate picture of the physical world. As physicist Alastair Rae put it, "By the end of the nineteenth century it seemed that the basic fundamental principles governing the behavior of the physical universe were known."* Indeed, many scientists said that the study of physics was nearly completed: no big discoveries remained to be made, only details and finishing touches.

But late in the final decade, a few curiosities came to light. Roentgen discovered rays that passed through flesh; because they were unexplained, he called them X rays. Two months later, Henri Becquerel accidentally found that a piece of uranium ore emitted something that fogged photographic plates. And the electron, the carrier of electricity, was discovered in 1897.

Yet on the whole, physicists remained calm, expecting that these oddities would eventually be explained by existing theory. No one would have predicted that within five years their complacent view of the world would be shockingly upended, producing an entirely new conception of the universe and entirely new technologies that would transform daily life in the twentieth century in unimaginable ways.

If you were to say to a physicist in 1899 that in 1999, a hundred years later, moving images would be transmitted into

*Alastair I. M. Rae, *Quantum Physics: Illusion or Reality?* (Cambridge, Eng.: Cambridge University Press, 1994). See also Richard Feynman, *The Character of Physical Law* (Cambridge, Mass.: MIT Press, 1965). Also Rae, *Quantum Mechanics* (Bristol, Eng.: Hilger, 1986).

homes all over the world from satellites in the sky; that bombs of unimaginable power would threaten the species; that antibiotics would abolish infectious disease but that disease would fight back; that women would have the vote, and pills to control reproduction; that millions of people would take to the air every hour in aircraft capable of taking off and landing without human touch; that you could cross the Atlantic at two thousand miles an hour; that humankind would travel to the moon, and then lose interest; that microscopes would be able to see individual atoms; that people would carry telephones weighing a few ounces, and speak anywhere in the world without wires; or that most of these miracles depended on devices the size of a postage stamp, which utilized a new theory called quantum mechanics—if you said all this, the physicist would almost certainly pronounce you mad.

Most of these developments could not have been predicted in 1899, because prevailing scientific theory said they were impossible. And for the few developments that were not impossible, such as airplanes, the sheer scale of their eventual use would have defied comprehension. One might have imagined an airplane—but ten thousand airplanes in the air at the same time would have been beyond imagining.

So it is fair to say that even the most informed scientists, standing on the threshold of the twentieth century, had no idea what was to come.

:

Now that we stand on the threshold of the twenty-first century, the situation is oddly similar. Once again, physicists believe the physical world has been explained, and that no further revolutions lie ahead. Because of prior history, they no longer express this view publicly, but they think it just the same. Some observers have even gone so far as to argue that science as a discipline has finished its work; that there is nothing important left for science to discover.*

---

*John Horgan, *The End of Science* (New York: Addison-Wesley, 1996). See also Gunther Stent, *Paradoxes of Progress* (New York: W. H. Freeman, 1978).

But just as the late nineteenth century gave hints of what was to come, so the late twentieth century also provides some clues to the future. One of the most important is the interest in so-called quantum technology. This is an effort on many fronts to create a new technology that utilizes the fundamental nature of subatomic reality, and it promises to revolutionize our ideas of what is possible.

Quantum technology flatly contradicts our common sense ideas of how the world works. It posits a world where computers operate without being turned on and objects are found without looking for them. An unimaginably powerful computer can be built from a single molecule. Information moves instantly between two points, without wires or networks. Distant objects are examined without any contact. Computers do their calculations in other universes. And teleportation— "Beam me up, Scotty"—is ordinary and used in many different ways.

In the 1990s, research in quantum technology began to show results. In 1995, quantum ultrasecure messages were sent over a distance of eight miles, suggesting that a quantum Internet would be built in the coming century. In Los Alamos, physicists measured the thickness of a human hair using laser light that was never actually shone on the hair, but only *might* have been. This bizarre, "counterfactual" result initiated a new field of interaction-free detection: what has been called "finding something without looking."

And in 1998, quantum teleportation was demonstrated in three laboratories around the world—in Innsbruck, in Rome and at Cal Tech.* Physicist Jeff Kimble, leader of the Cal Tech team, said that quantum teleportation could be applied to solid objects: "The quantum state of one entity could be transported to another entity. . . . We think we know how to do that."† Kimble stopped well short of suggesting they

---

*Dik Bouwmeester et al., "Experimental Quantum Teleportation, *Nature* 390 (11 Dec. 1997): 575–9.

†Maggie Fox, "Spooky Teleportation Study Brings Future Closer," Reuters, 22 Oct. 1998. For Jeffrey R. Kimble, see A. Furusawa et al., "Unconditional Quantum Teleportation," *Science* 282 (23 Oct. 1998): 706–9.

could teleport a human being, but he imagined that someone might try with a bacterium.

These quantum curiosities, defying logic and common sense, have received little attention from the public, but they will. According to some estimates, by the first decades of the new century, the majority of physicists around the world will work in some aspect of quantum technology.*

∴

It is therefore not surprising that during the mid-1990s, several corporations undertook quantum research. Fujitsu Quantum Devices was established in 1991. IBM formed a quantum research team in 1993, under pioneer Charles Bennett.[†] ATT and other companies soon followed, as did universities such as Cal Tech, and government facilities like Los Alamos. And so did a New Mexico research company called ITC. Located only an hour's drive from Los Alamos, ITC made remarkable strides very early in the decade. Indeed, it is now clear that ITC was the first company to have a practical, working application employing advanced quantum technology, in 1998.

In retrospect, it was a combination of peculiar circumstances—and considerable luck—that gave ITC the lead in a dramatic new technology. Although the company took the position that their discoveries were entirely benign, their so-called recovery expedition showed the dangers only too clearly. Two people died, one vanished, and another suffered serious injuries. Certainly, for the young graduate students who undertook the expedition, this new quantum technology, harbinger of the twenty-first century, proved anything but benign.

---

*Colin P. Williams and Scott H. Clearwater, *Explorations in Quantum Computing* (New York: Springer-Verlag, 1998). See also Gerard J. Milburn, *Schrödinger's Machines* (New York: W. H. Freeman, 1997) and *The Feynman Processor* (Reading, Mass.: Perseus, 1998).

[†]C. H. Bennett et al., "Teleporting an Unknown Quantum State via Dual Classical and Einstein-Podolsky-Rosen Channels," *Physical Review Letters* 70 (1993): 1895.

A typical episode of private warfare occurred in 1357. Sir Oliver de Vannes, an English knight of nobility and character, had taken over the towns of Castelgard and La Roque, along the Dordogne River. By all accounts, this "borrowed lord" ruled with honest dignity, and was beloved by the people. In April, Sir Oliver's lands were invaded by a rampaging company of two thousand *brigandes*, renegade knights under the command of Arnaut de Cervole, a defrocked monk known as "the Archpriest." After burning Castelgard to the ground, Cervole razed the nearby Monastery of Sainte-Mère, murdering monks and destroying the famed water mill on the Dordogne. Cervole then pursued Sir Oliver to the fortress of La Roque, where a terrible battle followed.

Oliver defended his castle with skill and daring. Contemporary accounts credit Oliver's efforts to his military adviser, Edwardus de Johnes. Little is known of this man, around whom a Merlin-like mythology grew up: it was said he could vanish in a flash of light. The chronicler Audreim says Johnes came from Oxford, but other accounts say he was Milanese. Since he traveled with a team of young assistants, he was most likely an itinerant expert, hiring himself out to whoever paid for his services. He was schooled in the use of gunpowder and artillery, a technology new at that time. . . .

Ultimately, Oliver lost his impregnable castle when a spy opened an inside passage, allowing the Archpriest's soldiers to enter. Such betrayals were typical of the complex intrigues of that time.

From *The Hundred Years War in France*
by M. D. Backes, 1996

# TIMELINE

# CORAZÓN

"Anyone who is not shocked by quantum theory
does not understand it."

"Nobody understands quantum theory."

He should never have taken that shortcut.

Dan Baker winced as his new Mercedes S500 sedan bounced down the dirt road, heading deeper into the Navajo reservation in northern Arizona. Around them, the landscape was increasingly desolate: distant red mesas to the east, flat desert stretching away in the west. They had passed a village half an hour earlier—dusty houses, a church and a small school, huddled against a cliff—but since then, they'd seen nothing at all, not even a fence. Just empty red desert. They hadn't seen another car for an hour. Now it was noon, the sun glaring down at them. Baker, a forty-year-old building contractor in Phoenix, was beginning to feel uneasy. Especially since his wife, an architect, was one of those artistic people who wasn't practical about things like gas and water. His tank was half-empty. And the car was starting to run hot.

"Liz," he said, "are you sure this is the way?"

Sitting beside him, his wife was bent over the map, tracing the route with her finger. "It has to be," she said. "The guidebook said four miles beyond the Corazón Canyon turnoff."

"But we passed Corazón Canyon twenty minutes ago. We must have missed it."

"How could we miss a trading post?" she said.

"I don't know." Baker stared at the road ahead. "But there's nothing out here. Are you sure you want to do this? I mean, we can get great Navajo rugs in Sedona. They sell all kinds of rugs in Sedona."

"Sedona," she sniffed, "is not authentic."

"Of course it's authentic, honey. A rug is a rug."

"Weaving."

"Okay." He sighed. "A weaving."

"And no, it's not the same," she said. "Those Sedona stores carry tourist junk—they're acrylic, not wool. I want the weavings that they sell on the reservation. And supposedly the trading post has an old Sandpainting weaving from the twenties, by Hosteen Klah. And I want it."

"Okay, Liz." Personally, Baker didn't see why they needed another Navajo rug—weaving—anyway. They already had two dozen. She had them all over the house. And packed away in closets, too.

They drove on in silence. The road ahead shimmered in the heat, so it looked like a silver lake. And there were mirages, houses or people rising up on the road, but always when you came closer, there was nothing there.

Dan Baker sighed again. "We must've passed it."

"Let's give it a few more miles," his wife said.

"How many more?"

"I don't know. A few more."

"How many, Liz? Let's decide how far we'll go with this thing."

"Ten more minutes," she said.

"Okay," he said, "ten minutes."

He was looking at his gas gauge when Liz threw her hand to her mouth and said, "Dan!" Baker turned back to the road just in time to see a shape flash by—a man, in brown, at the side of the road—and hear a loud thump from the side of the car.

"Oh my God!" she said. "We hit him!"

"What?"

"We hit that guy."

"No, we didn't. We hit a pothole."

In the rearview mirror, Baker could see the man still standing at the side of the road. A figure in brown, rapidly disappearing in the dust cloud behind the car as they drove away.

"We couldn't have hit him," Baker said. "He's still standing."

"Dan. We hit him. I saw it."

"I don't think so, honey."

Baker looked again in the rearview mirror. But now he saw nothing except the cloud of dust behind the car.

"We better go back," she said.

"Why?"

Baker was pretty sure that his wife was wrong and that they hadn't hit the man on the road. But if they had hit him, and if he was even slightly injured—just a head cut, a scratch—then it was going to mean a very long delay in their trip. They'd never get to Phoenix by nightfall. Anybody out here was undoubtedly a Navajo; they'd have to take him to a hospital, or at least to the nearest big town, which was Gallup, and that was out of their way—

"I thought you wanted to go back," she said.

"I do."

"Then let's go back."

"I just don't want any problems, Liz."

"Dan. I don't believe this."

He sighed, and slowed the car. "Okay, I'm turning. I'm turning."

And he turned around, being careful not to get stuck in the red sand at the side of the road, and headed back the way they had come.

:

"Oh Jesus."

Baker pulled over, and jumped out into the dust cloud of his own car. He gasped as he felt the blast of heat on his face and body. It must be 120 degrees out here, he thought.

As the dust cleared, he saw the man lying at the side of the road, trying to raise himself up on his elbow. The guy was shaky, about seventy, balding and bearded. His skin was pale; he didn't look Navajo. His brown clothes were fashioned into long robes. Maybe he's a priest, Baker thought.

"Are you all right?" Baker said as he helped the man to sit up on the dirt road.

The old man coughed. "Yeah. I'm all right."

"Do you want to stand up?" he said. He was relieved not to see any blood.

"In a minute."

Baker looked around. "Where's your car?" he said.

The man coughed again. Head hanging limply, he stared at the dirt road.

"Dan, I think he's hurt," his wife said.

"Yeah," Baker said. The old guy certainly seemed to be confused. Baker looked around again: there was nothing but flat desert in all directions, stretching away into shimmering haze.

No car. Nothing.

"How'd he get out here?" Baker said.

"Come on," Liz said, "we have to take him to a hospital."

Baker put his hands under the man's armpits and helped the old guy to his feet. The man's clothes were heavy, made of a material like felt, but he wasn't sweating in the heat. In fact, his body felt cool, almost cold.

The old guy leaned heavily on Baker as they crossed the road. Liz opened the back door. The old man said, "I can walk. I can talk."

"Okay. Fine." Baker eased him into the back seat.

The man lay down on the leather, curling into a fetal position. Underneath his robes, he was wearing ordinary clothes: jeans, a checked shirt, Nikes. He closed the door, and Liz got back in the front seat. Baker hesitated, remaining outside in the heat. How was it possible the old guy was out here all alone? Wearing all those clothes and not sweating?

It was as if he had just stepped out of a car.

So maybe he'd been driving, Baker thought. Maybe he'd fallen asleep. Maybe his car had gone off the road and he'd had an accident. Maybe there was someone else still trapped in the car.

He heard the old guy muttering, "Left it, heft it. Go back now, get it now, and how."

Baker crossed the road to have a look. He stepped over a very large pothole, considered showing it to his wife, then decided not to.

Off the road, he didn't see any tire tracks, but he saw clearly the old man's footprints in the sand. The footprints ran back from the road into the desert. Thirty yards away, Baker saw the rim of an arroyo, a ravine cut into the landscape. The footprints seemed to come from there.

So he followed the footsteps back to the arroyo, stood at the edge, and looked down into it. There was no car. He saw nothing but a snake, slithering away from him among the rocks. He shivered.

Something white caught his eye, glinting in the sunlight a few feet down the slope. Baker scrambled down for a better look. It was a piece of white ceramic about an inch square. It looked like an electrical insulator. Baker picked it up, and was surprised to find it was cool to the touch. Maybe it was one of those new materials that didn't absorb heat.

Looking closely at the ceramic, he saw the letters ITC stamped on one edge. And there was a kind of button, recessed in the side. He wondered what would happen if he pushed the button. Standing in the heat, with big boulders all around him, he pushed it.

Nothing happened.

He pushed it again. Again nothing.

Baker climbed out of the ravine and went back to the car. The old guy was sleeping, snoring loudly. Liz was looking at the maps. "Nearest big town is Gallup."

Baker started the engine. "Gallup it is."

:

Back on the main highway, they made better time, heading south to Gallup. The old guy was still sleeping. Liz looked at him and said, "Dan . . ."

"What?"

"You see his hands?"

"What about them?"

"The fingertips."

Baker looked away from the road, glanced quickly into the back seat. The old guy's fingertips were red to the second knuckle. "So? He's sunburned."

"Just on the tips? Why not the whole hand?"

Baker shrugged.

"His fingers weren't like that before," she said. "They weren't red when we picked him up."

"Honey, you probably just didn't notice them."

"I did notice, because he had a manicure. And I thought it was interesting that some old guy in the desert would have a manicure."

"Uh-huh." Baker glanced at his watch. He wondered how long they would have to stay at the hospital in Gallup. Hours, probably.

He sighed.

The road continued straight ahead.

Halfway to Gallup, the old guy woke up. He coughed and said, "Are we there? Are we where?"

"How are you feeling?" Liz said.

"Feeling? I'm reeling. Fine, just fine."

"What's your name?" Liz said.

The man blinked at her. "The quondam phone made me roam."

"But what's your name?"

The man said, "Name same, blame game."

Baker said, "He's rhyming everything."

She said, "I noticed, Dan."

"I saw a TV show on this," Baker said. "Rhyming means he's schizophrenic."

"Rhyming is timing," the old man said. And then he began to sing loudly, almost shouting to the tune of the old John Denver song:

> "Quondam phone, makes me roam,
> to the place I belong,
> old Black Rocky, country byway,
> quondam phone, it's on roam."

"Oh boy," Baker said.

"Sir," Liz said again, "can you tell me your name?"

"Niobium may cause opprobrium. Hairy singularities don't permit parities."

Baker sighed. "Honey, this guy is nuts."

"A nut by any other name would smell like feet."

9

But his wife wouldn't give up. "Sir? Do you know your name?"

"Call Gordon," the man said, shouting now. "Call Gordon, call Stanley. Keep in the family."

"But, sir—"

"Liz," Baker said, "leave him alone. Let him settle down, okay? We still have a long drive."

Bellowing, the old man sang: "To the place I belong, old black magic, it's so tragic, country foam, makes me groan." And immediately, he started to sing it again.

"How much farther?" Liz said.

"Don't ask."

:

He telephoned ahead, so when he pulled the Mercedes under the red-and-cream-colored portico of the McKinley Hospital Trauma Unit, the orderlies were waiting there with a gurney. The old man remained passive as they eased him onto the gurney, but as soon as they began to strap him down, he became agitated, shouting, "Unhand me, unband me!"

"It's for your own safety, sir," one orderly said.

"So you say, out of my way! Safety is the last refuge of the scoundrel!"

Baker was impressed by the way the orderlies handled the guy, gently but still firmly, strapping him down. He was equally impressed by the petite dark-haired woman in a white coat who fell into step with them. "I'm Beverly Tsosie," she said, shaking hands with them. "I'm the physician on call." She was very calm, even though the man on the gurney continued to yell as they wheeled him into the trauma center. "Quondam phone, makes me roam. . . ."

Everybody in the waiting room was looking at him. Baker saw a young kid of ten or eleven, his arm in a sling, sitting in a chair with his mother, watching the old man curiously. The kid whispered something to his mother.

The old guy sang, "To the plaaaaace I belongggg. . . ."

Dr. Tsosie said, "How long has he been this way?"

"From the beginning. Ever since we picked him up."

"Except when he was sleeping," Liz said.

"Was he ever unconscious?"

"No."

"Any nausea, vomiting?"

"No."

"And you found him where? Out past Corazón Canyon?"

"About five, ten miles beyond."

"Not much out there," she said.

"You know it?" Baker said.

"I grew up around there." She smiled slightly. "Chinle."

They wheeled the old man, still shouting, through a swinging door. Dr. Tsosie said, "If you'll wait here, I'll get back to you as soon as I know something. It'll probably be a while. You might want to go get lunch."

:

Beverly Tsosie had a staff position at University Hospital in Albuquerque, but lately she'd been coming to Gallup two days a week to be with her elderly grandmother, and on those days she worked a shift in the McKinley Trauma Unit to make extra money. She liked McKinley, with its modern exterior painted in bold red and cream stripes. The hospital was really dedicated to the community. And she liked Gallup, a smaller town than Albuquerque, and a place where she felt more comfortable with a tribal background.

Most days, the Trauma Unit was pretty quiet. So the arrival of this old man, agitated and shouting, was causing a lot of commotion. She pushed through the curtains into the cubicle, where the orderlies had already stripped off the brown felt robes and removed his Nikes. But the old man was still struggling, fighting them, so they had to leave him strapped down. They were cutting his jeans and the plaid shirt away.

Nancy Hood, the senior unit nurse, said it didn't matter because his shirt had a big defect anyway; across the pocket there ran a jagged line where the pattern didn't match. "He already tore it and sewed it back together. You ask me, pretty lousy job, too."

"No," said one of the orderlies, holding up the shirt. "It's never been sewn together, it's all one piece of cloth. Weird, the pattern doesn't line up because one side is bigger than the other. . . ."

"Whatever, he won't miss it," Nancy Hood said, and tossed it on the floor. She turned to Tsosie. "You want to try and examine him?"

The man was far too wild. "Not yet. Let's get an IV in each arm. And go through his pockets. See if he's got any identification at all. If he doesn't, take his fingerprints and fax them to D.C.; maybe he'll show up on a database there."

:

Twenty minutes later, Beverly Tsosie was examining a kid who had broken his arm sliding into third. He was a bespectacled, nerdy-looking kid, and he seemed almost proud of his sports injury.

Nancy Hood came over and said, "We searched the John Doe."

"And?"

"Nothing helpful. No wallet, no credit cards, no keys. The only thing he had on him was this." She gave Beverly a folded piece of paper. It looked like a computer printout, and showed an odd pattern of dots in a gridlike pattern. At the bottom was written "mon. ste. mere."

" 'Monstemere?' Does that mean anything to you?"

Hood shook her head. "You ask me, he's psychotic."

Beverly Tsosie said, "Well, I can't sedate him until we know what's going on in his head. Better get skull films to rule out trauma and hematoma."

"Radiology's being remodeled, remember, Bev? X rays'll take forever. Why don't you do an MRI? Scan total body, you have it all."

"Order it," Tsosie said.

Nancy Hood turned to leave. "Oh, and surprise, surprise. Jimmy is here, from the police."

:

Dan Baker was restless. Just as he predicted, they'd had to spend hours sitting around the waiting room of McKinley Hospital. After they got lunch—burritos in red chile sauce—they had come back to see a policeman in the parking lot, looking over their car, running his hand along the side door panel. Just seeing him gave Baker a chill. He thought of going over to the cop but decided not to. Instead, they returned to the waiting room. He called his daughter and said they'd be late; in fact, they might not even get to Phoenix until tomorrow.

And they waited. Finally, around four o'clock, when Baker went to the desk to inquire about the old man, the woman said, "Are you a relative?"

"No, but—"

"Then please wait over there. Doctor will be with you shortly."

He went back and sat down, sighing. He got up again, walked over to the window, and looked at his car. The cop had gone, but now there was a fluttering tag under the windshield wiper. Baker drummed his fingers on the windowsill. These little towns, you get in trouble, anything could happen. And the longer he waited, the more his mind spun scenarios. The old guy was in a coma; they couldn't leave town until he woke up. The old guy died; they were charged with manslaughter. They weren't charged, but they had to appear at the inquest, in four days.

When somebody finally came to talk to them, it wasn't the petite doctor, it was the cop. He was a young policeman in his twenties, in a neatly pressed uniform. He had long hair, and his nametag said JAMES WAUNEKA. Baker wondered what kind of a name that was. Hopi or Navajo, probably.

"Mr. and Mrs. Baker?" Wauneka was very polite, introduced himself. "I've just been with the doctor. She's finished her examination, and the MRI results are back. There's absolutely no evidence he was struck by a car. And I looked at your car myself. No sign of any impact. I think you may have hit a pothole and just thought you hit him. Road's pretty bad out there."

Baker glared at his wife, who refused to meet his eye. Liz said, "Is he going to be all right?"

"Looks like it, yes."

"Then we can go?" Baker said.

"Honey," Liz said, "don't you want to give him that thing you found?"

"Oh, yes." Baker brought out the little ceramic square. "I found this, near where he was."

The cop turned the ceramic over in his hands. "ITC," he said, reading the stamp on the side. "Where exactly did you find this?"

"About thirty yards from the road. I thought he might have been in a car that went off the road, so I checked. But there was no car."

"Anything else?"

"No. That's all."

"Well, thanks," Wauneka said, slipping the ceramic in his pocket. And then he paused. "Oh, I almost forgot." He took a piece of paper out of his pocket and unfolded it carefully. "We found this in his clothing. I wondered if you had ever seen it."

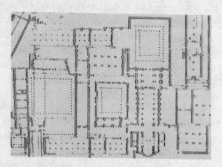

Baker glanced at the paper: a bunch of dots arranged in grids. "No," he said. "I've never seen it before."

"You didn't give it to him?"

"No."

"Any idea what it might be?"

"No," Baker said. "No idea at all."

"Well, I think I do," his wife said.

"You do?" the cop said.

"Yes," she said. "Do you mind if I, uh . . ." And she took the paper from the policeman.

Baker sighed. Now Liz was being the architect, squinting at the paper judiciously, turning it this way and that, looking at the dots upside down and sideways. Baker knew why. She was trying to distract attention from the fact that she had been wrong, that his car *had* hit a pothole, after all, and that they had wasted a whole day here. She was trying to justify a waste of time, to somehow give it importance.

"Yes," she said finally, "I know what it is. It's a church."

Baker looked at the dots on the paper. He said, "That's a church?"

"Well, the floor plan for one," she said. "See? Here's the long axis of the cross, the nave. . . . See? It's definitely a church, Dan. And the rest of this image, the squares within squares, all rectilinear, it looks like . . . you know, this might be a monastery."

The cop said, "A monastery?"

"I think so," she said. "And what about the label at the bottom: 'mon.ste.mere.' Isn't 'mon' an abbreviation for monastery? I bet it is. I'm telling you, I think this is a monastery." She handed the picture back to the cop.

Pointedly, Baker looked at his watch. "We really should be going."

"Of course," Wauneka said, taking the hint. He shook hands with them. "Thanks for all your help. Sorry for the delay. Have a pleasant trip."

Baker put his arm firmly around his wife's waist and led her out into the afternoon sunlight. It was cooler now; hot-air balloons were rising to the east. Gallup was a center for hot-air ballooning. He went to the car. The fluttering tag on the windshield was for a sale of turquoise jewelry at a local store. He pulled it from behind the wiper, crumpled it, and got behind the wheel. His wife was sitting with her arms crossed over her chest, staring forward. He started the engine.

She said, "Okay. I'm sorry." Her tone was grumpy, but Baker knew it was all he would get.

He leaned over and kissed her cheek. "No," he said. "You did the right thing. We saved the old guy's life."

His wife smiled.

He drove out of the parking lot, and headed for the highway.

In the hospital, the old man slept, his face partly covered by an oxygen mask. He was calm now; she'd given him a light sedative, and he was relaxed, his breathing easy. Beverly Tsosie stood at the foot of the bed, reviewing the case with Joe Nieto, a Mescalero Apache who was a skilled internist, and a very good diagnostician. "White male, ballpark seventy years old. Comes in confused, obtunded, disoriented times three. Mild congestive heart failure, slightly elevated liver enzymes, otherwise nothing."

"And they didn't hit him with the car?"

"Apparently not. But it's funny. They say they found him wandering around north of Corazón Canyon. There's nothing there for ten miles in any direction."

"So?"

"This guy's got no signs of exposure, Joe. No dehydration, no ketosis. He isn't even sunburned."

"You think somebody dumped him? Got tired of grandpa grabbing the remote?"

"Yeah. That's my guess."

"And what about his fingers?"

"I don't know," she said. "He has some kind of circulatory problem. His fingertips are cold, turning purple, they could even go gangrenous. Whatever it is, it's gotten worse since he's been in the hospital."

"He diabetic?"

"No."

"Raynaud's?"

"No."

17

Nieto went over to the bedside, looked at the fingers. "Only the tips are involved. All the damage is distal."

"Right," she said. "If he wasn't found in the desert, I'd call that frostbite."

"You check him for heavy metals, Bev? Because this could be toxic exposure to heavy metals. Cadmium, or arsenic. That would explain the fingers, and also his dementia."

"I drew the samples. But heavy metals go to UNH in Albuquerque. I won't have the report back for seventy-two hours."

"You have any ID, medical history, anything?"

"Nothing. We put a missing persons out on him, and we transmitted his fingerprints to Washington for a database check, but that could take a week."

Nieto nodded. "And when he was agitated, babbling? What'd he say?"

"It was all rhymes, the same things over. Something about Gordon and Stanley. And then he would say, 'Quondam phone makes me roam.' "

"Quondam? Isn't that Latin?"

She shrugged. "It's a long time since I was in church."

"I think quondam is a word in Latin," Nieto said.

And then they heard a voice say, "Excuse me?" It was the bespectacled kid in the bed across the hall, sitting with his mother.

"We're still waiting for the surgeon to come in, Kevin," Beverly said to him. "Then we can set your arm."

"He wasn't saying 'quondam phone,' " the kid said. "He was saying 'quantum foam.' "

"What?"

"Quantum foam. He was saying 'quantum foam.' "

They went over to him. Nieto seemed amused. "And what, exactly, is quantum foam?"

The kid looked at them earnestly, blinking behind his glasses. "At very small, subatomic dimensions, the structure of space-time is irregular. It's not smooth, it's sort of bubbly and foamy. And because it's way down at the quantum level, it's called quantum foam."

"How old are you?" Nieto said.

"Eleven."

His mother said, "He reads a lot. His father's at Los Alamos."

Nieto nodded. "And what's the point of this quantum foam, Kevin?"

"There isn't any point," the kid said. "It's just how the universe is, at the subatomic level."

"Why would this old guy be talking about it?"

"Because he's a well-known physicist," Wauneka said, coming toward them. He glanced at a sheet of paper in his hand. "It just came in on the M.P.D. Joseph A. Traub, seventy-one years old, materials physicist. Specialist in super-conducting metals. Reported missing by his employer, ITC Research in Black Rock, around noon today."

"Black Rock? That's way over near Sandia." It was several hours away, in central New Mexico. "How the hell did this guy get to Corazón Canyon in Arizona?"

"I don't know," Beverly said. "But he's—"

The alarms began to sound.

∴

It happened with a swiftness that stunned Jimmy Wauneka. The old man raised his head from the bed, stared at them, eyes wild, and then he vomited blood. His oxygen mask turned bright red; blood spurted past the mask, running in streaks across his cheeks and chin, spattering the pillow, the wall. He made a gurgling sound: he was drowning in his own blood.

Beverly was already running across the room. Wauneka ran after her. "Turn the head!" Nieto was saying, coming up to the bed. "Turn it!" Beverly had pulled off the oxygen mask and was trying to turn the old man's head, but he struggled, fighting her, still gurgling, eyes wide with panic. Wauneka pushed past her, grabbed the old man's head with both hands and wrenched hard, twisting him bodily to the side. The man vomited again; blood sprayed all over the monitors, and over Wauneka. "Suction!" Beverly shouted, pointing to a tube on the wall.

Wauneka tried to hold the old man and grab for the tube,

but the floor was slick with blood. He slipped, grabbed at the bed for support.

"Come *on*, people!" Tsosie shouted. "I need you! Suction!" She was on her knees, shoving her fingers in the man's mouth, pulling out his tongue. Wauneka scrambled to his feet, saw Nieto holding out a suction line. He grabbed it with blood-slippery fingers, and saw Nieto twist the wall valve. Beverly took the neoprene probe, started sucking out the guy's mouth and nose. Red blood ran up the tubes. The man gasped, coughed, but he was growing weaker.

"I don't like this," Beverly said, "we better—" The monitor alarms changed tone, high-pitched, steady. *Cardiac arrest.*

"Damn," she said. There was blood all over her jacket, her blouse. "Paddles! Get the paddles!"

Nieto was standing over the bed, holding the paddles in outstretched arms. Wauneka scrambled back from the bed as Nancy Hood pushed her way through; there were people clustered all around the man now. Wauneka smelled a sharp odor and knew the man's bowels had released. He suddenly realized the old man was going to die.

"Clear," Nieto said as he pushed down on the paddles. The body jolted on the table. The bottles on the wall clattered. The monitor alarms continued.

Beverly said, "Close the curtain, Jimmy."

He looked back, and saw the bespectacled kid across the room, staring, his mouth open. Wauneka yanked the drapes shut.

·

An hour later, an exhausted Beverly Tsosie dropped down at a desk in the corner to write up the case summary. It would have to be unusually complete, because the patient had died. As she thumbed through the chart, Jimmy Wauneka came by with a cup of coffee for her. "Thanks," she said. "By the way, do you have the phone number for that ITC company? I have to call them."

"I'll do that for you," Wauneka said, resting his hand briefly on her shoulder. "You've had a tough day."

Before she could say anything, Wauneka had gone to the next desk, flipped open his notepad, and started dialing. He smiled at her as he waited for the call to go through.

"ITC Research."

He identified himself, then said, "I'm calling about your missing employee, Joseph Traub."

"One moment please, I'll connect you to our director of human resources."

He then waited on hold for several minutes. Muzak played. He cupped his hand over the phone, and as casually as he could, said to Beverly, "Are you free for dinner, or are you seeing your granny?"

She continued to write, not looking up from the chart. "I'm seeing Granny."

He gave a little shrug. "Just thought I'd ask," he said.

"But she goes to bed early. About eight o'clock."

"Is that right?"

She smiled, still looking down at her notes. "Yes."

Wauneka grinned. "Well, okay."

"Okay."

The phone clicked again and he heard a woman say, "Hold please, I am putting you through to our senior vice president, Dr. Gordon."

"Thank you." He thought, Senior vice president.

Another click, then a gravelly voice: "This is John Gordon speaking."

"Dr. Gordon, this is James Wauneka of the Gallup Police Department. I'm calling you from McKinley Hospital, in Gallup," he said. "I'm afraid I have some bad news."

Seen through the picture windows of the ITC conference room, the yellow afternoon sun gleamed off the five glass and steel laboratory buildings of the Black Rock research complex. In the distance, afternoon thunderclouds were forming over the far desert. But inside the room, the twelve ITC board members were turned away from the view. They were having coffee at a side table, talking to one another while they waited for the meeting to begin. Board meetings always ran into the night, because the ITC president, Robert Doniger, was a notorious insomniac and he scheduled them that way. It was a tribute to Doniger's brilliance that the board members, all CEOs and major venture capitalists, came anyway.

Right now, Doniger had yet to make an appearance. John Gordon, Doniger's burly vice president, thought he knew why. Still talking on a cell phone, Gordon began to make his way toward the door. At one time Gordon had been an Air Force project manager, and he still had a military bearing. His blue business suit was freshly pressed, and his black shoes shone. Holding his cell phone to his ear, he said, "I understand, Officer," and he slipped out the door.

Just as he had thought, Doniger was in the hallway, pacing up and down like a hyperactive kid, while Diane Kramer, ITC's head attorney, stood to one side and listened to him. Gordon saw Doniger jabbing his finger in the air at her angrily. Clearly, he was giving her hell.

:

Robert Doniger was thirty-eight years old, a brilliant physicist, and a billionaire. Despite a potbelly and gray hair, his manner remained youthful—or juvenile, depending on whom you talked to. Certainly age had not mellowed him. ITC was his third startup company; he had grown rich from the others, but his management style was as caustic and nasty as ever. Nearly everybody in the company feared him.

In deference to the board meeting, Doniger had put on a blue suit, forgoing his usual khakis and sweats. But he looked uncomfortable in the suit, like a boy whose parents had made him dress up.

"Well, thank you very much, Officer Wauneka," Gordon said into the cell phone. "We'll make all the arrangements. Yes. We'll do that immediately. Thank you again." Gordon flipped the phone shut, and turned to Doniger. "Traub's dead, and they've identified his body."

"Where?"

"Gallup. That was a cop calling from the ER."

"What do they think he died of?"

"They don't know. They think massive cardiac arrest. But there was a problem with his fingers. A circulatory problem. They're going to do an autopsy. It's required by law."

Doniger waved his hand, a gesture of irritable dismissal. "Big fucking deal. The autopsy won't show anything. Traub had transcription errors. They'll never figure it out. Why are you wasting my time with this shit?"

"One of your employees just died, Bob," Gordon said.

"That's true," Doniger said coldly. "And you know what? There's fuck all I can do about it. I feel sorry. Oh me oh my. Send some flowers. Just handle it, okay?"

:

At moments like this, Gordon would take a deep breath, and remind himself that Doniger was no different from most other aggressive young entrepreneurs. He would remind himself that behind the sarcasm, Doniger was nearly always right. And he would remind himself that in any case, Doniger had behaved this way all his life.

Robert Doniger had shown early signs of genius, taking up engineering textbooks while still in grade school. By the time he was nine, he could fix any electronic appliance—a radio, or a TV—fiddling with the vacuum tubes and wires until he got it working. When his mother expressed concern that he would electrocute himself, he told her, "Don't be an idiot." And when his favorite grandmother died, a dry-eyed Doniger informed his mother that the old lady still owed him twenty-seven dollars, and he expected her to make good on it.

After graduating summa cum laude in physics from Stanford at the age of eighteen, Doniger had gone to Fermilab, near Chicago. He quit after six months, telling the director of the lab that "particle physics is for jerkoffs." He returned to Stanford, where he worked in what he regarded as a more promising area: superconducting magnetism.

This was a time when scientists of all sorts were leaving the university to start companies to exploit their discoveries. Doniger left after a year to found TechGate, a company that made the components for precision chip etching that Doniger had invented in passing. When Stanford protested that he'd made these discoveries while working at the lab, Doniger said, "If you've got a problem, sue me. Otherwise shut up."

It was at TechGate that Doniger's harsh management style became famous. During meetings with his scientists, he'd sit in the corner, tipped precariously back in his chair, firing off questions. "What about this?" "Why aren't you doing that?" "What's the reason for this?" If the answer satisfied him, he'd say, "Maybe. . . ." That was the highest praise anyone ever got from Doniger. But if he didn't like the answer—and he usually didn't—he'd snarl, "Are you brain-dead?" "Do you *aspire* to be an idiot?" "Do you want to die stupid?" "You're not even a half-wit." When really annoyed, he threw pencils and notebooks, and screamed, "Assholes! You're all fucking assholes!"

TechGate employees put up with the tantrums of "Death March Doniger" because he was a brilliant physicist, better than they were; because he knew the problems his teams were facing; and because his criticisms were invariably on point.

Unpleasant as it was, this stinging style worked; TechGate made remarkable advances in two years.

In 1984, he sold his company for a hundred million dollars. That same year, *Time* magazine listed him as one of fifty people under the age of twenty-five "who will shape the rest of the century." The list also included Bill Gates and Steve Jobs.

:

"Goddamn it," Doniger said, turning to Gordon. "Do I have to do everything myself? Jesus. Where did they find Traub?"

"In the desert. On the Navajo reservation."

"Where, *exactly*?"

"All I know is, ten miles north of Corazón. Apparently there's not much out there."

"All right," Doniger said. "Then get Baretto from security to drive Traub's car out to Corazón, and leave it in the desert. Puncture a tire and walk away."

Diane Kramer cleared her throat. She was dark-haired, in her early thirties, dressed in a black suit. "I don't know about that, Bob," she said, in her best lawyerly tone. "You're tampering with evidence—"

"Of course I'm tampering with evidence! That's the whole point! Somebody's going to ask how Traub got out there. So leave his car for them to find."

"But we don't know exactly where—"

"It doesn't matter exactly where. Just do it."

"That means Baretto plus somebody else knows about this. . . ."

"And who gives a damn? Nobody. Just do it, Diane."

There was a short silence. Kramer stared at the floor, frowning, clearly still unhappy.

"Look," Doniger said, turning to Gordon. "You remember when Garman was going to get the contract and my old company wasn't? You remember the press leak?"

"I remember," Gordon said.

"You were so worried about it," Doniger said, smirking. He explained to Kramer: "Garman was a fat pig. Then he lost a

lot of weight because his wife put him on a diet. We leaked
that Garman had inoperable cancer and his company was
going to fold. He denied it, but nobody believed him, because
of the way he looked. We got the contract. I sent a big basket
of fruit to his wife." He laughed. "But the point is, nobody
ever traced the leak to us. All's fair, Diane. Business is business. Get the goddamn car out in the desert."

She nodded, but she was still looking at the floor.

"And then," Doniger said, "I want to know how the hell
Traub got into the transit room in the first place. Because he'd
already made too many trips, and he had accumulated too
many transcription defects. He was past his limit. He wasn't
supposed to make any more trips. He wasn't cleared for
transit. We have a lot of security around that room. So how'd
he get in?"

"We think he had a maintenance clearance, to work on the
machines," Kramer said. "He waited until evening, between
shifts, and took a machine. But we're checking all that now."

"I don't want you to *check* it," Doniger said sarcastically. "I
want you to *fix* it, Diane."

"We'll fix it, Bob."

"You better, goddamn it," Doniger said. "Because this
company now faces three significant problems. And Traub is
the least of them. The other two are major. Ultra, ultra,
major."

:

Doniger had always had a gift for the long view. Back in
1984, he had sold TechGate because he foresaw that computer chips were going to "hit the wall." At the time, this
seemed nonsensical. Computer chips were doubling in power
every eighteen months, while the cost was halved. But
Doniger recognized that these advances were made by cram-
ming components closer and closer together on the chip. It
couldn't go on forever. Eventually, circuits would be so
densely packed that the chips would melt from the heat. This
implied an upper limit on computer power. Doniger knew

that society would demand ever more raw computational power, but he didn't see any way to accomplish it.

Frustrated, he returned to an earlier interest, superconducting magnetism. He started a second company, Advanced Magnetics, which owned several patents essential for the new Magnetic Resonance Imaging machines that were starting to revolutionize medicine. Advanced Magnetics was paid a quarter of a million dollars in royalties for every MRI machine made. It was "a cash cow," Doniger once said, "and about as interesting as milking a cow." Bored and seeking new challenges, he sold out in 1988. He was then twenty-eight years old, and worth a billion dollars. But in his view, he had yet to make his mark.

The following year, 1989, he started ITC.

:

One of Doniger's heroes was the physicist Richard Feynman. In the early eighties, Feynman had speculated that it might be possible to build a computer using the quantum attributes of atoms. Theoretically, such a "quantum computer" would be billions and billions of times more powerful than any computer ever made. But Feynman's idea implied a genuinely new technology—a technology that had to be built from scratch, a technology that changed all the rules. Because nobody could see a practical way to build a quantum computer, Feynman's idea was soon forgotten.

But not by Doniger.

In 1989, Doniger set out to build the first quantum computer. The idea was so radical—and so risky—that he never publicly announced his intention. He blandly named his new company ITC, for International Technology Corporation. He set up his main offices in Geneva, drawing from the pool of physicists working at CERN.

For several years afterward, nothing was heard from Doniger, or his company. People assumed he had retired, if they thought of him at all. It was, after all, common for prominent high-tech entrepreneurs to drop from view, after they had made their fortunes.

In 1994, *Time* magazine made a list of twenty-five people under the age of forty who were shaping our world. Robert Doniger was not among them. No one cared; no one remembered.

That same year he moved ITC back to the United States, establishing a laboratory facility in Black Rock, New Mexico, one hour north of Albuquerque. A thoughtful observer might have noticed that he had again moved to a location with a pool of available physicists. But there were no observers, thoughtful or otherwise.

So no one noticed when during the 1990s, ITC grew steadily in size. More labs were built on the New Mexico site; more physicists were hired. Doniger's board of directors grew from six to twelve. All were CEOs of companies that had invested in ITC, or venture capitalists. All had signed draconian nondisclosure agreements requiring them to post a significant personal bond in escrow, to submit to a polygraph test on request, and to allow ITC to tap their phones without notice. In addition, Doniger demanded a minimum investment of $300 million. That was, he explained arrogantly, the cost of a seat on the board. "You want to know what I'm up to, you want to be a part of what we're doing here, it's a third of a billion dollars. Take it or leave it. I don't give a damn either way."

But of course he did. ITC had a fearsome burn rate: they had gone through more than $3 billion in the last nine years. And Doniger knew he was going to need more.

:

"Problem number one," Doniger said. "Our capitalization. We'll need another billion before we see daylight." He nodded toward the boardroom. "They won't come up with it. I have to get them to approve three new board members."

Gordon said, "That's a tough sell, in that room."

"I know it is," Doniger said. "They see the burn rate, and they want to know when it ends. They want to see concrete results. And that's what I am going to give them today."

"What concrete results?"

"A victory," Doniger said. "These dipshits are going to need a victory. Some exciting news about one of the projects."

Kramer sucked in her breath. Gordon said, "Bob, the projects are all long-term."

"One of them must be nearing completion. Say, the Dordogne?"

"It's not. I don't advise this approach."

"And I need a victory," Doniger said. "Professor Johnston has been out there in France with his Yalies for three years on our nickel. We ought to have something to show for it."

"Not yet, Bob. Anyway, we don't have all the land."

"We have enough of the land."

"Bob . . ."

"Diane will go. She can pressure them nicely."

"Professor Johnston won't like it."

"I'm sure Diane can handle Johnston."

One of the assistants opened the door to the conference room and looked into the hall. Doniger said, "In a goddamn minute!" But he immediately began walking toward the door.

He looked back at them over his shoulder and said, "Just do it!" And then he went into the room and closed the door.

:

Gordon walked with Kramer down the corridor. Her high heels clicked on the floor. Gordon glanced down and saw that beneath the very correct and corporate black Jil Sander suit, she was wearing black slingback heels. It was the classic Kramer look: seductive and unattainable at the same time.

Gordon said, "Did you know about this before?"

She nodded. "But not for long. He told me an hour ago."

Gordon said nothing. He suppressed his irritation. Gordon had been with Doniger for twelve years now, since Advanced Magnetics days. At ITC, he had run a major industrial research operation on two continents, employing dozens of physicists, chemists, computer scientists. He'd had to teach himself about superconducting metals, fractal compression, quantum qubits, and high-flow ion exchange. He'd been up to his neck in theoretical physicists—the very worst kind—and yet milestones were reached; development was on schedule; cost overruns were manageable. But despite his success, Doniger still never really confided in him.

Kramer, on the other hand, had always enjoyed a special relationship with Doniger. She had begun as an attorney in an outside law firm, doing work for the company. Doniger thought she was smart and classy, so he hired her. She was his girlfriend for the next year, and even though that was long over, he still listened to her. She'd been able to head off several potential disasters over the years.

"For ten years," Gordon said, "we've kept this technology quiet. When you think about it, it's a miracle. Traub was the first incident to get away from us. Fortunately, it ended up in the hands of some doofus cop, and it won't go any further. But if Doniger starts pushing in France, people might start to put things together. We've already got that reporter in Paris chasing us. Bob could blow this wide open."

"I know he's considered all that. That's the second big problem."

"Going public?"

"Yes. Having it all come out."

"He's not worried?"

"Yes, he's worried. But he seems to have a plan to deal with it."

"I hope so," Gordon said. "Because we can't always count on having a doofus cop sifting through our dirty laundry."

Officer James Wauneka came into McKinley Hospital the next morning, looking for Beverly Tsosie. He thought he would check the autopsy results on the old guy who had died. But they told him that Beverly had gone up to the third-floor Imaging Unit. So he went up there.

He found her in a small beige room adjacent to the white scanner. She was talking to Calvin Chee, the MRI technician. He was sitting at the computer console, flicking black-and-white images up, one after another. The images showed five round circles in a row. As Chee ran through the images, the circles got smaller and smaller.

"Calvin," she was saying. "It's impossible. It has to be an artifact."

"You ask me to review the data," he said, "and then you don't believe me? I'm telling you, Bev, it's not an artifact. It's real. Here, look at the other hand."

Chee tapped the keyboard, and now a horizontal oval appeared on the screen, with five pale circles inside it. "Okay? This is the palm of the left hand, seen in a midsection cut." He turned to Wauneka. "Pretty much what you'd see if you put your hand on a butcher block and chopped straight down through it."

"Very nice, Calvin."

"Well, I want everybody to be clear."

He turned back to the screen. "Okay, landmarks. Five round circles are the five palmar bones. These things here are tendons going to the fingers. Remember, the muscles that work the hand are mostly in the forearm. Okay. That little

31

circle is the radial artery, which brings blood to the hand through the wrist. Okay. Now, we move outward from the wrist, in cut sections." The images changed. The oval grew narrower, and one by one, the bones pulled apart, like an amoeba dividing. Now there were four circles. "Okay. Now we're out past the palm, and we see only the fingers. Small arteries within each finger, dividing as we go out, getting smaller, but you can still see them. See, here and here? Okay. Now moving out toward the fingertips, the bones get larger, that's the proximal digit, the knuckle . . . and now . . . watch the arteries, see how they go . . . section by section . . . and *now*."

Wauneka frowned. "It looks like a glitch. Like something jumped."

"Something *did* jump," Chee said. "The arterioles are offset. They don't line up. I'll show you again." He went to the previous section, then the next. It was clear—the circles of the tiny arteries seemed to hop sideways. "That's why the guy had gangrene in his fingers. He had no circulation be-cause his arterioles didn't line up. It's like a mismatch or something."

Beverly shook her head. "Calvin."

"I'm telling you. And not only that, it's other places in his body, too. Like in the heart. Guy died of massive coronary? No surprise, because the ventricular walls don't line up, either."

"From old scar tissue," she said, shaking her head. "Cal-vin, come on. He was seventy-one years old. Whatever was wrong with his heart, it worked for more than seventy years. Same with his hands. If this arteriole offset was actually pres-ent, his fingers would have dropped off years ago. But they didn't. Anyway, this was a new injury; it got worse while he was in the hospital."

"So what are you going to tell me, the machine is wrong?"

"It has to be. Isn't it true that you can get registration errors from hardware? And there are sometimes bugs in scaling software?"

"I checked the machine, Bev. It's fine."

She shrugged. "Sorry, I'm not buying it. You've got a problem somewhere. Look, if you're so sure you're right, go down to pathology and check the guy out in person."

"I tried," Chee said. "The body was already picked up."

"It was?" Wauneka said. "When?"

"Five o'clock this morning. Somebody from his company."

"Well, that company's way over by Sandia," Wauneka said. "Maybe they're still driving the body—"

"No." Chee shook his head. "Cremated this morning."

"Really? Where?"

"Gallup Mortuary."

"They cremated him here?" Wauneka said.

"I'm telling you," Chee said, "there's definitely something weird about this guy."

Beverly Tsosie crossed her arms over her chest. She looked at the two men. "There's nothing weird," she said. "His company did it that way because they could arrange it all by phone, long-distance. Call the mortuary, they come over and cremate him. Happens all the time, especially when there's no family. Now cut the crap," she said, "and call the repair techs to fix the machine. You have a problem with your MRI—and that's all you have."

:

Jimmy Wauneka wanted to be finished with the Traub case as soon as possible. But back in the ER, he saw a plastic bag filled with the old guy's clothes and personal belongings. There was nothing to do but call ITC again. This time he spoke to another vice president, a Ms. Kramer. Dr. Gordon was in meetings and was unavailable.

"It's about Dr. Traub," he said.

"Oh yes." A sad sigh. "Poor Dr. Traub. Such a nice man."

"His body was cremated today, but we still have some of his personal effects. I don't know what you want us to do with them."

"Dr. Traub doesn't have any living relatives," Ms. Kramer said. "I doubt anybody here would want his clothes, or anything. What effects were you speaking of?"

"Well, there was a diagram in his pocket. It looks like a church, or maybe a monastery."

"Uh-huh."

"Do you know why he would have a diagram of a monastery?"

"No, I really couldn't say. To tell the truth, Dr. Traub got a little strange, the last few weeks. He was quite depressed, ever since his wife died. Are you sure it's a monastery?"

"No, I'm not. I don't know what it is. Do you want this diagram back?"

"If you wouldn't mind sending it along."

"And what about this ceramic thing?"

"Ceramic thing?"

"He had a piece of ceramic. It's about an inch square, and it's stamped 'ITC.' "

"Oh. Okay. That's no problem."

"I was wondering what that might be."

"What that might be? It's an ID tag."

"It doesn't look like any ID tag I ever saw."

"It's a new kind. We use them here to get through security doors, and so on."

"You want that back, too?"

"If it's not too much trouble. Tell you what, I'll give you our FedEx number, and you can just stick it in an envelope and drop it off."

Jimmy Wauneka hung up the phone and he thought, *Bullshit*.

:

He called Father Grogan, the priest at his local Catholic parish, and told him about the diagram, and the abbreviation at the bottom: mon.ste.mere.

"That would be the Monastery of Sainte-Mère," he said promptly.

"So it *is* a monastery?"

"Oh absolutely."

"Where?"

"I have no idea. It's not a Spanish name. 'Mère' is French

for 'Mother.' Saint Mother means the Virgin Mary. Perhaps it's in Louisiana."

"How would I locate it?" Wauneka said.

"I have a listing of monasteries here someplace. Give me an hour or two to dig it up."

:

"I'm sorry, Jimmy. I don't see any mystery here."

Carlos Chavez was the assistant chief of police in Gallup, about to retire from the force, and he had been Jimmy Wauneka's adviser from the start. Now he was sitting back with his boots up on his desk, listening to Wauneka with a very skeptical look.

"Well, here's the thing," Wauneka said. "They pick up this guy out by Corazón Canyon, demented and raving, but there's no sunburn, no dehydration, no exposure."

"So he was dumped. His family pushed him out of the car."

"No. No living family."

"Okay, then he drove himself out there."

"Nobody saw a car."

"Who's nobody?"

"The people who picked him up."

Chavez sighed. "Did you go out to Corazón Canyon yourself, and look for a car?"

Wauneka hesitated. "No."

"You took somebody's word for it."

"Yes. I guess I did."

"You guess? Meaning a car could still be out there."

"Maybe. Yeah."

"Okay. So what did you do next?"

"I called his company, ITC."

"And they told you what?"

"They said he was depressed, because his wife had died."

"Figures."

"I don't know," Wauneka said. "Because I called the apartment building where Traub lived. I talked to the building manager. The wife died a year ago."

"So this happened close to the anniversary of her death, right? That's when it usually happens, Jimmy."

"I think I ought to go over and talk to some folks at ITC Research."

"Why? They're two hundred and fifty miles from where this guy was found."

"I know, but—"

"But what? How many times we get some tourist stranded out in the reservations? Three, four times a year? And half the time they're dead, right? Or they die afterward, right?"

"Yes. . . ."

"And it's always one of two reasons. Either they're New Age flakes from Sedona who come to commune with the eagle god and got stuck, their car broke down. Or they're depressed. One or the other. And this guy was depressed."

"So they say. . . ."

"Because his wife died. Hey, I believe it." Carlos sighed. "Some guys are depressed, some guys are overjoyed."

"But there's unanswered questions," Wauneka said. "There's some kind of diagram, and a ceramic chip—"

"Jimmy. There's always unanswered questions." Chavez squinted at him. "What's going on? Are you trying to impress that cute little doctor?"

"What little doctor?"

"You know who I mean."

"Hell no. She thinks there's nothing to all this."

"She's right. Drop it."

"But—"

"Jimmy." Carlos Chavez shook his head. "Listen to me. Drop it."

"Okay."

"I'm serious."

"Okay," Wauneka said. "Okay, I'll drop it."

:

The next day, the police in Shiprock picked up a bunch of thirteen-year-old kids joyriding in a car with New Mexico plates. The registration in the glove compartment was in the name of Joseph Traub. The kids said they had found the car on the side of the road past Corazón Canyon, with the keys still in it. The kids had been drinking, and the inside of the car was a mess, sticky with spilled beer.

Wauneka didn't bother to drive over and see it.

:

A day after that, Father Grogan called him back. "I've been checking for you," he said, "and there is no Monastery of Sainte-Mère, anywhere in the world."

"Okay," Wauneka said. "Thanks." It was what he'd been expecting, anyway. Another dead end.

"At one time, there was a monastery of that name in France, but it was burned to the ground in the fourteenth century. It's just a ruin now. In fact, it's being excavated by archaeologists from Yale and the University of Toulouse. But I gather there's not much there."

"Uh-huh. . . ." But then he remembered some of the things the old guy had said, before he died. Some of the nonsense rhymes. "Yale in France, has no chance." Something like that.

"Where is it?" he said.

"Somewhere in southwest France, near the Dordogne River."

"Dordogne? How do you spell that?" Wauneka said.

# DORDOGNE

"The glory of the past is an illusion.
So is the glory of the present."

EDWARD JOHNSTON

The helicopter thumped through thick gray fog. In the rear seat, Diane Kramer shifted uneasily. Whenever the mist thinned, she saw the treetops of the forest very close beneath her. She said, "Do we have to be so low?"

Sitting in front alongside the pilot, André Marek laughed. "Don't worry, it's perfectly safe." But then, Marek didn't look like the sort of man to worry about anything. He was twenty-nine years old, tall, and very strong; muscles rippled beneath his T-shirt. Certainly, you would never think he was an assistant professor of history at Yale. Or second in command of the Dordogne project, which was where they were headed now.

"This mist will clear in a minute," Marek said, speaking with just a trace of his native Dutch accent. Kramer knew all about him: a graduate of Utrecht, Marek was one of the new breed of "experimental" historians, who set out to re-create parts of the past, to experience it firsthand and understand it better. Marek was a fanatic about it; he had learned medieval dress, language and customs in detail; supposedly, he even knew how to joust. Looking at him, she could believe it.

She said, "I'm surprised Professor Johnston didn't come with us." Kramer had really expected to deal with Johnston himself. She was, after all, a high-level executive from the company that funded their research. Protocol required that Johnston himself give the tour. And she had planned to start working on him in the helicopter.

"Unfortunately, Professor Johnston had a prior appointment."

"Oh?"

"With François Bellin, the minister of antiquities. He's coming down from Paris."

"I see." Kramer felt better. Obviously, Johnston must first deal with authorities. The Dordogne project was entirely dependent on good relations with the French government. She said, "Is there a problem?"

"I doubt it. They're old friends. Ah, here we go."

The helicopter burst through the fog into morning sunlight. The stone farmhouses cast long shadows.

As they passed over one farm, the geese in the barnyard flapped, and a woman in an apron shook her fist at them.

"She's not happy about us," Marek said, pointing with his massive muscular arm.

Sitting in the seat behind him, Kramer put on her sunglasses and said, "Well, it *is* six o'clock in the morning. Why did we go so early?"

"For the light," Marek said. "Early shadows reveal contours, crop marks, all that." He pointed down past his feet. Three heavy yellow housings were clamped to the front struts of the helicopter. "Right now we're carrying stereo terrain mappers, infrared, UV, and side-scan radar."

Kramer pointed out the rear window, toward a six-foot-long silver tube that dangled beneath the helicopter at the rear. "And what's that?"

"Proton magnetometer."

"Uh-huh. And it does what?"

"Looks for magnetic anomalies in the ground below us that could indicate buried walls, or ceramics, or metal."

"Any equipment you'd like that you don't have?"

Marek smiled. "No, Ms. Kramer. We've gotten everything we asked for, thank you."

The helicopter had been skimming over the rolling contours of dense forest. But now she saw outcrops of gray rock, cliff faces that cut across the landscape. Marek was giving what struck her as a practiced guided tour, talking almost continuously.

"Those limestone cliffs are the remains of an ancient beach," he said. "Millions of years ago, this part of France was covered by a sea. When the sea receded, it left behind a beach. Compressed over eons, the beach became limestone. It's very soft stone. The cliffs are honeycombed with caves."

Kramer could indeed see many caves, dark openings in the rock. "There're a lot of them," she said.

Marek nodded. "This part of southern France is one of the most continuously inhabited places on the planet. Human beings have lived here for at least four hundred thousand years. There is a continuous record from Neanderthal man right up to the present."

Kramer nodded impatiently. "And where is the project?" she said.

"Coming up."

The forest ended in scattered farms, open fields. Now they were heading toward a village atop a hill; she saw a cluster of stone houses, narrow roads, and the stone tower of a castle rising into the sky.

"That's Beynac," Marek said, his back to her. "And here comes our Doppler signal." Kramer heard electronic beeps in her headphones, coming faster and faster.

"Stand by," the pilot said.

Marek flicked on his equipment. A half dozen lights glowed green.

"Okay," the pilot said. "Starting first transect. Three . . . two . . . one."

The rolling forested hills fell away in a sheer cliff, and Diane Kramer saw the valley of the Dordogne spread out beneath them.

:

The Dordogne River twisted in loops like a brown snake in the valley it had cut hundreds of thousands of years before. Even at this early hour, there were kayakers paddling along it.

"In medieval times the Dordogne was the military frontier," Marek said. "This side of the river was French and the other side was English. Fighting went back and forth. Directly beneath us is Beynac, a French stronghold."

Kramer looked down on a picturesque tourist town with

quaint stone buildings and dark stone roofs. The narrow, twisting streets were empty of tourists. The town of Beynac was built against the cliff face, rising from the river up to the walls of an old castle.

"And over there," Marek said, pointing across the river, "you see the opposing town of Castelnaud. An English stronghold."

High on a far hill, Kramer saw a second castle, this one built entirely of yellow stone. The castle was small but beautifully restored, its three circular towers rising gracefully into the air, connected by high walls. It, too, had a quaint tourist town built around its base.

She said, "But this isn't our project. . . ."

"No," Marek said. "I'm just showing you the general layout in this region. All along the Dordogne, you find these paired, opposing castles. Our project also involves a pair of opposing castles, but it's a few miles downstream from here. We'll go there now."

:

The helicopter banked, heading west over rolling hills. They left the tourist area behind; Kramer was pleased to see the land beneath her was mostly forest. They passed a small town called Envaux near the river, and then climbed up into the hills again. As they came over one rise, she suddenly saw an open expanse of cleared green field. In the center of the field were the remains of ruined stone houses, walls set at odd angles to one another. This had clearly once been a town, its houses located beneath the walls of a castle. But the walls were just a line of rubble, and nearly nothing of the castle remained; she saw only the bases of two round towers and bits of broken wall connecting them. Here and there, white tents had been pitched among the ruins. She saw several dozen people working there.

"All this was owned by a goat farmer, until three years ago," Marek said. "The French had mostly forgotten about these ruins, which were overgrown by forest. We've been clearing it away, and doing some rebuilding. What you see was once the famous English stronghold of Castelgard."

"This is Castelgard?" Kramer sighed. So little remained. A few standing walls to indicate the town. And of the castle itself, almost nothing.

"I thought there would be more," she said.

"Eventually, there will be. Castelgard was a large town in its day, with a very imposing castle," Marek said. "But it'll be several years before it's restored."

Kramer was wondering how she would explain this to Doniger. The Dordogne project was not as far advanced as Doniger had imagined it to be. It would be extremely difficult to begin major reconstruction while the site was still so fragmented. And she was certain Professor Johnston would resist any suggestion to begin.

Marek was saying, "We've set up our headquarters in that farm over there." He pointed to a farmhouse with several stone buildings, not far from the ruins. A green tent stood beside one building. "Want to circle Castelgard for another look?"

"No," Kramer said, trying to keep the disappointment out of her voice. "Let's move on."

"Okay, then, we'll go to the mill."

The helicopter turned, heading north toward the river. The land sloped downward, then flattened along the banks of the Dordogne. They crossed the river, broad and dark brown, and came to a heavily wooded island near the far shore. Between the island and the northern shore was a narrower, rushing stream perhaps fifteen feet wide. And here she saw ruins of another structure—so ruined, in fact, that it was hard to tell what it once had been. "And this?" she said, looking down. "What's this?"

"That's the water mill. There was once a bridge over the river, with water wheels beneath. They used water power to grind grain, and to pump big bellows for making steel."

"Nothing's been rebuilt here at all," Kramer said. She sighed.

"No," Marek said. "But we've been studying it. Chris

Hughes, one of our graduate students, has investigated it quite extensively. That's Chris down there now, with the Professor."

Kramer saw a compact, dark-haired young man, standing beside the tall, imposing figure she recognized as Professor Johnston. Neither man looked up at the helicopter passing overhead; they were focused on their work.

Now the helicopter left the river behind, and moved on to the flat land to the east. They passed over a complex of low rectangular walls, visible as dark lines in the slanting morning light. Kramer guessed that the walls were no more than a few inches high. But it clearly outlined what looked like a small town.

"And this? Another town?"

"Just about. That's the Monastery of Sainte-Mère," Marek said. "One of the wealthiest and most powerful monasteries in France. It was burned to the ground in the fourteenth century."

"Lot of digging down there," Kramer said.

"Yes, it's our most important site."

As they flew by, she could see the big square pits they had dug down to the catacombs beneath the monastery. Kramer knew the team devoted a great deal of attention here because they hoped to find more buried caches of monastic documents; they had already discovered quite a few.

The helicopter swung away, and approached the limestone cliffs on the French side, and a small town. The helicopter rose up to the top of the cliffs.

"We come to the fourth and final site," Marek said. "The fortress above the town of Bezenac. In the Middle Ages it was called La Roque. Although it's on the French side of the river, it was actually built by the English, who were intent on maintaining a permanent foothold in French territory. As you see, it's quite extensive."

And it was: a huge military complex on top of the hill, with two sets of concentric walls, one inside the other, spread out over fifty acres. She gave a little sigh of relief. The fortress of La Roque was in better condition than the other sites of the project, and it had more standing walls. It was easier to see what it once had been.

But it was also crawling with tourists.

"You let the tourists in?" she asked in dismay.

"Not really our decision," Marek said. "As you know, this is a new site, and the French government wanted it opened to the public. But of course we'll close it again when we begin reconstruction."

"And when will that be?"

"Oh . . . between two and five years from now."

She said nothing. The helicopter circled and rose higher.

"So," Marek said, "we've come to the end. From up here you can see the entire project: the fortress of La Roque, the monastery in the flats, the mill, and across the river, the fortress of Castelgard. Want to see it again?"

"No," Diane Kramer said. "We can go back. I've seen enough."

Edward Johnston, Regius Professor of History at Yale, squinted as the helicopter thumped by overhead. It was heading south, toward Domme, where there was a landing field. Johnston glanced at his watch and said, "Let's continue, Chris."

"Okay," Chris Hughes said. He turned back to the computer mounted on the tripod in front of them, attached the GPS, and flicked the power button. "It'll take me a minute to set up."

Christopher Stewart Hughes was one of Johnston's graduate students. The Professor—he was invariably known by that name—had five graduate students working on the site, as well as two dozen undergraduates who had become enamored of him during his introductory Western Civilization class.

It was easy, Chris thought, to become enamored of Edward Johnston. Although well past sixty, Johnston was broad-shouldered and fit; he moved quickly, giving the impression of vigor and energy. Tanned, with dark eyes and sardonic manner, he often seemed more like Mephistopheles than a history professor.

Yet he dressed the part of a typical college professor: even here in the field, he wore a button-down shirt and tie every day. His only concession to field work were his jeans and hiking boots.

What made Johnston so beloved by his students was the way he involved himself in their lives: he fed them at his house once a week; he looked after them; if any of them had a problem with studies, or finances, or family back home, he was always ready to help solve the difficulty, without ever seeming to do anything at all.

Chris carefully unpacked the metal case at his feet, removing first a transparent liquid crystal screen, which he mounted vertically, fitting it into brackets above the computer. Then he restarted the computer, so that it would recognize the screen.

"It'll just be a few seconds now," he said. "The GPS is calibrating."

Johnston just nodded patiently, and smiled.

Chris was a graduate student in the history of science—a bitterly controversial field—but he neatly sidestepped the disputes by focusing not on modern science, but on medieval science and technology. Thus he was becoming expert in techniques of metallurgy, the manufacture of armor, three-field crop rotation, the chemistry of tanning, and a dozen other subjects from the period. He had decided to do his doctoral dissertation on the technology of medieval mills—a fascinating, much-neglected area.

And his particular interest was, of course, the mill of Sainte-Mère.

Johnston waited calmly.

Chris had been an undergraduate, in his junior year, when his parents were killed in an automobile accident. Chris, an only child, was devastated; he thought he would drop out of school. Johnston moved the young student into his house for three months, and served as a substitute father for many years afterward, advising him on everything from settling his parents' estate to problems with his girlfriends. And there had been a lot of problems with girlfriends.

In the aftermath of his parents' death, Chris had gotten involved with many women. The subsequent complexity of his life—dirty looks in a seminar from a jilted lover; frantic midnight calls to his room because of a missed period, while he was in bed with someone else; clandestine hotel-room meetings with an associate professor of philosophy who was in the midst of a nasty divorce—all this became a familiar texture to his life. Inevitably his grades suffered, and then Johnston took him aside, spending several evenings talking things through with him.

But Chris wasn't inclined to listen; soon after, he was named in the divorce. Only the Professor's personal intervention prevented him from being expelled from Yale. Chris's response to this sudden jeopardy was to bury himself in his studies; his grades swiftly improved; he eventually graduated fifth in his class. But in the process he became conservative. Now, at twenty-four, he tended toward fussiness, and stomach trouble. He was reckless only with women.

:

"Finally," Chris said. "It's coming up."

The liquid crystal display showed an outline in bright green. Through the transparent display, they could see the ruins of the mill, with the green outline superimposed. This was the latest method for modeling archaeological structures. Formerly, they had relied on ordinary architectural models, made of white foamcore, cut and assembled by hand. But the technique was slow, and modifications were difficult.

These days, all models were made in the computer. The models could be quickly assembled, and easily revised. In addition, they allowed this method for looking at models in the field. The computer was fed mapped coordinates from the ruin; using the GPS-fixed tripod position, the image that came up on the screen was in exact perspective.

They watched the green outline fill in, making solid forms. It showed a substantial covered bridge, built of stone, with three water wheels beneath it. "Chris," Johnston said, "you've made it fortified." He sounded pleased.

"I know it's a risk . . . ," he said.

"No, no," the Professor said, "I think it makes sense."

There were references in the literature to fortified mills, and certainly there were records of innumerable battles over mills and mill rights. But few fortified mills were actually known: one in Buerge and another recently discovered near

Montauban, in the next valley. Most medieval historians believed such fortified mill buildings were rare.

"The column bases at the water's edge are very large," Chris said. "Like everything else around here, once the mill was abandoned, the local people used it as a quarry. They took away the stones to build their own houses. But the rocks in the column bases were left behind, because they were simply too large to move. To me, that implies a massive bridge. Probably fortified."

"You may be right," Johnston said. "And I think—"

The radio clipped to his waist crackled. "Chris? Is the Professor with you? The minister is on-site."

Johnston looked across the monastery excavation, toward the dirt road that ran along the edge of the river. A green Land Rover with white lettering on the side panels was racing toward them, raising a large plume of dust. "Yes indeed," he said. "That will be François. Always in a rush."

:

"Edouard! Edouard!" François Bellin grabbed the Professor by the shoulders, and kissed him on both cheeks. Bellin was a large, balding, exuberant man. He spoke rapid French. "My dear friend, it is always too long. You are well?"

"I am, François," Johnston said, taking a step back from this effusiveness. Whenever Bellin was excessively friendly, it meant there was a problem ahead. "And you, François?" Johnston said. "How does it go?"

"The same, the same. But at my age, that suffices." He looked around the site, then placed his hand on Johnston's shoulder in a conspiratorial way. "Edouard, I must ask you a favor. I have a small difficulty."

"Oh?"

"You know this reporter, from *L'Express*—"

"No," Johnston said. "Absolutely not."

"But Edouard—"

"I already talked to her on the phone. She's one of those conspiracy people. Capitalism is bad, all corporations are evil—"

"Yes, yes, Edouard, what you say is true." He leaned closer. "But she sleeps with the minister of culture."

"That doesn't narrow the field much," Johnston said.

"Edouard, please. People are starting to listen to her. She can cause trouble. For me. For you. For this project."

Johnston sighed.

"You know there is a sentiment here that Americans destroy all culture, having none of their own. There is trouble with movies and music. And there has been discussion of banning Americans from working on French cultural sites. Hmm?"

Johnston said, "This is old news."

"And your own sponsor, ITC, has asked you to speak to her."

"They have?"

"Yes. A Ms. Kramer requested you speak to her."

Johnston sighed again.

"It will only take a few minutes of your time, I promise you," Bellin said, waving to the Land Rover. "She is in the car."

Johnston said, "You brought her personally?"

"Edouard, I am trying to tell you," Bellin said. "It is necessary to take this woman seriously. Her name is Louise Delvert."

As she climbed out of the car, Chris saw a woman in her mid-forties, slender and dark, her face handsome, with strong features. She was stylish in the way of certain mature European women, conveying a sophisticated, understated sexuality. She appeared dressed for an expedition, in khaki shirt and pants, straps around her neck for camera, video and tape recorder. She carried her notepad in her hand as she strode toward them, all business.

But as she came closer, she slowed down.

Delvert extended her hand. "Professor Johnston," she said, in unaccented English. Her smile was genuine and warm. "I cannot tell you how much I appreciate your taking the time to see me."

"Not at all," Johnston said, taking her hand in his. "You

have come a long way, Miss Delvert. I am pleased to help you in any way I can."

Johnston continued to hold her hand. She continued to smile at him. This went on for ten seconds more, while she said that he was too kind and he said on the contrary, it was the very least he could do for her.

⋮

They walked through the monastery excavations, a tight little group: the Professor and Miss Delvert in the front, Bellin and Chris following behind, not too close, but still trying to hear the discussion. Bellin wore a quiet, satisfied smile; it occurred to Chris that there was more than one way to deal with a troublesome culture minister.

As for the Professor, his wife had been dead for many years, and although there were rumors, Chris had never seen him with another woman. He was fascinated to watch him now. Johnston did not change his manner; he simply gave the reporter his undivided attention. He conveyed the impression that there was nothing in the world more important than she was. And Chris had a feeling that Delvert's questions were much less contentious than she had planned.

"As you know, Professor," she said, "for some time now, my newspaper has been working on a story about the American company ITC."

"Yes, I'm aware of that."

"Am I correct that ITC sponsors this site?"

"Yes, they do."

She said, "We have been told they contribute a million dollars a year."

"That's about right."

They walked on for a moment. She seemed to be trying to frame her next question carefully.

"There are some at the newspaper," she said, "who think that's a great deal of money to spend on medieval archaeology."

"Well, you can tell them at the newspaper," Johnston said, "that it's not. In fact, it's average for a large site like this. ITC gives us two hundred and fifty in direct costs, a hundred and a quarter in indirect costs paid to the university, another eighty in scholarships, stipends, and travel and living expenses, and fifty for laboratory and archiving costs."

"But surely there is much more than that," she said, playing with her hair with her pen, and blinking rapidly. Chris thought, She's batting her eyes at him. He'd never seen a woman do that. You had to be French to pull it off.

The Professor appeared not to notice. "Yes, there is certainly more," he said, "but it doesn't go to us. The rest is reconstruction costs for the site itself. That is separately accounted, since as you know, reconstruction costs are shared with the French government."

"Of course," she said. "So the half million dollars your own team spends is in your view quite usual?"

"Well, we can ask François," Johnston said. "But there are twenty-seven archaeological sites being worked in this corner of France. They range from the Paleolithic dig that the University of Zurich is doing with Carnegie-Mellon, to the Roman *castrum*, the fort, that the University of Bordeaux is doing with Oxford. The average annual cost of these projects is about half a million dollars a year."

"I did not know that." She was staring into his eyes, openly admiring. Too openly, Chris thought. It suddenly occurred to him that he might have misjudged what was happening. This might simply be her way of getting a story.

Johnston glanced back at Bellin, who was walking behind him. "François? What would you say?"

"I believe you know what you are doing—I mean, saying," Bellin said. "Funding varies from four to six hundred thousand U.S. Scandinavians, Germans and Americans cost more. Paleolithic costs more. But yes, half a million could be an average number."

Miss Delvert remained focused on Johnston: "And for your funding, Professor Johnston, how much contact are you required to have with ITC?"

"Almost none."

"Almost none? Truly?"

"Their president, Robert Doniger, came out two years ago. He's a history buff, and he was very enthusiastic, like a kid. And ITC sends a vice president about once a month. One is here right now. But by and large, they leave us alone."

"And what do you know about ITC itself?"

Johnston shrugged. "They do research in quantum physics. They make components used in MRIs, medical devices, and so forth. And they are developing several quantum-based dating techniques, to precisely date any artifact. We're helping with that."

"I see. And these techniques, they work?"

"We have prototype devices in our farmhouse office. So far they've proven too delicate for field work. They're always breaking down."

"But this is why ITC funds you—to test their equipment?"

"No," Johnston said. "It's the other way around. ITC is making dating equipment for the same reason ITC funds us—because Bob Doniger is enthusiastic about history. We're his hobby."

"An expensive hobby."

"Not for him," Johnston said. "He's a billionaire. He bought a Gutenberg Bible for twenty-three million. He bought the Rouen Tapestry at auction for seventeen million. Our project's just small change."

"Perhaps so. But Mr. Doniger is also a tough business-man."

"Yes."

"Do you really think he supports you out of personal interest?" Her tone was light, almost teasing.

Johnston looked directly at her. "You never know, Miss Delvert, what someone's reasons are."

Chris thought, He's suspicious, too.

Delvert seemed to sense it as well, and she immediately reverted to a more businesslike manner. "Of course, yes. But I ask this for a reason. Isn't it true that you do not own the results of your research? Anything you find, anything you discover, is owned by ITC."

"Yes, that's correct."

"This doesn't bother you?"

"If I worked for Microsoft, Bill Gates would own the results of my research. Anything I found and discovered, Bill Gates would own."

"Yes. But this is hardly the same."

"Why not? ITC is a technical company, and Doniger set up this fund the way technical companies do such things. The arrangement doesn't bother me. We have the right to publish our findings—they even pay for publication."

"After they approve them."

"Yes. We send our reports to them first. But they have never commented."

"So you see no greater ITC plan behind all this?" she asked.

Johnston said, "Do you?"

"I don't know," she said. "That is why I am asking you. Because of course there are some extremely puzzling aspects to the behavior of ITC as a company."

"What aspects?"

"For example," she said, "they are one of the world's largest consumers of xenon."

"Xenon? You mean the gas?"

"Yes. It is used in lasers and electron tubes."

Johnston shrugged. "They can have all the xenon gas they want. I can't see how it concerns me."

"What about their interest in exotic metals? ITC recently purchased a Nigerian company to assure their supply of niobium."

"Niobium." Johnston shook his head. "What's niobium?"

"It is a metal similar to titanium."

"What's it used for?"

"Superconducting magnets, and nuclear reactors."

"And you wonder what ITC is using it for?" Johnston shook his head again. "You'd have to ask them, Miss Delvert."

"I did. They said it was for 'research in advanced magnetics.' "

"There you are. Any reason not to believe them?"

"No," she said. "But as you said yourself, ITC is a research company. They employ two hundred physicists at their main facility, a place called Black Rock, in New Mexico. It is clearly and unquestionably a high-technology company."

"Yes. . . ."

"So I wonder: Why would a high-technology company want so much land?"

"Land?"

"ITC has purchased large land parcels in remote locations around the world: the mountains of Sumatra, northern Cambodia, southeast Pakistan, the jungles of central Guatemala, the highlands of Peru."

Johnston frowned. "Are you sure?"

"Yes. They have made acquisitions in Europe, as well. West of Rome, five hundred hectares. In Germany near Heidelberg, seven hundred hectares. In France, a thousand hectares in the limestone hills above the River Lot. And finally, right here."

"Here?"

"Yes. Using British and Swedish holding companies, they have very quietly acquired five hundred hectares, all around your site. It is mostly forest and farmland, at the moment."

"Holding companies?" he said.

"That makes it very difficult to trace. Whatever ITC is doing, it clearly requires secrecy. But why would this company fund your research, and also buy the land all around the site?"

"I have no idea," Johnston said. "Especially since ITC doesn't own the site itself. You'll recall they gave the entire area—Castelgard, Sainte-Mère and La Roque—to the French government last year."

"Of course. For a tax exemption."

"But still, ITC does not own the site. Why should they buy land around it?"

"I will be happy to show you everything I have."

"Perhaps," Johnston said, "you should."

"My research is just in the car."

They started together toward the Land Rover. Watching

them go, Bellin clucked his tongue. "Ah, dear, dear. It is so difficult to trust these days."

Chris was about to answer in his bad French when his radio clicked. "Chris?" It was David Stern, the project technologist. "Chris, is the Professor with you? Ask him if he knows somebody named James Wauneka."

Chris pressed the button on his radio. "The Professor's busy right now. What's it about?"

"He's some guy in Gallup. He's called twice. Wants to send us a picture of our monastery that he says he found in the desert."

"What? In the desert?"

"He might be a little cracked. He claims he's a cop, and he keeps babbling on about some dead ITC employee."

"Have him send it to our e-mail address," Chris said. "You take a look at it."

He clicked the radio off. Bellin was looking at his watch, clucking again, then looking at the car, where Johnston and Delvert were standing, their heads almost touching as they pored over papers. "I have appointments," he said mournfully. "Who knows how long this will take?"

"I think," Chris said, "perhaps not long."

∴

Twenty minutes later, Bellin was driving off with Miss Delvert at his side, and Chris was standing with the Professor, waving good-bye. "I think that went rather well," Johnston said.

"What'd she show you?"

"Some land-purchase records, for the area around here. But it's not persuasive. Four parcels were bought by a German investment group about which little is known. Two parcels were bought by a British attorney who claims he's going to retire here; another by a Dutch banker for his grown daughter; and so on."

"The British and the Dutch have been buying land in the Périgord for years," Chris said. "It's nothing new."

"Exactly. She has some idea that all the purchases could be

traced to ITC. But it's pretty tenuous. You have to be a believer."

The car was gone. They turned and walked toward the river. The sun was higher in the sky now, and it was getting warm.

Cautiously, Chris said, "Charming woman."

"I think," Johnston said, "that she works too hard at her job."

They got into the rowboat tied up at the river's edge, and Chris rowed them across to Castelgard.

∴

They left the rowboat behind, and began climbing toward the top of Castelgard hill. They saw the first sign of castle walls. On this side, all that remained of the walls were grassy embankments that ended in long scars of exposed, crumbled rock. After six hundred years, it almost looked like a natural feature. But it was in fact the remains of a wall.

"You know," the Professor said, "what she really doesn't like is corporate sponsorship. But archaeological research has always depended on outside benefactors. A hundred years ago, the benefactors were all individuals: Carnegie, Peabody, Stanford. But these days wealth is corporate, so Nippon TV finances the Sistine Chapel, British Telecom finances York, Philips Electronics finances the Toulouse *castrum*, and ITC finances us."

"Speak of the devil," Chris said. As they came over the hill, they saw the dark form of Diane Kramer, standing with André Marek.

The Professor sighed. "This day is completely wasted. How long is she going to be here?"

"Her plane is at Bergerac. She's scheduled to leave this afternoon at three."

∴

"I'm sorry about that woman," Diane Kramer said, when Johnston came up to join her. "She's annoying everybody, but we've been unable to do anything about her."

"Bellin said you wanted me to talk to her."

"We want everybody to talk to her," Kramer said. "We're doing everything we can to show her there are no secrets."

"She seemed mostly concerned," Johnston said, "that ITC was making land purchases in this area."

"Land purchases? ITC?" Kramer laughed. "I haven't heard that one before. Did she ask you about niobium and nuclear reactors?"

"As a matter of fact, she did. She said you'd bought a company in Nigeria, to assure your supply."

"Nigeria," Kramer repeated, shaking her head. "Oh dear. Our niobium comes from Canada. Niobium's not exactly a rare metal, you know. It sells for seventy-five dollars a pound." She shook her head. "We offered to give her a tour of our facility, interview with our president, bring a photographer, her own experts, whatever she wants. But no. It's modern journalism: don't let the facts get in your way."

Kramer turned, and gestured to the ruins of Castelgard all around them. "Anyway," she said. "I've taken Dr. Marek's excellent tour, in the helicopter and on foot. It's evident you're doing absolutely spectacular work. Progress is good, the work's of extremely high academic quality, recordkeeping is first rate, your people are happy, the site is managed well. Just fabulous. I couldn't be happier. But Dr. Marek tells me he is going to be late for his—what is it?"

"My broadsword lesson," Marek said.

"His broadsword lesson. Yes. I think he should certainly do that. It doesn't sound like something you can change, like a piano lesson. In the meantime, shall we walk the site together?"

"Of course," Johnston said.

Chris's radio beeped. A voice said, "Chris? It's Sophie for you."

"I'll call her back."

"No, no," Kramer said. "You go ahead. I'll speak to the Professor alone."

Johnston said quickly, "I usually have Chris with me, to take notes."

"I don't think we'll need notes today."

"All right. Fine." He turned to Chris. "But give me your radio, in case."

"No problem," Chris said. He unclipped the radio from his belt and handed it to Johnston. As Johnston took it in his hand, he clearly flicked on the voice-activation switch. Then he slipped it on his belt.

"Thanks," Johnston said. "Now, you better go call Sophie. You know she doesn't like to be kept waiting."

"Right," Chris said.

As Johnston and Kramer began to walk through the ruins, he sprinted across the field toward the stone farmhouse that served as the project office.

:

Just beyond the crumbling walls of Castelgard town, the team had bought a dilapidated stone storehouse and had rebuilt the roof, and repaired the stonework. Here they housed all their electronics, lab equipment and archival computers. Unprocessed records and artifacts were spread out on the ground beneath a broad green tent adjacent to the farmhouse.

Chris went into the storehouse, which was one large room that they had divided into two. To the left, Elsie Kastner, the team's linguist and graphology expert, sat in her own room, hunched over parchment documents. Chris ignored her and went straight ahead to the room crammed with electronic equipment. There David Stern, the thin and bespectacled technical expert on the project, was talking on a telephone.

"Well," Stern was saying, "you'll have to scan your document at a fairly high resolution, and send it to us. Do you have a scanner there?"

Hastily, Chris rummaged through the equipment on the field table, looking for a spare radio. He didn't see one; all the charger boxes were empty.

"The police department doesn't have a scanner?" Stern was saying, surprised. "Oh, you're not at the—well, why don't you go there and use the police scanner?"

Chris tapped Stern on the shoulder. He mouthed, *Radio*.

Stern nodded and unclipped his own radio from his belt.

"Well yes, the hospital scanner would be fine. Maybe they will have someone who can help you. We need twelve-eighty by ten-twenty-four, saved as a JPEG file. Then you transmit that to us. . . ."

Chris ran outside, flicking through the channels on the radio as he went.

From the storehouse door, he could look down over the entire site. He saw Johnston and Kramer walking along the edge of the plateau overlooking the monastery. She had a notebook open and was showing him something on paper.

And then he found them on channel eight.

"—ignificant acceleration in the pace of research," she was saying.

And the Professor said, "What?"

:

Professor Johnston looked over his wire-frame spectacles at the woman standing before him. "That's impossible," he said.

She took a deep breath. "Perhaps I haven't explained it very well. You are already doing some reconstruction. What Bob would like to do," she said, "is to enlarge that to be a full program of reconstruction."

"Yes. And that's impossible."

"Tell me why."

"Because we don't know enough, that's why," Johnston said angrily. "Look: the only reconstruction we've done so far has been for safety. We've rebuilt walls so they don't fall on our researchers. But we're not ready to actually begin rebuilding the site itself."

"But surely a part," she said. "I mean, look at the monastery over there. You could certainly rebuild the church, and the cloister beside it, and the refectory, and—"

"What?" Johnston said. "The refectory?" The refectory was the dining room where the monks took their meals. Johnston pointed down at the site, where low walls and crisscrossing trenches made a confusing pattern. "Who said the refectory was next to the cloister?"

"Well, I—"

"You see? This is exactly my point," Johnston said. "We still aren't sure where the refectory is yet. It's only just recently that we've started to think it might be next to the cloister, but we aren't sure."

She said irritably, "Professor, academic study can go on indefinitely, but in the real world of results—"

"I'm all for results," Johnston said. "But the whole point of a dig like this is that we don't repeat the mistakes of the past. A hundred years ago, an architect named Viollet-le-Duc rebuilt monuments all over France. Some he did well. But when he didn't have enough information, he just made it up. The buildings were just his fantasy."

"I understand you want to be accurate—"

"If I knew ITC wanted Disneyland, I'd never have agreed."

"We don't want Disneyland."

"If you rebuild now, that's what you'll get, Ms. Kramer. You'll get a fantasy. Medieval Land."

"No," she said. "I can assure you in the strongest possible terms. We do not want a fantasy. We want an historically accurate reconstruction of the site."

"But it can't be done."

"We believe it can."

"How?"

"With all due respect, Professor, you're being overcautious. You know more than you think you do. For example, the town of Castelgard, beneath the castle itself. That could certainly be rebuilt."

"I suppose . . . Part of it could, yes."

"And that's all we're asking. Just to rebuild a part."

:

David Stern wandered out of the storehouse, to find Chris listening with the radio pressed to his ear. "Eavesdropping, Chris?"

"Shhh," Chris said. "This is important."

Stern shrugged his shoulders. He always felt a little detached from the enthusiasms of the graduate students around him. The others were historians, but Stern was trained as a physicist, and he tended to see things differently. He just couldn't get very excited about finding another medieval hearth, or a few bones from a burial site. In any case, Stern had only taken this job—which required him to run the electronic equipment, do various chemical analyses, carbon dating, and so on—to be near his girlfriend, who was attending summer school in Toulouse. He had been intrigued by the idea of quantum dating, but so far the equipment had failed to work.

On the radio, Kramer was saying, "And if you rebuild part of the town, then you could also rebuild part of the outer castle wall, where it is adjacent to the town. That section there." She was pointing to a low, ragged wall running north–south across the site.

The Professor said, "Well, I suppose we could. . . ."

"And," Kramer continued, "you could extend the wall to the south, where it goes into the woods over there. You could clear the woods, and rebuild the tower."

Stern and Chris looked at each other.

"What's she talking about?" Stern said. "What tower?"

"Nobody's even surveyed the woods yet," Chris said. "We were going to clear it at the end of the summer, and then have it surveyed in the fall."

Over the radio, they heard the Professor say, "Your proposal is very interesting, Ms. Kramer. Let me discuss it with the others, and we'll meet again at lunch."

And then in the field below, Chris saw the Professor turn, look directly at them, and point a stabbing finger toward the woods.

:

Leaving the open field of ruins behind, they climbed a green embankment, and entered the woods. The trees were slender, but they grew close together, and beneath their canopy it was dark and cool. Chris Hughes followed the old outer castle wall as it diminished progressively from a waist-high wall to a low outcrop of stones, and then finally to nothing, disappearing beneath the underbrush.

From then on, he had to bend over, pushing aside the ferns and small plants with his hands in order to see the path of the wall.

The woods grew thicker around them. He felt a sense of peace here. He remembered that when he had first seen Castelgard, nearly the entire site had been within forest like this. The few standing walls were covered in moss and lichen, and seemed to emerge from the earth like organic forms. There had been a mystery to the site back then. But that had been lost once they cleared the land and began excavations.

Stern trailed along behind him. Stern didn't get out of the lab much, and he seemed to be enjoying it. "Why are all the trees so small?" he said.

"Because it's a new forest," Chris said. "Nearly all the forests in the Périgord are less than a hundred years old. All this land used to be cleared, for vineyards."

"And?"

Chris shrugged. "Disease. That blight, phylloxera, killed all the vines around the turn of the century. And the forest grew back." And he added, "The French wine industry almost vanished. They were saved by importing vines that were phylloxera-resistant, from California. Something they'd rather forget."

As he talked, he continued looking at the ground, finding a piece of stone here and there, just enough to enable him to follow the line of the old wall.

But suddenly, the wall was gone. He'd lost it entirely. Now he would have to double back, pick it up again.

"Damn."

"What?" Stern said.

"I can't find the wall. It was running right this way"—he pointed with the flat of his hand—"and now it's gone."

They were standing in an area of particularly thick under-growth, high ferns intermixed with some kind of thorny vine that scratched at his bare legs. Stern was wearing trousers, and he walked forward, saying, "I don't know, Chris, it's got to be around here. . . ."

Chris knew he had to double back. He had just turned to re-trace his steps when he heard Stern yell.

Chris looked back.

Stern was gone. Vanished.

Chris was standing alone in the woods.

⋮

"David?"

A groan. "Ah . . . damn."

"What happened?"

"I banged my knee. It hurts like a *mother*."

Chris couldn't see him anywhere. "Where are you?"

"In a hole," Stern said. "I fell. Be careful, if you come this way. In fact . . ." A grunt. Swearing. "Don't bother. I can stand. I'm okay. In fact—*hey*."

"What?"

"Wait a minute."

"What is it?"

"Just wait, okay?"

Chris saw the underbrush move, the ferns shifting back and forth, as Stern headed to the left. Then Stern spoke. His voice sounded odd. "Uh, Chris?"

"What is it?"

"It's a section of wall. Curved."

"What are you saying?"

"I think I'm standing at the bottom of what was once a round tower, Chris."

"No kidding," Chris said. He thought, How did Kramer know about *that*?

⋮

"Check the computer," the Professor said. "See if we have any helicopter survey scans—infrared or radar—that show a tower. It may already be recorded, and we just never paid at-tention to it."

"Late-afternoon infrared is your best bet," Stern said. He was sitting in a chair with an ice pack on his knee.

"Why late afternoon?"

"Because this limestone holds heat. That's why the cave-men liked it so much here. Even in winter, a cave in Péri-gord limestone was ten degrees warmer than the outside temperature."

"So in the afternoon . . ."

"The wall holds heat as the forest cools. And it'll show up on infrared."

"Even buried?"

Stern shrugged.

Chris sat at the computer console, started hitting keys. The computer made a soft beep. The image switched abruptly.

"Oops. We're in e-mail."

Chris clicked on the mailbox. There was just one message, and it took a long time to download. "What's this?"

"I bet it's that guy Wauneka," Stern said. "I told him to send a pretty big graphic. He probably didn't compress it."

Then the image popped up on the screen: a series of dots arranged in a geometric pattern. They all recognized it at once. It was unquestionably the Monastery of Sainte-Mère. Their own site.

In greater detail than their own survey.

Johnston peered at the image. He drummed his fingers on the tabletop. "It's odd," he said finally, "that Bellin and Kramer would both just happen to show up here on the same day."

The graduate students looked at each other. "What's odd about it?" Chris said.

"Bellin didn't ask to meet her. And he always wants to meet sources of funding."

Chris shrugged. "He seemed very busy."

"Yes. That's the way he seemed." He turned to Stern. "Anyway, print that out," he said. "We'll see what our archi-tect has to say."

•

Katherine Erickson—ash-blond, blue-eyed, and darkly tanned—hung fifty feet in the air, her face just inches below the broken Gothic ceiling of the Castelgard chapel. She lay on her back in a harness and calmly jotted down notes about the construction above her.

Erickson was the newest graduate student on the site, having joined the project just a few months before. Originally, she had gone to Yale to study architecture, but found she disliked her chosen field, and transferred to the history department. There, Johnston had sought her out, convincing her to join him the way he had convinced all the others: "Why don't you put aside these old books and do some real history? Some hands-on history?"

So, hands-on it was—hanging way up here. Not that she minded: Kate had grown up in Colorado and was an avid climber. She spent every Sunday climbing the rock cliffs all around the Dordogne. There was rarely anyone else around, which was great: at home, you had to wait in line for the good pitches.

Using her pick, she chipped off a few flakes of mortar from different areas to take back for spectroscopic analysis. She dropped each into one of the rows of plastic containers, like film containers, that she wore over her shoulders and across her chest like a bandolier.

She was labeling the containers when she heard a voice say, "How do you get down from there? I want to show you something."

She glanced over her shoulder, saw Johnston on the floor below. "Easy," she said. Kate released her lines and slid smoothly to the ground, landing lightly. She brushed strands of blond hair back from her face. Kate Erickson was not a pretty girl—as her mother, a homecoming queen at UC, had so often told her—but she had a fresh, all-American quality that men found attractive.

"I think you'd climb anything," Johnston said.

She unclipped from the harness. "It's the only way to get this data."

"If you say so."

"Seriously," she said. "If you want an architectural history of this chapel, then I have to get up there and take mortar samples. Because that ceiling's been rebuilt many times—either because it was badly made and kept falling in, or because it was broken in warfare, from siege engines."

"Surely sieges," Johnston said.

"Well, I'm not so sure," Kate said. "The main castle structures—the great hall, the inner apartments—are solid, but several of the walls aren't well constructed. In some cases, it looks like walls were added to make secret passages. This castle's got several. There's even one that goes to the kitchen! Whoever made those changes must have been pretty paranoid. And maybe they did it too quickly." She wiped her hands on her shorts. "So. What've you got to show me?"

Johnston handed her a sheet of paper. It was a computer printout, a series of dots arranged in a regular, geometric pattern. "What's this?" she said.

"You tell me."

"It looks like Sainte-Mère."

"Is it?"

"I'd say so, yes. But the thing is . . ."

She walked out of the chapel, and looked down on the monastery excavation, about a mile away in the flats below. It was spread out almost as clearly as the drawing she held in her hand.

"Huh."

"What?"

"There's features on this drawing that we haven't uncovered yet," she said. "An apsidal chapel appended to the church, a second cloister in the northeast quadrant, and . . . this looks like a garden, inside the walls. . . . Where'd you get this picture, anyway?"

:

The restaurant in Marqueyssac stood on the edge of a plateau, with a view over the entire Dordogne valley. Kramer looked up from her table and was surprised to see the Professor arriving with both Marek and Chris. She frowned. She had expected to have a private lunch. She was at a table for two.

They all sat down together, Marek bringing two chairs from the next table. The Professor leaned forward and looked at her intently.

"Ms. Kramer," the Professor said, "how did you know where the refectory is?"

"The refectory?" She shrugged. "Well, I don't know. Wasn't it in the weekly progress report? No? Then maybe Dr. Marek mentioned it to me." She looked at the solemn faces staring at her. "Gentlemen, monasteries aren't exactly my specialty. I must have heard it somewhere."

"And the tower in the woods?"

"It must be in one of the surveys. Or the old photographs."

"We checked. It's not."

The Professor slid the drawing across the table to her. "And why does an ITC employee named Joseph Traub have a drawing of the monastery that is more complete than our own?"

"I don't know. . . . Where did you get this?"

"From a policeman in Gallup, New Mexico, who is asking some of the same questions I am."

She said nothing. She just stared at him.

"Ms. Kramer," he said finally. "I think you're holding out on us. I think you have been doing your own analysis behind our backs, and not sharing what you've found. And I think the reason is that you and Bellin have been negotiating to exploit the site in the event that I'm not cooperative. And the French government would be only too happy to throw Americans off their heritage site."

"Professor, that is absolutely not true. I can assure you—"

"No, Ms. Kramer. You can't." He looked at his watch. "What time does your plane go back to ITC?"

"Three o'clock."

"I'm ready to leave now."

He pushed his chair away from the table.

"But I'm going to New York."

"Then I think you'd better change your plans and go to New Mexico."

"You'll want to see Bob Doniger, and I don't know his schedule. . . ."

"Ms. Kramer." He leaned across the table. *"Fix it."*

:

As the Professor left, Marek said, "I pray God look with favor upon your journey and deliver you safe back." That was what he always said to departing friends. It had been a favorite phrase of the Count Geoffrey de la Tour, six hundred years before.

Some thought Marek carried his fascination with the past to the point of obsession. But in fact it was natural to him: even as a child, Marek had been strongly drawn to the medieval period, and in many ways he now seemed to inhabit it. In a restaurant, he once told a friend he would not grow a beard because it was not fashionable at the time. Astonished, the friend protested, "Of course it's fashionable, just look at all the beards around you." To which Marek replied, "No, no, I mean it is not fashionable in *my* time." By which he meant the thirteenth and fourteenth centuries.

Many medieval scholars could read old languages, but Marek could *speak* them: Middle English, Old French, Occitan, and Latin. He was expert in the fine points of period dress and manners. And with his size and athletic prowess, he set out to master the martial skills of the period. After all, he said, it was a time of perpetual war. Already he could ride the huge Percherons that had been used as destriers, or warhorses. And he was reasonably skilled at jousting, having spent hours practicing with the spinning tournament dummy called the quintain. Marek was so good with a longbow that he had begun to teach the skill to the others. And now he was learning to fight with a broadsword.

But his detailed knowledge of the past put him oddly out of touch with the present. The Professor's sudden departure left everyone on the project feeling bereft and uneasy; wild rumors flew, especially among the undergraduates: ITC was pulling its funding. ITC was turning the project into Medieval

Land. ITC had killed somebody in the desert and was in trouble. Work stopped; people just stood around talking.

Marek finally decided he'd better hold a meeting to squelch the rumors, so in the early afternoon, he called everyone together under the big green tent outside the storehouse. Marek explained that a dispute had arisen between the Professor and ITC, and the Professor had gone back to ITC headquarters to clear it up. Marek said it was just a misunderstanding, which would be resolved in a few days. He said they would be in constant touch with the Professor, who had arranged to call them every twelve hours; and that he expected the Professor to return soon, and things to be normal once again.

It didn't help. The deep sense of unease remained. Several of the undergraduates suggested the afternoon was really too hot to work, and better suited for kayaking on the river; Marek, finally sensing the mood, said they might as well go.

One by one, the graduate students decided to take the rest of the day off, too. Kate appeared, with several pounds of metal clanking around her waist, and announced she was going to climb the cliff behind Gageac. She asked Chris if he wanted to come with her (to hold her ropes—she knew he would never climb), but he said he was going to the riding stables with Marek. Stern declared he was driving to Toulouse for dinner. Rick Chang headed off to Les Eyzies to visit a colleague at a Paleolithic site. Only Elsie Kastner, the graphologist, remained behind in the storehouse, patiently going over documents. Marek asked if she wanted to come with him. But she told him, "Don't be silly, André," and kept working.

:

The Equestrian Center outside Souillac was four miles away, and it was here that Marek trained twice a week. In the far corner of a little-used field, he had set up an odd T-shaped bar on a revolving stand. At one end of the T-bar was a padded square; at the other end, a leather teardrop that looked like a punching bag.

This was a quintain, a device so ancient that it had been drawn by monks at the edges of illuminated manuscripts a thousand years earlier. Indeed, it was from just such drawings that Marek had fashioned his own version.

Making the quintain had been simple enough; it was much more difficult to get a decent lance. This was the kind of problem Marek faced again and again in experimental history. Even the simplest and most common items from the past were impossible to reproduce in the modern world. Even when money was no object, thanks to the ITC research fund.

In medieval times, tournament lances were turned on wood lathes more than eleven feet long, which was the standard length of a jousting lance. But wood lathes of that size hardly existed anymore. After much searching, Marek located a specialty woodworking plant in northern Italy, near the Austrian border. They were able to turn out lances of pine to the dimensions he specified, but were astonished to hear he wanted an initial order of twenty. "Lances break," he told them. "I'll need a lot of them." To deal with splinters, he fitted a piece of screening to the faceplate of a football helmet. When he wore this helmet riding, he drew considerable attention. He looked like a demented beekeeper.

Eventually, Marek succumbed to modern technology, and he had his lances turned in aluminum, by a company that made baseball bats. The aluminum lances had better balance and felt more authentic to him, even though they were wrong for the period. And since splintering was no longer a problem, he could just wear a standard riding helmet.

Which was what he was wearing now.

Standing at the end of the field, he waved to Chris, who was over by the quintain. "Chris? Ready?"

Chris nodded and set the T-bar at right angles to Marek. He waved. Marek lowered his lance, and spurred his horse forward.

Training with the quintain was deceptively simple. The rider galloped toward the T-bar, attempting to strike the padded square with the tip of his lance. If he succeeded, he set the T-bar spinning, obliging him to spur his mount past before the leather bag swung around and hit him in the head. In the old days, Marek knew, the bag had been heavy enough to

knock a young rider from his mount. But Marek made it just
heavy enough to deliver a stinging rebuke.

On his first run, he hit the pad squarely, but he was not quick
enough to avoid the bag, which boxed him on the left ear. He
reined up, and trotted back. "Why don't you try one, Chris?"

"Maybe later," Chris said, repositioning the T-bar for the
next run.

Once or twice in recent days, Marek had gotten Chris to try a
run at the quintain. But he suspected that was only because of
Chris's sudden recent interest in all aspects of horsemanship.

Marek turned his charger, reared, and charged again. When
he first began, galloping full tilt toward a foot-square target
had seemed absurdly difficult. Now he was getting the hang
of it. He generally hit the target four out of five times.

The horse thundered ahead. He lowered his lance.

"Chris! Hallo!"

Chris turned, and waved to the girl riding up on horseback.
At that moment, Marek's lance hit the pad, and the leather bag
swung around, knocking Chris flat on his face.

:

Chris lay there, stunned, hearing peals of girlish laughter. But
she quickly dismounted and helped him to his feet again. "Oh
Chris, I'm sorry to laugh," she said in her elegant British accent. "It was all my fault, in any case. I oughtn't to have dis-
tracted you."

"I'm all right," he said, a little sulky. He brushed dirt from
his chin and faced her, managing to smile.

As always, he was struck by her beauty, especially at this
moment, her blond hair backlit in the afternoon sun so her
perfect complexion seemed to glow, setting off her deep
violet eyes. Sophie Rhys-Hampton was the most beautiful
woman he had ever met in his life. And the most intelligent.
And the most accomplished. And the most seductive.

"Oh, Chris, Chris," she said, brushing his face with cool
fingertips. "I really do apologize. There, now. Any better?"

Sophie was a student at Cheltenham College; twenty years
old, four years younger than he. Her father, Hugh Hampton,

was a London barrister; he owned the farmhouse that the project rented for the summer. Sophie had come down to stay with friends in a farmhouse nearby. One day she had come round to collect something from her father's study. Chris had seen her, and promptly walked into a tree trunk.

Which seemed to have set the tone for their relationship, he thought ruefully. She looked at him now and said, "I'm flattered I have this effect on you, Chris. But I worry for your safety." She giggled, and kissed him lightly on the cheek. "I called you today."

"I know, I got tied up. We had a crisis."

"A crisis? What constitutes an archaeological crisis?"

"Oh, you know. Funding hassles."

"Oh yes. That ITC bunch. From New Mexico." She made it sound like the ends of the earth. "Do you know, they asked to buy my father's farm?"

"Did they?"

"They said they needed to rent it for so many years ahead, they might as well buy it. Of course he said no."

"Of course." He smiled at her. "Dinner?"

"Oh, Chris. I can't tonight. But we can ride tomorrow. Shall we?"

"Of course."

"In the morning? Ten o'clock?"

"All right," he said. "I'll see you at ten."

"I'm not interrupting your work?"

"You know you are."

"It's quite all right to do it another day."

"No, no," he said. "Ten o'clock tomorrow."

"Done," she said, with a dazzling smile.

In fact, Sophie Hampton was almost too pretty, her figure too perfect, her manner too charming to be quite real. Marek, for one, was put off by her.

But Chris was entranced.

After she rode away, Marek charged by again. This time Chris got out of the way of the swinging quintain. When Marek trotted back, he said, "You're being jerked around, my friend."

"Maybe," Chris said. But the truth was, he didn't care.

The next day found Marek at the monastery, helping Rick Chang with the excavations into the catacombs. They had been digging here for weeks now. And it was slow going, because they kept finding human remains. Whenever they came upon bones, they stopped digging with shovels, and switched to trowels and toothbrushes.

Rick Chang was the physical anthropologist on the team. He was trained to deal with human finds; he could look at a pea-sized piece of bone and tell you whether it came from the right wrist or the left, male or female, child or adult, ancient or contemporary.

But the human remains they were finding here were puzzling. For one thing, they were all male; and some of the long bones had evidence of battle injuries. Several of the skulls showed arrow wounds. That was how most soldiers had died in the fourteenth century, from arrows. But there was no record of any battle ever fought at the monastery. At least none that they knew of.

They had just found what looked like a bit of rusted helmet when Marek's cell phone rang. It was the Professor.

"How is it going?" Marek said.

"Fine, so far."

"Did you meet with Doniger?"

"Yes. This afternoon."

"And?"

"I don't know yet."

"They still want to go forward with the reconstruction?"

"Well, I'm not sure. Things are not quite what I expected here." The Professor seemed vague, preoccupied.

"How's that?"

"I can't discuss it over the line," the Professor said. "But I wanted to tell you: I won't be calling in the next twelve hours. Probably not for the next twenty-four hours."

"Uh-huh. Okay. Everything all right?"

"Everything is fine, André."

Marek wasn't so sure. "Do you need aspirin?" That was one of their established code phrases, a way to ask if something was wrong, in case the other person couldn't speak freely.

"No, no. Not at all."

"You sound a little detached."

"Surprised, I would say. But everything's fine. At least, I think it's fine." He paused, then, "And what about the site? What's going on with you?"

"I'm with Rick at the monastery now. We're digging in the catacombs of quadrant four. I think we'll be down later today, or tomorrow at the latest."

"Excellent. Keep up the good work, André. I'll talk to you in a day or two."

And he rang off.

Marek clipped the phone back on his belt and frowned. What the hell did all that mean?

The helicopter thumped by overhead, its sensor boxes hanging beneath. Stern had kept it for another day, to do morning and afternoon runs; he wanted to survey the features that Kramer had mentioned, to see exactly how much showed up in an instrument run.

Marek wondered how it was going, but to talk to him, he needed a radio. The nearest one was in the storehouse.

:

"Elsie," Marek said as he walked into the storehouse. "Where's the radio to talk to David?"

Of course, Elsie Kastner didn't answer him. She just continued to stare at the document in front of her. Elsie was a pretty, heavyset woman who was capable of intense concentration. She sat in this storehouse for hours, deciphering the handwriting on parchments. Her job required her to know not only the six principal languages of medieval Europe, but also long-forgotten local dialects, slang and abbreviations. Marek felt lucky to have her, even though she stayed aloof from the rest of the team. And she could be a little strange at times. He said, "Elsie?"

She looked up suddenly. "What? Oh, sorry, André. I'm just, uh, I mean a little . . ." She gestured to the parchment in front of her. "This is a bill from the monastery to a German count. For putting up his personal retinue for the night: twenty-nine people and thirty-five horses. That's what this count was taking with him through the countryside. But it's written in a combination of Latin and Occitan, and the handwriting is impossible."

Elsie picked up the parchment and carried it to the photography stand in the corner. A camera was mounted on a four-legged stand above the table, with strobe lights aiming from all sides. She set the parchment down, straightened it, arranged the bar code ID at the bottom, put a two-inch checkerboard ruler down for standardization, and snapped the picture.

"Elsie? Where's the radio to talk to David?"

"Oh, sorry. It's on the far table. It's the one with the adhesive strip that says DS."

Marek went over, pressed the button. "David? It's André."

"Hi, André." Marek could hardly hear him with the thumping of the helicopter.

"What've you found?"

"Zip. Nada. Absolutely nothing," Stern said. "We checked the monastery and we checked the forest. None of Kramer's landmarks show up: not on SLS, or on radar, infrared, or UV. I have no idea how they made these discoveries."

:

They were galloping full tilt along a grassy ridge overlooking the river. At least, Sophie was galloping; Chris bounced and jolted, hanging on for dear life. Ordinarily, she never galloped on their outings together, in deference to his lesser ability, but today she was shrieking with delight as she raced headlong across the fields.

Chris tried to stay with her, praying she would stop soon, and finally she did, reining up her snorting and sweaty black stallion, patting it on the neck, waiting for him to catch up.

"Wasn't that exciting?" she said.

"It was," he said, gasping for breath. "It certainly was that."

"You did very well, Chris, I must say. Your seat is improving."

All he could do was nod. His seat was painful after all the bouncing, and his thighs ached from squeezing so hard.

"It's beautiful here," she said, pointing to the river, the dark castles on the far cliffs. "Isn't it glorious?"

And then she glanced at her watch, which annoyed him. But walking turned out to be surprisingly pleasant. She rode very close to him, the horses almost touching, and she leaned over to whisper in his ear; once she threw her arm around his shoulder and kissed him on the mouth, before glancing away, apparently embarrassed by her moment of boldness.

From their present position, they overlooked the entire site: the ruins of Castelgard, the monastery, and on the far hill, La Roque. Clouds raced overhead, moving shadows across the landscape. The air was warm and soft, and it was quiet, except for the distant rumble of an automobile.

"Oh, Chris," she said, and kissed him again. When they broke, she looked away in the distance, and suddenly waved.

A yellow convertible was winding up the road toward them. It was some sort of racing car, low-slung, its engine growling. A short distance away, it stopped, and the driver stood up behind the wheel, sitting on the back of the seat.

"Nigel!" she cried happily.

The man in the car waved back lazily, his hand tracing a slow arc.

"Oh Chris, would you be a dear?" Sophie handed Chris the reins of her horse, dismounted, and ran down the hill to the car, where she embraced the driver. The two of them got in the car. As they drove off, she looked back at Chris and blew him a kiss.

The restored medieval town of Sarlat was particularly charming at night, when its cramped buildings and narrow alleys were lit softly by gas lamps. On the rue Tourny, Marek and the graduate students sat in an outdoor restaurant under white umbrellas, drinking the dark red wine of Cahors into the night.

Usually, Chris Hughes enjoyed these evenings, but tonight nothing seemed right to him. The evening was too warm; his metal chair uncomfortable. He had ordered his favorite dish, *pintade aux cèpes*, but the guinea hen tasted dry, and the mushrooms were bland. Even the conversation irritated him: usually, the graduate students talked over the day's work, but tonight their young architect, Kate Erickson, had met some friends from New York, two American couples in their late twenties—stock traders with their girlfriends. He disliked them almost immediately.

The men were constantly getting up from the table to talk on cell phones. The women were both publicists in the same PR firm; they had just finished a very big party for Martha Stewart's new book. The group's bustling sense of their own self-importance quickly got on Chris's nerves; and, like many successful business people, they tended to treat academics as if they were slightly retarded, unable to function in the real world, to play the real games. Or perhaps, he thought, they just found it inexplicable that anyone would choose an occupation that wouldn't make them a millionaire by age twenty-four.

Yet he had to admit they were perfectly pleasant; they were

drinking a lot of wine, and asking a lot of questions about the project. Unfortunately, they were the usual questions, the ones tourists always asked: *What's so special about that place? How do you know where to dig? How do you know what to look for? How deep do you dig and how do you know when to stop?*

"Why are you working there? What's so special about that place, anyway?" one of the women asked.

"The site is very typical for the period," Kate said, "with two opposing castles. But what makes it a real find is that it has been a neglected site, never previously excavated."

"That's good? That it was neglected?" The woman was frowning; she came from a world where neglect was bad.

"It's very desirable," Marek said. "In our work, the real opportunities arise only when the world passes an area by. Like Sarlat, for instance. This town."

"It's very sweet here," one of the women said. The men stepped away to talk on their phones.

"But the point," Kate said, "is that it's an accident that this old town exists at all. Originally, Sarlat was a pilgrimage town that grew up around a monastery with relics; eventually it got so big that the monastery left, looking for peace and quiet elsewhere. Sarlat continued as a prosperous market center for the Dordogne region. But its importance diminished steadily over the years, and in the twentieth century, the world passed Sarlat by. It was so unimportant and poor that the town didn't have the money to rebuild its old sections. The old buildings just remained standing, with no modern plumbing and electricity. A lot of them were abandoned."

Kate explained that in the 1950s, the city was finally going to tear the old quarter down and put up modern housing. "André Malraux stopped it. He convinced the French government to put aside funds for restoration. People thought he was crazy. Now, Sarlat's the most accurate medieval town in France, and one of the biggest tourist attractions in the country."

"It's nice," the woman said, vaguely. Suddenly, both men

returned to the table together, sat down, and put their phones in their pockets with an air of finality.

"What happened?" Kate said.

"Market closed," one explained. "So. You were saying about Castelgard. What's so special about it?"

Marek said, "We were discussing the fact that it's never been excavated before. But it's also important to us because Castelgard is a typical fourteenth-century walled town. The town is older than that, but between 1300 and 1400 most of its structures were built, or modified, for greater defense: thicker walls, concentric walls, more complicated moats and gates."

"This is when? The Dark Ages?" one of the men said, pouring wine.

"No," Marek said. "Technically, it's the High Middle Ages."

"Not as high as I'm going to be," the man said. "So what comes before that, the Low Middle Ages?"

"That's right," Marek said.

"Hey," the man said, raising his wineglass. "Right the first time!"

:

Starting around 40 B.C., Europe had been ruled by Rome. The region of France where they now were, Aquitaine, was originally the Roman colony of Aquitania. All across Europe, the Romans built roads, supervised trade, and maintained law and order. Europe prospered.

Then, around A.D. 400, Rome began to withdraw its soldiers and abandon its garrisons. After the empire collapsed, Europe sank into lawlessness, which lasted for the next five hundred years. Population fell, trade died, towns shrank. The countryside was invaded by barbarian hordes: Goths and Vandals, Huns and Vikings. That dark period was the Low Middle Ages.

"But toward the last millennium—I mean A.D. 1000—things began to get better," Marek said. "A new organization coalesced that we call the feudal system—although back then, people never used that word."

Under feudalism, powerful lords provided local order. The new system worked. Agriculture improved. Trade and cities flourished. By A.D. 1200, Europe was thriving again, with a larger population than it had had during the Roman Empire. "So the year 1200 is the beginning of the High Middle Ages— a time of growth, when culture flourished."

The Americans were skeptical. "If it was so great, why was everybody building more defenses?"

"Because of the Hundred Years War," Marek said, "which was fought between England and France."

"What was it, a religious war?"

"No," Marek said. "Religion had nothing to do with it. Everyone at the time was Catholic."

"Really? What about the Protestants?"

"There were no Protestants."

"Where were they?"

Marek said, "They hadn't invented themselves yet."

"Really? Then what was the war about?"

"Sovereignty," Marek said. "It was about the fact that England owned a large part of France."

One of the men frowned skeptically. "What are you telling me? England used to own France?"

Marek sighed.

:

He had a term for people like this: temporal provincials— people who were ignorant of the past, and proud of it.

Temporal provincials were convinced that the present was the only time that mattered, and that anything that had occurred earlier could be safely ignored. The modern world was compelling and new, and the past had no bearing on it. Studying history was as pointless as learning Morse code, or how to drive a horse-drawn wagon. And the medieval period— all those knights in clanking armor and ladies in gowns and pointy hats—was so obviously irrelevant as to be beneath consideration.

Yet the truth was that the modern world was invented in the Middle Ages. Everything from the legal system, to nation-states, to reliance on technology, to the concept of romantic love had first been established in medieval times. These stockbrokers owed the very notion of a market economy to the Middle Ages. And if they didn't know that, then they didn't know the basic facts of who they were. Why they did what they did. Where they had come from.

Professor Johnston often said that if you didn't know history, you didn't know anything. You were a leaf that didn't know it was part of a tree.

:

The stock trader continued, pushing in the stubborn way that some people did when confronted with their own ignorance: "Really? England used to own part of France? That doesn't make any sense. The English and French have always hated each other."

"Not always," Marek said. "This was six hundred years ago. It was a completely different world. The English and French were much closer then. Ever since soldiers from Normandy conquered England in 1066, all the English nobility were basically French. They spoke French, ate French food, followed French fashions. It wasn't surprising they owned French territory. Here in the south, they had ruled Aquitaine for more than a century."

"So? What was the war about? The French decided they wanted it all for themselves?"

"More or less, yes."

"Figures," the man said, with a knowing nod.

:

Marek lectured on. Chris passed the time trying to catch Kate's eye. Here in candlelight, the angles of her face, which looked hard, even tough, in sunlight, were softened. He found her unexpectedly attractive.

But she did not return his look. Her attention was focused on her stockbroker friends. Typical, Chris thought. No matter what they said, women were only attracted to men with power and money. Even manic and sleazy men like these two.

He found himself studying their watches. Both men wore big, heavy Rolexes, but the metal watchbands were fitted loosely, so the watches flopped and dangled down their wrists, like a woman's bracelet. It was a sign of indifference and wealth, a casual sloppiness that suggested they were permanently on vacation. It annoyed him.

When one of the men began to play with his watch, flipping it around on his wrist, Chris finally could stand it no longer. Abruptly, he got up from the table. He mumbled some excuse about having to check on his analyses back at the site, and headed down the rue Tourny toward the parking lot at the edge of the old quarter.

All along the street, it seemed to him that he saw only lovers, couples strolling arm in arm, the woman with her head on the man's shoulder. They were at ease with each other, having no need to speak, just enjoying the surroundings. Each one he passed made him more irritable, and made him walk faster.

It was a relief when he finally got to his car, and drove home. Nigel!

What kind of an idiot had a name like Nigel?

The following morning, Kate was again hanging in the Castelgard chapel when her radio crackled and she heard the cry "Hot tamales! Hot tamales! Grid four. Come and get it! *Lunch is served.*"

That was the team's signal that a new discovery had been made. They used code words for all their important transmissions, because they knew local officials sometimes monitored them. At other sites, the government had occasionally sent agents in to confiscate discoveries at the moment they were first found, before the researchers had a chance to document and evaluate them. Although the French government had an enlightened approach to antiquities—in many ways better than Americans—individual field inspectors were notoriously inconsistent. And, of course, there was often some feeling about foreigners appropriating the noble history of France.

Grid four, she knew, was over at the monastery. She debated whether to stay in the chapel or to go all the way over there, but finally she decided to go. The truth was that much of their daily work was dull and uneventful. They all needed the renewed enthusiasm that came with the excitement of discoveries.

She walked through the ruins of Castelgard town. Unlike many others, Kate could rebuild the ruins in her mind, and see the town whole. She liked Castelgard; this was a nononsense town, conceived and built in time of war. It had all the straightforward authenticity that she had found missing in architecture school.

She felt the hot sun on her neck and her legs and thought for the hundredth time how glad she was to be in France, and not sitting in New Haven at her cramped little workspace on the sixth floor of the A & A Building, with big picture windows overlooking fake-colonial Davenport College and fake-Gothic Payne Whitney Gym. Kate had found architecture school depressing, she had found the Arts and Architecture Building *very* depressing, and she had never regretted her switch to history.

Certainly, you couldn't argue with a summer in southern France. She fitted into the team here at the Dordogne quite well. So far it had been a pleasant summer.

Of course, there had been some men to fend off. Marek had made a pass early on, and then Rick Chang, and soon she would have to deal with Chris Hughes as well. Chris took the British girl's rejection hard—he was apparently the only one in the Périgord who hadn't seen it coming—and now he was behaving like a wounded puppy. He'd been staring at her last night, during dinner. Men didn't seem to realize that rebound behavior was slightly insulting.

Lost in her thoughts, she walked down to the river, where the team kept the little rowboat that they used to ferry across.

And waiting there, smiling at her, was Chris Hughes.

:

"I'll row," he offered as they climbed into the boat. She let him. He began to pull across the river in easy strokes. She said nothing, just closed her eyes, turned her face up to the sun. It felt warm, relaxing.

"Beautiful day," she heard him say.

"Yes, beautiful."

"You know, Kate," he began, "I really enjoyed dinner last night. I was thinking maybe—"

"That's very flattering, Chris," she said. "But I have to be honest with you."

"Really? About what?"

"I've just broken up with someone."

"Oh. Uh-huh. . . ."

"And I want to take some time off."

"Oh," he said. "Sure. I understand. But maybe we could still—"

She gave him her nicest smile. "I don't think so," she said.

"Oh. Okay." She saw that he was starting to pout. Then he said, "You know, you're right. I really think it's best that we just stay colleagues."

"Colleagues," she said, shaking hands with him.

The boat touched the far shore.

⋮

At the monastery, a large crowd was standing around at the top of grid four, looking down into the excavation pit.

The excavation was a precise square, twenty feet on a side, going down to a depth of ten feet. On the north and east sides, the excavators had uncovered flat sides of stone arches, which indicated the dig was now within the catacomb structure, beneath the original monastery. The arches themselves were filled in with solid earth. Last week, they had dug a trench through the north arch, but it seemed to lead nowhere. Shored up with timbers, it was now ignored.

Now all the excitement was directed to the east arch, where in recent days they had dug another trench under the arch. Work had been slow because they kept finding human remains, which Rick Chang identified as the bodies of soldiers.

Looking down, Kate saw that the walls of the trench had collapsed on both sides, the earth falling inward, covering the trench itself. There was now a great mound of earth, like a landslide, blocking further progress, and as the earth collapsed, brownish skulls and long bones—lots of them—had tumbled out.

She saw Rick Chang down there, and Marek, and Elsie, who had left her lair to come out here. Elsie had her digital camera on a tripod, snapping off shots. These would later be stitched together in the computer to make 360-degree panoramas. They would be taken at hourly intervals, to record every phase of the excavation.

Marek looked up and saw Kate on the rim. "Hey," he said. "I've been looking for you. Get down here."

She scrambled down the ladder to the earthen floor of the pit. In the hot midafternoon sun, she smelled dirt, and the faint odor of organic decay. One of the skulls broke free and rolled to the ground at her feet. But she didn't touch it; she knew the remains should stay as they were until Chang removed them.

"This may be the catacombs," Kate said, "but these bones weren't stored. Was there ever a battle here?"

Marek shrugged. "There were battles everywhere. I'm more interested in *that*." He pointed ahead to the arch, which was without decoration, rounded and slightly flattened.

Kate said, "Cistercian, could even be twelfth century. . . ."

"Okay, sure. But what about *that*?" Directly beneath the central curve of the arch, the collapse of the trench had left a black opening about three feet wide.

She said, "What are you thinking?"

"I'm thinking we better get in there. Right away."

"Why?" she said. "What's the hurry?"

Chang said to her, "It looks like there's space beyond the opening. A room, maybe several rooms."

"So?"

"Now it's exposed to the air. For the first time in maybe six hundred years."

Marek said, "And air has oxygen."

"You think there's artifacts in there?"

"I don't know what's in there," Marek said. "But you could have considerable damage within a few hours." He turned to Chang. "Have we got a snake?"

"No, it's in Toulouse, being repaired." The snake was a fiber optic cable that could be hooked to a camera. They used it to view otherwise inaccessible spaces.

Kate said, "Why don't you just pump the room full of nitrogen?" Nitrogen was an inert gas, heavier than air. If they pumped it through the opening, it would fill the space up, like water. And protect any artifacts from the corrosive effects of oxygen.

"I would," Marek said, "if I had enough gas. The biggest cylinder we've got is fifty liters."

That wasn't enough.

She pointed to the skulls. "I know, but if you do anything now, you'll disturb—"

"I wouldn't worry about these skeletons," Chang said. "They've already been moved out of position. And they look like they were mass-graved, after a battle. But there isn't that much we can learn from them." He turned and looked up. "Chris, who's got the reflector?"

Up above, Chris said, "Not me. I think they were last used here."

One of the students said, "No, it's over by grid three."

"Let's get it. Elsie, are you about finished with your pictures?"

"Pushy, pushy."

"Are you, or not?"

"One minute more."

Chang was calling to the students above, telling them to bring the reflectors. Four of them ran off excitedly.

Marek was saying to the others, "Okay, you people, I want flashlights, I want excavation packs, portable oxygen, filter headsets, lead lines, the works—*now*."

Through the excitement, Kate continued to eye the opening beneath the arch. The arch itself looked weak to her, the stones held loosely together. Normally, an arch kept its shape by the weight of the walls pressing in on the center stone, the keystone of the arch. But here, the whole upper curve above the opening could just collapse. The landslide of earth underneath the opening was loose. She watched pebbles break free and trickle down here and there. It didn't look good to her.

"André, I don't think it's safe to climb over that. . . ."

"Who's talking about climbing over? We'll lower you from above."

"Me?"

"Yeah. You hang from above the arch, and then go inside." She must have looked stricken, because he grinned. "Don't worry, I'll go with you."

"You realize, if we're wrong . . ." She was thinking, *We could be buried alive*.

"What's this?" Marek said. "Losing your nerve?"

That was all he had to say.

:

Ten minutes later, she was hanging in midair by the edge of the exposed arch. She wore the excavation backpack, which was fitted with an oxygen bottle on the back and had two flashlights dangling like hand grenades from the waist straps. She had her filter headset pushed up on her forehead. Wires ran from the radio to a battery in her pocket. With so much equipment she felt clunky, uncomfortable. Marek stood above her, holding her safety line. And down in the pit, Rick and his students were watching her tensely.

She looked up at Marek. "Give me five." He released five feet of line, and she slid down until she was lightly touching the dirt mound. Little rivulets of earth trickled away beneath her feet. She eased herself forward.

"Three more."

She dropped to hands and knees, giving the mound her full weight. It held. But she looked up at the arch uneasily. The keystone was crumbling at the edges.

"Everything all right?" Marek called.

"Okay," she said. "I'll go in now."

She crawled back toward the gaping hole at the arch. She looked up at Marek, unhooked the flashlight. "I don't know if you can do this, André. The dirt may not support your weight."

"Very funny. You don't do this alone, Kate."

"Well, at least let me get in there first."

She flicked on her light, turned on her radio, pulled down her headset so she was breathing through filters, and crawled through the hole, into the blackness beyond.

:

The air was surprisingly cool. The yellow beam of her flashlight played on bare stone walls, a stone floor. Chang was right: this was open space beneath the monastery. And it seemed to continue for some distance, before dirt and collapsed rubble blocked the far passage. Somehow this chamber had not been filled with dirt like the others. She shone her light up at the roof, trying to see its condition. She couldn't really tell. Not great.

She crept forward on hands and knees, then began to descend, sliding a little, down the dirt toward the ground. Moments later, she was standing inside the catacombs.

"I'm here."

It was dark around her, and the air felt wet. There was a dank odor that was unpleasant, even through the filters. The filters took out bacteria and viruses. At most excavation sites, no one bothered with masks, but they were required here, because plague had come several times in the fourteenth century, killing a third of the population. Although one form of the epidemic was originally transmitted by infected rats, another form was transmitted through the air, through coughs and sneezes, and so anybody who went into an old, sealed space had to worry about—

She heard a clattering behind her. She saw Marek coming through the hole above. He began to slide, so he jumped to the ground. In the silence afterward, they heard the soft sounds of pebbles and earth, trickling down the mound.

"You realize," she said, "we could be buried alive in here."

"Always look on the bright side," Marek said. He moved forward, holding a big fluorescent light with reflectors. It illuminated a whole section of the room. Now that they could see clearly, the room appeared disappointingly bare. To the left was the stone sarcophagus of a knight; he was carved in relief on the lid, which had been removed. When they looked inside the sarcophagus, it was empty. Then there was a rough wooden table leaning against a wall. It was bare. An open corridor going down to their left, ending in a stone staircase, which led upward until it disappeared in a mound of dirt. More mounds of earth in this chamber, over to the right, blocking another passageway, another arch.

Marek sighed. "All this excitement . . . for nothing."

But Kate was still worried about the earth breaking free and coming into the room. It made her look closely at the earth mounds to the right.

And that was why she saw it.

"André," she said. "Come here."

:

It was an earth-colored protrusion, brown against the brown of the mound, but the surface had a faint sheen. She brushed it with her hand. It was oilcloth. She exposed a sharp corner. Oilcloth, wrapping something.

Marek looked over her shoulder. "Very good, very good."

"Did they have oilcloth then?"

"Oh yes. Oilcloth is a Viking invention, perhaps ninth century. Quite common in Europe by our period. Although I don't think we have found anything else in the monastery that's wrapped in oilcloth."

He helped her dig. They proceeded cautiously, not wanting the mound to come down on them, but soon they had it exposed. It was a rectangle roughly two feet square, wrapped with oil-soaked string.

"I am guessing it's documents," Marek said. His fingers were twitching in the fluorescent light, he wanted to open it so badly, but he restrained himself. "We'll take it back with us."

He slipped it under his arm and headed back toward the entrance. She gave one last look at the earth mound, wondering if she had missed something. But she hadn't. She swung her light away and—

She stopped.

Out of the corner of her eye, she'd caught a glimpse of something shiny. She turned, looked again. For a moment, she couldn't find it, but then she did.

It was a small piece of glass, protruding from the earth.

"André?" she said. "I think there's more."

:

The glass was thin, and perfectly clear. The edge was curved and smooth, almost modern in its quality. She brushed the dirt away with her fingertips and exposed one lens of an eyeglass.

It was a bifocal lens.

"What is it?" André said, coming back to her.

"You tell me."

He squinted at it, shone his light very near. His face was so close to the glass, his nose almost touched it. "Where did you find this?" He sounded concerned.

"Right here."

"Lying in the open, just like now?" His voice was tense, almost accusing.

"No, only the edge was exposed. I cleaned it off."

"How?"

"With my finger."

"So: you are telling me it was partly buried?" He sounded like he didn't believe her.

"Hey, what is this?"

"Just answer, please."

"No, André. It was *mostly* buried. Everything but that left edge was buried."

"I wish you had not touched it."

"I do, too, if I'd known you were going to act like—"

"This must be explained," he said. "Turn around."

"What?"

*"Turn around."* He took her by the shoulder, turned her roughly, so she was facing away from him.

"Jesus." She glanced over her shoulder to see what he was doing. He held his light very close to her backpack and moved over the surface slowly, examining it minutely, then down to her shorts. "Uh, are you going to tell me—"

"Be quiet, please."

It was a full minute before he finished. "The lower left zip pocket of your pack is open. Did you open it?"

"No."

"Then it has been open all the time? Ever since you put the pack on?"

"I guess. . . ."

"Did you brush against the wall at any time?"

"I don't think so." She had been careful about it, because she hadn't wanted the wall to break loose.

"Are you sure?" he said.

"For Christ's sake. No, André, I'm not sure."

"All right. Now you check me." He handed her his light, and turned his back to her.

"Check you how?" she said.

"That glass is contamination," he said. "We have to explain how it got here. Look to see if any part of my pack is open."

She looked. Nothing was.

"Did you look carefully?"

"Yes, I looked carefully," she said, annoyed.

"I think you didn't take enough time."

"André. I did."

Marek stared at the earthen mound in front of them. Small pebbles trickled down as he watched. "It could have fallen from one of our packs and then been covered. . . ."

"Yes, I guess it could."

"If you could clean it with a fingertip, it was not tightly buried. . . ."

"No, no. Very loose."

"All right. Then somehow, that is the explanation."

"What is?"

"Somehow, we brought this lens in with us, and while we were working on the oilskin documents, it fell from the pack, and was covered by dirt. Then you saw it, and cleaned it. It is the only explanation."

"Okay. . . ."

He took out a camera, photographed the glass several times from different distances—very close, then progressively farther back. Only then did he bring out a plastic baggie, lift the glass carefully with tweezers, and drop it into the bag. He brought out a small roll of bubble wrap, encased the bag, sealed it all with tape, and handed the bundle to her. "You bring it out. Please be careful." He seemed more relaxed. He was being nicer to her.

"Okay," she said. They climbed the dirt slope again, heading back outside.

.
.

They were greeted by cheers from the undergraduates, and the oilskin package was handed over to Elsie, who quickly took it back to the farmhouse. Everyone was laughing and smiling, except Chang and Chris Hughes. They were wearing headsets, and had heard everything inside the cave. They looked gloomy and upset.

Site contamination was extremely serious, and they all knew it. Because it implied sloppy excavation technique, it called into question any other, legitimate discoveries made by the team. A typical instance was a minor scandal at Les Eyzies the year before.

Les Eyzies was a Paleolithic site, a habitation of early man beneath a cliff ledge. The archaeologists had been digging at a level that dated to 320,000 B.P., when one of them found a half-buried condom. It was still in its metallic wrapper, and nobody thought for a moment that it belonged at that level. But the fact that it had been found there—half-buried—suggested that they were not being careful in their technique. It caused a near panic among the team, which persisted even after a graduate student was sent back to Paris in disgrace.

"Where is this glass lens?" Chris said to Marek.

"Kate has it."

She gave it to Chris. While everyone else was cheering, he turned away, unwrapped the package, and held the baggie up to the light.

"Definitely modern," he said. He shook his head unhappily. "I'll check it out. Just make sure you include it in the site report."

Marek said he would.

Then Rick Chang turned away and clapped his hands. "All right, everybody. Excitement's over. Back to work!"

In the afternoon, Marek scheduled archery practice. The undergraduates were amused by it, and they never missed a session; recently Kate had taken it up, as well. The target today was a straw-filled scarecrow, set about fifty yards away. The kids were all lined up, holding their bows, and Marek strode down behind them.

"To kill a man," he said, "you have to remember: he is almost certainly wearing plate armor on his chest. He's less likely to have armor on his head and neck, or on his legs. So to kill him, you must shoot him in the head, or on the side of his torso, where the plates don't cover."

Kate listened to Marek, amused. André took everything so seriously. *To kill a man.* As if he really meant it. Standing in the yellow afternoon sunlight of southern France, hearing the distant honk of cars on the road, the idea seemed slightly absurd.

"But if you want to stop a man," Marek continued, "then shoot him in the leg. He'll go right down. Today we'll use the fifty-pound bows."

Fifty pounds referred to the draw weight, what was needed to pull the string back. The bows were certainly heavy, and difficult to draw. The arrows were almost three feet long. Many of the kids had trouble with it, especially at first. Marek usually finished each practice session with some weight lifting, to build up their muscles.

Marek himself could draw a hundred-pound bow. Although it was difficult to believe, he insisted that this was the size of actual fourteenth-century weapons—far beyond what any of them could use.

"All right," Marek said, "nock your arrows, aim, and loose them, please." Arrows flew through the air. "No, no, no, David, don't pull until you tremble. Maintain control. Carl, look at your stance. Bob, too high. Deanna, remember your fingers. Rick, that was much better. All right, here we go again, nock your arrows, aim, and . . . loose them!"

:

It was late in the afternoon when Stern called Marek on the radio, and asked him to come to the farmhouse. He said he had good news. Marek found him at the microscope, examining the lens.

"What is it?"

"Here. Look for yourself." He stepped aside, and Marek looked. He saw the lens, and the sharp line of the bifocal cut. Here and there, the lens was lightly spotted with white circles, as if from bacteria.

"What am I supposed to see?" Marek said.

"Left edge."

He moved the stage, bringing the left edge into view. Refracted in the light, the edge looked very white. Then he noticed that the whiteness spilled over the edge, onto the surface of the lens itself.

"That's bacteria growing on the lens," Stern said. "It's like rock varnish."

Rock varnish was the term for the patina of bacteria and mold that grew on the underside of rocks. Because it was organic, rock varnish could be dated.

"Can this be dated?" Marek said.

"It could," Stern said, "if there was enough of it for a C-14 run. But I can tell you now, there isn't. You can't get a decent date from that amount. There isn't any use trying."

"So?"

"The point is, that was the exposed edge of the lens, right? The edge that Kate said was sticking out of the earth?"

"Right. . . ."

"So it's old, André. I don't know how old, but it's not site contamination. Rick is looking at all the bones that were exposed today, and he thinks some of them are later than our period, eighteenth century, maybe even nineteenth century. Which means one of them could have been wearing bifocals."

"I don't know. This lens looks pretty sharply done. . . ."

"Doesn't mean it's new," Stern said. "They've had good grinding techniques for two hundred years. I'm arranging for this lens to be checked by an optics guy back in New Haven. I've asked Elsie to jump ahead and do the oilskin documents, just to see if there's anything unusual there. In the meantime, I think we can all ease up."

"That's good news," Marek said, grinning.

"I thought you'd want to know. See you at dinner."

They had arranged to have dinner in the old town square of Domme, a village on top of a cliff a few miles from their site. By nightfall, Chris, grumpy all day, had recovered from his bad mood and was looking forward to dinner. He wondered if Marek had heard from the Professor, and if not, what they were going to do about it. He had a sense of expectancy.

His good mood vanished when he arrived to find the stockbroker couples again, sitting at their table. Apparently they'd been invited for a second night. Chris was about to turn around and leave, but Kate got up and quickly put her arm around his waist, and steered him toward the table.

"I'd rather not," he said in a low voice. "I can't stand these people." But then she gave him a little hug, and eased him into a chair. He saw that the stockbrokers must be buying the wine tonight—Château Lafite-Rothschild '95, easily two thousand francs a bottle.

And he thought, What the hell.

"Well, this is a charming town," one of the women was saying. "We went and saw the walls around the outside. They go on for quite a distance. High, too. And that very pretty gate coming into town, you know, with the two round towers on either side."

Kate nodded. "It's sort of ironic," she said, "that a lot of the villages that we find so charming now were actually the shopping malls of the fourteenth century."

"Shopping malls? How do you mean?" the woman asked.

At that moment, Marek's radio, clipped to his belt, crackled with static.

101

"André? Are you there?"

It was Elsie. She never came to dinner with the others, but worked late on her cataloging. Marek held up the radio. "Yes, Elsie."

"I just found something very weird, here."

"Yes. . . ."

"Would you ask David to come over? I need his help testing. But I'm telling you guys—if this is a joke, I don't appreciate it."

With a click, the radio went dead.

"Elsie?"

No answer.

Marek looked around the table. "Anybody play a joke on her?"

They all shook their heads no.

Chris Hughes said, "Maybe she's cracking up. It wouldn't surprise me, all those hours staring at parchment."

"I'll see what she wants," David Stern said, getting up from the table. He headed off into the darkness.

Chris thought of going with him, but Kate looked at him quickly, and gave him a smile. So he eased back in his seat and reached for his wine.

:

"You were saying—these towns were like shopping malls?"

"A lot of them were, yes," Kate Erickson said. "These towns were speculative ventures to make money for land developers. Just like shopping malls today. And like malls, they were all built on a similar pattern."

She turned in her chair and pointed to the Domme town square behind them. "See the covered wooden market in the center of the town square? You'll find similar covered markets in lots of towns around here. It means the town is a *bastide*, a new, fortified village. Nearly a thousand *bastide* towns were built in France during the fourteenth century. Some of them were built to hold territory. But many of them were built simply to make money."

That got the attention of the stock pickers.

One of the men looked up sharply and said, "Wait a minute. How does building a village make anybody money?"

Kate smiled. "Fourteenth-century economics," she said. "It worked like this. Let's say you're a nobleman who owns a lot of land. Fourteenth-century France is mostly forest, which means that your land is mostly forest, inhabited by wolves. Maybe you have a few farmers here and there who pay you some measly rents. But that's no way to get rich. And because you're a nobleman, you're always desperately in need of money, to fight wars and to entertain in the lavish style that's expected of you.

"So what can you do to increase the income from your lands? You build a new town. You attract people to live in your new town by offering them special tax breaks, special liberties spelled out in the town charter. Basically, you free the townspeople from feudal obligations."

"Why do you give them these breaks?" one of the men said.

"Because pretty soon you'll have merchants and markets in the town, and the taxes and fees generate much more money for you. You charge for everything. For the use of the road to come to the town. For the right to enter the town walls. For the right to set up a stall in the market. For the cost of soldiers to keep order. For providing moneylenders to the market."

"Not bad," one of the men said.

"Not bad at all. And in addition, you take a percentage of everything that's sold in the market."

"Really? What percentage?"

"It depended on the place, and the particular merchandise. In general, one to five percent. So the market is really the reason for the town. You can see it clearly, in the way the town is laid out. Look at the church over there," she said, pointing off to the side. "In earlier centuries, the church was the center of the town. People went to Mass at least once a day. All life revolved around the church. But here in Domme, the church is off to one side. The market is now the center of town."

"So all the money comes from the market?"

"Not entirely, because the fortified town offers protection

for the area, which means farmers will clear the nearby land and start new farms. So you increase your farming rents, as well. All in all, a new town was a reliable investment. Which is why so many of these towns were built."

"Is that the only reason the towns were built?"

"No, many were built for military considerations as—"

Marek's radio crackled. It was Elsie again. "André?"

"Yes," Marek said.

"You better get over here right away. Because I don't know how to handle this."

"Why? What is it?"

"Just come. *Now.*"

The generator chugged loudly, and the farmhouse seemed brilliantly lit in the dark field, under a sky of stars.

They all crowded into the farmhouse. Elsie was sitting at her desk in the center, staring at them. Her eyes seemed distant.

"Elsie?"

"It's impossible," she said.

"What's impossible? What happened here?"

Marek looked over at David Stern, but he was still working at some analysis in the corner of the room.

Elsie sighed. "I don't know, I don't know. . . ."

"Well," Marek said, "start at the beginning."

"Okay," she said. "The beginning." She stood up and crossed the room, where she pointed to a stack of parchments resting on a piece of plastic tarp on the floor. "This is the beginning. The document bundle I designated M-031, dug up from the monastery earlier today. David asked me to do it as soon as possible."

Nobody said anything. They just watched her.

"Okay," she said. "I've been going through the bundle. This is how I do it. I take about ten parchments at a time and bring them over here to my desk." She brought ten over. "Now, I sit down at the desk, and I go through them, one by one. Then, after I've summarized the contents of one sheet, and entered the summary into the computer, I take the sheet to be photographed, over here." She went to the next table, slipped a parchment under the camera.

Marek said, "We're familiar with—"

"No, you're not," she said sharply. "You're not familiar at all." Elsie went back to her table, took the next parchment off the stack. "Okay. So I go through them one by one. This particular stack consists of all kinds of documents: bills, copies of letters, replies to orders from the bishop, records of crop yields, lists of monastery assets. All dating from about the year 1357."

She took the parchments from the stack, one after the other.

"And then"—she removed the last one—"I see this."

They stared.

Nobody said anything.

The parchment was identical in size to the others in the stack, but instead of dense writing in Latin or Old French, this one had only two words, scrawled in plain English:

HELP ME
4/7/1357

"In case you're wondering," she said, "that's the Professor's handwriting."

The room was silent. No one moved or shifted. They all just stared in complete silence.

Marek was thinking very fast, running through the possibilities. Because of his detailed, encyclopedic knowledge of the medieval period, for many years he had served as an outside consultant on medieval artifacts to the Metropolitan Museum of Art in New York. As a result, Marek had considerable experience with fakes of all kinds. It was true that he was rarely shown faked documents from the medieval period—the fakes were usually precious stones set in a bracelet that was ten years old, or a suit of armor that turned out to have been made in Brooklyn—but his experience had given him a clear way to think it through.

Marek said, "Okay. Begin at the beginning. Are you sure that's his handwriting?"

"Yes," Elsie said. "Without question."

"How do you know?"

She sniffed. "I'm a graphologist, André. But here. See for yourself."

She brought out a note that Johnston had scrawled a few days earlier, a note written in block letters, attached to a bill: "PLS CHK THIS CHARGE." She set it beside the parchment signature. "Block letters are actually easier to analyze. His *H*, for example, has a faint diagonal beneath. He draws one vertical line, lifts his pen, draws the second vertical, then drags his pen back to draw the crossbar, making the diagonal below. Or look at the *P*. He makes a downward stroke, then goes up and back to position to make the semicircle. Or the *E*, which he draws as an *L* and then zigzags back up to make the two added lines. There's no question. It's his handwriting."

"Someone couldn't have forged it?"

"No. Forgery, you have pen lifts and other signs. This writing is his."

Kate said, "Would he play a joke on us?"

"If he did, it isn't funny."

"What about this parchment it's written on?" Marek said. "Is it as old as the other sheets in the stack?"

"Yes," David Stern said, coming over. "Short of carbon dating, I'd say yes—it's the same age as the others."

Marek thought: *How can that be?* He said, "Are you sure? This parchment looks different. The surface looks rougher to me."

"It is rougher," Stern said. "Because it's been poorly scraped. Parchment was valuable material in medieval times. Generally it was used, scraped clean, and then used again. But if we look at this parchment under ultraviolet. . . . Would somebody get the lights?" Kate turned them off, and in the darkness Stern swung a purple lamp over the table.

Marek immediately saw more writing, faint but clearly there on the parchment.

"This was originally a bill for lodging," Elsie said. "It's been scraped clean, quickly and crudely, as if somebody was in a hurry."

Chris said, "Are you saying the Professor scraped it?"

"I have no idea who scraped it. But it's not expertly done."

"All right," Marek said. "There's one definitive way to decide this, once and for all." He turned to Stern. "What about the ink, David? Is it genuine?"

Stern hesitated. "I'm not sure."

"Not sure? Why not?"

:

"Chemically speaking," Stern said, "it's exactly what you'd expect: iron in the form of ferrous oxide, mixed with gall as an organic binder. Some added carbon for blackness, and five percent sucrose. In those days, they used sugar to give the inks a shiny surface. So it's ordinary iron-gall ink, correct for the period. But that in itself doesn't mean much."

"Right." Stern was saying it could be faked.

"So I ran gall and iron titers," Stern said, "which I usually do in questionable cases. They tell us the exact amounts present in the ink. The titers indicate that this particular ink is similar but not identical to the ink on the other documents."

"Similar but not identical," Marek said. "How similar?"

"As you know, medieval inks were mixed by hand before use, because they didn't keep. Gall is organic—it's the ground-up nuts of an oak tree—which means the inks would eventually go bad. Sometimes they added wine to the ink as a preservative. Anyway, there's usually a fairly large variation in gall and iron content from one document to another. You find as much as twenty or thirty percent difference between documents. It's reliable enough that we can use these percentages to tell if two documents were written on the same day, from the same ink supply. This particular ink is about twenty-nine percent different from the documents on either side of it."

"Meaningless," Marek said. "Those numbers don't confirm either authenticity or forgery. Did you do a spectrographic analysis?"

"Yes. Just finished it. Here's the spectra for three documents, with the Professor's in the middle." Three lines, a series of spikes and dips. "Again, similar but not identical."

"Not *that* similar," Marek said, looking at the pattern of spikes. "Because along with the percentage difference in iron content, you've got lots of trace elements in the Professor's ink, including—what's this spike, for instance?"

"Chromium."

Marek sighed. "Which means it's modern."

"Not necessarily, no."

"There's no chromium in the inks before and after."

"That's true. But chromium *is* found in manuscript inks. Fairly commonly."

"Is there chromium in this valley?"

"No," Stern said, "but chromium was imported all over Europe, because it was used for fabric dyes as well as inks."

"But what about all these other contaminants?" Marek said, pointing to the other spikes. He shook his head. "I'm sorry. I'm just not buying this."

Stern said, "I agree. This has to be a joke."

"But we're not going to know for sure without a carbon date," Marek said. Carbon-14 would enable them to date both ink and parchment within about fifty years. That would be good enough to settle the question of forgery.

"I'd also like to do thermoluminescence, and maybe a laser activation while we're at it," Stern said.

"You can't do that here."

"No, I'll take it over to Les Eyzies." Les Eyzies, the town in the next valley that was the center of prehistoric studies in southern France, had a well-equipped lab that did carbon-14 and potassium-argon dating, as well as neutron activation and other difficult tests. The field results weren't as accurate as the labs in Paris or Toulouse, but scientists could get an answer in a few hours.

"Any chance you can run it tonight?" Marek said.

"I'll try."

Chris came back to join the group; he had been telephoning the Professor on a cell phone. "Nothing," he said. "I just got his voicemail."

"All right," Marek said. "There's nothing more we can do right now. I assume this message is a bizarre joke. I can't imagine who played it on us—but somebody did. Tomorrow we'll run carbon and date the message. I have no doubt it will prove to be recent. And with all due respect to Elsie, it's probably a forgery."

Elsie started to sputter.

"But in any case," Marek continued, "the Professor is due to call in tomorrow, and we'll ask him. In the meantime, I suggest we all go to bed and get a good night's rest."

In the farmhouse, Marek closed the door softly behind him before turning on the lights. Then he looked around.

The room was immaculate, as he would have expected. It had the tidiness of a monk's cell. Beside the bed stood five or six research papers, neatly stacked. On a desk to the right, more research papers sat beside a closed laptop computer. The desk had a drawer, which he opened and rummaged through quickly.

But he didn't find what he was looking for.

He went next to the armoire. The Professor's clothes were neatly arranged inside, with space between each hanging garment. Marek went from one to the next, patting the pockets, but he still did not find it. Perhaps it wasn't here, he thought. Perhaps he had taken it with him to New Mexico.

There was a bureau opposite the door. He opened the top drawer: coins in a small shallow dish, American dollar bills wrapped in a rubber band, and a few personal objects, including a knife, a pen and a spare watch—nothing out of the ordinary.

Then he saw a plastic case, tucked over to one side.

He brought the case out, opened it up. The case contained eyeglasses. He set the glasses out on the counter.

The lenses were bifocals, oval in shape.

He reached into his shirt pocket and brought out a plastic bag. He heard a creak behind him, and turned to see Kate Erickson coming in through the door.

"Going through his underwear?" she said, raising her eyebrows. "I saw the light under the door. So I had a look."

"Without knocking?" Marek said.

"What are you doing in here?" she said. Then she saw the plastic. "Is that what I think it is?"

"Yes."

Marek took the single bifocal lens out of the plastic bag, holding it with a pair of tweezers, and placed it on top of the bureau, beside the Professor's eyeglasses.

"Not identical," she said. "But I'd say the lens is his."

"So would I."

"But isn't that what you always thought? I mean, he's the only one on the site who wears bifocals. The contamination has to be from his eyeglasses."

"But there isn't any contamination," Marek said. "This lens is old."

"What?"

"David says that white edge is bacterial growth. This lens is not modern, Kate. It's old."

She looked closely. "It can't be," she said. "Look at the way the lenses are cut. It's the same in the Professor's glasses and this lens. It must be modern."

"I know, but David insists it's old."

"How old?"

"He can't tell."

"He can't date it?"

Marek shook his head. "Not enough organic material."

"So in that case," she said, "you came to his room because . . ." She paused, staring at the eyeglasses, then at him. She frowned. "I thought you said that signature was a forgery, André."

"I did, yes."

"But you also asked if David could do the carbon test *tonight*, didn't you."

"Yes. . . ."

"And then you came here, with the glass, because you're worried. . . ." She shook her head as if to clear it. "About what? What do you think is going on?"

Marek looked at her. "I have absolutely no idea. Nothing makes sense."

"But you're worried."

"Yes," Marek said. "I'm worried."

The following day dawned bright and hot, a glaring sun beneath a cloudless sky. The Professor didn't call in the morning. Marek called him twice, but always got his voicemail: "Leave me a message, and I'll call you back."

Nor was there any word from Stern. When they called the lab at Les Eyzies they were told he was busy. A frustrated technician said, "He is repeating the tests again! Three times now!"

Why? Marek wondered. He considered going over to Les Eyzies to see for himself—it was just a short drive—but decided to stay at the storehouse in case the Professor called.

He never called.

In the middle of the morning, Elsie said, "Huh."

"What?"

She was looking at another piece of parchment. "This was the document on the stack right before the Professor's," she said.

Marek came over. "What about it?"

"It looks like there are ink spots from the Professor's pen. See, here, and here?"

Marek shrugged. "He was probably looking at this right before he wrote his note."

"But they're in the margin," she said, "almost like a notation."

"Notation to what?" he said. "What's the document about?"

"It's a piece of natural history," she said. "A description of an underground river by one of the monks. Says you have to

113

be cautious at various points, marked off in paces, so on and so forth."

"An underground river. . . ." Marek wasn't interested. The monks were the scholars of the region, and they often wrote little essays on local geography, or carpentry, the proper time to prune orchard trees, how best to store grain in winter, and so on. They were curiosities, and often wrong.

" 'Marcellus has the key,' " she said, reading the text. "Wonder what that means. It's right where the Professor put his marks. Then . . . something about . . . giant feet . . . no . . . the giant's feet? . . . The feet of the giant? . . . And it says *vivix*, which is Latin for . . . let me see. . . . That's a new one. . . ."

She consulted a dictionary.

Restless, Marek went outside and paced up and down. He was edgy, nervous.

"That's odd," she said, "there is no word *vivix*. At least not in this dictionary." She made a note, in her methodical way.

Marek sighed.

The hours crawled by.

The Professor never called.

Finally it was three o'clock; the students were wandering up to the big tent for their afternoon break. Marek stood in the door and watched them. They seemed carefree, laughing, punching each other, making jokes.

The phone rang. He immediately turned back. Elsie picked it up. He heard her say, "Yes, he's here with me right now. . . ."

He hurried into her room. "The Professor?"

She was shaking her head. "No. It's someone from ITC." And she handed him the phone.

"This is André Marek speaking," he said.

"Oh yes. Please hold, Mr. Marek. I know Mr. Doniger is eager to speak to you."

"He is?"

"Yes. We've been trying to reach you for several hours. Please hold while I find him for you."

A long pause. Some classical music played. Marek put his hand over the phone and said to Elsie, "It's Doniger."

"Hey," she said. "You must rate. The big cheese himself."

"Why is Doniger calling me?"

Five minutes later, he was still waiting on hold, when Stern walked into the room, shaking his head. "You're not going to believe this."

"Yes? What?" Marek said, holding the phone.

Stern just handed him a sheet of paper. It said:

$$638 \pm 47 \text{ BP}$$

"What is this supposed to be?" Marek said.

"The date on the ink."

"What are you talking about?"

"The ink on that parchment," Stern said. "It's six hundred and thirty-eight years old, plus or minus forty-seven years."

"What?" Marek said.

"That's right. The ink has a date of A.D. 1361."

*"What?"*

"I know, I know," Stern said. "But we ran the test three times. There's no question about it. If the Professor really wrote that, he wrote it six hundred years ago." Marek flipped the paper over. On the other side, it said:

$$AD \ 1361 \pm 47 \text{ years}$$

On the phone, the music ended with a click, and a taut voice said, "This is Bob Doniger. Mr. Marek?"

"Yes," Marek said.

"You may not remember, but we met a couple of years ago, when I visited the site."

"I remember very well," Marek said.

"I'm calling about Professor Johnston. We are very concerned for his safety."

"Is he missing?"

"No, he's not. We know exactly where he is."

Something in his tone sent a shiver down Marek's spine. Marek said, "Then can I speak to him?"

"Not at the moment, I'm afraid."

"Is the Professor in danger?"

"It's difficult to say. I hope not. But we're going to need the help of you and your group. I've already sent the plane to get you."

∴

Marek said, "Mr. Doniger, we seem to have a message from Professor Johnston that is six hundred years—"

"Not on a cell phone," Doniger said, cutting him off. But Marek noticed that he didn't seem at all surprised. "It's three o'clock now in France, is that right?"

"Just after, yes."

"All right," Doniger said. "Pick the three members of your team who know the Dordogne region best. Drive to the airport at Bergerac. Don't bother to pack. We'll supply everything when you get here. The plane lands at six p.m. your time, and will bring you back to New Mexico. Is that clear?"

"Yes, but—"

"I'll see you then."

And Doniger hung up.

∴

David Stern looked at Marek. "What was that all about?" he said.

Marek said, "Go get your passport."

"What?"

"Go get your passport. Then come back with the car."

"We going somewhere?"

"Yes, we are," Marek said.

And he reached for his radio.

∴

Kate Erickson looked down from the ramparts of La Roque Castle into the inner bailey, the broad grassy center of the castle, twenty feet below. The grass was swarming with tourists of a dozen nationalities, all in bright clothes and shorts. Cameras clicking in every direction.

Beneath her, she heard a young girl say, "*Another* castle. Why do we have to go to all these stupid castles, Mom?"

The mother said, "Because Daddy is interested."

"But they're all the same, Mom."

"I know, dear. . . ."

The father, a short distance away, was standing inside low walls that outlined a former room. "And this," he announced to his family, "was the great hall."

Looking down, Kate saw at once that it wasn't. The man was standing inside the remains of the kitchen. It was obvious from the three ovens still visible in the wall to the left. And the stone sluice that had brought water could be seen just behind the man as he spoke.

"What happened in the great hall?" his daughter asked.

"This is where they held their banquets, and where visiting knights paid homage to the king."

Kate sighed. There was no evidence a king had ever been to La Roque. On the contrary, documents indicated that it had always been a private castle, built in the eleventh century by someone named Armand de Cléry, and later heavily rebuilt early in the fourteenth century, with another ring of outer walls, and additional drawbridges. That added work was done by a knight named François le Gros, or Francis the Fat, around 1302.

Despite his name, François was an English knight, and he built La Roque in the new English style of castles, established by Edward I. The Edwardian castles were large, with spacious inner courtyards and pleasant quarters for the lord. This suited François, who by all accounts had an artistic temperament, a lazy disposition, and a propensity for money troubles. François was forced to mortgage his castle, and later to sell it outright. During the Hundred Years War, La Roque was controlled by a succession of knights. But the fortifications held: the castle was never captured in battle, only in commercial transactions.

As for the great hall, she saw it was off to the left, badly ruined, but clearly indicating the outlines of a much larger room, almost a hundred feet long. The monumental fireplace—nine feet high and twelve feet wide—was still visible. Kate knew that any great hall of this size would have had stone walls and a timber roof. And yes, as she looked, she saw notches in the stone high up, to hold the big horizontal timbers. Then there would have been cross-bracing above that, to support the roof.

A British tour group squeezed past her on the narrow ramparts. She heard the guide say, "These ramparts were built by Sir Francis the Bad in 1363. Francis was a thoroughly nasty piece of work. He liked to torture men and women, and even children, in his vast dungeons. Now if you look to the left, you will see Lover's Leap, where Madame de Renaud fell to her death in 1292, disgraced because she was pregnant by her husband's stable boy. But it is disputed whether she fell or was pushed by her outraged spouse. . . ."

Kate sighed. Where did they come up with this stuff? She turned to her sketchbook notes, where she was recording the outlines of the walls. This castle, too, had its secret passages. But Francis the Fat was a skilled architect. His passages were mostly for defense. One passage ran from the ramparts down behind the far wall of the great hall, past the rear of the fireplace. Another passage followed the battlements on the south ramparts.

But the most important passage still eluded her. According to the fourteenth-century writer Froissart, the castle of La Roque had never been taken by siege because its attackers could never find the secret passage that permitted food and water to be brought to the castle. It was rumored that this secret passage was linked to the network of caves in the limestone rock below the castle; also that it ran some distance, ending in a concealed opening in the cliffs.

Somewhere.

The easiest way to find it now would be to locate where it ended inside the castle and to follow it back. But to find that opening, she would need technical help. Probably the best thing would be ground radar. But to do that, she'd need the castle empty. It was closed on Mondays; they might do it next Monday, if—

Her radio crackled. "Kate?"

It was Marek.

She held the radio to her face, pressed the button. "Yes, this is Kate."

"Come back to the farmhouse now. It's an emergency."
And he clicked off.

:

Nine feet underwater, Chris Hughes heard the gurgling hiss
of his regulator as he adjusted the tether that held him in place
against the current of the Dordogne. The water clarity was not
bad today, about twelve feet, and he was able to see the entire
large pylon of the fortified mill bridge, at the water's edge.
The pylon ended in a jumble of large cut rocks that ran in a
straight line across the river. These rocks were the remains of
the former bridge span.

Chris moved along this line, examining the rocks slowly.
He was looking for grooves or notches that would help
him determine where timbers had been used. From time to
time, he tried to turn one rock over, but it was very difficult
underwater because he could get no leverage.

On the surface above, he had a plastic float with a red-
striped diver's flag. It was there to protect him from the vaca-
tioning kayakers. At least, that was the idea.

He felt a sudden jerk, yanking him away from the bottom.
He broke surface and bumped his head against the yellow
hull of a kayak. The rider was holding the plastic float, shouting at him in what sounded like German.

Chris pulled his mouthpiece out and said, "Just leave that
alone, will you?"

He was answered in rapid German. The kayaker was pointing irritably toward the shore.

"Listen, pal, I don't know what you're—"

The man kept shouting and pointing toward the shore, his
finger stabbing the air.

Chris looked back.

One of the students was standing on the shore, holding a
radio in his hand. He was shouting. It took Chris a moment to
understand. "Marek wants you back to the farmhouse. Now."

"Jesus, how about in half an hour, when I finish—"

"He says *now*."

Dark clouds hung over the distant mesas, and it looked like there would be rain. In his office, Doniger hung up the phone and said, "They've agreed to come."

"Good," Diane Kramer said. She was standing facing him, her back to the mountains. "We need their help."

"Unfortunately," Doniger said, "we do." He got up from his desk and began to pace. He was always restless when he was thinking hard.

"I just don't understand how we lost the Professor in the first place," Kramer said. "He must have stepped into the world. You told him not to do it. You told him not to go in the first place. And he must have stepped into the world."

"We don't know what happened," Doniger said. "We have no damn idea."

"Except that he wrote a message," Kramer said.

"Yes. According to Kastner. When did you talk to her?"

"Late yesterday," Kramer said. "She called me as soon as she knew. She's been a very reliable connection for us, and she—"

"Never mind," Doniger said, waving his hand irritably. "It's not core."

That was the expression he always used when he thought something was irrelevant. Kramer said, "What's core?"

"Getting him back," Doniger said. "It is essential that we get that man back. That is core."

"No question," Kramer said. "Essential."

"Personally, I thought the old fart was an asshole," Doniger said. "But if we don't get him back, it's a publicity nightmare."

120

"Yes. A nightmare."

"But I can deal with it," Doniger said.

"You can deal with it, I'm sure."

Over the years, Kramer had fallen into the habit of re-peating whatever Doniger said when he was in one of his "pacing moods." To an outsider, it looked like sycophancy, but Doniger found it useful. Frequently, when Doniger heard her say it back, he would disagree. Kramer understood that in this process, she was just a bystander. It might look like a conversation between two people, but it wasn't. Doniger was talking only to himself.

"The problem," Doniger said, "is that we're increasing the number of outsiders who know about the technology, but we're not getting a commensurate return. For all we know, those students won't be able to get him back, either."

"Their chances are better."

"That's a presumption." He paced. "It's weak."

"I agree, Bob. Weak."

"And the search team you sent back? Who did you send?"

"Gomez and Baretto. They didn't see the Professor anywhere."

"How long were they there?"

"I believe about an hour."

"They didn't step into the world?"

Kramer shook her head. "Why take the risk? There's no point. They're a couple of ex-marines, Bob. They wouldn't know where to look even if they did step in. They wouldn't even know what to be afraid of. It's completely different back there."

"But these graduate students may know where to look."

"That's the idea," Kramer said.

Distant thunder rumbled. The first fat drops of rain streaked the office windows. Doniger stared at the rain. "What if we lose the graduate students, too?"

"A publicity nightmare."

"Maybe," Doniger said. "But we have to prepare for the possibility."

The jet engines whined as the Gulfstream V rolled toward them, "ITC" in big silver letters on the tail. The stairs lowered, and a uniformed flight attendant rolled out a strip of red carpet at the bottom of the stairs.

The graduate students stared.

"No kidding," Chris Hughes said. "There really *is* a red carpet."

"Let's go," Marek said. He threw his backpack over his shoulder and led them aboard.

Marek had refused to answer their questions, pleading ignorance. He told them the results of the carbon dating. He told them he couldn't explain it. He told them that ITC wanted them to come to help the Professor, and that it was urgent. He didn't say any more. And he noticed that Stern, too, was keeping silent.

Inside, the plane was all gray and silver. The flight attendant asked them what they wanted to drink. All this luxury contrasted with the tough-looking man with cropped gray hair who came forward to greet them. Although the man wore a business suit, Marek detected a military manner as he shook hands with each of them.

"My name's Gordon," he said. "Vice president at ITC. Welcome aboard. Flying time to New Mexico is nine hours, forty minutes. Better fasten your seat belts."

They dropped into seats, already feeling the aircraft begin to move on the runway. Moments later, the engines roared, and Marek looked out the window to see the French countryside fall away beneath them.

:

It could be worse, Gordon thought, sitting at the back of the plane and looking at the group. True, they were academics. They were a little befuddled. And there was no coordination, no team feeling among them.

But on the other hand, they all seemed to be in decent physical condition, particularly the foreign guy, Marek. He looked strong. And the woman wasn't bad, either. Good muscle tone in the arms, calluses on her hands. Competent manner. So she might hold up under pressure, he thought.

But the good-looking kid would be useless. Gordon sighed as Chris Hughes looked out the window, caught his own reflection in the glass, and brushed back his hair with his hand.

And Gordon couldn't decide about the fourth kid, the nerdy one. He'd obviously spent time outdoors; his clothes were faded and his glasses scratched. But Gordon recognized him as a tech guy. Knew everything about equipment and circuits, nothing about the world. It was hard to say how he'd react if things got tough.

The big man, Marek, said, "Are you going to tell us what's going on?"

"I think you already know, Mr. Marek," Gordon said. "Don't you?"

"I have a piece of six-hundred-year-old parchment with the Professor's writing on it. In six-hundred-year-old ink."

"Yes. You do."

Marek shook his head. "But I have trouble believing it."

"At this point," Gordon said, "it's simply a technological reality. It's real. It can be done." He got out of his seat and moved to sit with the group.

"You mean time travel," Marek said.

"No," Gordon said. "I don't mean time travel at all. Time travel is impossible. Everyone knows that."

:

"The very concept of time travel makes no sense, since time doesn't flow. The fact that we think time passes is just an accident of our nervous systems—of the way things look to us. In reality, time doesn't pass; we pass. Time itself is invariant. It just *is*. Therefore, past and future aren't separate locations, the way New York and Paris are separate locations. And since the past isn't a location, you can't travel to it."

They were silent. They just stared at him.

"It is important to be clear about this," Gordon said. "The ITC technology has nothing to do with time travel, at least not directly. What we have developed is a form of space travel. To be precise, we use quantum technology to manipulate an orthogonal multiverse coordinate change."

They looked at him blankly.

"It means," Gordon said, "that we travel to another place in the multiverse."

"And what's the multiverse?" Kate said.

"The multiverse is the world defined by quantum mechanics. It means that—"

"Quantum mechanics?" Chris said. "What's quantum mechanics?"

Gordon paused. "That's fairly difficult. But since you're historians," he said, "let me try to explain it historically."

.

"A hundred years ago," Gordon said, "physicists understood that energy—like light or magnetism or electricity—took the form of continuously flowing waves. We still refer to 'radio waves' and 'light waves.' In fact, the recognition that all forms of energy shared this wavelike nature was one of the great achievements of nineteenth-century physics.

"But there was a small problem," he said. It turned out that if you shined light on a metal plate, you got an electric current. The physicist Max Planck studied the relationship between the amount of light shining on the plate and the amount of electricity produced, and he concluded that energy wasn't a continuous wave. Instead, energy seemed to be composed of individual units, which he called quanta. "The discovery that energy came in quanta was the start of quantum physics," Gordon said.

"A few years later, Einstein showed that you could explain the photoelectric effect by assuming that light was composed of particles, which he called photons. These photons of light struck the metal plate and knocked off electrons, producing electricity. Mathematically, the equations worked. They fit the view that light consisted of particles. Okay so far?"

"Yes. . . ."

"And pretty soon, physicists began to realize that not only light, but all energy was composed of particles. In fact, all matter in the universe took the form of particles. Atoms were composed of heavy particles in the nucleus, light electrons buzzing around on the outside. So, according to the new thinking, everything is particles. Okay?"

"Okay. . . ."

"The particles are discrete units, or quanta. And the theory that describes how these particles behave is quantum theory. A major discovery of twentieth-century physics."

They were all nodding.

"Physicists continue to study these particles, and begin to realize they're very strange entities. You can't be sure where they are, you can't measure them exactly, and you can't predict what they will do. Sometimes they behave like particles, sometimes like waves. Sometimes two particles will interact with each other even though they're a million miles apart, with no connection between them. And so on. The theory is starting to seem extremely weird.

"Now, two things happen to quantum theory. The first is that it gets confirmed, over and over. It's the most proven theory in the history of science. Supermarket scanners, lasers and computer chips all rely on quantum mechanics. So there is absolutely no doubt that quantum theory is the correct mathematical description of the universe.

"But the problem is, it's *only* a mathematical description. It's just a set of equations. And physicists couldn't visualize the world that was implied by those equations—it was too weird, too contradictory. Einstein, for one, didn't like that. He felt it meant the theory was flawed. But the theory kept getting confirmed, and the situation got worse and worse. Eventually, even scientists who won the Nobel Prize for contributions to quantum theory had to admit they didn't understand it.

"So, this made a very odd situation. For most of the twentieth century, there's a theory of the universe that everyone uses, and everyone agrees is correct—but nobody can tell you what it is saying about the world."

"What does all this have to do with multiple universes?" Marek said.

"I'm getting there," Gordon said.

:

Many physicists tried to explain the equations, Gordon said. Each explanation failed for one reason or another. Then in 1957, a physicist named Hugh Everett proposed a daring new explanation. Everett claimed that our universe—the universe we see, the universe of rocks and trees and people and galaxies out in space—was just one of an infinite number of universes, existing side by side.

Each of these universes was constantly splitting, so there was a universe where Hitler lost the war, and another where he won; a universe where Kennedy died, and another where he lived. And also a world where you brushed your teeth in the morning, and one where you didn't. And so forth, on and on and on. An infinity of worlds.

Everett called this the "many worlds" interpretation of quantum mechanics. His explanation was consistent with the quantum equations, but physicists found it very hard to accept. They didn't like the idea of all these worlds constantly splitting all the time. They found it unbelievable that reality could take this form.

"Most physicists still refuse to accept it," Gordon said. "Even though no one has ever shown it is wrong."

Everett himself had no patience with his colleagues' objections. He insisted the theory was true, whether you liked it or not. If you disbelieved his theory, you were just being stodgy and old-fashioned, exactly like the scientists who disbelieved the Copernican theory that placed the sun at the center of the solar system—and which had also seemed unbelievable at the time. "Because Everett claimed the many worlds concept was *actually true*. There really *were* multiple universes. And they were running right alongside our own. All these multiple universes were eventually referred to as a 'multiverse.'"

"Wait a minute," Chris said. "Are you telling us this is true?"

"Yes," Gordon said. "It's true."

"How do you know?" Marek said.

"I'll show you," Gordon said. And he reached for a manila file that said "ITC/CTC Technology."

⋮

He took out a blank piece of paper, and began drawing. "Very simple experiment, it's been done for two hundred years. Set up two walls, one in front of the other. The first wall has a single vertical slit in it."

He showed them the drawing.

"Now you shine a light at the slit. On the wall behind, you'll see—"

"A white line," Marek said. "From the light coming through the slit."

"Correct. It would look something like this." Gordon pulled out a photo on a card.

Gordon continued to sketch. "Now, instead of one slit, you have a wall with *two* vertical slits in it. Shine a light on it, and on the wall behind, you see—"

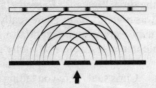

"Two vertical lines," Marek said.

"No. You'll see a series of light and dark bars." He showed them:

"And," Gordon continued, "if you shine your light through *four* slits, you get half as many bars as before. Because every other bar goes black."

Marek frowned. "More slits mean fewer bars? Why?"

"The usual explanation is what I've drawn—the light passing through the slits acts like two waves that overlap. In some places they add to each other, and in other places they cancel each other out. And that makes a pattern of alternating light and dark on the wall. We say the waves interfere with each other, and that this is an interference pattern."

Chris Hughes said, "So? What's wrong with all that?"

"What's wrong," Gordon said, "is that I just gave you a nineteenth-century explanation. It was perfectly acceptable when everybody believed that light was a wave. But since Einstein, we know that light consists of particles called photons. How do you explain a bunch of photons making this pattern?"

There was silence. They were shaking their heads.

David Stern spoke for the first time. "Particles aren't as simple as the way you have described them. Particles have some wavelike properties, depending on the situation. Particles can interfere with one another. In this case, the photons in the beam of light are interfering with one another to produce the same pattern."

"That does seem logical," Gordon said. "After all, a beam of light is zillions and zillions of little photons. It's not hard to imagine that they would interact with one another in some fashion, and produce the interference pattern."

They were all nodding. Yes, not hard to imagine.

"But is it really true?" Gordon said. "Is that what's going on? One way to find out is to eliminate any interaction among the photons. Let's just deal with one photon at a time. This has been done experimentally. You make a beam of light so weak that only one photon comes out at a time. And you can put very sensitive detectors behind the slits—so sensitive, they can register a single photon hitting them. Okay?"

They nodded, more slowly this time.

"Now, there can't be any interference from other photons, because we are dealing with a single photon only. So: the photons come through, one at a time. The detectors record where the photons land. And after a few hours, we get a result, something like this."

"What we see," Gordon said, "is that the individual photons land only in certain places, and never others. They behave exactly the same as they do in a regular beam of light. But they are coming in one at a time. There are no other photons to interfere with them. Yet *something* is interfering with them, because they are making the usual interference pattern. So: What is interfering with a single photon?"

Silence.

"Mr. Stern?"

Stern shook his head. "If you calculate the probabilities—"

"Let's not escape into mathematics. Let's stay with reality. After all, this experiment has been performed—with real photons, striking real detectors. And something real interferes with them. The question is, What is it?"

"It has to be other photons," Stern said.

"Yes," Gordon said, "but where are they? We have detectors, and we don't detect any other photons. So where are the interfering photons?"

Stern sighed. "Okay," he said. He threw up his hands.

Chris said, "What do you mean, Okay? Okay what?"

Gordon nodded to Stern. "Tell them."

"What he is saying is that single-photon interference proves that reality is much greater than just what we see in our universe. The interference is happening, but we can't see any cause for it in our universe. Therefore, the interfering photons must be in other universes. And that proves that the other universes exist."

"Correct," Gordon said. "And they sometimes interact with our own universe."

:

"I'm sorry," Marek said. "Would you do that again? Why is some other universe interfering with our universe?"

"It's the nature of the multiverse," Gordon said. "Remember, within the multiverse, the universes are constantly splitting, which means that many other universes are very similar to ours. And it is the similar ones that interact. Each time we make a beam of light in our universe, beams of light are simultaneously made in many similar universes, and the photons from those other universes interfere with the photons in our universe and produce the pattern that we see."

"And you are telling us this is true?"

"Absolutely true. The experiment has been done many times."

Marek frowned. Kate stared at the table. Chris scratched his head.

Finally David Stern said, "Not all the universes are similar to ours?"

"No."

"Are they all *simultaneous* to ours?"

"Not all, no."

"Therefore some universes exist at an earlier time?"

"Yes. Actually, since they are infinite in number, the universes exist at all earlier times."

Stern thought for a moment. "And you are telling us that ITC has the technology to travel to these other universes."

"Yes," Gordon said. "That's what I'm telling you."

"How?"

"We make wormhole connections in quantum foam."

"You mean Wheeler foam? Subatomic fluctuations of space-time?"

"Yes."

"But that's impossible."

Gordon smiled. "You'll see for yourself, soon enough."

"We will? What do you mean?" Marek said.

"I thought you understood," Gordon said. "Professor Johnston is in the fourteenth century. We want you to go back there, to get him out."

⁝

No one spoke. The flight attendant pushed a button and all the windows in the cabin slid closed at the same time, blocking out the sunshine. She went around the cabin, putting sheets and blankets on the couches, making them up as beds. Beside each she placed large padded headphones.

"We're going back?" Chris Hughes said. "How?"

"It will be easier just to show you," Gordon said. He handed them each a small cellophane packet of pills. "Right now, I want you to take these."

"What are they?" Chris said.

"Three kinds of sedative," he said. "Then I want you all to lie down and listen on the headphones. Sleep if you like. The flight's only ten hours, so you won't absorb very much, anyway. But at least you'll get used to the language and pronunciation."

"What language?" Chris said, taking his pills.

"Old English, and Middle French."

Marek said, "I already know those languages."

"I doubt you know correct pronunciation. Wear the headphones."

"But nobody knows the correct pronunciation," Marek said. As soon as he said it, he caught himself.

"I think you will find," Gordon said, "that *we* know."

Chris lay down on one bed. He pulled up the blanket and slipped the headphones over his ears. At least they blotted out the sound of the jet.

These pills must be strong, he thought, because he suddenly felt very relaxed. He couldn't keep his eyes open. He listened as a tape began to play. A voice said, "Take a deep breath. Imagine you are in a beautiful warm garden. Everything is familiar and comforting to you. Directly ahead, you see a door going down to the basement. You open the door. You know the basement well, because it is your basement. You begin to walk down the stone steps, into the warm and comforting basement. With each step, you hear voices. You find them pleasant to listen to, easy to listen to."

Then male and female voices began to alternate.

"Give me my hat. *Yiff may mean haht.*"

"Here is your hat. *Hair baye thynhatt.*"

"Thank you. *Grah mersy.*"

"You are welcome. *Ayepray thee.*"

The sentences became longer. Soon Chris found it difficult to follow them.

"I am cold. I would rather have a coat. *Ayeam chillingcold, ee wolld leifer half a coot.*"

Chris was drifting gently, imperceptibly, to sleep, with the sensation that he was still walking down a flight of stairs, deeper and deeper into a cavernous, echoing, comforting place. He was peaceful, though the last two sentences he remembered gave a tinge of concern:

"Prepare to fight. *Dicht theeselv to ficht.*"

"Where is my sword? *Whar beest mee swearde?*"

But then he exhaled, and slept.

# BLACK ROCK

"Risk everything, or gain nothing."

GEOFFREY DE CHARNY, 1358

The night was cold and the sky filled with stars as they stepped off the airplane onto the wet runway. To the east, Marek saw the dark outlines of mesas beneath low-hanging clouds. A Land Cruiser was waiting off to one side.

Soon they were driving down a highway, dense forest on both sides of the road. "Where exactly are we?" Marek said.

"About an hour north of Albuquerque," Gordon said. "The nearest town is Black Rock. That's where our research facility is."

"Looks like the middle of nowhere," Marek said.

"Only at night. Actually, there are fifteen high-tech research companies in Black Rock. And of course, Sandia is just down the road. Los Alamos is about an hour away. Farther away, White Sands, all that."

They continued down the road for several more miles. They came to a prominent green-and-white highway sign that read ITC BLACK ROCK LABORATORY. The Land Cruiser turned right, heading up a twisting road into the forested hills.

⋮

From the back seat, Stern said, "You told us before that you can connect to other universes."

"Yes."

"Through quantum foam."

"That's right."

"But that doesn't make any sense," Stern said.

"Why? What *is* quantum foam?" Kate said, stifling a yawn.

"It's a remnant of the birth of the universe," Stern said. He explained that the universe had begun as a single, very dense pinpoint of matter. Then, eighteen billion years ago, it exploded outward from that pinpoint—in what was known as the big bang.

"After the explosion, the universe expanded as a sphere. Except it wasn't an absolutely perfect sphere. Inside the sphere, the universe wasn't absolutely homogeneous—which is why we now have galaxies clumped and clustered irregularly in the universe, instead of being uniformly distributed. Anyway, the point is, the expanding sphere had tiny, tiny imperfections in it. And the imperfections never got ironed out. They're still a part of the universe."

"They are? Where?"

"At subatomic dimensions. Quantum foam is just a way of saying that at very small dimensions, space-time has ripples and bubbles. But the foam is smaller than an individual atomic particle. There may or may not be wormholes in that foam."

"There are," Gordon said.

"But how could you use them for travel? You can't put a person through a hole that small. You can't put *anything* through it."

"Correct," Gordon said. "You also can't put a piece of paper through a telephone line. But you can send a fax."

Stern frowned. "That's entirely different."

"Why?" Gordon said. "You can transmit anything, as long as you have a way to compress and encode it. Isn't that so?"

"In theory, yes," Stern said. "But you're talking about compressing and encoding the information for an entire human being."

"That's right."

"That can't be done."

Gordon was smiling, amused now. "Why not?"

"Because the complete description of a human being—all the billions of cells, how they are interconnected, all the chemicals and molecules they contain, their biochemical state—consists of far too much information for any computer to handle."

"It's just information," Gordon said, shrugging.

"Yes. Too much information."

"We compress it by using a lossless fractal algorithm."

"Even so, it's still an enormous—"

"Excuse me," Chris said. "Are you saying you compress a person?"

"No. We compress the information equivalent of a person."

"And how is that done?" Chris said.

"With compression algorithms—methods to pack data on a computer, so they take up less space. Like JPEG and MPEG for visual material. Are you familiar with those?"

"I've got software that uses it, but that's it."

"Okay," Gordon said. "All compression programs work the same way. They look for similarities in data. Suppose you have a picture of a rose, made up of a million pixels. Each pixel has a location and a color. That's three million pieces of information—a lot of data. But most of those pixels are going to be red, surrounded by other red pixels. So the program scans the picture line by line, and sees whether adjacent pixels are the same color. If they are, it writes an instruction to the computer that says make this pixel red, and also the next fifty pixels in the line. Then switch to gray, and make the next ten pixels gray. And so on. It doesn't store information for each individual point. It stores instructions for how to re-create the picture. And the data is cut to a tenth of what it was."

"Even so," Stern said, "you're not talking about a two-dimensional picture, you're talking about a three-dimensional living object, and its description requires so much data—"

"That you'd need massive parallel processing," Gordon said, nodding. "That's true."

Chris frowned. "Parallel processing is what?"

"You hook several computers together and divide the job up among them, so it gets done faster. A big parallel-processing computer would have sixteen thousand processors hooked together. For a really big one, thirty-two thousand processors. We have *thirty-two billion* processors hooked together."

"Billion?" Chris said.

Stern leaned forward. "That's impossible. Even if you tried to make one . . ." He stared at the roof of the car, calculating. "Say, allow one inch between motherboards . . . that makes a stack . . . uh . . . two thousand six hundred . . . that makes a stack half a mile high. Even reconfigured into a cube, it'd be a huge building. You'd never build it. You'd never cool it. And it'd never work anyway, because the processors would end up too far apart."

Gordon sat and smiled. He was looking at Stern, waiting.

"The only possible way to do that much processing," Stern said, "would be to use the quantum characteristics of individual electrons. But then you'd be talking about a quantum computer. And no one's ever made one."

Gordon just smiled.

"Have they?" Stern said.

:

"Let me explain what David is talking about," Gordon said to the others. "Ordinary computers make calculations using two electron states, which are designated one and zero. That's how all computers work, by pushing around ones and zeros. But twenty years ago, Richard Feynman suggested it might be possible to make an extremely powerful computer using all thirty-two quantum states of an electron. Many laboratories are now trying to build these quantum computers. Their advantage is unimaginably great power—so great that you can indeed describe and compress a three-dimensional living object into an electron stream. Exactly like a fax. You can then transmit the electron stream through a quantum foam wormhole and reconstruct it in another universe. And that's what we do. It's not quantum teleportation. It's not particle entanglement. It's direct transmission to another universe."

:

The group was silent, staring at him. The Land Cruiser came into a clearing. They saw a number of two-story buildings, brick and glass. They looked surprisingly ordinary. This could be any one of those small industrial parks found on the outskirts of many American cities. Marek said, "This is ITC?"

"We like to keep a low profile," Gordon said. "Actually, we chose this spot because there is an old mine here. Good mines are getting hard to find now. So many physics projects require them."

Off to one side, working in the glare of floodlights, several men were getting ready to launch a weather balloon. The balloon was six feet in diameter, pale white. As they watched, it moved swiftly up into the sky, a small instrument bundle hanging beneath. Marek said, "What's that about?"

"We monitor the cloud cover every hour, especially when it's stormy. It's an ongoing research project, to see if the weather is the cause of any interference."

"Interference with what?" Marek asked.

The car pulled up in front of the largest building. A security guard opened the door. "Welcome to ITC," he said with a big smile. "Mr. Doniger is waiting for you."

Doniger walked quickly down the hallway with Gordon. Kramer followed behind. As he walked, Doniger scanned a sheet of paper that listed everybody's names and backgrounds. "How do they look, John?"

"Better than I expected. They're in good physical shape. They know the area. They know the time period."

"And how much persuading will they need?"

"I think they're ready. You just have to be careful talking about the risks."

"Are you suggesting I should be less than entirely honest?" Doniger said.

"Just be careful how you put it," Gordon said. "They're very bright."

"Are they? Well, let's have a look."

And he threw the door open.

:

Kate and the others had been left alone in a plain, bare conference room—scratched Formica table, folding chairs all around. On one side was a large markerboard with formulas scrawled on it. The formulas were so long that they ran the entire width of the board. It was completely mysterious to her. She was about to ask Stern what the formulas were for, when Robert Doniger swept into the room.

Kate was surprised by how young he was. He didn't look much older than they were, especially dressed in sneakers, jeans and a Quicksilver T-shirt. Even late at night, he seemed full of energy, going around the table quickly, shaking hands with each of them, addressing them by name. "Kate," he said, smiling at her. "Good to meet you. I've read your preliminary study on the chapel. It's very impressive."

Surprised, she managed to say, "Thank you," but Doniger had already moved on.

"And Chris. It's nice to see you again. I like the computer-simulation approach to that mill bridge; I think it will pay off."

Chris had time only to nod before Doniger was saying, "And David Stern. We haven't met. But I gather you're also a physicist, as I am."

"That's right. . . ."

"Welcome aboard. And André. Not getting any shorter! Your paper on the tournaments of Edward I certainly set Monsieur Contamine straight. Good work. So: please, all of you, please sit down."

They sat, and Doniger moved to the head of the table.

"I will get right to the point," Doniger said. "I need your help. And I will tell you why. For the last ten years, my company has been developing a revolutionary new technology. It is not a technology of war. Nor is it a commercial technology, to be sold for profit. On the contrary, it is an entirely benign and peaceful technology that will provide a great benefit to mankind. A *great* benefit. But I need your help."

:

"Consider for a moment," Doniger continued, "how unevenly technology has impacted the various fields of knowledge in the twentieth century. Physics employs the most advanced technology—including accelerator rings many miles in diameter. The same with chemistry and biology. A hundred years ago, Faraday and Maxwell had tiny private labs. Darwin worked with a notebook and a microscope. But today, no important scientific discovery could be made with such simple tools. The sciences are utterly dependent on advanced technology. But what about the humanities? During this same time, what has happened to them?"

Doniger paused, rhetorically. "The answer is, nothing.

There has been no significant technology. The scholar of literature or history works *exactly* as his predecessors did a hundred years before. Oh, there have been some minor changes in authentication of documents, and the use of CD-ROMs, and so forth. But the basic, day-to-day work of the scholar is *exactly the same*."

He looked at each of them in turn. "So we have an inequity. The fields of human knowledge are unbalanced. Medieval scholars are proud that in the twentieth century their views have undergone a revolution. But physics has undergone *three* revolutions in the same century. A hundred years ago, physicists argued about the age of the universe and the source of the sun's energy. No one on earth knew the answers. Today, every schoolchild knows. Today, we have seen the length and breadth of the universe, we understand it from the level of galaxies to the level of subatomic particles. We have learned so much that we can speak in detail about what happened during the first few minutes of the birth of the exploding universe. Can medieval scholars match this advance within their own field? In a word, no. Why not? Because no new technology assists them. No one has ever developed a new technology for the benefit of historians—until now."

:

A masterful performance, Gordon thought. One of Doniger's best—charming, energetic, even excessive at moments. Yet the fact was, Doniger had just given them an exciting explanation for the project—without ever revealing its true purpose. Without ever telling them what was really going on.

"But I told you I needed your help. And I do."

Doniger's mood changed. He spoke slowly now, somber, concerned. "You know that Professor Johnston came here to see us because he thought we were withholding information. And in a way, we were. We did have certain information that we hadn't shared, because we couldn't explain how we got it."

And, Gordon thought, because Kramer screwed up.

"Professor Johnston pushed us," Doniger was saying. "I'm sure you know his way. He even threatened to go to the press.

Finally we showed him the technology we are about to show you. And he was excited—just as you will be. But he insisted on going back, to see for himself."

Doniger paused. "We didn't want him to go. Again, he threatened. In the end, we had no choice but to let him go. That was three days ago. He is still back there. He asked you for help, in a message he knew you would find. You know that site and time better than anyone else in the world. You have to go back and get him. You are his only chance."

∴

"What exactly happened to him after he went back?" Marek said.

"We don't know," Doniger said. "But he broke the rules."

"Rules?"

"You have to understand that this technology is still very new. We've been cautious about how we use it. We have been sending observers back for about two years now—using ex-marines, trained military people. But of course they are not historians, and we have kept them on a tight leash."

"Meaning what?"

"We haven't ever let our observers enter the world back there. We haven't allowed anyone to stay longer than an hour. And we haven't allowed anyone to go more than fifty yards from the machine. Nobody has ever just left the machine behind and gone off into the world."

"But the Professor did?" Marek said.

"He must have, yes."

"And we'll have to, too, if we're going to find him. We'll have to enter the world."

"Yes," Doniger said.

"And you're saying we're the first people ever to do this? The first people ever to step into the world?"

"Yes. You, and the Professor before you."

Silence.

Suddenly, Marek broke into a broad grin. "Terrific," he said. "I can't wait!"

But the others said nothing. They looked uneasy, edgy.

Stern said, "About this guy they found in the desert. . . ."

"Joe Traub," Doniger said. "He was one of our best scientists."

"What was he doing in the desert?"

"Apparently, he drove there. They found his car. But we don't know why he went."

Stern said, "Supposedly, he was all messed up, there was something about his fingers. . . ."

"That wasn't in the autopsy report," Doniger said. "He died of a heart attack."

"Then his death had nothing to do with your technology?"

"Nothing at all," Doniger said.

⋮

There was another silence. Chris shifted in his chair. "In layman's terms—how safe is this technology?"

"Safer than driving your car," Doniger said without hesitation. "You will be thoroughly briefed, and we'll send you back with our experienced observers. The trip will last a maximum of two hours. You'll just go back and get him."

Chris Hughes drummed his fingers on the table. Kate bit her lip. Nobody spoke.

"Look, this is all voluntary," Doniger said. "It's entirely up to you whether you go or not. But the Professor has asked for your help. And I don't think you would let him down."

"Why don't you just send the observers?" Stern said.

"Because they don't know enough, David. As you're aware, it's an entirely different world back there. You have the advantage of your knowledge. You know the site, and you know the time, in detail. You know languages and customs."

"But our knowledge is academic," Chris said.

"Not anymore," Doniger said.

⋮

The group filed out of the room, heading off with Gordon to see the machines. Doniger watched them go, then turned as Kramer entered the room. She had been watching everything on the closed-circuit television.

"What do you think, Diane?" Doniger said. "Will they go?"

"Yeah. They'll go."

"Can they pull it off?"

Kramer paused. "I'd say it's fifty-fifty."

They walked down a broad concrete ramp, large enough for a truck to drive down. At the bottom was a pair of heavy steel doors. Marek saw a half-dozen security cameras mounted in different locations around the ramp. The cameras turned, following them as they walked down to the doors. At the bottom of the ramp, Gordon looked up at the security cameras, and waited.

The doors opened.

Gordon led them through into a small room beyond. The steel doors clanged shut behind them. Gordon went forward to an inner set of doors, again waited.

Marek said, "You can't open them yourself?"

"No."

"Why? They don't trust you?"

"They don't trust anybody," Gordon said. "Believe me, nobody gets in here unless we intend for them to get in."

The doors opened.

They walked into an industrial-looking metal cage. The air was cold, faintly musty. The doors closed behind them. With a whir, the cage began to descend.

Marek saw that they were standing in an elevator.

"We're going down a thousand feet," Gordon said. "Be patient."

:

The elevator stopped and the doors opened. They walked down a long concrete tunnel, their footsteps echoing. Gordon said, "This is the control and maintenance level. The actual machines are another five hundred feet below us."

They came to a pair of heavy doors that were dark blue and transparent. At first, Marek thought they were made of extremely thick glass. But as the doors slid open on a motorized track, he saw slight movement beneath the surface. "Water," Gordon said. "We use a lot of water shielding here. Quantum technology is very sensitive to random outside influences—cosmic rays, spurious electronic fields, all of that. That's why we're down here in the first place."

Up ahead, they saw what appeared to be the doors to an ordinary laboratory hallway. Passing through another set of glass doors, they entered a hallway painted antiseptic white, with doors opening off on either side. The first door on the left said PREPACK. The second, FIELDPREP. And further down the hallway, they saw a sign marked simply TRANSIT.

Gordon rubbed his hands together. He said, "Let's get right to the packing."

:

The room was small and reminded Marek of a hospital laboratory; it made him uneasy. In the center of the room stood a vertical tube, about seven feet high and five feet in diameter. It was hinged open. Inside were dull strips. Marek said, "A suntanning machine?"

"Actually, it's an advanced resonance imager. Basically it's a high-powered MRI. But you'll find it's good practice for the machine itself. Perhaps you should go first, Dr. Marek."

"Go in there?" Marek pointed to the tube. Seen up close, it looked more like a white coffin.

"Just remove your clothes and step inside. It's exactly like an MRI—you won't feel anything at all. The entire process takes about a minute. We'll be next door."

They went through a side door with a small window, into another room. Marek couldn't see what was in there. The door clanged shut.

He saw a chair in the corner. He went over and took his clothes off, then walked into the scanner. There was the click of an intercom and he heard Gordon say, "Dr. Marek, if you will look at your feet."

Marek looked down at his feet.

"You see the circle on the floor? Please make sure your feet are entirely within that circle." Marek shifted his position. "Thank you, that's fine. The door will close now."

With a mechanical hum, the hinged door swung shut. Marek heard a hiss as it sealed. He said, "Airtight?"

"Yes, it has to be. You may feel some cold air coming in now. We'll give you added oxygen while we calibrate. You're not claustrophobic, are you?"

"I wasn't, until now." Marek was looking around at the interior. The dull strips, he now saw, were plastic-covered openings. Behind the plastic he saw lights, small whirring machines. The air became noticeably cooler.

"We're calibrating now," Gordon said. "Try not to move."

Suddenly, the individual strips around him began to rotate, the machines clicking. The strips spun faster and faster, then suddenly jerked to a stop.

"That's good. Feel all right?"

"It's like being inside a pepper mill," Marek said.

Gordon laughed. "Calibration is completed. The rest is dependent on exact timing, so the sequence is automatic. Just follow the instructions as you hear them. Okay?"

"Okay."

A click. Marek was alone.

A recorded voice said, "The scan sequence has begun. We are turning on lasers. Look straight ahead. And do not look up."

Instantly, the interior of the tube was a bright, glowing blue. The air itself seemed to be glowing.

"Lasers are polarizing the xenon gas, which is now being pumped into the compartment. Five seconds."

Marek thought, Xenon gas?

The bright blue color all around him increased in intensity. He looked down at his hand and could hardly see it for the shimmering air.

"We have reached xenon concentration. Now we will ask you to take a deep breath."

Marek thought, Take a deep breath? Of xenon?

"Hold your position without moving for thirty seconds. Ready? Stand still—eyes open—deep breath—hold it. . . . *Now!*"

The strips suddenly began to spin wildly, then one by one, each strip started to jerk back and forth, almost as if it were looking, and sometimes had to go back for a second look. Each strip seemed to be moving individually. Marek had the uncanny sense of being examined by hundreds of eyes.

The recorded voice said, "Very still, please. Twenty seconds remaining."

All around him, the strips hummed and whirred. And then suddenly, they all stopped. Several seconds of silence. The machinery clicked. Now the strips began to move forward and back, as well as laterally.

"Very still, please. Ten seconds."

The strips began to spin in circles now, slowly synchronizing, until finally they were all rotating together as a unit. Then they stopped.

"The scan is completed. Thank you for your cooperation."

The blue light clicked off, and the hinged door hissed open. Marek stepped out.

⋮

In the adjacent room, Gordon sat in front of a computer console. The others had pulled up chairs around him.

"Most people," Gordon said, "don't realize that the ordinary hospital MRI works by changing the quantum state of atoms in your body—generally, the angular momentum of nuclear particles. Experience with MRIs tells us that changing your quantum state has no ill effect. In fact, you don't even notice it happening.

"But the ordinary MRI does this with a very powerful magnetic field—say, 1.5 tesla, about twenty-five thousand times as strong as the earth's magnetic field. We don't need that. We use superconducting quantum interference devices, or SQUIDs, that are so sensitive they can measure resonance just from the earth's magnetic field. We don't have any magnets in there."

Marek came into the room. "How do I look?" he said.

The image on the screen showed a translucent picture of Marek's limbs, in speckled red. "You're looking at the marrow, inside the long bones, the spine, and the skull," Gordon said. "Now it builds outward, by organ systems. Here's the bones"—they saw a complete skeleton—"and now we're adding muscles. . . ."

Watching the organ systems appear, Stern said, "Your computer's incredibly fast."

"Oh, we've slowed this way down," Gordon said. "Otherwise you wouldn't be able to see it happening. The actual processing time is essentially zero."

Stern stared. "Zero?"

"Different world," Gordon said, nodding. "Old assumptions don't apply." He turned to the others. "Who's next?"

·
:

They walked down to the end of the corridor, to the room marked TRANSIT. Kate said, "Why did we just do all that?"

"We call it prepacking," Gordon said. "It enables us to transmit faster, because most of the information about you is already loaded into the machine. We just do a final scan for differences, and then we transmit."

They entered another elevator, and passed through another set of water-filled doors. "Okay," Gordon said. "Here we are."

·
:

They came out into an enormous, brightly lit, cavernous space. Sounds echoed. The air was cold. They were walking on a metal passageway, suspended a hundred feet above the floor. Looking down, Chris saw three semicircular water-filled walls, arranged to form a circle, with gaps between large enough for a person to walk through. Inside this outer wall were three smaller semicircles, forming a second wall. And inside the second wall was a third. Each successive semicircle was rotated so that the gaps never lined up, giving the whole thing a mazelike appearance.

In the center of the concentric circles was a space about twenty feet across. Here, half a dozen cagelike devices stood, each about the size of a phone booth. They were arranged in no particular pattern. They had dull-colored metal tops. White mist drifted across the enclosure. Tanks lay on the floor, and heavy black power cables snaked everywhere. It looked like a workroom. And in fact, some men were working on one of the cages.

"This is our transmission area," Gordon said. "Heavily shielded, as you can see. We're building a second area over there but it won't be ready for several months." He pointed across the cavernous space, where a second series of concentric walls were going up. These walls were clear; they hadn't been filled with water yet.

From the gangway, a cable elevator went down to the space in the center of the glass walls.

Marek said, "Can we go down there?"

"Not yet, no."

A technician looked up and waved. Gordon said, "How long until the burn check, Norm?"

"Couple of minutes. Gomez is on her way now."

"Okay." Gordon turned to the others. "Let's go up to the control booth to watch."

:

Bathed in deep blue light, the machines stood on a raised platform. They were dull gray in color and hummed softly. White vapor seeped along the floor, obscuring their bases. Two workmen in blue parkas were down on their hands and knees, working inside the opened base of one of them.

The machines were essentially open cylinders, with metal at the top and bottom. Each machine stood on a thick metal base. Three rods around the perimeter supported the metal roof.

Technicians were dragging a tangle of black cables down from an overhead grid and then attaching the cables to the roof of one machine, like gas station attendants filling a car.

The space between the base and the roof was completely empty. In fact, the whole machine seemed disappointingly plain. The rods were odd, triangular-shaped, and studded along their length. Pale blue smoke seemed to be coming from under the roof of the machine.

The machines didn't look like anything Kate had ever seen. She stared at the huge screens inside the narrow control room. Behind her, two technicians in shirtsleeves sat at two console desks. The screens in front of her gave the impression you were looking out a window, though in fact the control room was windowless.

"You are looking at the latest version of our CTC technology," Gordon said. "That stands for Closed Timelike Curve—the topology of space-time that we employ to go back. We've had to develop entirely new technologies to build these machines. What you see here is actually the sixth version, since the first working prototype was built three years ago."

Chris stared at the machines and said nothing. Kate Erickson was looking around the control room. Stern was anxious, rubbing his upper lip. Marek kept his eye on Stern.

"All the significant technology," Gordon continued, "is located in the base, including the indium-gallium-arsenide quantum memory, the computer lasers and the battery cells. The vaporizing lasers, of course, are in the metal strips. The dull-colored metal is niobium; pressure tanks are aluminum; storage elements are polymer."

A young woman with short dark red hair and a tough manner walked into the room. She wore a khaki shirt, shorts and boots; she looked as if she were dressed for a safari. "Gomez will be one of your aides when you go take your trip. She's going back right now to do what we call a 'burn check.' She's already burned her navigation marker, fixing the target date, and now she's going to make sure it's accurate." He pushed the intercom. "Sue? Show us your nav marker, would you?"

The woman held up a white rectangular wafer, hardly larger than a postage stamp. She cupped it easily in her palm.

"She'll use that to go back. And to call the machine for the return—show us the button, would you, Sue?"

"It's a little hard to see," she said, turning the wafer on edge. "There's a tiny button here, you push it with your thumbnail. That calls the machine when you're ready to return."

"Thank you, Sue."

One of the technicians said, "Field buck."

They turned and looked. On his console, one screen showed an undulating three-dimensional surface with a jagged up-swinging in the middle, like a mountain peak. "Nice one," Gordon said. "Classic." He explained to the others. "Because our field-sensing equipment is SQUID-based, we're able to detect extremely subtle discontinuities in the local magnetic field—we call them 'field bucks.' We'll register them starting as early as two hours before an event. And in fact, these started about two hours ago. It means a machine is returning here."

"What machine?" Kate said.

"Sue's machine."

"But she hasn't left yet."

"I know," he said. "It doesn't seem to make sense. Quantum events are all counterintuitive."

"You're saying you get an indicator that she is returning before she has left?"

"Yes."

"Why?" Kate said.

Gordon sighed. "It's complicated. Actually, what we are seeing in the field is a probability function—the likelihood that a machine is going to return. We don't usually think about it that way. We just say it's coming back. But to be accurate, a field buck is really telling us that it is highly probable a machine is coming back."

Kate was shaking her head. "I don't get it."

Gordon said, "Let's just say that in the ordinary world, we have beliefs about cause and effect. Causes occur first, effects second. But that order of events does not always occur in the quantum world. Effects can be simultaneous with causes, and effects can precede causes. This is one minor example of that."

⁙

The woman, Gomez, stepped into one of the machines. She pushed the white wafer into a slot in the base in front of her. "She's just installed her nav marker, which guides the machine out and back."

"And how do you know you'll get back?" Stern said.

"A multiverse transfer," Gordon said, "creates a sort of potential energy, like a stretched spring that wants to snap back. So the machines can come home relatively easily. Outbound is the tricky part. That's what's encoded in the ceramic."

He leaned forward to press an intercom button. "Sue? How long are you gone?"

"I'll be a minute, maybe two."

"Okay. Synch elapsed."

Now the technicians began to talk, flipping switches at a console, looking at video readouts in front of them.

"Helium check."

"Read as full," a technician said, looking at her console.

"EMR check."

"Check."

"Stand by for laser alignment."

One of the technicians flipped a switch, and from the metal strips, a dense array of green lasers fired into the center of the machine, putting dozens of green spots on Gomez's face and body as she stood still, her eyes closed.

The bars began to revolve slowly. The woman in the center remained still. The lasers made green horizontal streaks over her body. Then the bars stopped.

"Lasers aligned."

Gordon said, "See you in a minute, Sue." He turned to the others. "Okay. Here we go."

⁙

The curved water shields around the cage began to glow a faint blue. Once again the machine began to rotate slowly. The woman in the center stood motionless; the machine moved around her.

The humming grew louder. The rotation increased in speed. The woman stood, calm and relaxed.

"For this trip," Gordon said, "she'll use up only a minute or two. But she actually has thirty-seven hours in her battery cells. That's the limit these machines can remain in a location without returning."

The bars were spinning swiftly. They now heard a rapid chattering sound, like a machine gun.

"That's the clearance check: infrared sensors verify the space around the machine. They won't proceed without two meters on all sides. They check both ways. It's a safety measure. We wouldn't want the machine emerging in the middle of a stone wall. All right. They're releasing xenon. Here she goes."

The humming was now very loud. The enclosure spun so rapidly, the metal strips were blurred. They could see the woman inside quite clearly.

They heard a recorded voice say, "Stand still—eyes open—deep breath—hold it. . . . *Now!*"

From the top of the machine, a single ring descended, scanning quickly to her feet.

"Now watch closely. It's fast," Gordon said.

Kate saw deep violet lasers fire inward from all the bars toward the center. The woman inside seemed to glow white-hot for an instant, and then a burst of blinding white light flashed inside the machine. Kate closed her eyes, turned away. When she looked back again, there were spots in front of her eyes, and for a moment she couldn't see what had happened. Then she realized that the machine was smaller. It had pulled away from the cables at the top, which now dangled free.

Another laser flash.

The machine was smaller. The woman inside was smaller. She was now only about three feet high, and shrinking before their eyes in a series of bright laser flashes.

"Jesus," Stern said, watching. "What does *that* feel like?"

"Nothing," Gordon said. "You don't feel a thing. Nerve conduction time from skin to brain is on the order of a hundred milliseconds. Laser vaporization is five nanoseconds. You're long gone."

"But she's still there."

"No, she's not. She was gone in the first laser burst. The computer's just processing the data now. What you see is an artifact of compression stepping. The compression's about three to the minus two. . . ."

There was another bright flash. The cage now shrank rapidly. It was three feet high, then two. Now it was close to the floor—less than a foot tall. The woman inside looked like a little doll in khakis.

"Minus four," Gordon said. There was another bright burst, near the floor. Now Kate couldn't see the cage at all.

"What happened to it?"

"It's there. Barely."

Another burst, this time just a pinpoint flash on the floor.

"Minus five."

The flashes came more quickly now, winking like a firefly, diminishing in strength. Gordon counted them out.

"And minus fourteen. . . . Gone."

There were no more flashes.

Nothing.

The cage had vanished. The floor was dark rubber, empty.

Kate said, "We're supposed to do *that*?"

.
.
.

"It's not an unpleasant experience," Gordon said. "You're entirely conscious all the way down, which is something we can't explain. By the final data compressions, you are in very small domains—subatomic regions—and consciousness should not be possible. Yet it occurs. We think it may be an artifact, a hallucination that bridges the transition. If so, it's analogous to the phantom limb that amputees feel, even though the limb isn't there. This may be a kind of phantom brain. Of course, we are talking about very brief time periods, nanoseconds. But nobody understands consciousness anyway."

Kate was frowning. For some time now, she had been looking at what she saw as architecture, a kind of "form follows function" approach: wasn't it remarkable how these huge underground structures had concentric symmetry— slightly reminiscent of medieval castles—even though these modern structures had been built without any aesthetic plan at all. They had simply been built to solve a scientific problem. She found the resulting appearance fascinating.

But now that she was confronted by what these machines were actually *used for*, she struggled to make sense of what her eyes had just seen. And her architectural training was absolutely no help to her. "But this, uh, method of shrinking a person, it requires you to break her down—"

"No. We destroy her," Gordon said bluntly. "You have to destroy the original, so that it can be reconstructed at the other end. You can't have one without the other."

"So she actually died?"

"I wouldn't say that, no. You see—"

"But if you destroy the person at one end," Kate said, "don't they die?"

Gordon sighed. "It's difficult to think of this in traditional terms," he said. "Since you're instantaneously reconstructed *at the very moment* you are destroyed, how can you be said to have died? You haven't died. You've just moved somewhere else."

:

Stern felt certain—it was a visceral sense—that Gordon wasn't being entirely honest about this technology. Just looking at the curved water shields, at all the different machines standing on the floor, gave him the sense that there was quite a bit more that was being left unexplained. He tried to find it.

"So she is in the other universe now?" he asked.

"That's right."

"You transmitted her, and she arrived in the other universe? Just like a fax?"

"Exactly."

"But to rebuild her, you need a fax machine at the other end."

Gordon shook his head. "No, you don't," he said.

"Why not?"

"Because she's already there."

Stern frowned. "She's already there? How could that be?"

"At the moment of transmission, the person is already in the other universe. And therefore the person doesn't need to be rebuilt by us."

"Why?" Stern said.

"For now, just call it a characteristic of the multiverse. We can discuss it later if you like. I'm not sure everybody needs to be bothered with these details," he said, nodding to the others.

Stern thought, There *is* something more. Something he doesn't want to say to us. Stern looked back at the transmission area. Trying to find the odd detail, the thing that was out of place. Because he was sure that something here was out of place.

"Didn't you tell us that you've only sent a few people back?"

"That's right, yes."

"More than one at a time?"

"Almost never. Very rarely two."

"Then why do you have so many machines?" Stern said. "I count eight in there. Wouldn't two be enough?"

"You're just seeing the results of our research program," Gordon said. "We are constantly working to refine our design."

Gordon had answered smoothly enough, but Stern was certain he had seen something—some buried glint of uneasiness—in Gordon's eyes.

*There is definitely something more.*

"I would have thought," Stern said, "that you'd make refinements to the same machines."

Gordon shrugged again, but did not answer.

*Definitely.*

"What are those repairmen doing in there?" Stern said, still probing. He pointed to the men on their hands and knees, working on the base of one machine. "I mean by the machine in the corner. What exactly are they repairing?"

"David," Gordon began. "I really think—"

"Is this technology *really* safe?" Stern said.

Gordon sighed. "See for yourself."

On the big screen, a sequence of rapid flashes appeared on the floor of the transit room.

"Here she comes," Gordon said.

The flashes grew brighter. They heard the chattering sound again, first faintly, then louder. And then the cage was full-size; the humming died away; the ground mist swirled, and the woman climbed out, waving to the spectators.

Stern squinted at her. She appeared absolutely fine. Her appearance was identical to what it had been before.

Gordon looked at him. "Believe me," he said. "It's perfectly safe." He turned to the screen. "How'd it look back there, Sue?"

"Excellent," she said. "Transit site is on the north side of the river. Secluded spot, in the woods. And the weather's pretty good, for April." She glanced at her watch. "Get your team together, Dr. Gordon. I'm going to go burn the spare nav marker. Then let's go back there and pull that old guy out before somebody hurts him."

"Lie on your left side, please." Kate rolled over on the table and watched uneasily as an elderly man in a white lab coat raised what looked like a glue gun and placed it over her ear. "This will feel warm."

Warm? She felt a burning rush of heat in her ear. "What is *that*?"

"It's an organic polymer," the man said. "Nontoxic and nonallergenic. Give it eight seconds. All right, now please make chewing motions. We want a looser fit. Very good, keep chewing."

She heard him going down the line. Chris was on the table behind her, then Stern, then Marek. She heard the old man say, "Lie on your left side, please. This will feel warm. . . ."

Not long after, he was back. He had her turn over, and injected the hot polymer into her other ear. Gordon was watching from the corner of the room. He said, "This is still a bit experimental but so far it works quite well. It's made of a polymer that begins to biodegrade after a week."

Later, the man had them stand up. He expertly popped the plastic implants out of their ears, moving down the line.

Kate said to Gordon, "My hearing is fine, I don't need a hearing aid."

"It's not a hearing aid," Gordon said.

Across the room, the man was drilling out the center of the plastic earpieces and inserting electronics. He worked surprisingly quickly. When the electronics were in place, he capped the hole with more plastic.

"It's a machine language translator and a radio mike. In case you need to understand what people are saying to you."

"But even if I understand what they're saying," she said, "how can I answer back?"

Marek nudged her. "Don't worry. I speak Occitan. And Middle French."

"Oh, that's good," she said sarcastically. "You going to teach it to me in the next fifteen minutes?" She was tense, she was about to be destroyed or vaporized or whatever the hell they did in that machine, and the words just popped out of her mouth.

Marek looked surprised. "No," he said seriously. "But if you stay with me, I will take care of you."

Something about his earnestness reassured her. He was such a straight arrow. She thought, He probably will take care of me. She felt herself relaxing.

Soon after, they were all fitted with flesh-colored plastic earpieces. "They're turned off now," Gordon said. "To turn them on, just tap your ear with your finger. Now, if you'll come over here . . ."

:

Gordon handed them each a small leather pouch. "We've been working on a first-aid kit; these are the prototypes. You're the first to enter the world, so you may have a use for them. You can keep them out of sight, under your clothing."

He opened one pouch and brought out a small aluminum canister about four inches high and an inch in diameter. It looked like a little shaving cream can. "This is the only defense we can provide you. It contains twelve doses of ethylene dihydride with a protein substrate. We can demonstrate for you with the cat, H.G. Where are you, H.G?"

A black cat jumped onto the table. Gordon stroked it, and then shot a burst of gas at its nose. The cat blinked, made a snuffling sound, and fell over on its side.

"Unconsciousness within six seconds," Gordon said, "and it leaves a retroactive amnesia. But bear in mind that it's short acting. And you must fire right in the person's face to ensure any effect."

The cat was already starting to twitch and revive as Gordon turned back to the pouch and held up three red paper cubes, roughly the size of sugar cubes, each covered in a layer of pale wax. They looked like fireworks.

"If you need to start a fire," he said, "these will do it. Pull the little string, and they catch fire. They're marked fifteen, thirty, sixty—the number of seconds before the fire starts. Wax, so they're waterproof. A word of warning: sometimes they don't work."

Chris Hughes said, "What's wrong with a Bic?"

"Not correct for the period. You can't take plastic back there." Gordon returned to the kit. "Then we have basic first aid, nothing fancy. Anti-inflammatory, antidiarrhea, antispasmodic, antipain. You don't want to be vomiting in a castle," he said. "And we can't give you pills for the water."

Stern took all this in with a sense of unreality. Vomiting in a castle? he thought. "Listen, uh—"

"And finally, an all-purpose pocket tool, including knife and picklock." It looked like a steel Swiss army knife. Gordon put everything back in the kit. "You'll probably never use any of this stuff, but you've got it anyway. Now let's get you dressed."

:

Stern could not shake off his persistent sense of unease. A kindly, grandmotherly woman had gotten up from her sewing machine and was handing them all clothing: first, white linen undershorts—sort of boxer shorts, but without elastic—then a leather belt, and then black woolen leggings.

"What're these?" Stern said. "Tights?"

"They're called hose, dear."

There was no elastic on them, either. "How do they stay up?"

"You slip them under your belt, beneath the doublet. Or tie them to the points of your doublet."

"Points?"

"That's right, dear. Of your doublet."

Stern glanced at the others. They were calmly collecting the clothes in a pile as each article was given to them. They seemed to know what everything was for; they were as calm as if they were in a department store. But Stern was lost, and he felt panicky. Now he was given a white linen shirt that came to his upper thigh, and a larger overshirt, called a doublet, made of quilted felt. And finally a dagger on a steel chain. He looked at it askance.

"Everyone carries one. You'll need it for eating, if nothing else."

He put it absently on top of the pile, and poked through the clothing, still trying to find the "points."

Gordon said, "These clothes are intended to be status-neutral, neither expensive nor poor. We want them to approximate the dress of a middling merchant, a court page, or a down-at-the-heels nobleman." Stern was handed shoes, which looked like leather slippers with pointed toes, except they buckled. Like court jester's shoes, he thought unhappily.

The grandmotherly woman smiled: "Don't worry, they have air soles built in, just like your Nikes."

"Why is everything dirty?" Stern said, frowning at his overshirt.

"Well, you want to fit in, don't you?"

.

They changed in a locker room. Stern watched the other men. "How exactly do we, uh . . ."

"You want to know how you dress in the fourteenth century?" Marek said. "It's simple." Marek had stripped off all his clothes and was walking around naked, relaxed. The man was bulging with muscles. Stern felt intimidated as he slowly took off his trousers.

"First," Marek said, "put on your undershorts. This is very nice quality linen. They had good linen in those days. To hold the shorts up, tie your belt around your waist and roll the top of the undershorts around the belt a couple of times, so it holds. All right?"

"Your belt goes *under* your clothes?"

"That's right. Holding up your shorts. Next, put on your hose." Marek began to pull on his black wool tights. The hose had feet at the bottom, like a child's pajamas. "They have these strings at the top, you see?"

"My hose is baggy," Stern said, tugging them up, poking at the knees.

"That's fine. These aren't dress hose, so they aren't skin-tight. Next, your linen overshirt. Just pull it over your head and let it hang down. No, no, David. The slit at the neck goes in the front."

Stern pulled his arms out and twisted the shirt around, fumbling.

"And finally," Marek said, picking up a felt outershirt, "you put on your doublet. Combination suit coat and windbreaker. You wear it indoors and out, never take it off except when it is very hot. See the points? They're the laces, under the felt. Now, tie your hose to the points of the doublet, through the slits in your overshirt."

Marek managed this in only a few moments; it was as if he'd done it every day of his life. It took Chris much longer, Stern noted with satisfaction. Stern himself struggled to twist his torso, to tie the knots at his backside.

"You call this simple?" he said, grunting.

"You just haven't looked at your own clothes lately," Marek said. "The average Westerner in the twentieth century wears nine to twelve items of daily clothing. Here, there are only six."

Stern pulled on his doublet, tugging it down over his waist, so it came to his thighs. In doing so, he wrinkled his under-shirt, and eventually Marek had to help him straighten it all out, as well as lace his hose tighter.

Finally, Marek looped the dagger and the chain loosely around Stern's waist, and stood back to admire him.

"There," Marek said, nodding. "How do you feel?"

Stern wriggled his shoulders uncomfortably. "I feel like a trussed chicken."

Marek laughed. "You'll get used to it."

:

Kate was finishing dressing when Susan Gomez, the young woman who had taken the trip back, came in. Gomez was wearing period clothes and a wig. She tossed another wig to Kate.

Kate made a face.

"You have to wear it," Gomez said. "Short hair on a woman is a sign of disgrace, or heresy. Don't ever let anyone back there see your true hair length."

Kate pulled on the wig, which brought dark blond hair to her shoulders. She turned to look in the mirror, and saw the face of a stranger. She looked younger, softer. Weaker.

"It's either that," Gomez said, "or cut your hair really short, like a man. Your call."

"I'll wear the wig," Kate said.

Diane Kramer looked at Victor Baretto and said, "But this has always been a rule, Victor. You know that."

"Yes, but the problem," Baretto said, "is that you're giving us a new mission." Baretto was a lean, tough-looking man in his thirties, an ex-ranger who had been with the company for two years. During that time, he had acquired a reputation as a competent security man, but a bit of a prima donna. "Now, you're asking us to go into the world, but you won't let us take weapons."

"That's right, Victor. No anachronisms. No modern artifacts going back. That's been our rule from the beginning." Kramer tried to conceal her frustration. These military types were difficult, particularly the men. The women, like Gomez, were okay. But the men kept trying to, as they put it, "apply their training" to the ITC trips back, and it never really worked. Privately, Kramer thought it was just a way for the men to conceal their anxiety, but of course she could never say that. It was difficult enough for them to take orders from a woman like her in the first place.

The men also had more trouble keeping their work secret. It was easier for women, but the men all wanted to brag about going back to the past. Of course, they were forbidden by all sorts of contractual arrangements, but contracts could be forgotten after a few drinks in a bar. That was why Kramer had informed them all about the existence of several specially burned nav wafers. These wafers had entered the mythology of the company, including their names: Tunguska, Vesuvius, Tokyo. The Vesuvius wafer put you on the Bay of Naples at

7:00 a.m. on August 24, A.D. 79, just before burning ash killed everyone. Tunguska left you in Siberia in 1908, just before the giant meteor struck, causing a shock wave that killed every living thing for hundreds of miles. Tokyo put you in that city in 1923, just before the earthquake flattened it. The idea was if word of the project became public, you might end up with the wrong wafer on your next trip out. None of the military types were quite sure whether any of this was true, or just company mythology.

Which was just how Kramer liked it.

"This is a new mission," Baretto said again, as if she hadn't heard him before. "You're asking us to go into the world—to go behind enemy lines, so to speak—without weapons."

"But you're all trained in hand-to-hand. You, Gomez, all of you."

"I don't think that's sufficient."

"Victor—"

"With all due respect, Ms. Kramer, you're not facing up to the situation here," Baretto said stubbornly. "You've already lost two people. Three, if you count Traub."

"No, Victor. We've never lost anybody."

"You certainly lost Traub."

"We didn't lose Dr. Traub," she said. "Traub volunteered, and Traub was depressed."

"You assume he was depressed."

"We know he was, Victor. After his wife died, he was severely depressed, and suicidal. Even though he had passed his trip limit, he wanted to go back, to see if he could improve the technology. He had an idea that he could modify the machines to have fewer transcription errors. But apparently, his idea was wrong. That's why he ended up in the Arizona desert. Personally, I don't think he ever really intended to come back at all. I think it was suicide."

"And you lost Rob," Baretto said. "He wasn't any damn suicide."

Kramer sighed. Rob Deckard was one of the first of the observers to go back, almost two years earlier. And he was one of the first to show transcription errors. "That was much earlier in the project, Victor. The technology was less refined. And you know what happened. After he'd made several trips, Rob began to show minor effects. He insisted on continuing. But we didn't lose him."

"He went out, and he never came back," Baretto said. "That's the bottom line."

"Rob knew exactly what he was doing."

"And now the Professor."

"We haven't lost the Professor," she said. "He's still alive."

"You hope. And you don't know why he didn't come back in the first place."

"Victor—"

"I'm just saying," Baretto said, "in this case the logistics don't fit the mission profile. You're asking us to take an unnecessary risk."

"You don't have to go," Kramer said mildly.

"No, hell. I never said that."

"You don't have to."

"No. I'm going."

"Well, then, those are the rules. No modern technology goes into the world. Understood?"

"Understood."

"And none of this gets mentioned to the academics."

"No, no. Hell no. I'm professional."

"Okay," Kramer said.

She watched him leave. He was sulking, but he was going to go along with it. They always did, in the end. And the rule was important, she thought. Even though Doniger liked to give a little speech about how you couldn't change history, the fact was, nobody really knew—and nobody wanted to risk it. They didn't want modern weapons, or artifacts, or plastic to go back.

And they never had.

Stern sat with the others on hard-backed chairs in a room with maps. Susan Gomez, the woman who had just returned in the machine, spoke in a crisp, quick manner that Stern found rushed.

"We are going," she said, "to the Monastery of Sainte-Mère, on the Dordogne River, in southwestern France. We will arrive at 8:04 a.m. on the morning of Thursday, April 7, 1357—that's the day of the Professor's message. It's fortunate for us, because there's a tournament that day in Castelgard, and the spectacle will draw large crowds from the surrounding countryside, so we won't be noticed."

She tapped one map. "Just for orientation, the monastery is here. Castelgard is over here, across the river. And the fortress of La Roque is on the bluffs here, above the monastery. Questions so far?"

They shook their heads.

"All right. The situation in the area is a little unsettled. As you know, April of 1357 puts us roughly twenty years into the Hundred Years War. It's seven months after the English victory at Poitiers, where they took the king of France prisoner. The French king is now being held for ransom. And France, without a king, is in an uproar.

"Right now, Castelgard is in the hands of Sir Oliver de Vannes, a British knight born in France. Oliver has also taken over La Roque, where he is strengthening the castle's defenses. Sir Oliver's an unpleasant character, with a famously bad temper. They call him the 'Butcher of Crécy,' for his excesses in that battle."

"So Oliver is in control of both towns?" Marek said.

"At the moment, yes. However, a company of renegade knights, led by a defrocked priest called Arnaut de Cervole—"

"The Archpriest," Marek said.

"Yes, exactly, the Archpriest—is moving into the area, and will undoubtedly attempt to take the castles from Oliver. We believe the Archpriest is still several days away. But fighting may break out at any time, so we will work quickly."

She moved to another map, with a larger scale. It showed the monastery buildings.

"We arrive approximately here, at the edge of the Forêt de Sainte-Mère. From our arrival point, we should be able to look right down on the monastery. Since the Professor's message came from the monastery, we will go directly there first. As you know, the monastery takes its main meal of the day at ten o'clock in the morning, and the Professor is likely to be present at that time. With luck, we'll find him there and bring him back."

Marek said, "How do you know all this? I thought nobody's ever gone into the world."

"That's correct. No one has. But observers close to the machines have still brought back enough that we know the background at this particular time. Any other questions?"

They shook their heads no.

"All right. It is very important we recover the Professor while he is still at the monastery. If he moves to either Castelgard or La Roque, it will be much more difficult. We have a tight mission profile. I expect to be on the ground between two and three hours. We will stay together at all times. If any of us is separated from the others, use your earpieces to get together again. We will find the Professor, and come right back. Okay?"

"Got it."

"You'll have two escorts, myself and Victor Baretto, over there in the corner. Say hello, Vic."

The second escort was a surly man who looked like an ex-marine—a tough and able man. Baretto's period clothes were more peasantlike, loose-fitting, made of a fabric like burlap. He gave a nod and a slight wave. He seemed to be in a bad mood.

"Okay?" Gomez said. "Other questions."

Chris said, "Professor Johnston has been there three days?"

"That's right."

"Who do the locals think he is?"

"We don't know," Gomez said. "We don't know why he left the machine in the first place. He must have had a reason. But since he is in the world, the simplest thing for him would be to pose as a clerk or scholar from London, on a pilgrimage to Santiago de Compostela in Spain. Sainte-Mère is on the pilgrimage route, and it is not unusual for pilgrims to break their trip, to stay a day or a week, especially if they strike up a friendship with the Abbot, who is quite a character. The Professor may have done that. Or he may not. We just don't know."

"But wait a minute," Chris Hughes said. "Won't his presence there change the local history? Won't he influence the outcome of events?"

"No. He won't."

"How do you know?"

"Because he can't."

"But what about the time paradoxes?"

"Time paradoxes?"

"That's right," Stern said. "You know, like going back in time and killing your grandfather, so that you can't be born and couldn't go back and kill your grandfather—"

"Oh, *that*." She shook her head impatiently. "There are no time paradoxes."

"What do you mean? Of course there are."

"No, there aren't," came a firm voice behind them. They turned; Doniger was there. "Time paradoxes do not occur."

:

"What do you mean?" Stern said. He was feeling put out that his question had been so roughly treated.

"The so-called time paradoxes," Doniger said, "do not

really involve time. They involve ideas about history that are seductive but wrong. Seductive, because they flatter you into thinking you can have an impact on the course of events. And wrong, because of course, you can't."

"You can't have an impact on events?"

"No."

"Of course you can."

"No. You can't. It's easiest to see if you take a contemporary example. Say you go to a baseball game. The Yankees and the Mets—the Yankees are going to win, obviously. You want to change the outcome so that the Mets win. What can you do? You're just one person in a crowd. If you try to go to the dugout, you will be stopped. If you try to go onto the field, you will be hauled away. Most ordinary actions available to you will end in failure and will not alter the outcome of the game.

"Let's say you choose a more extreme action: you'll shoot the Yankee pitcher. But the minute you pull a gun, you are likely to be overpowered by nearby fans. Even if you get off a shot, you'll almost certainly miss. And even if you succeed in hitting the pitcher, what is the result? Another pitcher will take his place. And the Yankees will win the game.

"Let's say you choose an even more extreme action. You will release a nerve gas and kill everyone in the stadium. Once again, you're unlikely to succeed, for all the reasons you're unlikely to get a shot off. But even if you do manage to kill everybody, you still have not changed the outcome of the game. You may argue that you have pushed history in another direction—and perhaps so—but you haven't enabled the Mets to win the game. In reality, there is nothing you can do to make the Mets win. You remain what you always were: a spectator.

"And this same principle applies to the great majority of historical circumstances. A single person can do little to alter events in any meaningful way. Of course, great masses of people can 'change the course of history.' But one person? No."

"Maybe so," Stern said, "but I *can* kill my grandfather. And if he's dead then I couldn't be born, so I would not exist, and therefore I couldn't have shot him. And that's a paradox."

"Yes, it is—assuming you actually kill your grandfather. But that may prove difficult in practice. So many things go wrong in life. You may not meet up with him at the right time. You may be hit by a bus on your way. Or you may fall in love. You may be arrested by the police. You may kill him too late, after your parent has already been conceived. Or you may come face to face with him, and find you can't pull the trigger."

"But *in theory* . . ."

"When we are dealing with history, theories are worthless," Doniger said with a contemptuous wave. "A theory is only valuable if it has the ability to predict future outcomes. But history is the record of human action—and no theory can predict human action."

He rubbed his hands together.

"Now then. Shall we end all this speculation and be on our way?"

There were murmurs from the others.

Stern cleared his throat. "Actually," he said, "I don't think I'm going."

:

Marek had been expecting it. He'd watched Stern during the briefing, noticing the way he kept shifting in his chair, as if he couldn't get comfortable. Stern's anxiety had been steadily growing ever since the tour began.

Marek himself had no doubts about going. Since his youth, he had lived and breathed the medieval world, imagining himself in Warburg and Carcassonne, Avignon and Milan. He had joined the Welsh wars with Edward I. He had seen the burghers of Calais give up their city, and he had attended the Champagne Fairs. He had lived at the splendid courts of Eleanor of Aquitaine and the Duc de Berry. Marek was going to take this trip, no matter what. As for Stern—

"I'm sorry," Stern was saying, "but this isn't my affair. I only signed on to the Professor's team because my girlfriend was going to summer school in Toulouse. I'm not a historian. I'm a scientist. And anyway, I don't think it's safe."

Doniger said, "You don't think the machines are safe?"

"No, the place. The year 1357. There was civil war in France after Poitiers. Free companies of soldiers pillaging the countryside. Bandits, cutthroats, lawlessness everywhere."

Marek nodded. If anything, Stern was understating the situation. The fourteenth century was a vanished world, and a dangerous one. It was a religious world; most people went to church at least once a day. But it was an incredibly violent world, where invading armies killed everyone, where women and children were routinely hacked to death, where pregnant women were eviscerated for sport. It was a world that gave lip service to the ideals of chivalry while indiscriminately pillaging and murdering, where women were imagined to be powerless and delicate, yet they ruled fortunes, commanded castles, took lovers at will and plotted assassination and rebellion. It was a world of shifting boundaries and shifting allegiances, often changing from one day to the next. It was a world of death, of sweeping plagues, of disease, of constant warfare.

Gordon said to Stern, "I certainly wouldn't want to force you."

"But remember," Doniger said, "you won't be alone. We'll be sending escorts with you."

"I'm sorry," Stern kept saying. "I'm sorry."

Finally Marek said, "Let him stay. He's right. It's not his period, and it's not his affair."

"Now that you mention it," Chris said, "I've been thinking: It's not my period, either. I'm much more late thirteenth than true fourteenth century. Maybe I should stay with David—"

"Forget it," Marek said, throwing an arm over Chris's shoulder. "You'll be fine." Marek treated it like a joke, even though he knew Chris wasn't exactly joking.

Not exactly.

The room was cold. Chilly mist covered their feet and ankles. They left ripples in the mist as they walked toward the machines.

Four cages had been linked together at the bases, and a fifth cage stood by itself. Baretto said, "That's mine," and stepped into the single cage. He stood erect, staring forward, waiting.

Susan Gomez stepped into one of the clustered cages, and said, "The rest of you come with me." Marek, Kate and Chris climbed into the cages next to her. The machines seemed to be on springs; they rocked slightly as each got on.

"Everybody all set?"

The others murmured, nodded.

Baretto said, "Ladies first."

"You got that right," Gomez said. There didn't seem to be any love lost between them. "Okay," she said to the others. "We're off."

Chris's heart began to pound. He felt light-headed and panicky. He balled his hands into fists.

Gomez said, "Relax. I think you'll find it's quite enjoyable." She slipped the ceramic into the slot at her feet, and stood back up.

"Here we go. Remember: everyone very still when the time comes."

The machines began to hum. Chris felt a slight vibration in the base, beneath his feet. The humming of the machines grew louder. The mist swirled away from the bases of the machines. The machines began to creak and squeal, as if metal was being twisted. The sound built quickly, until it was as steady and loud as a scream.

"That's from the liquid helium," Gomez said. "Chilling the metal to superconduction temperatures."

Abruptly, the screaming ended and the chattering sound began.

"Infrared clearance," she said. "This is it."

Chris felt his whole body begin to tremble involuntarily. He tried to control it, but his legs were shaking. He had a moment of panic—maybe he should call it off—but then he heard a recorded voice say, "Stand still—eyes open—"

Too late, he thought. Too late.

"—deep breath—hold it. . . . *Now!*"

The circular ring descended from above his head, moving swiftly to his feet. It clicked as it touched the base. And a moment later, there was a blinding flash of light—brighter than the sun—coming from all around him—but he felt nothing at all. In fact, he had a sudden strange sense of cold detachment, as if he were now observing a distant scene.

The world around him was completely, utterly silent.

He saw Baretto's nearby machine was growing larger, starting to loom over him. Baretto, a giant, his huge face with monstrous pores, was bending over, looking down at them.

More flashes.

As Baretto's machine grew larger, it also appeared to move away from them, revealing a widening expanse of floor: a vast plain of dark rubber floor, stretching away into the distance.

More flashes.

The rubber floor had a pattern of raised circles. Now these circles began to rise up around them like black cliffs. Soon the black cliffs had grown so high that they seemed like black skyscrapers, joining overhead, closing off the light above. Finally, the skyscrapers touched one another, and the world was dark.

More flashes.

They sank into inky blackness for a moment before he distinguished flickering pinpoints of light, arranged in a gridlike pattern, stretching away in all directions. It was as if they were inside some enormous glowing crystalline structure. As Chris watched, the points of light grew brighter and larger, their edges blurring, until each became a fuzzy glowing ball. He wondered if these were atoms.

He could no longer see the grid, just a few nearby balls. His cage moved directly toward one glowing ball, which appeared to be pulsing, changing its shape in flickering patterns.

Then they were inside the ball, immersed in a bright glowing fog that seemed to throb with energy.

And then the glow faded, and was gone.

They hung in featureless blackness. Nothing.

Blackness.

But then he saw that they were still sinking downward, now heading toward the churning surface of a black ocean in a black night. The ocean whipped and boiled, making a frothy blue-tinged foam. As they descended to the surface, the foam grew larger. Chris saw that one bubble in particular had an especially bright blue glow.

His machine moved toward that glow at accelerating speed, flying faster and faster, and he had the odd sensation that they were going to crash in the foam, and then they entered the bubble and he heard a loud piercing shriek.

Then silence.

Darkness.

Nothing.

In the control room, David Stern watched the flashes on the rubber floor become smaller and weaker, and finally vanish entirely. The machines were gone. The technicians immediately turned to Baretto and began his transmission countdown.

But Stern kept staring at the spot in the rubber floor where Chris and the others had been.

"And where are they now?" he asked Gordon.

"Oh, they've arrived now," Gordon said. "They are *there* now."

"They've been rebuilt?"

"Yes."

"Without a fax machine at the other end."

"That's right."

"Tell me why," Stern said. "Tell me the details the others didn't need to be bothered with."

"All right," Gordon said. "It isn't anything bad. I just thought the others might find it, well, *disturbing*."

"Uh-huh."

"Let's go back," Gordon said, "to the interference patterns, which you remember showed us that other universes can affect our own universe. We don't have to do anything to get the interference pattern to occur. It just happens by itself."

"Yes."

"And this interaction is very reliable; it will always occur, whenever you set up a pair of slits."

Stern nodded. He was trying to see where this was going, but he couldn't foresee the direction Gordon was taking.

"So we know that in certain situations, we can count on

other universes to make something happen. We hold up the slits, and the other universes make the pattern we see, every time."

"Okay. . . ."

"And, if we transmit through a wormhole, the person is always reconstituted at the other end. We can count on that happening, too."

There was a pause.

Stern frowned.

"Wait a minute," he said. "Are you saying that when you transmit, the person is being reconstituted *by* another universe?"

"In effect, yes. I mean, it has to be. We can't very well reconstitute them, because we're not there. We're in this universe."

"So *you're* not reconstituting. . . ."

"No."

"Because you don't know how," Stern said.

"Because we don't find it necessary," Gordon said. "Just as we don't find it necessary to glue plates to a table to make them stay put. They stay by themselves. We make use of a characteristic of the universe, gravity. And in this case, we are making use of a characteristic of the multiverse."

Stern frowned. He immediately distrusted the analogy; it was too glib, too easy.

"Look," Gordon said, "the whole point of quantum technology is that it overlaps universes. When a quantum computer calculates—when all thirty-two quantum states of the electron are being used—the computer is technically carrying out those calculations in other universes, right?"

"Yes, technically, but—"

"No. Not technically. Really."

There was a pause.

"It may be easier to understand," Gordon said, "by seeing it from the point of view of the other universe. That universe sees a person suddenly arrive. A person from another universe."

"Yes. . . ."

"And that's what happened. The person *has* come from another universe. Just not ours."

"Say again?"

"The person didn't come from our universe," Gordon said.

Stern blinked. "Then where?"

"They came from a universe that is almost identical to ours —identical in every respect—except that they know how to reconstitute it at the other end."

"You're joking."

"No."

"The Kate who lands there isn't the Kate who left here? She's a Kate from another universe?"

"Yes."

"So she's almost Kate? Sort of Kate? Semi-Kate?"

"No. She's Kate. As far as we have been able to tell with our testing, she is absolutely identical to our Kate. Because our universe and their universe are almost identical."

"But she's still not the Kate who left here."

"How could she be? She's been destroyed, and reconstructed."

"Do you feel any different when this happens?" Stern said.

"Only for a second or two," Gordon said.

Blackness.

Silence, and then in the distance, glaring white light.

Coming closer. Fast.

Chris shivered as a strong electric shock rippled through his body, and made his fingers twitch. For a moment, he suddenly *felt* his body, the way one feels clothes when you first put them on; he felt the encompassing flesh, felt the weight of it, the pull of gravity downward, the pressure of his body on the soles of his feet. Then a blinding headache, a single pulse, and then it was gone and he was surrounded by intense purple light. He winced, and blinked his eyes.

He was standing in sunlight. The air was cool and damp. Birds chirruped in the huge trees rising above him. Shafts of sunlight came down through the thick foliage, dappling the ground. He was standing in one beam. The machine stood beside a narrow muddy path that wound through a forest. Directly ahead, through a gap in the trees, he saw a medieval village.

First, a cluster of farm plots and huts, plumes of gray smoke rising from thatched roofs. Then a stone wall and the dark stone roofs of the town itself inside, and finally, in the distance, the castle with circular turrets.

He recognized it at once: the town and the fortress of Castelgard. And it was no longer a ruin. Its walls were complete.

*He was here.*

# CASTELGARD

"Nothing in the world is as certain as death."

JEAN FROISSART, 1359

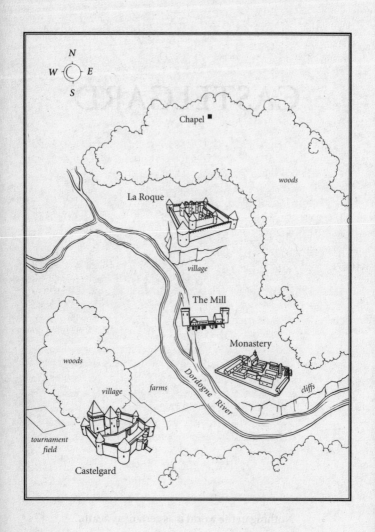

**CASTELGARD**

N
W · E
S

Chapel ■

woods

La Roque

village

The Mill

Monastery

woods

village   farms

Dordogne River

cliffs

tournament
field

Castelgard

# 37:00:00

Gomez hopped lightly out of the machine. Marek and Kate stepped slowly out of their cages, seemingly dazed as they looked around. Chris climbed out, too. His feet touched the mossy ground. It was springy underfoot.

Marek said, "Fantastic!" and immediately moved away from the machine, crossing the muddy path for a better look at the town. Kate followed behind him. She still seemed to be in shock.

But Chris wanted to stay close to the machine. He turned slowly, looking at the forest. It struck him as dark, dense, primeval. The trees, he noticed, were huge. Some of them had trunks so thick, you could hide three or four people behind them. They rose high into the sky, spreading a leafy canopy above them that darkened most of the ground below.

"Beautiful, isn't it?" Gomez said. She seemed to sense that he was uneasy.

"Yes, beautiful," he answered. But he didn't feel that way at all; something about this forest struck him as sinister. He turned round and round, trying to understand why he had the distinct feeling that something was wrong with what he was seeing—something was missing, or out of place. Finally, he said, "What's *wrong*?"

She laughed. "Oh, that," she said. "Listen."

Chris stood silently for a moment, listening. There was the chirp of birds, the soft rustle of a faint breeze in the trees. But other than that . . .

"I don't hear anything."

"That's right," Gomez said. "It upsets some people when

they first arrive. There's no ambient noise here: no radio or TV, no airplanes, no machinery, no passing cars. In the twentieth century, we're so accustomed to hearing sound all the time, the silence feels creepy."

"I guess that's right." At least, that was exactly how he was feeling. He turned away from the trees and looked at the muddy path, a sunlit track through the forest. In many places, the mud was two feet deep, churned by many hooves.

This was a world of horses, he thought.

No machine sounds. Lots of hoofprints.

He took a deep breath, and let it out slowly. Even the air seemed different. Heady, bright-feeling, as if it had more oxygen in it.

He turned, and saw that the machine was gone. Gomez appeared unconcerned. "Where's the machine?" he said, trying not to sound worried.

"It drifted."

"It *drifted*?"

"When the machines are fully charged, they're a little unstable. They tend to slide off the present moment. So we can't see them."

"Where are they?" Chris said.

She shrugged. "We don't know, exactly. They must be in another universe. Wherever they are, they're fine. They always come back."

To demonstrate, she held up her ceramic marker and pressed the button with her thumbnail. In increasingly bright flashes of light, the machine returned: all four cages, standing exactly where they had been a few minutes before.

"Now, it'll stay here like this for maybe a minute, maybe two," Gomez said. "But eventually it will drift again. I just let them go. Gets 'em out of the way."

Chris nodded; she seemed to know what she was talking about. But the thought that the machines drifted made Chris vaguely uneasy; those machines were his ticket back home, and he didn't like to think that they behaved according to their own rules and could disappear at random. He thought, Would anybody fly on an airplane if the pilot said that it was "unstable"? He felt a coolness on his forehead, and he knew in a moment he would break out in a cold sweat.

To distract himself, Chris picked his way across the path, following the others, trying not to sink into the mud. On solid ground again, he pushed through thick ground cover, some kind of dense waist-high plant, like rhododendron. He glanced back at Gomez: "Anything to worry about in these woods?"

"Just vipers," she said. "They're usually in the lower branches of the trees. They fall down on your shoulders and bite you."

"Great," he said. "Are they poisonous?"

"Very."

"Fatal?"

"Don't worry, they're very rare," she said.

Chris decided not to ask any more questions. Anyway, by now he had reached a sunlit opening in the foliage. He looked down and saw the Dordogne River two hundred feet below him, twisting through farmland, and looking, he thought, not very different from the way he was used to seeing it.

But if the river was the same, everything else in this landscape was different. Castelgard was entirely intact, and so was its town. Beyond the walls were farming plots; some of the fields were being plowed now.

But his attention was drawn to the right, where he looked down on the great rectangular complex of the monastery—and the fortified mill bridge. *His* fortified bridge, he thought. The bridge he had been studying all summer—

And unfortunately, looking very different from the way he had reconstructed it in the computer.

Chris saw four water wheels, not three, churning in the current that ran beneath a bridge. And the bridge above was not a single unified structure. There seemed to be at least two independent structures, like little houses. The larger was made of stone and the other of wood, suggesting the structures had been built at different times. From the stone building, smoke belched in a continuous gray plume. So maybe they really were making steel there, he thought. If you had water-powered bellows, then you could have an actual blast furnace. That would explain the separate structures, too. Because mills that ground grain or corn never permitted any open fire or flame inside—not even a candle. That was why grinding mills operated only during daylight hours.

Absorbed in the details, he felt himself relax.

∴

On the far side of the muddy path, Marek stared at the village of Castelgard with a slow sense of astonishment.

*He was here.*

He felt light-headed, almost giddy with excitement as he took in the details. In the fields below, peasants wore patched leggings and tunics in red and blue, orange and rose. The vivid colors stood out against the dark earth. Most of the fields were already planted, their furrows closed over. This was early April, so the spring planting of barley, peas, oats and beans—the so-called Lenten crops—would be nearly finished.

He watched a new field being plowed, the black iron blade hauled by two oxen. The plow itself turned the earth of the furrow neatly on both sides. He was pleased to see a low wooden guard mounted above the blade. That was a mold-board, and it was characteristic of this particular time.

Walking behind the plowman, a peasant sowed seed with rhythmic sweeps of his arm. The sack of seed hung from his shoulder. A short distance behind the sower, birds fluttered down to the furrow, eating the seed. But not for long. In a nearby field, Marek saw the harrower: a man riding a horse that dragged a wooden T-frame weighted down by a large rock. The harrower closed the furrows, protecting the seed.

Everything appeared to move in the same gentle, steady rhythm: the hand throwing seed, the plow turning the furrow, the harrow scraping the ground. And there was almost no sound in the still morning, just the hum of insects and the twitter of birds.

Beyond the fields, Marek saw the twenty-foot-high stone wall encircling the town of Castelgard. The stone was a dark, weathered gray. In one section, the wall was being repaired; the new stone was lighter in color, yellow-gray. Masons were hunched over, working quickly. Atop the wall itself, guards in chain mail strode back and forth, sometimes pausing to stare nervously into the distance.

And rising above everything, the castle itself, with its circular towers and black stone roofs. Flags fluttered from the turrets. All the flags showed the same emblem: a maroon-and-gray shield with a silver rose.

It gave the castle a festive appearance, and indeed, in a field just outside the town walls, a large wooden viewing stand, like bleachers, was being erected for the tournament. A crowd had already begun to gather. A few knights were there, horses tied beside the brightly colored striped tents that were pitched all around the tournament field itself. Pages and grooms threaded their way among the tents, carrying armor, and water for the horses.

Marek took it all in and gave a long, satisfied sigh.

Everything he saw was accurate, down to the smallest detail. Everything was real.

*He was here.*

⋮

Kate Erickson stared at Castelgard with a sense of puzzlement. Beside her, Marek was sighing like a lover, but she wasn't sure why. Of course, Castelgard was now a lively village, restored to its former glory, its houses and castle complete. But overall, the scene before her didn't look that different from any rural French landscape. Perhaps a little more backward than most, with horses and oxen instead of tractors. But otherwise . . . well, it just wasn't that different.

Architecturally, the biggest difference she saw in the scene before her and the present was that all the houses had *lauzes* roofs, made of stacked black stone. These stone roofs were incredibly heavy and required a great deal of internal bracing, which was why houses in the Périgord no longer used them, except in tourist areas. She was accustomed to seeing French houses with ocher roofs of curved Roman tile, or the flat tile of the French style.

Yet here, *lauzes* roofs were everywhere. There was no tile at all.

As she continued to look at the scene, she slowly noticed other details. For example, there were a lot of horses: really a lot, when you considered the horses in the fields, the horses at the tournament, the horses ridden on the dirt roads, and the horses put out to pasture. There must be a hundred horses in her view right now, she thought. She couldn't remember seeing so many horses at one time, even in her native Colorado. All kinds of horses, from beautiful sleek warhorses at the tournament to barnyard nags in the fields.

And while many of the people working in the fields were drably dressed, others wore colors so brilliant they almost reminded her of the Caribbean. These clothes were patched and patched again, but always in a contrasting color, so that the patchwork was visible even from a distance. It became a kind of design.

Then, too, she became aware of a clear demarcation between the relatively small areas of human habitation—towns and fields—and the surrounding forest, a dense, vast green carpet, stretching away in all directions. In this landscape, the forest predominated. She had the sense of encompassing wilderness, in which human beings were interlopers. And minor interlopers at that.

And as she looked again at the town of Castelgard itself, she sensed there was something odd that she couldn't put her finger on. Until she finally realized, there were no chimneys!

No chimneys anywhere.

The peasant houses simply had holes in the thatched roofs from which smoke issued. Within the town, the houses were similar, even though their roofs were stone: the smoke issued from a hole, or from a vent in a wall. The castle lacked chimneys, too.

She was looking at a time before chimneys appeared in this part of France. For some reason this trivial architectural detail made her shiver with a kind of horror. A world before chimneys. When had chimneys been invented, anyway? She couldn't remember exactly. Certainly by 1600, they were common. But that was a long time from now.

This "now," she reminded herself.

Behind her, she heard Gomez say, "What the hell do you think you're doing?"

:

Kate looked back and saw that the surly guy, Baretto, had arrived. His single cage was visible on the other side of the path, a few yards back in the woods.

"I'll do what I damn well want to do," he said to Gomez.

He had pulled up his burlap tunic, revealing a heavy leather belt with a holstered pistol and two black grenades. He was checking the pistol.

"If we're going into the world," Baretto said, "I'm going to be prepared."

"You're not bringing that stuff with you," Gomez said.

"The hell I'm not, sister."

"You're not. You know that's not allowed. Gordon would never permit modern weapons to be taken into the world."

"But Gordon's not here, is he?" Baretto said.

"Look, goddamn it," Gomez said, and she pulled out her white ceramic marker, waving it at Baretto.

It looked as if she was threatening to go back.

# 36:50:22

In the control room, one of the technicians at the monitors said, "We're getting field bucks."

"Oh, really? That's good news," Gordon said.

"Why?" Stern said.

"It means," Gordon said, "that someone is headed back in the next two hours. Undoubtedly your friends."

"So they will get the Professor and be back here within two hours?"

"Yes, that's exactly—" Gordon broke off, staring at the undulating image on the monitor. A little undulating surface, with a spike that stuck up. "Is that it?"

"Yes," the technician said.

"But the amplitude's much too large," Gordon said.

"Yes. And the interval's getting shorter. Fast."

"You mean someone is coming back *now*?"

"Yeah. Soon, it looks like."

Stern glanced at his watch. The team had been gone only a few minutes. They couldn't have recovered the Professor so quickly.

"What does that mean?" Stern asked him.

"I don't know," Gordon said. The truth was, he didn't like this development at all. "They must be having some sort of trouble."

"What kind of trouble?"

"This soon, it's probably mechanical. Maybe a transcription error."

Stern said, "What's a transcription error?"

The technician said, "I'm calculating an arrival in twenty minutes fifty-seven seconds." He was measuring the field strengths, and the pulse intervals.

"How many are coming back?" Gordon said. "All of them?"

"No," the technician said. "Just one."

# 36:49:19

Chris Hughes couldn't help it; he was anxious again. Despite the cool morning air, he was sweating, his skin cold, his heart pounding. Listening to Baretto and Gomez argue did nothing to increase his confidence.

He went back to the path, stepping around the pools of thick mud. Marek and Kate were coming back, too. They all stood a little apart from the argument.

"All right, *all right,* goddamn it," Baretto was saying. He took off his weapons and put them carefully on the floor of his cage. "All right. Does *that* satisfy you?"

Gomez was still speaking quietly, barely a whisper. Chris couldn't hear her.

"It's *fine,*" Baretto said, almost snarling.

Gomez again spoke softly. Baretto was grinding his teeth. It was very uncomfortable to be standing there. Chris moved a few steps farther away, turning his back to the argument, waiting for it to be over.

He was surprised to see that the path sloped downward rather steeply, and he could see through a break in the trees to the flatland below. The monastery was there—a geometric arrangement of courtyards, covered passageways, and cloisters, all built of beige stone, surrounded by a high stone wall. It looked like a dense, compact little city. It was surprisingly close, perhaps a quarter of a mile. No more than that.

"Screw it, I'm walking," Kate said, and she started down the path. Marek and Chris looked at each other, then followed after her.

"You people stay in sight, damn it," Baretto called to them.

Gomez said, "I think we'd better go."

Baretto put a restraining hand on her arm. "Not until we get something cleared up," he said. "About how things are handled on this expedition."

"I think it's pretty well cleared up," Gomez said.

Baretto leaned close and said, "Because I didn't like the way you . . ." And the rest was too low to hear, just the furious hiss of his voice.

Chris was grateful to move around the curve in the path and leave them behind.

:

Kate started at a brisk walk, feeling the tension leave her body as she moved. The argument left her feeling cramped and edgy. A few paces behind her, she heard Chris and Marek talking. Chris was anxious, and Marek was trying to calm him down. She didn't want to hear it. She picked up the pace a little. After all, to be here, in these fantastic woods, surrounded by these huge trees . . .

After a minute or two, she had left Marek and Chris behind, but she knew they were near enough, and it was nice to be alone. The woods around her felt cool and relaxing. She listened to the chitter of birds and the sound of her own feet padding along on the path. Once she thought she heard something else, too. She slowed a bit to listen.

Yes, there was another sound: running feet. They seemed to be coming from farther down the path. She heard someone panting, gasping for breath.

And also a fainter sound, like the rumble of distant thunder. She was trying to place that rumble when a teenage boy burst around the corner, racing toward her.

The boy was wearing black hose, a bright green quilted jacket and a black cap. He was red-faced with exertion; he'd clearly been running for some time. He seemed startled to find her walking on the path. As he came toward her, he cried, *"Aydethee amsel! Grassa due! Aydethee!"*

An instant later, she heard his voice translated in her earpiece: "Hide, woman! For the sake of God! Hide!"

Hide from what? Kate wondered. These woods were deserted. What could he mean? Maybe she hadn't understood him right. Maybe the translator wasn't correct. As the boy passed her, he again cried, "Hide!" and shoved Kate hard, pushing her off the path and into the woods. She tripped on a gnarled root, tumbled into the undergrowth. She banged her head, felt sharp pain and a wave of dizziness. She was getting slowly to her feet when she realized what the rumbling sound was.

Horses.

Riding at full gallop toward her.

:

Chris saw the young boy running up the path, and almost immediately, he heard the sound of pursuing horses. The boy, finally out of breath, stopped for a moment beside them, doubled over, and finally managed to gasp, "Hide! Hide!" before he darted away into the woods.

Marek ignored the boy. He was looking down the path.

Chris frowned. "What is all that about—"

"*Now,*" Marek said, and throwing an arm around Chris's shoulders, he pulled him bodily off the path and into the foliage.

"Jesus," Chris said, "would you mind telling me—"

"*Shhh!*" Marek put his hand over Chris's mouth. "*Do you want to get us killed?*"

No, Chris thought, he was clear on that: he did not want to get anybody killed. Charging up the hill toward them were six horsemen in full armor: steel helmets, chain mail and cloth surcoats of maroon and gray. The horses were draped in black cloth studded with silver. The effect was ominous. The lead rider, wearing a helmet with a black plume, pointed ahead and screamed, "*Godin!*"

Baretto and Gomez were still standing beside the path, just standing there, apparently in shock at what they saw galloping toward them. The black rider leaned over in the saddle and swung his broadsword in an arc at Gomez as he rode past her.

Chris saw Gomez's headless torso, spurting blood, as it toppled to the ground. Baretto, spattered with blood, swore loudly as he ran into the woods. More riders galloped up the hill. Now they were all shouting, *"Godin! Godin!"* One rider wheeled on his horse, drawing his bow.

The arrow struck Baretto's left shoulder as he ran, the steel point punching through the other side, the impact knocking him to his knees. Cursing, Baretto staggered to his feet again, and finally reached his machine.

He picked up his belt, yanked one of the grenades free, and turned to throw it. An arrow struck him full in the chest. Baretto looked surprised, coughed, and fell back, sprawled in a seated position against the bars. He made a feeble effort to pull the arrow out of his chest. The next arrow passed through his throat. The grenade dropped from his hand.

Back on the path, the horses reared and whinnied, their riders wheeling in circles, shouting and pointing.

There was a bright flash of light.

Chris looked back in time to see Baretto still seated, unmoving, as the machine flashed repeatedly, shrinking in size.

In moments, the machine was gone. The riders now had looks of fear on their faces. The black-plumed rider shouted something to the others, and as a group, they whipped their horses and raced on up the hill, out of sight.

As the black rider turned to go, his horse stumbled over Gomez's body. Cursing, the rider wheeled and reared his horse repeatedly, stomping the body again and again. Blood flew in the air; the horse's forelegs turned dark red. At last the black rider turned, and with a final curse, he galloped up the hill again to rejoin the others.

*"Jesus."* The suddenness of it, the casual violence—

Chris scrambled to his feet, ran back to the path.

Gomez's body lay in a muddy pool, crushed almost beyond recognition. But one hand was flung outward and lay open on the ground. And next to her hand lay the white ceramic marker.

It was cracked open, its electronic innards exposed.

Chris picked it up. The ceramic fell apart in his hands, bits of white and silver fluttering to the ground, falling into the muddy pool. And in that moment, their situation was clear to him.

Their guides were both dead.

One machine was gone.

Their return marker was shattered.

Which meant they were stuck in this place. Trapped here, without guides or assistance. And with no prospect of ever getting back.

Not ever.

# 36:30:42

"Stand by," a technician said. "Coming in now."

In the rubber floor, in the center of the curved water shields, small flashes of light appeared.

Gordon glanced at Stern. "We'll know what happened in just a minute."

The flashes grew brighter, and a machine began to emerge above the rubber. It was about two feet high when Gordon said, "Goddamn it! That guy is nothing but trouble."

Stern said something, but Gordon paid no attention. He saw Baretto sitting there, propped up against a bar, clearly dead. The machine reached full size. He saw the pistol in his hand. He knew of course what had happened. Even though Kramer had specifically warned Baretto, the son of a bitch had taken modern weapons back with him. So of course Gomez sent him back, and—

A small dark object rolled out onto the floor.

"What's that?" Stern said.

"I don't know," Gordon said, staring at the screens. "It almost looks like a gre—"

The explosion flashed in the transit room, blooming white on the video screens, washing everything out. Inside the control room, the sound was oddly distorted, more like a burst of static. The transit room was immediately filled with pale smoke.

"Shit," Gordon said. He banged his fist down on the console.

The technicians in the transit room were screaming. One man's face was covered with blood. In the next moment, the man was swept off his feet in the rush of water as the shields collapsed, shattered by grenade fragments. Water three feet deep sloshed back and forth like surf. But almost immediately, it began to drain out, leaving the newly bare floor hissing and steaming.

"It's the cells," Gordon said. "They've leaked hydrofluoric acid."

Obscured by smoke, figures in gas masks were running into the room, helping the injured technicians. Overhead beams began to crash down, shattering the remaining water shields. Other beams smashed down into the center of the floor.

In the control room, someone gave a gas mask to Gordon, and another to Stern. Gordon pulled his on.

"We have to go now," he said. "The air is contaminated."

Stern was staring at the screens. Through the smoke, he could see the other machines shattered, toppled over, leaking steam and pale green gas. There was only one still standing, off to one side, and as he watched, a connecting beam crashed down on it, crumpling it.

"There are no more machines," Stern said. "Does this mean—"

"Yes," Gordon said. "For now, I'm afraid your friends are on their own."

# 36:30:00

"Just take it easy, Chris," Marek said.

"Take it easy? Take it *easy*?" Chris was almost shouting. "Look at it, for Christ's sake, André—her marker's trashed. We have no marker. Which means we have no way to get home. Which means we are totally screwed, André. And you want me to *take it easy*?"

"That's right, Chris," Marek said, his voice very quiet, very steady. "That's what I want. I want you to take it easy, please. I want you to pull yourself together."

"Why the hell should I?" Chris said. "For what? Face the facts, André: we're all going to get killed here. You know that, don't you? We're going to get goddamn killed. And there is *no way out of here*."

"Yes, there is."

"I mean, we don't even have any *food*, we don't have god-damn anything, we're stuck in this—this *shithole*, without a goddamn paddle, and—" He stopped and turned toward Marek. "What did you say?"

"I said, there's a way out."

"How?"

"You're not thinking. The other machine has gone back. To New Mexico."

"So?"

"They'll see his condition—"

"Dead, André. They'll see he's *dead*."

"The point is, they'll know something is wrong. And they will come for us. They'll send another machine to get us," Marek said.

"How do you know?"

"Because they will." Marek turned and started down the hill.

"Where are you going?"

"To find Kate. We have to keep together."

"I'm going to stay right here."

"As you like. Just as long as you don't leave."

"Don't worry, I'll be right here."

Chris pointed to the ground in front of him. "This is exactly where the machine arrived before. And that's where I'm staying."

Marek trotted off, disappearing around the curve in the path. Chris was alone. Almost immediately, he wondered if he ought to run and catch up with Marek. Maybe it was better not to be alone. Stay together, as Marek had said.

He took a couple of steps down the path after Marek, then stopped. No, he thought. He'd said he would stay where he was. He stood in the path, trying to slow his breathing.

Looking down, he saw he was standing on Gomez's hand. He stepped quickly away. He walked a few yards back up the path, trying to find a spot where he could no longer see the body. His breathing slowed still more. He was able to think things over. Marek was right, he decided. They would send another machine, and probably very soon. Would it land right here? Was this a known spot for landings? Or would it be somewhere in the general area?

In either case, Chris felt certain he should stay exactly where he was.

He looked down the path, toward where Marek had gone. Where was Kate now? Probably some distance down the path. Couple of hundred yards, maybe more.

Jesus, he wanted to go home.

Then, in the woods to his right, he heard a crashing sound. Someone was approaching.

He tensed, aware that he had no weapon. Then he remembered his pack, which was tied to his belt, beneath his clothes. He had that gas canister. It was better than nothing. He fumbled, lifting his overshirt, searching for the—

*"Ssss."*

He turned.

It was the teenage boy, coming out of the woods. His face was smooth and beardless; he couldn't be more than twelve, Chris realized. The boy whispered, *"Arkith. Thou. Earwashmann."*

Chris frowned, not understanding, but an instant later he heard a tinny voice inside his ear: "Hey. You. Irishman." The earpiece was translating, he realized.

"What?" he said.

*"Coumen hastealey."* In his ear he heard, "Come quickly." The boy was beckoning to him, tense, urgently.

"But . . ."

"Come. Sir Guy will soon realize he has lost the trail. Then he will return to find it again."

"But . . ."

"You cannot stay here. He will kill you. Come!"

"But . . ." Chris gestured helplessly toward the path where Marek had gone.

"Your manservant will find you. Come!"

Now he heard the distant rumble of horses' hooves, rapidly growing louder.

"Are you dumb?" the boy asked, staring at him. "Come!"

The rumble was closer.

Chris stood frozen in place, not certain what to do.

The boy lost patience. With a disgusted shake of his head, he turned and ran off through the forest. He immediately vanished in dense undergrowth.

Chris stood alone on the trail. He looked down the path. He didn't see Marek. He looked up the path, toward the sound of the approaching horses. His heart was pounding again.

He had to decide. Now.

"I'm coming!" he shouted to the boy.

Then he turned and ran into the woods.

·

Kate sat on a fallen tree, touching her head gingerly, her wig askew. There was blood on her fingertips.

"Are you hurt?" Marek said as he came up to her.

"I don't think so."

"Let me see."

Lifting the wig away, Marek saw matted blood and a three-inch gash across the scalp. The wound was no longer bleeding freely; the blood had begun to coagulate against the mesh of the wig. The injury deserved sutures, but she would be all right without them.

"You'll survive." He pushed the wig back down on her head.

She said, "What happened?"

"Those other two are dead. It's just us now. Chris is a little panicked."

"Chris is a little panicked." She nodded, as if she had expected it. "Then we better go get him."

They started up the path. As they walked, Kate said, "What about the markers?"

"The guy went back, and he took his. Gomez's body was trampled, her marker was destroyed."

"What about the other one?" Kate said.

"What other one?"

"She had a spare."

"How do you know?"

"She said so. Don't you remember? When she came back from that reconnaissance trip, or whatever it was, she said that everything was fine and that we should hurry up and get ready. And she said, 'I'm going to go burn the spare.' Or something like that."

Marek frowned.

"It makes sense there would be a spare," Kate said.

"Well, Chris will be glad to hear it," Marek said. They walked around the final curve. Then they stopped and stared.

Chris was gone.

.
.

Plunging through the undergrowth, ignoring the brambles that scratched his legs and plucked at his hose, Chris Hughes at last glimpsed the boy running, fifty yards ahead. But the boy did not heed him, did not stop, but continued to run forward. He was heading toward the village. Chris struggled to keep up. He kept running.

Behind on the trail, he heard the horses stamping and snorting, and the shouts of the men. He heard one cry, "In the wood!" and another answered with a curse. But off the trail, the ground was densely covered. Chris had to scramble over fallen trees, rotting trunks, snapped branches as thick as his thigh, dense patches of bramble. Was this ground too difficult for horses? Would they dismount? Would they give up? Or would they chase?

Hell, they would chase.

He kept running. He was in a boggy area now. He pushed through the waist-high plants with their skunklike smell, slipped in mud that grew deeper with each step. He heard the sound of his panting breath, and the suck and slap of his feet in the mud.

But he didn't hear anyone behind him.

Soon the footing was dry again, and he was able to run faster. Now the boy was only ten paces ahead of him, still going fast. Chris was panting, struggling to keep up, but he held his own.

He ran on. There was a crackling in his left ear. "Chris."

It was Marek.

"Chris, where are you?"

How did he answer? Was there a microphone? Then he remembered they'd said something about bone conduction. He said aloud, "I'm . . . I'm running. . . ."

"I hear that. Where are you running?"

"The boy . . . the village . . ."

"You're going to the village?"

"I don't know. I think so."

"You think so? Chris, where are you?"

And then, behind him, Chris heard a crashing, the shouts of men, and the whinny of horses.

The riders were coming after him. And he had left a trail of snapped branches and muddy footprints. It would be easy to follow.

*Shit.*

Chris ran harder, pushing himself to the limit. And suddenly he realized the young boy was no longer visible ahead.

He stopped, gasping for breath, and spun around in a circle. Looking—

Gone.

The boy had vanished.

Chris was alone in the forest.

And the riders were coming.

.
.

On the muddy path overlooking the monastery, Marek and Kate stood listening to their earpieces. There was silence now; Kate clapped her hand over her ear to hear better. "I don't get anything."

"He may be out of range," Marek said.

"Why is he going to the village? It sounds like he's following that boy," she said. "Why would he do that?"

Marek looked toward the monastery. It was no more than a ten-minute walk from where they were standing. "The Professor is probably down there right now. We could just go get him, and go home." He kicked a tree stump irritably. "It would have been so easy."

"Not anymore," Kate said.

The sharp crack of static in their earpieces made them wince. They heard Chris panting again.

Marek said, "Chris. Are you there?"

"I can't . . . can't talk now."

He was whispering. And he sounded scared.

.
.

"No, no, *no*!" the boy whispered, reaching down from the branches of a very large tree. He had whistled, finally taking pity on Chris as he spun in panicky circles on the ground below. And he had waved him to the tree.

Chris was now struggling to climb the tree, trying to pull himself up on the lowest branches, getting extra leverage by bracing his legs against the trunk. But the way he did it upset the boy.

"No, no! Hands! Use only the hands!" the boy whispered, exasperated. "You *are* dumb—look now the marks on the trunk, by your feet."

Hanging from a branch, Chris looked down. The boy was right. There were muddy streaks, very clear on the bark of the trunk.

"By the rood, we are lost," the boy cried, swinging over Chris's head and dropping lightly to the ground.

"What are you doing?" Chris said.

But the boy was already running off, through the brambles, moving from tree to tree. Chris dropped back to the ground and followed.

The boy muttered irritably to himself as he inspected the branches of each tree. Apparently he wanted a very large tree with relatively low branches; none suited him. The sound of the riders was growing louder.

Soon they had traveled a hundred yards or more, into an area carpeted with gnarled, scrubby ground pines. It was more exposed and sunnier here because there were fewer trees to his right, and then Chris saw they were running near the edge of a cliff that overlooked the town and the river. The boy darted away from the sunlight, back into the darker forest. Almost at once, he found a tree he liked, and signaled Chris to come forward. "You go first. And no feet!"

The boy bent his knees, laced the fingers of his hands, and tensed his body, bracing himself. Chris felt the youth was too slender to take his weight, but the boy jerked his head impatiently. Chris put his foot in the boy's hands, and reaching upward, grasped the lowest branch. With the help of the boy, he pulled himself up, until with a final grunt he swung himself over so he lay on his stomach, bent double over the branch. He looked down at the boy, who hissed, "Move!" Chris struggled to his knees, then got to his feet on the branch. The next branch above was within easy reach, and he continued to climb.

Below, the boy leapt into the air, gripped the branch, and pulled quickly up. Although slim, he was surprisingly strong, and he moved from branch to branch surely. Chris was now about twenty feet above the ground. His arms burned, he was gasping as he went up, but he kept on going, branch to branch.

The boy gripped his calf, and he froze. Slowly, cautiously, he looked back over his shoulder, and saw the boy rigid on the branch beneath him. Then Chris heard the soft snort of a horse and realized the sound was close.

Very close.

∶

On the ground below, six riders moved slowly and silently forward. They were still some distance away, intermittently visible through gaps in the foliage. When a horse snorted, its rider leaned forward to pat its neck to quiet it.

The riders knew they were close to their prey. They leaned over in their saddles, scanning the ground, looking to one side and the other. Fortunately they were now among the scrubby low pines; no trail was visible.

Communicating by hand gestures, they moved apart, separating themselves as they came forward. Now they formed a rough line, passing beneath the tree on both sides. Chris held his breath. *If they looked up . . .*

But they didn't.

They moved onward, deeper into the forest, and finally one of them spoke aloud. It was the rider with the black plume on his helmet, the one who had cut off Gomez's head. His visor was up.

"Here is enough. They have slipped us."

"How? Over the cliff?"

The black knight shook his head. "The child is not so foolish." Chris saw his face was dark: dark complexion and dark eyes.

"Nor quite a child, my Lord."

"If he fell, it was by error. It could not be otherwise. But I think we have gone awry. Let us return as we came."

"My Lord."

The riders turned their mounts and started back. They

passed beneath the tree again, and then rode off, still widely spaced, heading into sunlight.

"Perhaps in better light, we shall find their track."

Chris gave a long sigh of relief.

The boy below tapped him on the leg and nodded to him, as if to say, Good work. They waited until the riders were at least a hundred yards away, nearly out of sight. Then the boy slipped quietly down the tree, and Chris followed as best he could.

Once on the ground, Chris saw the riders moving off. They were coming to the tree with the muddy footprints. The black knight passed it, not noticing. Then the next—

The boy grabbed his arm, pulled him away, slipping off in the underbrush.

Then: "Sir Guy! Look you here! The tree! They are in the tree!"

One of the knights had noticed.

*Shit.*

The riders spun on their mounts, looking up at the tree. The black knight came back, skeptical. "Eh? Show me."

"I do not see them up there, my Lord."

The knights turned, looked back, looked in all directions, looked behind them. . . .

And they saw them.

"There!"

The riders charged.

The boy ran hard. "God's truth, we are lost now," he said, glancing over his shoulder as he raced forward. "Can you swim?"

"Swim?" Chris said.

Of course he could swim. But that was not what he was thinking about. Because right now they were running hard, flat out—toward the clearing, toward the break in the trees.

Toward the cliff.

The land sloped downward, gently at first, then more steeply. The ground cover became thinner, with exposed patches of yellow-white limestone. The sunlight was glaring.

The black knight bellowed something. Chris didn't understand it.

They came at last to the edge of the clearing. Without hesitation, the boy leapt into space.

Chris hesitated, not wanting to follow. Glancing back, he
saw the knights charging him, their broadswords raised.

*No choice.*

Chris turned and ran forward toward the cliff edge.

⋮

Marek winced as he heard Chris's scream in his earpiece. The
scream was loud at first, then abruptly ended with a grunt and
a crashing sound.

An impact.

He stood with Kate by the trail, listening. Waiting.

They heard nothing more. Not even the crackle of static.

Nothing at all.

"Is he dead?" Kate said.

Marek didn't answer her. He walked quickly to Gomez's
body, crouched down, and started searching in the mud.
"Come on," he said. "Help me find that spare marker."

⋮

They searched for the next few minutes, and then Marek
grabbed Gomez's hand, already turning pale gray, the muscles
stiffening. He lifted her arm, feeling the coldness of her skin,
and turned her torso over. The body splashed back in the mud.

That was when he noticed that Gomez had a bracelet of
braided twine on her wrist. Marek hadn't noticed it before; it
seemed to be part of her period costume. Of course, it was
completely wrong for the period. Even a modest peasant
woman would wear a bracelet of metal, or carved stone or
wood, if she wore anything at all. This was a hippie-dippy
modern thing.

Marek touched it curiously, and he was surprised to find it
was stiff, almost like cardboard. He turned it on her wrist,
looking for the latch, and a sort of lid flicked open in the

braided twine, and he realized that the bracelet covered a small electronic timer, like a wristwatch.

The timer read: 36:10:37.

And it was counting backward.

He knew at once what it was. It was an elapsed counter for the machine, showing how much time they had left. They had thirty-seven hours initially, and now they had lost about fifty minutes.

We should hold on to this, he thought. He untied the bracelet from her arm, then wrapped it around his own wrist. He flipped the little lid shut.

"We've got a timer," Kate said. "But no marker."

They searched for the next five minutes. And finally, reluctantly, Marek had to admit the hard truth.

There was no marker. And without a marker, the machines would not come back.

Chris was right: they were trapped there.


# 36:28:04


In the control room, an alarm rang insistently. The technicians both got up from their consoles and started out of the room. Stern felt Gordon grab him firmly by the arm.

"We have to go," Gordon said. "The air's contaminated from the hydrofluoric acid. The transit pad is toxic. And the fumes will be up here, too, soon enough." He began to lead Stern out of the control room.

Stern glanced back at the screen, at the jumble of girders in smoke in the transit site. "But what if they try to come back when everybody is gone?"

"Don't worry," Gordon said. "That can't happen. The

wreckage will trigger the infrared. The sensors need six feet on all sides, remember? Two meters. They don't have it. So the sensors won't let the machines come back. Not until we get all that cleared away."

"How long will it take to clear it away?"

"First, we have to exchange the air in the cave."

Gordon took Stern back to the long corridor leading to the main elevator. There were a lot of people in the corridor, all leaving. Their voices echoed in the tunnel.

"Exchange the air in the cave?" Stern said. "That's a huge volume. How long will that take?"

Gordon said, "In theory, it takes nine hours."

"In theory?"

"We've never had to do it before," Gordon said. "But we have the capacity, of course. The big fans should cut in any minute."

A few seconds later, a roaring sound filled the tunnel. Stern felt a blast of wind press his body, tug at his clothes.

"And after they exchange all the air? What then?"

"We rebuild the transit pad and wait for them to come back," Gordon said. "Just the way we were planning to do."

"And if they try to come back before you're ready for them?"

"It's not a problem, David. The machine will just refuse. It'll pop them right back to where they were. For the time being."

"So they're stranded," Stern said.

"For the moment," Gordon said. "Yes. They're stranded. And there's nothing we can do about it."

# 36:13:17

Chris Hughes ran to the edge of the cliff and threw himself into space, screaming, arms and legs flailing in the sunlight. He saw the Dordogne, two hundred feet below, snaking through the green countryside. It was too far to fall. He knew the river was too shallow. There was no question he would die.

But then he saw the cliff face beneath him was not sheer—there was a protruding shelf of land, twenty feet below, jutting out from the upper rim of the cliff. It was steeply angled bare rock, with a sparse cover of scrubby trees and brush.

He slammed down on the shelf, landing on his side, the impact blasting the air from his lungs. Immediately, he began rolling helplessly toward the edge. He tried to stop the roll, clutching desperately at underbrush, but it was all too weak, and it tore away in his hands. As he tumbled toward the edge, he was aware of the boy reaching for him, but Chris missed his outstretched arms. He continued to roll, his world spinning out of control. Now the boy was behind him, with a horrified look on his face. Chris knew he was going to go over the edge; he was going to fall—

With a grunt, he slammed into a tree. He felt a sharp pain in his stomach, then it streaked through his whole body. For a moment, he did not know where he was; he felt only pain. The world was greenish white. He came back to it slowly.

The tree had broken his descent, but for a moment he still could not breathe at all. The pain was intense. Stars swam before his eyes, then slowly faded, and finally he saw his legs were dangling over the edge of the cliff.

And moving.

Moving downward.

The tree was a spindly pine, and his weight was slowly, slowly bending it over. He felt himself begin to slide along the trunk. He was helpless to stop it. He grabbed at the trunk and held tightly. And it worked: he wasn't sliding anymore. He pulled himself along the trunk, working his way back to the rock.

Then, to his horror, he saw the roots of the tree begin to break free of the rocky crevices, one by one snapping loose, pale in the sunlight. It was only a matter of time before the entire trunk broke free.

Then he felt a tug at his collar and saw the boy standing above him, hauling him back to his feet. The boy looked exasperated. "Come, now!"

"Jesus," Chris said. He flopped onto a flat rock, gasping for breath. "Just give me a minute—"

An arrow whined past his ear like a bullet. He felt the wind of its passage. He was stunned by the power of it. Energized by fear, he scrambled along the shelf, bent over, pulling himself from tree to tree. Another arrow snapped down through the trees.

On the cliff above, the horsemen were looking down on them. The black knight shouted, "Fool! Idiot!" and cuffed the archer angrily, knocking the bow from his hands. There were no more arrows.

The boy pulled Chris forward by the arm. Chris didn't know where the path along the cliff went, but the boy seemed to have a plan. Above him, the horsemen wheeled, turned away, heading back into the woods.

Now the shelf ended in a narrow ledge, no more than a foot wide, which curved around an angle in the cliff. Below the ledge was a sheer drop to the river. Chris stared at the river, but the boy grabbed his chin, jerked his head up. "Do not look down. Come." The boy pressed himself flat against the cliff face, hugging the rock, and moved gingerly along on the ledge. Chris followed his example, still gasping for breath. He knew if he hesitated at all, panic would overcome him. The wind tugged at his clothes, pulling him away from the cliff. He pressed his cheek to the warm rock, clutching at fingerholds, fighting panic.

He saw the boy disappear around the corner. Chris kept going. The corner was sharp, and the path beneath had fallen away, leaving a gap. He had to step across it carefully, but then he rounded the corner, and sighed in relief.

He saw the cliff now ended in a long green slope of forested land, which continued all the way down to the river. The boy was waving to him. Chris moved ahead, rejoining the boy.

"From here it is easier." The boy started down, Chris behind him. Almost at once, he realized the slope was not as gentle as it had appeared. It was dark beneath the trees, steep and muddy. The boy slipped, slid along the muddy track, and vanished into the forest below. Chris continued to pick his way downward, grabbing branches for support. Then he, too, lost his footing, slapped down in the mud on his backside, and slid. For some reason he thought, *I am a graduate student at Yale. I am an historian specializing in the history of technology.* It was as if he was trying to hold on to an identity that was rapidly fading from his awareness, like a dream from which he had awakened, and was now forgetting.

Sliding headlong in the mud, Chris banged into trees, felt branches scratch at his face, but could do nothing to slow his descent. He went down the hill, and down.

⋮

With a sigh, Marek got to his feet. There was no marker on Gomez's body. He was sure of it. Kate stood beside him, biting her lip. "I *know* she said there was a spare. I *know* it."

"I don't know where it is," Marek said.

Unconsciously, Kate started to scratch her head, then felt the wig, and the pain from the bump on her head. "This damn wig . . ."

She stopped. She stared at Marek.

And then she walked away into the woods along the edge of the path. "Where did it go?" she said.

"What?"

"Her head."

She found it a moment later, surprised at how small it seemed. A head without a body wasn't very big. She tried not to look at the stump of the neck.

Fighting revulsion, she crouched down and turned the head over, so that she was looking at the gray face, the sightless eyes. The tongue half-protruded from the slack jaw. Flies buzzed inside the mouth.

She lifted the wig away and immediately saw the ceramic marker. It was taped to the mesh inside the wig. She pulled it free.

"Got it," she said.

Kate turned it over in her hand. She saw the button in the side of the marker, where there was a small light. The button was so small and narrow, it could only be pushed with a thumbnail.

This was it. They had definitely found it.

Marek came over and stared at the ceramic.

"Looks like it to me," he said.

"So we can go back," Kate said. "Anytime we want."

"Do you want to go back?" Marek asked her.

She thought it over. "We came here to get the Professor," she said. "And I think that's what we ought to do."

Marek grinned.

And then they heard thundering hooves, and they dived into the bushes just moments before six dark horsemen galloped down the muddy path, heading toward the river below.

:

Chris staggered forward, knee-deep in boggy marsh at the edge of the river. Mud clung to his face, his hair, his clothes. He was covered in so much mud that he felt its weight. He saw the boy ahead of him, already splashing in the water, washing.

Pushing past the last of the tangles along the water's edge, Chris slid into the river. The water was icy cold, but he didn't care. He ducked his head under, ran his hand through his hair, rubbed his face, trying to get the mud off him.

By now the boy had climbed out on the opposite bank and

was sitting in the sun on a rocky outcrop. The boy said something that Chris could not hear, but his earpiece translated, "You do not remove your clothes to bathe?"

"Why? You did not."

At this, the boy shrugged. "But you may, if you wish it."

Chris swam to the far side, and climbed out. His clothes were still very muddy, and he felt chilled now that he was out in the open air. He stripped off his clothes down to his belt and linen shorts, rinsed the outergarments in the river, then set them on the rocks to dry. His body was covered with scratches, welts and bruises. But already his skin was drying, and the sun felt warm. He turned his face upward, closed his eyes. He heard the soft song of women in the fields. He heard birds. The gentle lap of the river at the banks. And for a moment, he felt a peace descend on him that was deeper, and more complete, than anything he had ever felt in his life.

He lay down on the rocks, and he must have fallen asleep for a few minutes, because when he awoke he heard:

*"Howbite thou speakst foolsimple ohcopan, eek invich array thouart. Essay thousooth Earisher?"*

The boy was speaking. An instant later, he heard the tinny voice in his ear, translating: "The way you speak plainly to your friend, and the way you dress. Tell the truth. You are Irish, is it so?"

Chris nodded slowly, thinking that over. Apparently, the boy had overheard him speaking to Marek on the path and had concluded they were Irish. There didn't seem to be any harm in letting him think that.

"Aye," he said.

*"Aie?"* the boy repeated. He formed the syllable slowly, pulling his lips back, showing his teeth. *"Aie?"* The word seemed strange to him.

Chris thought, He doesn't understand "aye"? He would try something else. He said, *"Oui?"*

*"Oui . . . oui. . . ."* The boy seemed confused by this word, as well. Then he brightened. *"Ourie? Seyngthou ourie?"* and the translation came, "Shabby? Are you saying shabby?"

Chris shook his head no. "I am saying 'yes.' " This was getting very confusing.

*"Yezz?"* the boy said, speaking it like a hiss.

"Yes," Chris said, nodding.

"Ah. *Earisher.*" The translation came: "Ah. Irish."

"Yes."

*"Wee sayen yeaso. Oriwis, thousay trew."*

Chris said, *"Thousay trew."* His earpiece translated his own words: "You speak the truth."

The boy nodded, satisfied with the answer. They sat in silence a moment. He looked Chris up and down. "So you are gentle."

Gentle? Chris shrugged. Of course he was gentle. He certainly wasn't a fighter. *"Thousay trew."*

The boy nodded judiciously. "I thought as much. Your manner speaks it, even if your attire ill-suits your degree."

Chris said nothing in reply. He wasn't sure what was meant here.

"How are you called?" the boy asked him.

"Christopher Hughes."

"Ah. Christopher de Hewes," the boy said, speaking slowly. He seemed to be assessing the name in some way that Chris didn't understand. "Where is Hewes? In the Irish land?"

*"Thousay trew."*

Another short silence fell over them while they sat in the sun.

"Are you a knight?" the boy asked finally.

"No."

"Then you are a squire," the boy said, nodding to himself. "That will do." He turned to Chris. "And of what age? Twenty-one year?"

"Close enough. Twenty-four year."

This news caused the boy to blink in surprise. Chris thought, What's wrong with being twenty-four?

"Then, good squire, I am very glad of your assistance, for saving me from Sir Guy and his band." He pointed across the river, where six dark horsemen stood watching them at the water's edge. They were letting their horses drink from the river, but their eyes were fixed on Chris and the boy.

"But I didn't save you," Chris said. "You saved me."

"*Didnt?*" Another puzzled look.

Chris sighed. Apparently these people didn't use contractions. It was so difficult to express even the simplest thought; he found the effort exhausting. But he tried again: "Yet I did not save you, you saved me."

"Good squire, you are too humble," the boy replied. "I am in your debt for my very life, and it shall be my pleasure to see to your needs, once we are to the castle."

Chris said, "The castle?"

.

Cautiously, Kate and Marek moved out of the woods, heading toward the monastery. They saw no sign of the riders who had galloped down the trail. The scene was peaceful; directly ahead were the monastery's farm plots, demarcated by low stone walls. At the corner of one plot was a tall hexagonal monument, carved as ornately as the spire of a Gothic church.

"Is that a *montjoie*?" she said.

"Very good," Marek said. "Yes. It's a milestone, or a land marker. You see them all over."

They moved between the plots, heading toward the ten-foot-high wall that surrounded the entire monastery. The peasants in the field paid no attention to them. On the river, a barge drifted downstream, its cargo bundled in cloth. A boatman standing in the stern sang cheerfully.

Near the monastery wall were clustered the huts of the peasants who worked in the field. Beyond the huts he saw a small door in the wall. The monastery covered such a large area that it had doors on all four sides. This was not the main entrance, but Marek thought it would be better to try here first.

They were moving among the huts when he heard the snort of a horse and the soft reassuring voice of a groom. Marek held out his hand, stopping Kate.

"What?" she whispered.

He pointed. About twenty yards away, hidden from easy

view behind one of the huts, five horses were held by a
groom. The horses were richly appointed, with saddles covered in red velvet trimmed with silver. Strips of red cloth ran
down the flanks.

"Those aren't farm horses," Marek said. But he didn't see
the riders anywhere.

"What do we do?" Kate said.

•

Chris Hughes was following the boy toward the village of
Castelgard when his earpiece suddenly crackled. He heard
Kate say, "What do we do?" and Marek answered, "I'm not
sure."

Chris said, "Have you found the Professor?"

The boy turned and looked back at him. "Do you speak to
me, squire?"

"No, boy," Chris said. "Just to myself."

"Justo myself?" the boy repeated, shaking his head. "Your
speech is difficult to comprehend."

In the earpiece, Marek said, "Chris. Where the hell are
you?"

"Going to the castle," Chris said aloud. "On this lovely
day." He looked up at the sky as he spoke, trying to make it
appear as if he was talking to himself.

He heard Marek say, "Why are you going there? Are you
still with the boy?"

"Yes, very lovely."

The boy turned back again, with a worried look on his face.
"Do you speak to the air? Are you with sound mind?"

"Yes," Chris said. "I am with sound mind. I wish only that
my companions might join me in the castle."

"Why?" Marek said in his earpiece.

"I am sure they shall join you in good time," the boy said.
"Tell me of your companions. Are they Irisher, too? Are they
gentles like you, or servants?"

In his ear, Marek said, "Why did you tell him you are
gentle?"

"Because it describes me."

"Chris. 'Gentle' means you are nobility," Marek said. "Gentle man, gentle woman. It means of noble birth. You'll draw attention to yourself and get embarrassing questions about your family, which you can't answer."

"Oh," Chris said.

"I am sure it does describe you," the boy said. "And your *copains* as well? They are gentles?"

"You speak true," Chris said. "My companions are gentles, too."

"Chris, goddamn it," Marek said through the earpiece. "Don't fool with what you don't understand. You're asking for trouble. And if you keep on this way, you will get it."

⋮

Standing at the edge of the peasant huts, Marek heard Chris say, "You just get the Professor, will you?" and then the boy asked Chris another question, but it was obscured by a burst of static.

Marek turned and looked across the river toward Castelgard. He could see the boy, walking slightly ahead of Chris.

"Chris," Marek said. "I see you. Turn around and come back. Join us here. We have to stay together."

"Most difficult."

"Why?" Marek said, frustrated.

Chris didn't answer him directly. "And who, good sir, may be the horsemen on the far bank?" Apparently, he was talking to the boy.

Marek shifted his gaze, saw mounted riders at the river's edge, letting their horses drink, watching them go.

"That is Sir Guy de Malegant, called 'Guy Tête Noire.' He is retained in the service of my Lord Oliver. Sir Guy is a knight of renown—for his many acts of murder and villainy."

Listening, Kate said, "He can't come back to us here, because of the knights on horseback."

"You speak true," Chris said.

Marek shook his head. "He should never have left us in the first place."

The creak of a door behind them made Marek turn. He saw

the familiar figure of Professor Edward Johnston coming
through the side door of the monastery wall and stepping into
sunlight. He was alone.

# 35:31:11

Edward Johnston was wearing a doublet of dark blue, and
black hose; the clothes were plain, with little decoration or
embroidery, lending him a conservative, scholarly air. He
could indeed pass for a London clerk on a pilgrimage, Marek
thought. Probably that was the way Geoffrey Chaucer, another clerk of the time, had dressed on his own pilgrimage.

The Professor stepped carelessly into the morning sun,
and then staggered a little. They rushed up to his side and saw
that he was panting. His first words were, "Do you have a
marker?"

"Yes," Marek said.

"It's just the two of you?"

"No. Chris also. But he's not here."

Johnston shook his head in quick irritation. "All right.
Quickly, this is how it is. Oliver's in Castelgard"—he nodded
to the town across the river—"but he wants to move to La
Roque, before Arnaut arrives. His great fear is that secret passage that goes into La Roque. Oliver wants to know where it
is. Everyone around here is mad to discover it, because both
Oliver and Arnaut want it so badly. It's the key to everything.
People here think I'm wise. The Abbot asked me to search the
old documents, and I found—"

The door behind them opened and soldiers in maroon-and-
gray surcoats rushed them. The soldiers cuffed Marek and
Kate, knocking them away roughly, and Kate nearly lost her

wig. But they were careful with the Professor, never touching him, walking on either side of him. The soldiers seemed respectful, as if they were a protective escort. Getting to his feet and dusting himself off, Marek had the feeling they had been instructed not to injure him.

Marek watched in silence as Johnston and the soldiers mounted up and set off on the road.

"What do we do?" Kate whispered.

The Professor tapped the side of his head. They heard him say in a singsong, as if praying, "Follow me. I'll try to get us all together. You get Chris."

# 35:25:18

Following the boy, Chris came to the entrance to Castelgard: double wooden doors, heavily reinforced with iron braces. The doors now stood open, guarded by a soldier in a surcoat of burgundy and gray. The guard greeted them by saying, "Setting a tent? Laying a ground cloth? It is five sols to sell in the market on tournament day."

*"Non sumus mercatores,"* the boy said. "We are not merchants."

Chris heard the guard reply, *"Anthoubeest, ye schule payen. Quinquesols maintenant, aut decem postea."* But the translation did not follow immediately in his ear; he realized the guard was speaking an odd mixture of English, French and Latin.

Then he heard, "If you are, you must pay. Five sols now, or ten later."

The boy shook his head. "Do you see merchant wares?"

*"Herkle, non."* In the earpiece: "By Hercules, I do not."

"Then you are answered."

Despite his youth the boy spoke sharply, as if accustomed to commanding. The guard merely shrugged and turned away. The boy and Chris passed through the doors and entered the village.

Immediately inside the walls were several farmhouses and fenced plots. This area smelled strongly of swine. They made their way past thatched houses and pens of grunting pigs, then climbed steps to a winding cobblestone street with stone buildings on both sides. Now they were in the town itself.

The street was narrow and busy, and the buildings two stories high, with the second story overhanging, so no sunlight reached the ground. The buildings were all open shops on the ground floor: a blacksmith, a carpenter who also made barrels, a tailor and a butcher. The butcher, wearing a spattered oilskin apron, was slaughtering a squealing pig on the cobblestones in front of his shop; they stepped around the flowing blood and coils of pale intestine.

The street was noisy and crowded, the odor almost overpowering to Chris, as the boy led him onward. They emerged in a cobbled square with a covered market in the center. Back at their excavations, this was just a field. He paused, looking around, trying to match what he knew with what he now saw.

Across the square, a well-dressed young girl, carrying a basket of vegetables, hurried over to the boy and said with concern, "My dear *sir*, your long absence does vex Sir Daniel sorely."

The boy looked annoyed to see her. He replied irritably, "Then tell my uncle I will attend him in good time."

"He will be most glad of it," the girl said, and hurried away down a narrow passage.

The boy led Chris in another direction. He made no reference to his conversation, just walked onward, muttering to himself.

They came now to an open ground, directly in front of the castle. It was a bright and colorful place, with knights parading on horses, carrying rippling banners. "Many visitors today," the boy said, "for the tournament."

Directly ahead was the drawbridge leading into the castle. Chris looked up at the looming walls, the high turrets. Soldiers walked the ramparts, staring down at the crowds. The boy led him forward without hesitation. Chris heard his feet thump hollowly on the wood of the drawbridge. There were two guards at the gate. He felt his body tense as he came closer.

But the guards paid no attention at all. One nodded to them absently; the other had his back turned and was scraping mud from his shoe.

Chris was surprised at their indifference. "They do not guard the entry?"

"Why should they?" the boy said. "It is daytime. And we are not under attack."

Three women, their heads wrapped in white cloth, so that only their faces showed, walked out of the castle, carrying baskets. The guards again hardly noticed. Chattering and laughing, the women walked out—unchallenged.

Chris realized that he was confronted by one of those historical anachronisms so deeply ingrained no one ever thought to question it. Castles were strongholds, and they always had a defensible entrance—a moat, drawbridge, and so on. And everybody assumed that the entrance was fiercely guarded at all times.

But, as the boy had said, why should it be? In times of peace, the castle was a busy social center, people coming and going to see the lord, to deliver goods. There was no reason to guard it. Especially, as the boy said, during daytime.

Chris found himself thinking of modern office buildings, which had guards only at night; during the day, the guards were present, but only to give information. And that was probably what these guards did, too.

On the other hand . . .

As he walked through the entrance, he glanced up at the spikes of the portcullis—the large iron grate now raised above his head. That grate could be lowered in a moment, he knew. And if it was, there would be no entry into the castle. And no escape.

He had entered the castle easily enough. But he was not sure it would be as easy to leave.

: :

They entered a large courtyard, stone on all sides. There were many horses here; soldiers wearing maroon-and-gray tunics sat in small groups, eating their midday meal. He saw passageways of wood high above him, running the length of the walls. Directly ahead he saw another building, with three-story-high stone walls, and turrets above. It was a castle within the castle. The boy led him toward it.

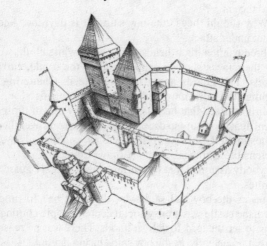

To one side, a door stood open. A single guard munched a piece of chicken. The boy said, "We are to the Lady Claire. She wishes this Irisher to do her service."

"So be it," the guard grunted, uninterested; they went inside. Chris saw an archway directly ahead, leading to the great hall, where a crowd of men and women stood talking. Everyone seemed richly dressed; their voices echoed off the stone walls.

But the boy did not give him much opportunity to look. He led Chris up a winding, narrow stair to the second floor, then down a stone corridor, and finally into a suite of rooms.

Three maids, all dressed in white, rushed forward to the boy and embraced him. They appeared very relieved. "By the grace of God, my Lady, you are returned!"

Chris said, "My Lady?"

Even as he said it, the black hat was thrown away, and golden hair tumbled down over her shoulders. She gave a little bow that turned into a curtsy. "I am heartfelt sorry, and beg your forgiveness for this deception."

"Who are you?" Chris said, stunned.

"I am called Claire."

She rose from her curtsy and looked directly into his eyes. He saw that she was older than he had thought, perhaps twenty-two or -three. And very beautiful.

He gaped and said nothing. He had no idea what to say, or to do. He felt foolish and awkward.

In the silence, one of the maids came forward, curtsied and said, "If it please you, she is the Lady Claire of Eltham, newly widowed of Sir Geoffrey of Eltham, who holds great estates in Guyenne and Middlesex. Sir Geoffrey died of his wounds from Poitiers, and now Sir Oliver—ruler of this castle— serves as my Lady's guardian. Sir Oliver feels she must be married again, and he has chosen Sir Guy de Malegant, a nobleman well known in these regions. But this match, my Lady refuses."

Claire turned and shot the girl a warning glance. But the girl, oblivious, chattered on. "My Lady says to all the world that Sir Guy lacks the means to defend her estates in France and England. Yet Sir Oliver will have his fee from this match, and Guy has—"

*"Elaine."*

"My Lady," the girl said, scurrying backward. She rejoined the other maids, who whispered in the corner, apparently chastising her.

"Enough talk," Claire said. "Here is my savior of this day, Squire Christopher of Hewes. He has delivered me from the predations of Sir Guy, who sought to take by force what he could not win freely at court."

Chris said, "No, no, that is not what happened at all—"

He broke off, as he realized that everyone was staring at him, their mouths open, their eyes wide.

"Sooth, he speaks queerly," Claire said, "for he comes from some remote part in the lands of Eire. And he is modest, as befits a gentle. He *did* save me, so I shall today introduce him to my guardian, once Christopher has proper attire." She turned to one of the ladies. "Is not our horse master, Squire Brandon, of his same length? Go to and fetch me his indigo doublet, his silver belt, and his best white hose." She handed the girl a purse. "Pay what he asks, but be quick."

The girl scurried off. As she left, she passed a gloomy elderly man, standing in the shadows, watching. He wore a rich robe of maroon velvet with silver fleurs-de-lis embroidered on it, and an ermine collar. "How now, my Lady?" he said, coming forward.

She curtsied to him. "Well, Sir Daniel."

"You are safely returned."

"I give thanks to God."

The gloomy man snorted. "As well you should. You strain even His patience. And did your trip yield success equal to its dangers?"

Claire bit her lip. "I fear not."

"Did you see the Abbot?"

A slight hesitation. "No."

"Speak me the truth, Claire."

The girl shook her head. "Sir, I did not. He was abroad, on a hunt."

"A pity," Sir Daniel said. "Why did you not await him?"

"I dared not do so, for Lord Oliver's men broke sanctuary, to take the Magister away by force. I feared discovery, and so fled."

"Yes, yes, this troublesome Magister," Sir Daniel reflected gloomily. "He is on every tongue. Do you know what they say? That he can make himself appear in a flash of light." Sir Daniel shook his head. It was impossible to tell whether he believed it or not. "He must be a skilled Magister of the gun-powder." He pronounced it *gonne-poulder*, and spoke the word slowly, as if it were exotic and unfamiliar. "Did you set eyes upon this Magister?"

"Indeed. I spoke to him."

"Oh?"

"With the Abbot gone, I sought him out. For they say the Magister has befriended the Abbot, these recent days."

Chris Hughes was struggling to follow this conversation, and he realized belatedly that they were talking about the Professor. He said, "Magister?"

Claire said, "Do you know the Magister? Edward de Johnes?"

He immediately backpedaled. "Uh . . . no . . . no, I don't, and—"

At this, Sir Daniel stared at Chris in open astonishment. He turned to Claire. "What does he say?"

"He says he does not know the Magister."

The old man remained astonished. "In what tongue?"

"A kind of English, Sir Daniel, with some Gaelic, so I believe."

"No Gaelic as I have ever heard," he said. He turned to Chris. "Speak you *la Langue-doc*? No? *Loquerisquide Latine?*"

He was asking if he spoke Latin. Chris had an academic knowledge of Latin, a reading knowledge. He'd never tried to speak it. Faltering, he said, *"Non, Senior Danielis, solum per-paululum. Perdoleo."* Only a little. Sorry.

*"Per, per . . . dicendo ille Ciceroni persimilis est."* He speaks like Cicero.

*"Perdoleo."* Sorry.

"Then you may profitably be silent." The old man turned back to Claire. "What did the Magister say to you?"

"He could not assist me."

"Did he know the secret we seek?"

"He said he did not."

"But the Abbot knows," said Sir Daniel. "The Abbot *must* know. It was his predecessor, the Bishop of Laon, who served as architect for the last repairs of La Roque."

Claire said, "The Magister said that Laon was not the architect."

"No?" Sir Daniel frowned. "And how does the Magister know that?"

"I believe the Abbot told him. Or perhaps he saw it among the old papers. The Magister has undertaken to sort and arrange the parchments of Sainte-Mère, for the benefit of the monks."

"Does he," Sir Daniel said thoughtfully. "I wonder why."

"I had no time to ask before Lord Oliver's men broke sanctuary."

"Well, the Magister will be here soon enough," Sir Daniel said. "And Lord Oliver himself will ask these questions. . . ." He frowned, clearly unhappy at this thought.

The old man turned abruptly to a young boy of nine or ten, standing behind him. "Take Squire Christopher to my chamber, where he may bathe and clean himself."

At this, Claire shot the old man a hard look. "Uncle, do not thwart my plans."

"Have I ever done so?"

"You know that you have tried."

"Dear child," he said, "my sole concern is ever for your safety—and your honor."

"And my honor, Uncle, is not yet pledged." With that, Claire walked boldly up to Chris, put her hand around his neck, and looked into his eyes. "I shall count every moment you are gone, and miss you with all my heart," she said softly, her eyes liquid. "Return to me soon."

She brushed her lips lightly across his mouth, and stepped back, releasing him reluctantly, fingers trailing away from his neck. He felt dazed, staring into her eyes, seeing how beautiful—

Sir Daniel coughed, turned to the boy. "See to Squire Christopher, and assist him in his bath."

The boy bowed to Chris. Everyone in the room was silent. This was apparently his cue to leave. He nodded, and said, "I thank you." He waited for the astonished looks, but for once, there were none; they seemed to understand what he had said. Sir Daniel gave him a frosty nod, and Chris left the room.

# 34:25:54

The horses clattered across the drawbridge. The Professor stared straight ahead, ignoring the soldiers who escorted him. The guards at the castle gate barely glanced up as the riders entered the castle. Then the Professor was gone from sight.

Standing near the drawbridge, Kate said, "What do we do now? Do we follow him?"

Marek didn't answer her. Looking back, she saw that he was staring fixedly at two knights on horseback, fighting with broadswords on the field outside the castle. It appeared to be some kind of demonstration or practice; the knights were surrounded by a circle of young men in livery—some wearing bright green, the others in yellow and gold, apparently the colors of the two knights. And a large crowd of spectators had gathered, laughing and shouting insults and encouragement to one knight or the other. The horses turned in tight circles, almost touching each other, bringing their armored riders face to face. The swords clanged again and again in the morning air.

Marek stared, without moving.

She tapped him on the shoulder. "Listen, André, the Professor—"

"In a minute."

"But—"

*"In a minute."*

:

For the first time, Marek felt a twinge of uncertainty. Until now, nothing he had seen in this world had seemed out of place, or unexpected. The monastery was just as he had expected. The peasants in the fields were as he had expected. The tournament being set up was as he had pictured it. And when he entered the town of Castelgard, he again found it exactly as he had thought it would be. Kate had been appalled by the butcher on the cobblestones, and the stench of the tanner's vats, but Marek was not. It was all as he had imagined it, years ago.

But not this, he thought, watching the knights fight.

*It was so fast!* The swordplay was so swift and continuous, attempting to slash with both downswing and backswing, so that it looked more like fencing than sword fighting. The clangs of impact came only a second or two apart. And the fight proceeded without hesitation or pause.

Marek had always imagined these fights as taking place in slow motion: ungainly armored men wielding swords so heavy that each swing was an effort, carrying dangerous momentum and requiring time to recover and reset before the next swing. He had read accounts of how exhausted men were after battle, and he had assumed it was the result of the extended effort of slow fights, encased in steel.

These warriors were big and powerful in every way. Their horses were enormous, and they themselves appeared to be six feet or more, and extremely strong.

Marek had never been fooled by the small size of the armor in museum display cases—he knew that any armor that found its way into a museum was ceremonial and had never been worn in anything more hazardous than a medieval parade. Marek also suspected, though he could not prove it, that much of the surviving armor—highly decorated, chiseled and chased—was intended only for display, and had been made at three-quarter scale, the better to show the delicacy of the craftsmen's designs.

Genuine battle armor never survived. And he had read enough accounts to know that the most celebrated warriors of medieval times were invariably big men—tall, muscular and unusually strong. They were from the nobility; they were better fed; and they were big. He had read how they trained, and how they delighted in performing feats of strength for the amusement of the ladies.

And yet, somehow, he had never imagined anything remotely like this. These men fought furiously, swiftly and continuously—and it looked as if they could go all day. Neither gave the least indication of fatigue; if anything, they seemed to be enjoying their exertions.

As he watched their aggressiveness and speed, Marek realized that left to his own devices, this was exactly the way he himself would choose to fight—quickly, with the conditioning and reserves of stamina to wear down an opponent. He had only imagined a slower fighting style from an unconscious assumption that men in the past were weaker or slower or less imaginative than he was, as a modern man.

Marek knew this assumption of superiority was a difficulty faced by every historian. He just hadn't thought he was guilty of it.

But clearly, he was.

It took him a while to realize, through the shouting of the crowd, that the combatants were in such superb physical condition that they could expend breath shouting as they fought; they hurled a stream of taunts and insults at each other between blows.

And then he saw that their swords were not blunted, that they were swinging real battle swords, with razor-sharp edges. Yet they clearly intended each other no harm; this was just an amusing warm-up to the coming tournament. Their cheerful, casual approach to deadly hazard was almost as unnerving as the speed and intensity with which they fought.

The battle continued for another ten minutes, until one mighty swing unhorsed one knight. He fell to the ground but immediately jumped up laughing, as easily as if he were wearing no armor. Money changed hands. There were cries of "Again! Again!" A fistfight broke out among the liveried boys. The two knights walked off, arm in arm, toward the inn.

Marek heard Kate say, "André. . . ."

He turned slowly toward her.

"André, is everything all right?"

"Everything is fine," he said. "But I have a lot to learn."

.
.
.

They walked down the castle drawbridge, approaching the guards. He felt Kate tense alongside him. "What do we do? What do we say?"

"Don't worry. I speak Occitan."

But as they came closer, another fight broke out on the field beyond the moat, and the guards watched it. They were entirely preoccupied as Marek and Kate passed through the stone arch and entered the castle courtyard.

"We just walked in," Kate said, surprised. She looked around the courtyard. "Now what?"

.
.
.

It was freezing, Chris thought. He sat naked, except for his undershorts, on a stool in Sir Daniel's small apartment. Beside him was a basin of steaming water, and a hand cloth for washing. The boy had brought the basin of water up from the kitchen, carrying it as if it were gold; his manner indicated that it was a sign of favor to be treated to hot water.

Chris had dutifully scrubbed himself, refusing the boy's offers of assistance. The bowl was small, and the water soon black. But eventually he'd managed to scrape the mud from beneath his fingernails, off his body and even off his face, with the aid of a tiny metal mirror the boy handed him.

Finally, he pronounced himself satisfied. But the boy, with a look of distress, said, "Master Christopher, *you are not clean.*" And he insisted on doing the rest.

So Chris sat shivering on his wooden stool while the boy scrubbed him for what seemed like an hour. Chris was perplexed; he'd always thought that medieval people were dirty and smelly, immersed in the filth of the age. Yet these people seemed to make a fetish of cleanliness. Everyone he saw in the castle was clean, and there were no odors.

Even the toilet, which the boy insisted he use before

bathing, was not as awful as Chris had expected. Located behind a wooden door in the bedroom, it was a narrow closet, fitted with a stone seat above a basin that drained into a pipe. Apparently, waste flowed down to the ground floor of the castle, where it was removed daily. The boy explained that each morning a servant flushed the pipe with scented water, then placed a fresh bouquet of sweet-smelling herbs in a clip on the wall. So the odor was not objectionable. In fact, he thought ruefully, he'd smelled much worse in airplane toilets.

And to top it all, these people wiped themselves with strips of white linen! No, he thought, things were not as he had expected.

One advantage of being forced to sit there was that he was able to try speaking to the boy. The boy was tolerant, and replied slowly to Chris, as if to an idiot. But this enabled Chris to hear him before the earpiece translation, and he quickly discovered that imitation helped; if he overcame his embarrassment and employed the archaic phrases he had read in texts—many of which the young boy himself used— then the boy understood him much more easily. So Chris gradually fell to saying "Methinks" instead of "I think," and "an" instead of "if," and "for sooth" instead of "in truth." And with each small change, the boy seemed to understand him better.

Chris was still sitting on the stool when Sir Daniel entered the room. He brought neatly folded clothes, rich and expensive-looking. He placed them on the bed.

"So, Christopher of Hewes. You have involved yourself with our clever beauty."

"She hath saved mine life." He pronounced it *say-ved*. And Sir Daniel seemed to understand.

"I hope it will not cause you trouble."

"Trouble?"

Sir Daniel sighed. "She tells me, friend Chris, that you are gentle, yet not a knight. You are a squire?"

"In sooth, yes."

"A very *old* squire," Sir Daniel said. "What is your training at arms?"

"My training at arms . . ." Chris frowned. "Well, I have, uh—"

"Have you any at all? Speak plain: What is your training?"

Chris decided he had better tell the truth. "In sooth, I am—I mean, trained—in my studies—as a scholar."

"A scholar?" The old man shook his head, incomprehending. *"Escolie? Esne discipulus? Studesne sub magistro?"* You study under a master?

*"Ita est."* Even so.

*"Ubi?"* Where?

"Uh . . . at, uh, Oxford."

"Oxford?" Sir Daniel snorted. "Then you have no business here, with such as my Lady. Believe me when I say this is no place for a *scolere*. Let me tell you how your circumstances now lie."

:

"Lord Oliver needs money to pay his soldiers, and he has plundered all he can from the nearby towns. So now he presses Claire to marry, that he may gain his fee. Guy de Malegant has tendered a handsome offer, very pleasing to Lord Oliver. But Guy is not wealthy, and he cannot make good on his fee unless he mortgages part of my Lady's holdings. To this she will not accede. Many believe that Lord Oliver and Guy have long since made a private agreement—one to sell the Lady Claire, the other to sell her lands."

Chris said nothing.

"There is a further impediment to the match. Claire despises Malegant, whom she suspects had a hand in her husband's death. Guy was in attendance of Geoffrey at the time of his death. Everyone was surprised by the suddenness of his departure from this world. Geoffrey was a young and vigorous knight. Although his wounds were serious, he made steady recovery. No one knows the truth of that day, yet there are rumors—many rumors—of poison."

"I see," Chris said.

"Do you? I doubt it. For consider: my Lady might as well be a prisoner of Lord Oliver in this castle. She may herself slip out, but she cannot secretly remove her entire retinue. If she secretly departs and returns to England—which is her wish—Lord Oliver will take his revenge against me, and others of her household. She knows this, and so she must stay.

"Lord Oliver wishes her to marry, and my Lady devises stratagems to postpone it. It is true she is clever. But Lord Oliver is not a patient man, and he will force the matter soon. Now, her only hope lies there." Sir Daniel walked over and pointed out the window.

Chris came to the window and looked.

From this high window, he saw a view over the courtyard, and the battlements of the outer castle wall. Beyond he saw the roofs of the town, then the town wall, with guards walking the parapets. Then fields and countryside stretching off into the distance.

Chris looked at Sir Daniel questioningly.

Sir Daniel said, "There, my *scolere*. The fires."

He was pointing in the far distance. Squinting, Chris could just make out faint columns of smoke disappearing into the blue haze. It was at the limit of what he could see.

"That is the company of Arnaut de Cervole," Sir Daniel said. "They are encamped no more than fifteen miles distant. They will reach here in a day—two days at most. All know it."

"And Sir Oliver?"

"He knows his battle with Arnaut will be fierce."

"And yet he holds a tournament—"

"That is a matter of his honor," Sir Daniel said. "His prickly honor. Certes, he would disband it, if he could. But he does not dare. And herein lies your hazard."

"My hazard?"

Sir Daniel sighed. He began pacing. "Dress you now, to meet my Lord Oliver in proper fashion. I shall try to avert the coming disaster."

The old man turned and walked out of the room. Chris looked at the boy. He had stopped scrubbing.

"What disaster?" he said.

# 33:12:51

It was a peculiarity of medieval scholarship in the twentieth century that there was not a single contemporary picture that showed what the interior of a fourteenth-century castle looked like. Not a painting, or an illuminated manuscript image, or a notebook sketch—there was nothing at all from that time. The earliest images of fourteenth-century life had actually been made in the fifteenth century, and the interiors —and food, and costumes—they portrayed were correct for the fifteenth century, not the fourteenth.

As a result, no modern scholar knew what furniture was used, how walls were decorated, or how people dressed and behaved. The absence of information was so complete that when the apartments of King Edward I were excavated in the Tower of London, the reconstructed walls had to be left as exposed plaster, because no one could say what decorations might have been there.

This was also why artists' reconstructions of the fourteenth century tended to show bleak interiors, rooms with bare walls and few furnishings—perhaps a chair, or a chest—but not much else. The very absence of contemporary imagery was taken to imply a sparseness to life at that time.

All this flashed through Kate Erickson's mind as she entered the great hall of Castelgard. What she was about to see, no historian had ever seen before. She walked in, slipping through the crowd, following Marek. And she stared, stunned by the richness and the chaos displayed before her.

The great hall sparkled like an enormous jewel. Sunlight streamed through high windows onto walls that gleamed with tapestries laced with gold, so that reflections danced on the red-and-gold-painted ceiling. One side of the room was hung with a vast patterned cloth: silver fleurs-de-lis on a background of deep blue. On the opposite wall, a tapestry depicting a battle: knights fighting in full regalia, their armor silver, their surcoats blue and white, red and gold; their fluttering banners threaded with gold.

At the end of the room stood a huge ornate fireplace, large enough for a person to walk into without ducking, its carved mantelpiece gilded and shimmering. In front of the fire stood a huge wicker screen, also gilded. And above the mantel hung a patterned tapestry of swans flying on a field of lacy red and gold flowers.

The room was inherently elegant, richly and beautifully executed—and rather feminine, to modern eyes. Its beauty and refinement stood in marked contrast to the behavior of the people in the room, which was noisy, boisterous, crude.

In front of the fire was laid the high table, draped in white linen, with dishes of gold, all heaped high with food. Little dogs scampered across the table, helping themselves to the food as they liked—until the man in the center of the table swatted them away with a curse.

Lord Oliver de Vannes was about thirty, with small eyes set in a fleshy, dissolute face. His mouth was permanently turned down in a sneer; he tended to keep his lips tight, since he was missing several teeth. His clothes were as ornate as the room: a robe of blue and gold, with a high-necked gold collar, and a fur hat. His necklace consisted of blue stones each the size of a robin's egg. He wore rings on several fingers, huge oval gems in heavy gold settings. He stabbed with his knife at food and ate noisily, grunting to his companions.

But despite the elegant accoutrements, the impression he conveyed was of a dangerous petulance—his red-rimmed eyes darted around the room as he ate, alert to any insult, spoiling for a fight. He was edgy and quick to strike; when one of the little dogs came back to eat again, Oliver unhesitatingly jabbed it in its rear with the point of his knife; the animal jumped off and ran yelping and bleeding from the room.

Lord Oliver laughed, wiped the dog's blood off the tip of his blade, and continued to eat.

The men seated at his table shared the joke. From the look of them, they were all soldiers, Oliver's contemporaries, and all were elegantly dressed—though none matched the finery of their leader. And three or four women, young, pretty and bawdy, in tight-fitting dresses and with loose, wanton hair, giggling as their hands groped beneath the table, completed the scene.

Kate stared, and a word came unbidden to her mind: *warlord*. This was a medieval warlord, sitting with his soldiers and their prostitutes in the castle he had captured.

A wooden staff banged on the floor, and a herald cried, "My Lord! Magister Edward de Johnes!" Turning, she saw Johnston shoved through the crowd, toward the table at the front.

Lord Oliver looked up, wiping gravy from his jowls with the back of his hand. "I bid you welcome, Magister Edwardus. Though I do not know if you are Magister or *magicien*."

"Lord Oliver," the Professor said, speaking in Occitan. He gave a slight nod of the head.

"Magister, why so cool," Oliver said, pretending to pout. "You wound me, you do. What have I done to deserve this reserve? Are you displeased I brought you from the monastery? You shall eat as well here, I assure you. Better. Anywise, the Abbot has no need of you—and I do."

Johnston stood erect, and did not speak.

"You have nothing to say?" Oliver said, glaring at Johnston. His face darkened. *"That will change,"* he growled.

Johnston remained unmoving, silent.

The moment passed. Lord Oliver seemed to collect himself. He smiled blandly. "But come, come, let us not quarrel. With all courtesy and respect, I seek your counsel," Oliver said. "You are wise, and I have much need of wisdom—so these worthies tell me." Guffaws at the table. "And I am told you can see the future."

"No man sees that," Johnston said.

"Oh so? I think you do, Magister. And I pray you, see your

own. I would not see a man of your distinction suffer much. Know you how your namesake, our late king, Edward the Foolish, met his end? I see by your face that you do. Yet you were not among those present in the castle. And I was." He smiled grimly and sat back in his chair. "There was never a mark upon his body."

Johnston nodded slowly. "His screams could be heard for miles."

Kate looked questioningly to Marek, who whispered, "They're talking about Edward II of England. He was imprisoned and killed. His captors didn't want any sign of foul play, so they stuck a tube up his rectum and inserted a red-hot poker into his bowels until he died."

Kate shivered.

"He was also gay," Marek whispered, "so it was thought the manner of his execution demonstrated great wit."

"Indeed, his screams were heard for miles," Oliver was saying. "So think on it. You know many things, and I would know them, too. You are my counselor, or you are not long for this world."

Lord Oliver was interrupted by a knight who slipped down the table and whispered in his ear. This knight was richly dressed in maroon and gray, but he had the tough, weathered face of a campaigner. A deep scar, almost a welt, ran down his face from forehead to chin and disappeared into his high collar. Oliver listened, and then said to him, "Oh? You think so, Robert?"

At this, the scarred knight whispered again, never taking his eyes off the Professor. Lord Oliver was also staring at the Professor while he listened. "Well, we shall see," Lord Oliver said.

The stocky knight continued to whisper, and Oliver nodded.

:

Standing in the crowd, Marek turned to the courtier beside him and, speaking in Occitan, said, "Pray, what worthy now has Sir Oliver's ear?"

"Faith, friend, that is Sir Robert de Kere."

"De Kere?" Marek said. "I do not know of him."

"He is new to the retinue, not yet in service a year, but he has found much favor in Sir Oliver's eyes."

"Oh so? Why is that?"

The man shrugged wearily, as if to say, Who knows why things happen at the high table? But he answered, "Sir Robert has a martial disposition, and he has been a trusted adviser to Lord Oliver on matters of warfare." The man lowered his voice. "But certes, I think he cannot be pleased to see another adviser, and one so eminent, before him now."

"Ah," Marek said, nodding. "I understand."

Sir Robert did indeed seem to be pressing his case, whispering urgently, until finally Oliver made a quick flicking sign with one hand, as if brushing away a mosquito. Instantly, the knight bowed and stepped back, standing behind Sir Oliver.

Oliver said, "Magister."

"My Lord."

"I am informed that you know the method of Greek Fire."

Standing in the crowd, Marek snorted. He whispered to Kate, "No one knows that." And no one did. Greek Fire was a famous historical conundrum, a devastating incendiary weapon from the sixth century, the precise nature of which was debated by historians even now. No one knew what Greek Fire really was, or how it was made.

"Yes," Johnston said. "I know this method."

Marek stared. What was this? Clearly the Professor had recognized a rival, but this was a dangerous game to be playing. He would undoubtedly be asked to prove it.

"You can yourself make Greek Fire?" Oliver said.

"My Lord, I can."

"Ah." Oliver turned and shot a glance back at Sir Robert. It seemed the trusted adviser had given wrong advice. Oliver turned back to the Professor.

"It will not be difficult," the Professor said, "if I have my assistants."

So that's it, Marek thought. The Professor was making promises, in an attempt to get them all together.

"Eh? Assistants? You have assistants?"

"I do, my Lord, and—"

"Well of course they can assist you, Magister. And if they do not, we shall provide you whatever help you need. Have no concern there. But what of Dew Fire—the fire of Nathos? You know it, as well?"

"I do, my Lord."

"And by demonstration you will show it to me?"

"Whenever you wish, my Lord."

"Very good, Magister. Very good." Lord Oliver paused, looking intently at the Professor. "And you also know the one secret that I wish to know above all others?"

"Sir Oliver, that secret I do not know."

*"You do! And you will answer me!"* he shouted, banging down a goblet. His face was bright red, the veins standing out on his forehead; his voice echoed in the hall, which had gone suddenly silent. *"I will have your answer this day!"* One of the small dogs on the table cringed; with the back of his hand, he smacked it, sending it yelping to the floor. When the girl beside him started to protest, he swore and slapped her hard across the face, the blow knocking her, chair and all, on her back. The girl did not make a sound, or move. She remained motionless, her feet up in the air.

*"Oh, I am wrothed! I am sore wrothed!"* Lord Oliver snarled, standing up. He looked around him angrily, his hand on his sword, his eyes sweeping the great hall, as if seeking some culprit.

Everyone inside the hall was silent, unmoving, staring down at their feet. It was as if the room had suddenly become a still life, in which only Lord Oliver moved. He puffed in fury, finally took out his sword, and crashed the blade down on the table. Plates and goblets jumped and clattered, the sword buried in the wood.

Oliver glared at the Professor, but he was gaining control, his fury passing. "Magister, *you will do my bidding*!" he cried. Then he nodded to the guards. "Take him away, and give him cause to meditate."

Roughly, guards grabbed the Professor and hauled him

back through the silent crowds. Kate and Marek stepped aside as he passed, but the Professor did not see them.

Lord Oliver glared at the silent room. "Be seated and be merry," he snarled, "before I am in temper!"

Immediately, the musicians began to play, and the noise of the crowd filled the hall.

⦂

Soon after, Robert de Kere hurried out of the room, following the Professor. Marek thought that departure meant nothing good. He nudged Kate, indicating that they should follow de Kere. They were moving toward the door when the herald's staff banged on the floor.

"My Lord! The Lady Claire d'Eltham and Squire Christopher de Hewes."

They paused. "Hell," Marek said.

A beautiful young woman came into the hall, with Chris Hughes walking at her side. Chris was now wearing rich, courtly clothes. He looked very distinguished—and very confused.

Standing beside Kate, Marek tapped his ear and whispered, "Chris. As long as you're in this room, don't speak, and don't act. Do you understand?"

Chris nodded slightly.

"Behave as if you don't understand anything. It shouldn't be difficult."

Chris and the woman passed through the crowd and walked directly to the high table, where Lord Oliver watched her approach with open annoyance. The woman saw it, dipped low, and stayed there, close to the ground, head bowed in submission.

"Come, come," Lord Oliver said irritably, waving a drumstick. "This obsecration ill-suits you."

"My Lord." She rose to her feet.

Oliver snorted. "And what have you dragged in with you today? Another dazzled conquest?"

"If it please my Lord, I present you Christopher of Hewes,

a squire of Eire, who saved me from villains who would have kidnapped me today, or worse."

"Eh? Villains? Kidnapped?" Amused, Lord Oliver looked down the table at his knights. "Sir Guy? What say you?"

A dark-complected man stood angrily. Sir Guy de Malegant was dressed entirely in black—black chain mail and a black surcoat, with a black eagle embroidered on his chest. "My Lord, I fear my Lady amuses herself at our expense. She knows full well I set my men to save her, seeing that she was alone and in distress." Sir Guy walked toward Chris, glaring at him. "It is this man, my Lord, who placed her at risk of her life. I cannot think she now defends him, except as display of her uncommon wit."

"Eh?" Oliver said. "Wit? My Lady Claire, what wit is here?"

The woman shrugged. "Only the witless, my Lord, see wit where none is writ."

The dark knight snorted. "Quick words, to quick conceal what lies beneath." Malegant walked up to Chris, until they were standing face to face, inches apart. He stared intensely as he slowly, deliberately began to take off his chain-mail glove. "Squire Christopher, is it how you are called?"

Chris said nothing, only nodded.

:

Chris was terrified. Trapped in a situation he did not understand, standing in a room full of bloodthirsty soldiers, no better than a bunch of street-corner thugs, and facing this dark, angry man whose breath stank of rotting teeth, garlic and wine—it was all he could do to keep his knees from shaking.

Through his earpiece, he heard Marek say, "Don't speak—no matter what."

Sir Guy squinted at him. "I asked of you a question, squire. Will you answer?" He was still taking off his glove, and Chris felt sure he was about to hit him with his bare fist.

Marek said, "Don't speak."

Chris was only too happy to follow that advice. He took a

deep breath, trying to control himself. His legs were tremulous, rubbery. He felt as if he might collapse in front of this man. He did his best to steady himself. Another deep breath.

Sir Guy turned to the woman. "Madam, does he speak, your savior squire? Or merely sigh?"

"If it please Sir Guy, he is of foreign parts, and often does not comprehend our tongue."

*"Dic mihi nomen tuum, scutari."* Tell me your name.

"Nor Latin, I fear, Sir Guy."

Malegant looked disgusted. *"Commodissime.* Most convenient, this dumb squire, for we cannot ask how he comes here, and for what purpose. This Irish squire is far from home. And yet he is not a pilgrim. He is not in service. What is he? Why is he here? See how he trembles. What can he fear? Nothing from us, my Lord—unless he be the creature of Arnaut, come to see how the land lies. This would make him dumb. A coward would not dare speak."

Marek whispered, "Do not respond. . . ."

Malegant poked Chris hard on the chest. "So, cowardly squire, I call you spy and scoundrel, and not man enough to admit your true cause. I would have contempt for you, were you not beneath it."

The knight finished removing his glove, and with a disgusted shake of his head, he dropped it on the floor. The chain-mail glove landed with a clunk on Chris's toes. Sir Guy turned insolently away and started back to the table.

Everyone in the room was staring at Chris.

Beside him, Claire whispered, "The glove. . . ."

He glanced at her sideways.

*"The glove!"*

What about the glove? he wondered, as he bent over and picked it up. It was heavy in his hand. He held the glove out to Claire, but she had already turned away, saying, "Knight, the squire has accepted your challenge."

Chris thought, What challenge?

Sir Guy said immediately, "Three lances untipped, *à outrance.*"

Marek said, "You poor bastard. Do you know what you just did?"

∴

Sir Guy turned to Lord Oliver at the high table. "My Lord, I pray you let the day's tourney begin with our challenge combat."

"So it shall be," Oliver said.

Sir Daniel slipped forward through the crowd and bowed. "My Lord Oliver, my niece carries this jest too far, with unworthy result. It may amuse her to see Sir Guy, a knight of renown, provoked into combat with a mere squire, and so dishonored by the doing. But it ill-serves Sir Guy to be taken in by her ruse."

"Is this so?" Lord Oliver said, looking at the dark knight.

Sir Guy Malegant spat on the floor. "A squire? Mark me, this is no squire. Here is a knight in hiding, a knave and a spy. His deceit shall have its reward. I will contest him this day."

Sir Daniel said, "If it please my Lord, I think it is not meet. Sooth he is a squire only, of little training at arms, and no match for your worthy knight."

Chris was still trying to understand what was going on, when Marek stepped forward, speaking fluently in a foreign language that sounded something like French, but not exactly. He guessed it was Occitan. Chris heard the translation in his earpiece.

"My Lord," Marek said, bowing smoothly, "this worthy gentleman speaks truth. Squire Christopher is my companion, but he is no warrior. In fairness, I ask you to allow Christopher to name a champion in his stead, to meet this challenge."

"Eh? Champion? What champion? I do not know you."

Chris saw that Lady Claire was staring at Marek with unconcealed interest. He returned a brief glance before speaking to Oliver.

"Please my Lord, I am Sir André de Marek, late of Hainaut. I offer myself as his champion, and God willing, I shall give good account with this noble knight."

Lord Oliver rubbed his chin, thinking.

Seeing his indecision, Sir Daniel pressed forward. "My Lord, to begin your tourney with unequal combat does not enhance the day, nor make it memorable in the minds of men. I think de Marek will give better sport."

Lord Oliver turned back to Marek to see what he would say to that.

"My Lord," Marek said, "if my friend Christopher is a spy, then so am I. In defaming him, Sir Guy has defamed me as well, and I beg leave to defend my good name."

Lord Oliver seemed entertained by this new complication. "How say you, Guy?"

"Faith," the dark knight said, "I grant you this de Marek may be a worthy second, if his arm has the skill of his tongue. But as a second, it is meet he fight my second, Sir Charles de Gaune."

A tall man stood at the end of the table. He had a pale face, a flat nose and pink eyes; he resembled a pit bull. His tone was contemptuous as he said, "I shall be second, with pleasure."

Marek made one final attempt. "So," he said, "it appears Sir Guy is afraid to fight me first."

At this, the Lady Claire openly smiled at Marek. She was clearly interested in him. And it seemed to annoy Sir Guy.

"I fear no man," Guy said, "least of all a Hainauter. If you survive my second—which I much doubt—then I will gladly fight you after, and bring your insolence to an end."

"So be it," Lord Oliver said, and turned away. His tone indicated that the discussion was ended.

# 32:16:01

The horses wheeled and charged, racing past each other on the grassy field. The ground shook as the big animals thundered past Marek and Chris, who were standing at the low fence, watching the practice runs. To Chris, the tournament field was huge—the size of a football field—and on two sides, the stands had been completed, and ladies were beginning to be seated. Spectators from the countryside, roughly dressed and noisy, lined the rail.

Another pair of riders charged, their horses snorting as they galloped. Marek said, "How well do you ride?"

He shrugged. "I rode with Sophie."

"Then I think I can keep you alive, Chris," Marek said. "But you must do exactly as I tell you."

"All right."

"So far, you haven't been doing what I tell you," Marek reminded him. "This time, you must."

"Okay, okay."

"All you have to do," Marek said, "is stay mounted on the horse long enough to take the hit. Sir Guy will have no choice but to aim for the chest when he sees how badly you ride, because the chest is the largest and steadiest target on a galloping rider. I want you to take his lance square on the chest, on the breastplate. You understand?"

"I take his lance on the chest," Chris said, looking very unhappy.

"When the lance strikes you, let yourself be unseated. It shouldn't be difficult. Fall to the ground and *do not move*, so you appear to have been knocked unconscious. Which you

may be. Under no circumstances get to your feet. Do you
understand?"

"Don't get to my feet."

"That's right. No matter what happens, you continue to lie
there. If Sir Guy has unhorsed you, and you are unconscious,
the match is over. But if you get up, he will call for another
lance, or he will fight you on foot with broadswords, and kill
you."

"Don't get up," Chris repeated.

"That's right," Marek said. "No matter what. Don't get up."
He clapped Chris on the shoulder. "With luck, you'll survive
just fine."

"Jesus," Chris said.

More horses charged past them, shaking the ground.

⁚

Leaving the field behind, they passed among the many tents
arranged outside the tournament ground. The tents were
small and round, boldly colored with stripes and zigzag designs. Pennants rippled in the air above each tent. Horses
were tied up outside. Pages and squires scurried to and fro,
carrying armor, saddles, hay, water. Several pages were rolling barrels over the ground. The barrels made a soft hissing
sound.

"That's sand," Marek explained. "They roll the chain mail
in sand to remove rust."

"Uh-huh." Chris tried to focus on details, to take his mind
off what was to come. But he felt as if he were going to his
own execution.

They entered a tent where three pages were waiting. A
warming fire burned in one corner; the armor was laid out on
a ground cloth. Marek inspected it briefly, then said, "It's
fine." He turned to leave.

"Where are you going?"

"To another tent, to dress."

"But I don't know how—"

"The pages will dress you," Marek said, and left.

Chris looked at the armor lying in pieces on the ground, especially at the helmet, which had one of those pointy snouts, like a large duck. There was only a little slit for the eyes. But beside it was another helmet, more ordinary-looking, and Chris thought that—

"Good my squire, if it please you." The head page, slightly older and better dressed than the others, was talking to him. He was a boy of about fourteen. "I pray you stand here." He pointed to the center of the tent.

Chris stood, and he felt many hands moving over his body. They quickly removed all his clothes down to his linen under-shirt and shorts, and then there were murmurs of concern as they saw his body.

"Have you been sick, squire?" one asked.

"Uh, no. . . ."

"A fever or an illness, to so weaken your body, as we see it now?"

"No," Chris said, frowning.

They began to dress him, saying nothing. First, thick felt leggings, and then a heavily padded long-sleeved undershirt that buttoned at the front. They told him to bend his arms. He could hardly do it, the cloth was so thick.

"It is stiff from washing, but it will soon be easier," one said.

Chris didn't think so. Jesus, he thought, I can hardly move, and they haven't put on the armor yet. Now they were strap-ping plates of metal on his thighs, calves and knees. Then they continued with his arms. As each piece went on, they asked him to move his limbs, to be sure the straps were not too tight.

Next a coat of chain mail was lowered over his head. It felt heavy on his shoulders. While the breastplate was being tied in place, the head page asked a series of questions, none of which Chris could answer.

"Do you sit high, or in cantle?"

"Will you couch your lance, or rest it?"

"Do you tie-brace the high pommel, or sit free?"

"Set your stirrups low, or forward?"

Chris made noncommittal noises. Meanwhile, more pieces of armor were added, with more questions.

"Flex sabaton or firm?"

"Vambrace guard or side plate?"

"Broadsword left or right?"

"Bascinet beneath your helm, or no?"

He felt increasingly burdened as more weight was added, and increasingly stiff as each joint was encased in metal. The pages worked quickly, and in a matter of minutes he was entirely dressed. They stepped away and surveyed him.

" 'Tis good, squire?"

"It is," he said.

"Now the helm." He was already wearing a kind of metal skullcap, but now they brought over the pointy-snout helmet and placed it over his head. Chris was plunged into darkness, and he felt the helmet's weight on his shoulders. He could see nothing except what was straight ahead, through a horizontal eye slit.

His heart began to pound. There was no air. He couldn't breathe. He tugged at the helmet, trying to lift the visor, but it did not move. He was trapped. He heard his breathing, amplified in the metal. His hot breath warmed the tight confines of the helmet. He was suffocating. *There was no air.* He grabbed at the helmet, struggling to remove it.

The pages lifted it off his head and looked at him curiously. "Is all well, squire?"

Chris coughed, and nodded, not trusting himself to speak. He never wanted that thing on his head again. But already they were leading him out of the tent, to a waiting horse.

Jesus Christ, he thought.

This horse was gigantic, and covered in more metal than he was. There was a decorated plate over the head, and more plates on the chest and sides. Even in armor, the animal was jumpy and high-spirited, snorting and jerking at the reins the page held. This was a true warhorse, a destrier, and it was far more spirited than any horse he had ever ridden before. But that was not what concerned him. What concerned him was the size—the damn horse was so big, he couldn't see over it. And the wooden saddle was raised, making it still higher. The

pages were all looking at him expectantly. Waiting for him.
To do what? Probably to climb up.

"How do I, uh. . . ."

They blinked, surprised. The head page stepped forward
and said smoothly, "Place your hand here, squire, on the
wood and swing up. . . ."

Chris extended his hand, but he could barely reach the
pommel, a rectangle of carved wood in the front of the saddle.
He closed his fingers around the wood, then raised his knee
and slipped his foot in the stirrup.

"Um. I think your left foot, squire."

Of course. Left foot. He knew that; he was just tense and
confused. He kicked the stirrup to get his right foot free. But
the armor had caught on the stirrup; he bent forward awkwardly and used his hand to tug the stirrup free. It still was
stuck. Finally, at the moment of release, he lost his balance
and fell on his back near the horse's rear hooves. The horrified
pages quickly dragged him clear.

They got him to his feet, and then they all helped him to
mount. He felt hands pressing against his buttocks as he rose
shakily into the air, swung his foot over—Jesus, that was
hard—and landed with a clank in the saddle.

Chris looked down at the ground, far below. He felt as if he
were ten feet in the air. As soon as he was mounted, the horse
began to whinny and shake its head, turning sideways and
snapping at Hughes's legs in the stirrups. He thought, *This
damn horse is trying to bite me*.

"Reins, squire! Reins! You must rein him!"

Chris tugged at the reins. The enormous horse paid no attention, pulling hard, still trying to bite him.

"Show him, squire! Strongly!"

Chris yanked the reins so sharply, he thought he'd break
the animal's neck. At this, the horse merely gave a final snort
and faced forward, suddenly calmed.

"Well done, squire."

Trumpets sounded, several long notes.

"That is the first call to arms," the page said. "We must to
the tourney field."

They took the horse's reins and led Chris toward the grassy field.

# 36:02:00

It was one in the morning. From inside his office at ITC, Robert Doniger stared down at the entrance to the cave, illuminated in the night by the flashing lights of six ambulances parked all around. He listened to the crackle of the paramedic radios and watched the people leaving the tunnel. He saw Gordon walking out with that new kid, Stern. Neither of them appeared to have been hurt.

He saw Kramer reflected in the glass of the window as she entered the room behind him. She was slightly out of breath. Without looking back at her, he said, "How many were injured?"

"Six. Two somewhat seriously."

"How seriously?"

"Shrapnel wounds. Burns from toxic inhalation."

"Then they'll have to go to UH." He meant University Hospital, in Albuquerque.

"Yes," Kramer said. "But I've briefed them about what they can say. Lab accident, all that. And I called Whittle at UH, reminded him of our last donation. I don't think there'll be a problem."

Doniger stared out the window. "There might be," he said.

"The PR people can handle it."

"Maybe not," Doniger said.

In recent years, ITC had built a publicity unit of twenty-six people around the world. Their job was not to get publicity for the company, but rather to deflect it. ITC, they explained to anyone who inquired, was a company that made superconducting quantum devices for magnetometers and medical scanners. These devices consisted of a complex electromechanical element about six inches long. Press handouts were stupefyingly boring, dense with quantum specifications.

For the rare reporter who remained interested, ITC enthusiastically scheduled a tour of their New Mexico facility. Reporters were taken to selected research labs. Then, in a large assembly room, they were shown how the devices were made—the gradiometer coils fitted into the cryostat, the superconducting shield and electrical leads outside. Explanations referred to the Maxwell equations and electric charge motion. Almost invariably, reporters abandoned their stories. In the words of one, "It's about as compelling as an assembly line for hair dryers."

In this way, Doniger had managed to keep silent about the most extraordinary scientific discovery of the late twentieth century. In part, his silence was self-preservation: other companies, like IBM and Fujitsu, had started their own quantum research, and even though Doniger had a four-year head start on them, it was in his interest that they not know exactly how far he had gone.

He also was aware that his plan was not yet completed, and he needed secrecy to finish. As he himself often said, grinning like a kid, "If people knew what we were up to, they'd *really* want to stop us."

But at the same time, Doniger knew that he could not maintain the secrecy forever. Sooner or later, perhaps by accident, it was all going to come out. And when that happened, it was up to him to manage it.

The question in Doniger's mind was whether it was happening now.

•

He watched as the ambulances pulled out, sirens whining.

"Think about it," he said to Kramer. "Two weeks ago, this company was buttoned down tight. Our only problem was that French reporter. Then we had Traub. That depressed old bastard put our whole company in jeopardy. Traub's death brought that cop from Gallup, who's still nosing around. Then Johnston. Then his four students. And now six techs going to the hospital. It's getting to be a lot of people out there, Diane. A lot of exposure."

"You think it's getting away from us," she said.

"Possibly," he said. "But not if I can help it. Especially since I've got three potential board members coming day after tomorrow. So let's button it back down."

She nodded. "I really think we can handle this."

"Okay," he said, turning away from the window. "See that Stern goes to bed in one of the spare rooms. Make sure he gets sleep, and put a block on the phone. Tomorrow, I want Gordon sticking to him like glue. Give him a tour of the place, whatever. But stay with him. I want a conference call with the PR people tomorrow at eight. I want a briefing about the transit pad at nine. And I want those media dipshits at noon. Call everybody now, so they can get ready."

"Right," she said.

"I may not be able to keep this under control," Doniger said, "but I'm sure as hell going to try."

He frowned at the glass, watching the people clustered outside the tunnel in the dark. "How long until they can go back in the cave?"

"Nine hours."

"And then we can mount a rescue operation? Send another team back?"

Kramer coughed. "Well . . ."

"Are you sick? Or does that mean no?"

"All the machines were destroyed in the explosion, Bob," she said.

"All of them?"

"I think so, yes."

"Then all we can do is rebuild the pad, and sit on our asses to see if they come back in one piece?"

"Yes. That's right. We have no way to rescue them."

"Then let's hope they know their stuff," Doniger said, "because they're on their own. Good fucking luck to them."

# 31:40:44

Through the narrow slit of his helmet visor, Chris Hughes could see that the tournament stands were filled—almost entirely with ladies—and the railings crowded with commoners ten deep. Everyone was shouting for the tournament to begin. Chris was now at the east end of the field, surrounded by his pages, trying to control the horse, which seemed upset by the shouting crowd and had begun to buck and rear. The pages tried to hand him a striped lance, which was absurdly long and ungainly in his hand. Chris took it, then fumbled it as the horse snorted and stomped beneath him.

Beyond the barrier, he saw Kate standing among the commoners. She was smiling encouragement at him, but the horse kept twisting and turning, so he could not return her gaze.

And not far off, he saw the armored figure of Marek, surrounded by pages.

As Chris's horse turned again—why didn't the pages grab the reins?—he saw the far end of the field, where Sir Guy de Malegant sat calmly on his mount. He was pulling on his black-plumed helmet.

Chris's horse bucked once more and turned him in circles. He heard more trumpets, and the spectators all looked toward the stands. He was dimly aware that Lord Oliver was taking his seat, to scattered applause.

Then the trumpets blared again.

"Squire, it is your signal," a page said, handing him the lance once more. This time, he managed to hold it long enough to rest it in a notch on his pommel, so that it crossed the horse's back and pointed ahead to his left. Then the horse spun, and the pages yelled and scattered as the lance swung in an arc over their heads.

More trumpets.

Hardly able to see, Chris tugged at his reins, trying to get the horse under control. He glimpsed Sir Guy at the far end of the field, just watching, his horse perfectly still. Chris wanted to get it over with, but his horse was wild. Angry and frustrated, he yanked hard at the reins one final time. "Goddamn it, *go*, will you?"

At this, the horse snapped his head up and down in two swift motions. The ears went flat.

And he charged.

:

Marek watched the charge tensely. He had not told Chris everything; there was no point in frightening him any more than necessary. But certainly Sir Guy would try to kill Chris, which meant he would aim his lance for the head. Chris was bouncing wildly in the saddle, his lance jerking up and down, his body swaying from side to side. He made a poor target, but if Guy was skilled—and Marek had no doubt that he was—then he would still aim for the head, risking a miss on the first pass in order to make the fatal hit.

He watched Chris jolt down the field, precariously hanging in the saddle. And he watched Sir Guy charging toward him, in perfect control, body leaning forward, lance couched in the crook of the arm.

Well, Marek thought, there was at least a chance that Chris would survive.

:

Chris could not see much of anything. Lurching wildly in the saddle, he had only blurred views of the stands, the ground, the other rider coming toward him. From his brief glimpses, he could not estimate how far away Guy was, or how long until the impact. He heard the thundering hoofbeats of his horse, the rhythmic snorting breath. He bounced in the saddle and tried to hold on to his lance. Everything was taking much longer than he expected. He felt as if he had been riding this horse for an hour.

At the last moment, he saw Guy very close, rushing up to him at frightful speed, and then his own lance recoiled in his hand, slamming painfully into his right side, and simultaneously he felt a sharp pain in his left shoulder and an impact that twisted him sideways in the saddle, and he heard the *crack!* of splintering wood.

The crowd roared.

His horse raced onward, to the far end of the field. Chris was dazed. What had happened? His shoulder burned fiercely. His lance had been snapped in two.

And he was still sitting in the saddle.

*Shit.*

:

Marek watched unhappily. It was bad luck; the impact had been too glancing to unseat Chris. Now they would have to charge another time. He glanced over at Sir Guy, who was cursing as he pulled a fresh lance from the hands of the pages, wheeling his horse, preparing to charge again.

At the far end of the field, Chris was again trying to get control of his new lance, which swung wildly in the air like a metronome. At last he brought it down across the saddle, but the horse was still twisting and bucking.

Guy was humiliated and angry. He was impatient, and did not wait. Kicking his spurs, he charged down the field.

You bastard, Marek thought.

:

The crowd roared in surprise at the one-sided attack. Chris heard it, and saw that Guy was already galloping toward him at full speed. His own horse was still twisting and unruly. He jerked on the reins and at that moment heard a *thwack* as one of the grooms whipped his horse on the hindquarters.

The horse whinnied. The ears flattened.

He charged down the field.

The second charge was worse—because this time, he knew what was coming.

:

The impact slammed him, streaking pain across his chest, as he was lifted bodily up into the air. Everything became slow. He saw the saddle moving away from him, then the horse's rear flanks revealed as he slid away, and then he was tilted back, staring up at sky.

He smashed onto the ground, flat on his back. His head clanged against the helmet. He saw bright blue spots, which spread and grew larger, then became gray. He heard Marek in his ear: *"Now stay there!"*

Somewhere he heard distant trumpets as the world faded gently, easily into blackness.

:

At the far end of the course, Guy was wheeling his horse to prepare for another charge, but already the trumpets had sounded for the next pair.

Marek lowered his lance, kicked his horse, and galloped forward. He saw his opposite, Sir Charles de Gaune, racing toward him. He heard the steady rumble of the horse, the building roar of the crowd—they knew this would be good—as he raced forward. This horse was running incredibly fast. Sir Charles charged forward, equally fast.

:

According to the medieval texts, the great challenge of the joust was not to carry the lance, or to aim it at this target or that. The challenge was to hold the line of the charge and not to veer away from the impact—not to give in to the panic that swept over nearly every rider as he galloped toward his opponent.

Marek had read the old texts, but now he suddenly understood them: he felt shivery and loose, weak in his limbs, his thighs trembling as he squeezed his mount. He forced himself to concentrate, to focus, to line up his lance with Sir Charles. But the tip of his lance whipped up and down as he charged. He raised it from the pommel, couched it in the crook of his arm. Steadier. His breathing was better. He felt his strength return. He lined up. Eighty yards now.

Charging hard.

He saw Sir Charles adjust his lance, angling it upward. He was going for the head. Or was it a feint? Jousting riders were known to change their aim at the last moment. Would he?

Sixty yards.

The head strike was risky if both riders were not aiming for it. A straight lance to the torso would impact a fraction of a second sooner than a lance to the head: it was a matter of the angles. The first impact would move both riders, making the head strike less certain. But a skilled knight might extend his lance farther forward, taking it out of couched position, to get six or eight inches of extra length, and thus the first impact. You had to have enormous arm strength to absorb the instant of impact, and control the lance as it socked back, so the horse would bear the brunt; but you were more likely to throw off the opponent's aim and timing.

Fifty yards.

Sir Charles still held his lance high. But now he couched it, leaning forward in the saddle. He had more control of the lance now. Would he feint again?

Forty yards.

There was no way to know. Marek decided to go for the chest strike. He put his lance in position. He would not move it again.

Thirty yards.

He heard the thunder of hooves, the roar of the crowd. The medieval texts warned, "Do not close your eyes at the moment of impact. Keep your eyes open to make the hit."

Twenty yards.

His eyes were open.

Ten.

The bastard raised his lance.

He was going for the head.

*Impact.*

:

The crack of wood sounded like a gunshot. Marek felt a pain in his left shoulder, stabbing upward and hard. He rode on to the end of the course, dropped his shattered lance, extended his hand out for another. But the pages were just staring at the field behind him.

Looking back, he saw that Sir Charles was down, lying on the ground, not moving.

And then he saw Sir Guy prancing and wheeling around Chris's fallen body. That would be his solution, Marek thought. He'd trample Chris to death.

Marek turned and drew his sword. He held it high.

With a howl of rage, Marek spurred his horse down the field.

:

The crowd screamed and pounded the railings like a drumbeat. Sir Guy turned, and he saw Marek coming. He looked back down at Chris, and kicked his horse, making it move sideways to stomp him.

"Fie! Fie!" the crowd shouted, and even Lord Oliver was on his feet, aghast.

But then Marek had reached Sir Guy, unable to stop his charge but sweeping past him, shouting, "Asshole" as he struck Guy's head with the flat of his sword. He knew it wouldn't hurt him, but it was an insulting blow, and it would make him abandon Chris. Which it did.

Sir Guy immediately turned away from Chris as Marek reined up, holding his sword. Sir Guy pulled his sword from the sheath and swung viciously, the blade whistling in the air. It clanged off Marek's blade. Marek felt his own sword vibrate in his hand with the impact. Marek lashed out in a backswing, going for the head. Guy parried; the horses wheeled; the swords clanged, again and again.

The battle had begun. And in some detached part of his mind, Marek knew that this would be a fight to the death.

:

Kate watched the battle from the railing. Marek was holding his own, and his physical strength was superior, but it was easy to see that he did not have the expertise of Sir Guy. His swings were wilder, his body position less sure. He seemed to know it, and so did Sir Guy, who kept backing his horse away, trying to open space for full swings. For his part, Marek pressed closer, keeping the distance between them tight, like a fighter staying in the clinch.

But Marek could not do it forever, she saw. Sooner or later, Guy would get enough distance, if only for a moment, and make a lethal blow.

∵

Marek's hair was soaked with sweat inside the helmet. Stinging drops dripped into his eyes. He could do nothing about it. He shook his head, trying to clear his vision. It didn't help much.

Soon he was gasping for breath. Through the slit of the helmet, Sir Guy appeared tireless and implacable, always on the attack, swinging repeatedly in a sure, practiced rhythm. Marek knew that he had to do something soon, before he became too tired. He had to break the knight's rhythm.

His right hand, holding the sword, already burned from constant exertion. His left hand was strong. Why not use his left hand?

It was worth a try.

Spurring his horse, Marek moved closer, until they were chest to chest. He waited until he had blocked one swing with his own sword, and then with the heel of his left hand, he punched upward at Sir Guy's helmet. The helmet snapped back; he felt the satisfying *thunk* as Guy's head struck the front of the helmet.

Immediately, Marek flipped his sword over and slammed the butt of the handle against Guy's helmet. There was a loud clang, and Guy's body jerked in the saddle. His shoulders slumped momentarily. Marek struck again, banged the helmet harder. He knew he was hurting him.

But not enough.

Too late, he saw Guy's sword hiss in a broad arc, toward his back. Marek felt the brutal sting like a whip across his shoulders. Did the chain mail hold? Was he hurt? He could still move his arms. He swung his own blade hard against the back of Guy's helmet. Guy did nothing to ward off the blow, which rang like a gong. He must be dazed, Marek thought.

Marek swung again, then wheeled his horse, coming around; and he swung broadly for the neck. Guy blocked it, but the force of the impact knocked him backward. Reeling, he slid sideways in the saddle, grabbed for the pommel, but could not prevent his fall to the ground.

Marek turned, started to dismount. The crowd roared again; looking back, he saw that Guy had leapt easily to his feet, his injuries a sham. He swung his blade at Marek while he was still dismounting. Marek, with one foot still raised in the stirrup, parried awkwardly, somehow got clear of his horse, and then swung back. Sir Guy was strong, sure of himself.

Marek realized his situation was now worse than before. He attacked fiercely, but Guy backed up easily, his footwork practiced and quick. Marek was gasping and wheezing inside his helmet; he was sure Guy could hear it, and would know what it meant.

Marek was wearing down.

All Sir Guy had to do was keep backing away, until Marek exhausted himself.

Unless . . .

Off to the left, Chris obediently still lay flat on his back.

Marek swung at Guy, moving to the right with every stroke. Guy continued to move lightly away. But now Marek was driving him back—toward Chris.

:

Chris awoke slowly to the clang of swords. Groggy, he took stock. He was lying on his back, staring at blue sky. But he was alive. What had happened? He turned his head inside his black helmet. With just a narrow slit for vision, it was hot and stuffy and claustrophobic.

He began to feel sick.

The sensation of nausea built quickly. He didn't want to

throw up inside the helmet. It was too tight around his head; he would drown in his own puke. He had to get his helmet off. Still lying there, he reached up and grabbed the helmet with both hands.

He tugged at it.

It didn't budge. Why? Had they tied it on him? Was it because he was lying down?

He was going to throw up. In the damn helmet.

Jesus.

Frantic, he rolled on the ground.

:

Marek swung his sword desperately. Behind Sir Guy, he saw Chris begin to move. Marek would have shouted to him to stay where he was, but he had no breath to speak.

Marek swung again, and again.

Now Chris was pulling at his helmet, trying to get it off. Guy was still ten yards from Chris. Dancing backward, enjoying himself, parrying Marek's blows easily.

Marek knew he was almost at the limits of his strength now. His swings were increasingly weak. Guy was still strong, still smooth. Just backing and parrying. Waiting for his chance.

Five yards.

Chris had rolled over on his stomach, and he was now getting up. He was on all fours. Hanging his head. Then there was a loud retching sound.

Guy heard it, too, turned his head a little to look—

Marek charged, butted him in the breastplate with his head, and Guy staggered backward, fell over Chris, and went down.

Malegant rolled quickly on the ground, but Marek was on him, stamping on Guy's right hand to pin the sword down, then swinging his other leg over to pin the opposite shoulder. Marek held his sword high, ready to plunge it down.

The crowd fell silent.

Guy did not move.

Slowly, Marek lowered his sword, cut the laces to Guy's helmet, and pushed it back with the tip of his blade. Guy's head was now exposed. Marek saw he was bleeding freely from his left ear.

Guy glared at him, and spat.

Marek raised his sword again. He was filled with rage, stinging sweat, burning arms, vision red with fury and exhaustion. He tightened his hands, prepared to swing down and cut the head from the body.

Guy saw it.

"Mercy!"

He shouted, so everyone would hear.

"I beg mercy!" he cried. "In the name of the Holy Trinity and the Virgin Mary! Mercy! Mercy!"

The crowd was silent.

Waiting.

Marek was not sure what to do. In the back of his mind, a voice said, *Kill this bastard or you will regret it later*. He knew that he must decide quickly; the longer he stood here, straddling Sir Guy, the more certain he would lose his nerve.

He looked at the crowd lining the railing. No one moved; they just stared. He looked at the stands, where Lord Oliver sat with the ladies. Everyone was motionless. Lord Oliver seemed frozen. Marek looked back at the cluster of pages standing by the railing. They, too, were frozen. Then, in a move that was almost subliminal, one page raised a hand to midchest and made a flicking wrist motion: cut it off.

He's giving you good advice, Marek thought.

But Marek hesitated. There was absolute silence in the field, except for the retches and groans of Chris. In the end, it was those retches that broke the moment. Marek stepped away from Sir Guy and extended a hand to help him up.

Sir Guy took his hand, got to his feet in front of Marek. He said, "You bastard, I'll see you in Hell," and turned on his heel and walked away.

# 31:15:58

The little stream wound through mossy grass and wild-flowers. Chris was on his knees, plunging his face into the water. He came back sputtering, coughing. He looked at Marek, who was squatting beside him, staring off into space.

"I've had it," Chris said. "I've *had* it."

"I imagine you have."

"I could have been killed," Chris said. "That's supposed to be a sport? You know what that is? It's a game of chicken on horses. Those people are *insane*." He dunked his head in the water again.

"Chris."

"I hate to throw up. I *hate* it."

"Chris."

"What? What is it now? You going to tell me I'll rust my armor? Because I don't give a shit, André."

"No," Marek said, "I'm going to tell you your felt under-shirt will swell, and it'll be difficult to take the armor off."

"Is that right? Well, I don't care. Those pages will come and get it off me." Chris sat back in the moss and coughed. "Jesus, I can't get rid of that smell. I need to take a bath or something."

Marek sat beside him, said nothing. He just let him un-wind. Chris's hands were shaking as he talked. It was better for him to get it out, he thought.

:

In the field below them, archers in maroon and gray were practicing. Ignoring the excitement of the nearby tournament, they patiently fired at targets, moved backward, fired again. It was just as the old texts said: the English archers were highly disciplined, and they practiced every day.

"Those men are the new military power," Marek said. "They decide battles now. Look at them."

Chris propped himself on his elbow. "You're kidding," he said. The archers were now more than two hundred yards from their circular targets—the length of two football fields. So far away, they were small figures, and yet they were confidently drawing their bows toward the sky. "Are they serious?"

The sky was black with whistling arrows. They struck the targets, or landed close by, sticking up in the grass.

"No kidding," Chris said.

Almost immediately, another thick volley filled the air. And another, and another. Marek was counting to himself. Three seconds between volleys. So it was true, he thought: English archers really could fire twenty rounds a minute. By now, the targets bristled with arrows.

"Charging knights can't stand up under that kind of attack," Marek said. "It kills the riders, and it kills the horses. That's why the English knights dismount to fight. The French still charge in the traditional way—and they're just slaughtered, before they ever get close to the English. Four thousand knights dead at Crécy, even more in Poitiers. Large numbers for this time."

"Why don't the French change tactics? Can't they see what's happening?"

"They do, but it means the end of a whole way of life—a whole culture, really," Marek said. "Knights are all nobility; their way of life is too expensive for commoners. A knight has to buy his armor and at least three warhorses, and he has to support his retinue of pages and aides. And these noble knights have been the determining factor in warfare, until now. Now it's over." He pointed to the archers in the field. "Those men are commoners. They win by coordination and discipline. There's no personal valor. They're paid a wage; they do a job. But they're the future of warfare—paid, disciplined, faceless troops. The knights are finished."

"Except for tournaments," Chris said sourly.

"Pretty much. And even there—all that plate armor, over the chain mail—that's all because of arrows. Arrows will go clean through an unprotected man, and they'll penetrate chain mail. So knights need plate armor. Horses need armor. But with a volley like that . . ." Marek pointed to the whistling rainfall of arrows and shrugged. "It's over."

Chris looked back at the tournament grounds. And then he said, "Well, it's about time!"

Marek turned and saw five liveried pages walking toward them, along with two guards in red-and-black surcoats. "Finally I'm going to get out of this damned metal."

Chris and Marek stood as the men came up. One of the guards said, "You have broken the rules of tourney, disgraced the chivalrous knight Guy Malegant, and the good offices of Lord Oliver. You are made arrest, and will come with us."

"Wait a minute," Chris said. "*We* disgraced *him*?"

"You will come with us."

"Wait a minute," Chris said.

The soldier cuffed him hard on the side of the head, and pushed him forward. Marek fell into step beside him. Surrounded by guards, they headed toward the castle.

:

Kate was still at the tournament, looking for Chris and André. At first, she thought to look in the tents ranged beyond the field, but there were only men—knights and squires and pages—in that area, and she decided against it. This was a different world, violence was in the air, and she felt a constant sense of risk. Nearly everyone in this world was young; the knights who swaggered about the field were in their twenties or early thirties, and the squires mere teenagers. She was dressed in ordinary fashion, and clearly not a member of the nobility. She had the feeling that if she were dragged off and raped, no one would take much notice.

Even though it was midday, she found herself behaving the way she did in New Haven at night. She tried never to be alone, but to move with a group; she skirted around the clusters of males, giving them wide berth.

She made her way behind the bleachers, hearing the cheers of the crowd as the next pair of knights began to fight. She looked into the area of tents to her left. She did not see Marek or Chris anywhere. Yet they had left the field only minutes before. Were they inside one of the tents? She had heard nothing in her earpiece for the last hour; she assumed it was because Marek and Chris had worn helmets, which blocked transmission. But surely their helmets were off now.

Then she saw them, a short distance down the hill, sitting by a meandering stream.

She headed down the hill. Her wig was hot and itchy in the sun. Perhaps she could get rid of the wig and just put her hair up under a cap. Or if she cut her hair a little shorter, she could pass for a young man, even without a cap.

It might be interesting, she thought, to be a man for a while.

She was thinking about where to get scissors when she saw the soldiers approaching Marek. She slowed her pace. She still heard nothing in her earpiece, but she was so close, she knew she should.

Was it turned off? She tapped her ear.

Immediately, she heard Chris say, "*We* disgraced *him*?" and then something garbled. She saw the soldiers push Chris toward the castle. Marek walked alongside him.

Kate waited a moment, then followed.

:

Castelgard was deserted, shops and storefronts locked, its streets echoing and empty. Everyone had gone to the tournament, which made it more difficult for her to follow Marek and Chris and the soldiers. She had to drop farther back, waiting until they had gone out of a street before she could follow them, hurrying ahead at a near run until she caught sight of them again, then duck back around a corner.

She knew her behavior looked suspicious. But there was

no one to see it. High in one window, she saw an old woman sitting in the sun, eyes closed. But she never looked down. Perhaps she was asleep.

She came to the open field in front of the castle. It, too, was now deserted. The knights on prancing horses, the mock combats, the flying banners were all gone. The soldiers crossed the drawbridge. As she followed after them, she heard the crowd roar from the field beyond the walls. The guards turned and shouted to soldiers on the ramparts, asking what was happening. The soldiers above could see down to the field; they shouted answers. All this was accompanied by much swearing; apparently, bets had been made.

In all the excitement, she walked through, into the castle.

*

She stood in the small courtyard known as the outer bailey. She saw horses there, tied to a post and unattended. But there were no soldiers in the bailey; everyone was up in the ramparts, watching the tournament.

She looked around for Marek and Chris but did not see them. Not knowing what else to do, she went through the door to the great hall. She heard footsteps echoing in the spiral staircase to her left.

She started up the stairs, going round and round, but the footsteps diminished.

They must have gone down, not up.

Quickly, she retraced her steps. The stairs spiraled downward, ending in a low-ceilinged stone passage, damp and moldy, with cells along one side. The cell doors were open; no one inside. Somewhere ahead, beyond a bend in the corridor, she heard echoing voices, and the clang of metal.

She moved cautiously forward. She must be beneath the great hall, she thought. In her mind she tried to reconstruct the area, from her memory of the ruined castle she had explored so carefully a few weeks earlier. But she did not remember ever seeing this passageway. Perhaps it had collapsed centuries before.

Another metal clang, and echoing laughter.

Then footsteps.

It took her a moment to realize they were coming toward her.

:

Marek fell back into soggy, rotting straw, slippery and stinking. Chris tumbled down alongside him, sliding on the mush. The cell door clanged shut. They were at the end of a corridor, with cells on all three sides. Through the bars, Marek saw the guards leaving, laughing as they went. One said, "Hey, Paolo, where do you think you are going? You stay here and guard them."

"Why? They are not going anywhere. I want to see the tourney."

"It is your watch. Oliver wants them guarded."

There was some protesting and swearing. More laughing, and footsteps going away. Then one heavyset guard came back, peered in through the bars at them, and swore. He wasn't happy; they were the reason he was missing the show. He spat on the floor of their cell, then walked a short distance away, to a wooden stool. Marek could not see him anymore, but he saw his shadow on the opposite wall.

It looked as though he was picking his teeth.

Marek walked up to the bars, trying to see into the other cells. He could not really see into the cell to the right, but directly across from them he saw a figure back against the wall, seated in the darkness.

As his eyes adjusted, he saw it was the Professor.

# 30:51:09

Stern sat in the private dining room of ITC. It was a small room with a single table, white tablecloth, set for four.

Gordon sat opposite him, eating hungrily, scrambled eggs and bacon. Stern watched the top of Gordon's crew-cut head bob up and down as he scooped the eggs with his fork. The man ate fast.

Outside, the sun was already climbing in the sky, above the mesas to the east. Stern glanced at his watch; it was six o'clock in the morning. The ITC technicians were releasing another weather balloon from the parking lot; he remembered that Gordon had told them they did it every hour. The balloon rose quickly into the sky, then disappeared into high clouds. The men who had released it didn't bother to watch it go, but walked back to a nearby laboratory building.

"How's your French toast?" Gordon said, looking up. "Rather have something else?"

"No, it's good," Stern said. "I'm just not very hungry."

"Take some advice from an old military man," Gordon said. "Always eat at a meal. Because you never know when your next one will be."

"I'm sure that's right," Stern said. "I'm just not hungry."

Gordon shrugged and resumed eating.

A man in a starched waiter's jacket came into the room. Gordon said, "Oh, Harold. Do you have coffee ready?"

The man in the jacket said, "I do, sir. Cappuccino if you prefer."

"I'll have it black."

"Certainly, sir."

"How about you, David?" Gordon said. "Coffee?"

"Nonfat latte, if you have it," Stern said.

"Certainly, sir." Harold went away.

Stern stared out the window. He listened to Gordon eat, listened to his fork scrape across the plate. Finally, he said, "Let me see if I understand this. At the moment, they *can't* come back, is that right?"

"That's right."

"Because there is no landing site."

"That's right."

"Because debris blocks it."

"That's right."

"And how long until they *can* come back?"

Gordon sighed. He pushed away from the table. "It's going to be all right, David," he said. "Things are going to turn out fine."

"Just tell me. How long?"

"Well, let's count it off. Another three hours to clear the air in the cave. Add an hour for good measure. Four hours. Then two hours to clear the debris. Six hours. Then you have to re-build the water shields."

"Rebuild the water shields?" Stern said.

"The three rings of water. They're absolutely essential."

"Why?"

"To minimize transcription errors."

Stern said, "And what exactly are transcription errors?"

"Errors on the rebuild. When the person is reconstructed by the machine."

"You told me there weren't any errors. That you could re-build exactly."

"For all intents and purposes, we can, yes. As long as we're shielded."

"And if we're not shielded?"

Gordon sighed. "But we *will* be shielded, David." He glanced at his watch. "I wish you'd stop worrying. There's several hours more before we can fix the transit site. You're upsetting yourself needlessly."

"It's just that I keep thinking," Stern said, "that there must be something we can do. Send a message, make some kind of contact. . . ."

Gordon shook his head. "No. No message, no contact. It's just not possible. For the moment, they're entirely cut off from us. And there's not a thing we can do about it."

# 30:40:39

Kate Erickson flattened herself against the wall, feeling damp stone on her back. She had ducked inside one of the cells in the corridor, and now she waited, holding her breath, while the guards who had locked up Marek and Chris walked back past her. The guards were laughing, and they seemed in good humor. She heard one of them say, "Sir Oliver was sore displeased with that Hainauter, to make a fool of his lieutenant."

"And the other one was worse! He rides like a flopping rag, and yet he breaks two lances with Tête Noire!" General laughter.

"Sooth, he made a fool of Tête Noire. For that, Lord Oliver will take their heads before nightfall."

"Else I miss my guess, he will chop their heads before supper."

"No, after. The crowd will be larger." More laughter.

They moved down the corridor, their voices fading. Soon she could hardly hear them. Now there was a short silence— had they started back up the stairs? No, not yet. She heard them laughing once again. And the laughter continued. It had an odd, forced quality.

Something was wrong.

She listened intently. They were saying something about Sir Guy and Lady Claire. She couldn't really make it out. She heard ". . . much vexed by our Lady . . ." and more laughter.

Kate frowned.

Their voices were no longer quite so faint.

Not good. They were coming back.

Why? she thought. What happened?

She glanced toward the door. And there, on the stone floor, she saw her own wet footprints, going into the cell.

Her shoes had been soaked from the grass near the stream. So had the shoes of everyone else, and the center of the stone corridor was a wet, muddy track of many footprints. But one set of footprints veered off, toward her cell.

And somehow they had noticed.

Damn.

A voice: "When does the tourney draw closed?"

"By high nones."

"Faith, then it is nigh finished."

"Lord Oliver will haste to sup, and prepare for the Archpriest."

She listened, trying to count the different voices. How many guards had there been? She tried to remember. At least three. Maybe five. She hadn't paid attention at the time.

*Damn.*

"They say the Archpriest brings a thousand men-at-arms. . . ."

A shadow crossed the floor, outside her door. That meant they were now on both sides of the cell door.

What could she do? All she knew was that she couldn't let herself be captured. She was a woman; she had no business here; they would rape her and kill her.

But, she reflected, they didn't know she was a woman. Not yet. There was silence outside the door, then a scuffling of feet. What would they do next? Probably send one man into the cell while the others waited outside. And meanwhile the others would get set, draw their swords, and raise them high—

She couldn't wait. Crouching low, she bolted.

She banged into a guard as he came through the door, hitting him at knee level from the side, and with a howl of pain and surprise, he fell backward. There were shouts from the other guards, but then she was through the door, a sword clanged down against stone behind her, spitting sparks, and she was running up the corridor.

"A woman! A woman!"

They ran after her.

She was in the spiral staircase now, going up fast. From

somewhere below, she heard the clank of their armor as they started up after her. But then she had reached the ground floor, and without thinking, she did the immediate thing: she ran straight into the great hall.

It was deserted, the tables set for a feast, the food not yet laid out. She ran past the tables, looking for a place to hide. Behind the tapestries? No, they were flat to the wall. Under the tablecloths? No, they would look there and find her. Where? *Where?* She saw the huge fireplace, the fire still burning high. Wasn't there a secret passage out of the dining room? Was that passage here in Castelgard, or was it in La Roque? She couldn't remember. She should have paid more attention.

In her mind's eye she saw herself, wearing khaki shorts and a Polo T-shirt and Nike sneakers, moving lazily through the ruins, taking notes on her pad. Her concerns—to the extent she'd had any at all—had been to satisfy her scholarly peers.

She should have paid more attention!

She heard the men approaching. There was no more time. She ran toward the nine-foot-high fireplace and stepped behind the huge gilded circular screen. The fire was blazing hot, waves of heat radiating against her body. She heard the men coming into the room, shouting, running, looking. She crouched behind the screen, held her breath and waited.

:

She heard kicking and banging, the clatter of dishes on tables as they searched. She could not make out their voices clearly; they merged with the roar of the flames behind her. There was a metal *clang* as something fell over; it sounded like a torch stand, something big.

She waited.

One man barked a question, and she heard no reply. Another shouted a question, and this time she heard a soft answer. It didn't sound like a man. Who were they talking to? It sounded like a woman. Kate listened: Yes, it was a woman's voice. She was sure of it.

Another exchange, and then the sound of clanking armor

as the men ran from the room. Peering around the edge of the gilded screen, she saw them vanish through the doorway.

She waited a moment, then stepped from behind the screen.

She saw a young girl of ten or eleven. She wore a white cloth that wrapped over her head, so only her face showed. She had a loose sort of dress, rose-colored, that came almost to the floor. She carried a gold pitcher, and was pouring water into goblets at the tables.

The girl met her eyes and just stared.

Kate waited for her to cry out, but she did not. She just stared curiously at Kate for a moment and then said, "They went upstairs."

Kate turned and ran.

⋮

Inside the cell, Marek heard the blare of trumpets, and the distant roar of the tournament crowds, drifting in from one of the high windows. The guard looked up unhappily, swore at Marek and the Professor, and then walked back to his stool.

The Professor said quietly, "Do you still have a marker?"

"Yes," Marek said. "I do. Do you have yours?"

"No, I lost it. About three minutes after I got here."

The Professor had landed, he said, in the forested flatlands near the monastery and the river. ITC had assured him this would be a deserted spot, but ideally situated. Without going far from the machine, he could see all the principal sites of his dig.

What happened was pure bad luck: the Professor landed just as a party of woodcutters was heading into the forest to work for the day, their axes over their shoulders.

"They saw the flashes of light, and then they saw me, and they all fell to their knees, praying. They thought they had seen a miracle. Then they decided they hadn't, and the axes came off their shoulders," the Professor said. "I thought they were going to kill me, but fortunately I knew Occitan. I convinced them to take me to the monastery. Let the monks settle it."

The monks took him away from the woodcutters, stripped

him, and searched his body for stigmata. "They were looking in rather unusual places," the Professor said. "That's when I demanded to see the Abbot. The Abbot wanted to know the location of the passage in La Roque. I suspect he's promised it to Arnaut. Anyway, I suggested it might be in the monastic documents." The Professor grinned. "I was willing to go through his parchments for him."

"Yes?"

"And I think I have found it."

"The passage?"

"I think so. It follows an underground river, so it is probably quite extensive. It starts in a place called the green chapel. And there is a key to finding the entrance."

"A key?"

The guard snarled something, and Marek broke off speaking for a moment. Chris got up, brushing the damp off his hose. He said, "We have to get out of here. Where is Kate?"

Marek shook his head. Kate was still free, unless the shouts from the guards he'd heard down the hallway meant that she'd been captured. But he didn't think they'd caught her. So if he could make contact with her, she might be able to help get them out.

That meant somehow overpowering the guard. The problem was that there were at least twenty yards from the bend in the corridor to where the guard was sitting on his stool. There was no way to take him by surprise. But if Kate was within range of their earpieces, then he could—

Chris was banging on the bars of the cell and shouting, "Hey! Guard! Hey, you!"

Before Marek could speak, the guard stepped into view, looking curiously at Chris, who had reached one hand through the bars and was beckoning him. "Hey, come here! Hey! Over here!"

The guard walked up to him, swatted Chris's hand, which extended through the bar, and then broke into a sudden fit of coughing as Chris sprayed him with the gas canister. The guard wobbled on his feet. Chris reached through the bars again, grabbed the guard by the collar, and sprayed a second time right in his face.

The guard's eyes rolled up in his head, and he dropped like a rock. Still holding on, Chris's arm banged against the cross-bars; he yelled in pain, then released the guard, who fell away from the bars and collapsed in the middle of the floor.

Far out of reach.

"Nice work," Marek said. "What's next?"

"You know, you might help me," Chris said. "You're very negative." He was down on his knees, reaching through the bars to his armpit, his hand grasping outside. His out-stretched fingers could almost reach the guard's foot. Almost, but not quite. Six inches from the sole of his foot. Chris stretched, grunting. "If we just had something—a stick, or a hook—something to pull him. . . ."

"It won't do any good," the Professor said from the other cell.

"Why not?"

He came forward into the light and looked through the bars. "Because he doesn't have the key."

"Doesn't have the key? Where is it?"

"Hanging on the wall," Johnston said, pointing down the corridor.

"Oh shit," Chris said.

On the floor, the guard's hand twitched. One leg kicked spasmodically. He was waking up.

Panicked, Chris said, "What do we do now?"

:

Marek said, "Kate, are you there?"

"I'm here."

"Where?"

"Just down the corridor. I came back because I figured they'd never look for me here."

"Kate," Marek said, "come here. Quickly."

Marek heard her footsteps as she ran toward them.

The guard coughed, rolled onto his back, then propped himself up on one elbow. He looked down the corridor and hastily began to get to his feet.

He was on his hands and knees when Kate kicked him, snapping his head back, and he fell onto the floor again. But he wasn't unconscious, only dazed. He started to get up, shaking his head to clear it.

"Kate," Marek said, "the keys. . . ."

"Where?"

"On the wall."

She backed away from the guard, got the keys on a heavy ring, and brought them to Marek's cell. She put one key in the lock and tried to turn it, but it didn't turn.

With a grunt, the guard threw himself at her, knocking her away from the cell, into the center of the room. They grappled, rolling on the floor. She was much smaller than he was. He held her down easily.

Marek was reaching through the bars with both hands, pulling the key out of the lock, trying another. It didn't fit, either.

Now the guard was straddling Kate, both hands around her neck, strangling her.

Marek tried another key. No luck. There were six more keys on the ring.

Kate was turning blue. She made rasping, choking sounds. She pounded her fists on the guard's arms, but her blows were ineffectual. She punched at his groin, but his surcoat protected him.

Marek shouted, "Knife! Knife!" but she didn't seem to understand. Marek tried another key. Still no success. From the opposite cell, Johnston yelled something in French to the guard.

The guard looked up and snarled a reply, and in that moment Kate brought her dagger out and slammed it into the guard's shoulder with all her strength. The blade didn't penetrate the chain mail. She tried again, and again. Furious, the guard began to pound her head against the stone floor to make her drop the knife.

Marek tried another key.

It turned with a loud creak.

The Professor was shouting, Chris was shouting, and

Marek flung the door open. The guard turned to face him, getting to his feet, releasing Kate. Coughing, she swung the knife at his unprotected legs, and he yelled in pain. Marek hit him twice in the head, very hard. The guard fell on the floor, not moving.

Chris unlocked the door for the Professor. Kate got to her feet, color slowly returning to her face.

Marek had pulled out the white wafer and had his thumb on the button. "Okay. We're finally all together." He was looking at the space between the cells. "Is this big enough? Can we call the machine right here?"

"No," Chris said. "It has to be six feet on each side, remember?"

"We need a bigger space." The Professor turned to Kate. "You know how to get out of here?"

She nodded. They started down the corridor.


# 30:21:02


She led them quickly up the first flight of spiral stairs, feeling a new confidence. The fight with the guard had somehow freed her; the worst had happened, and she had survived. Now, even though her head was throbbing, she felt calmer and clearer than before. And her research had all come back to her: she could remember where the passages were.

They came to the ground floor and looked out into the courtyard. It was even busier than she had expected. There were many soldiers, as well as knights in armor and courtiers in fine clothes, all returning from the tournament. She guessed it was about three in the afternoon; the courtyard was bathed in afternoon light, but shadows had begun to lengthen.

"We can't go out there," Marek said, shaking his head.

"Don't worry." She led them upstairs to the second floor, then quickly down a stone passageway with doors opening to the inside, windows on the outer side. She knew that behind the doors were a series of small apartments for family or guests.

Behind her, Chris said, "I've been here." He pointed to one of the doors. "Claire is in that room there."

Marek snorted. Kate continued on. At the far end of the corridor, a tapestry covered the left wall. She lifted the tapestry—it was surprisingly heavy—and then began to move along the wall, pressing the stones. "I'm pretty sure it's here," she said.

"Pretty sure?" Chris said.

"The passage to take us to the rear courtyard."

She reached the end of the wall. She didn't find a door. And she had to admit, looking back along the wall, that it didn't appear as if there was a doorway anywhere in this wall. The stones were smoothly and evenly mortared. The wall was flat, with no bulges or indentations. There was no sign of any additional or recent work. When she put her cheek against the wall and squinted along the length, it seemed all of a piece.

Was she wrong?

Was this the wrong place?

She couldn't be wrong. The door was here somewhere. She went back, pressing again. Nothing. When she finally discovered it, it was by pure accident. They heard voices from the other end of the corridor—voices coming up the stairwell. When she turned to look, her foot scraped against the stone at the base of the wall.

She felt the stone move.

With a soft metallic *clink*, a door appeared directly in front of her. It only opened a few inches. But she could see that the masonry had concealed the crack with cunning skill.

She pushed the door open. They all went through. Marek came last, dropping the tapestry as he closed the door.

:

They were in a dark, narrow passageway. Small holes in the wall every few yards allowed faint light to enter, so torches were not necessary.

When she had first mapped this passage, among the ruins of Castelgard, Kate had wondered why it existed. It seemed to make no sense. But now that she was here, she immediately understood its purpose.

This wasn't a passage to get from one place to another. It was a secret corridor to spy into the apartments on the second floor.

They moved forward quietly. From the adjacent room, Kate heard voices: a woman's and a man's. As they came to the small holes, they all paused, peered through.

She heard Chris give a sigh that was almost a groan.

·

At first, Chris saw only a man and woman silhouetted against a bright window. It took a moment for his eyes to adjust to the glare. Then he realized that it was Lady Claire and Sir Guy. They were holding hands, touching each other intimately. Sir Guy kissed her passionately, and she returned his kiss with equal fervor, her arms around his neck.

Chris just stared.

Now the lovers broke, and Sir Guy was speaking to her as she stared intently into his eyes. "My Lady," he was saying, "your public manner and sharp discourtesy provoke many to laugh behind my back, and talk of my unmanliness, that I should tolerate such abuse."

"It must be so," she said. "For both our sakes. This you know full well."

"Yet I would you were not quite so strong in your manner."

"Oh so? And how, then? Would you chance the fortune we both desire? There is other talk, good knight, as you know full well. So long as I oppose marriage, I share those suspicions that many harbor: that you had a black hand in my husband's death. Yet if Lord Oliver forces this marriage upon me, despite all my efforts, then no one can complain of my regard. 'Tis true?"

" 'Tis true," he said, nodding unhappily.

"Yet how different is the circumstance, if I show you favor now," she said. "The same tongues that wag will soon whisper that I too was party to my husband's untimely end, and such tales will quickly reach my husband's family in England. Already, they are of a mind to retake his estates. They lack only the excuse to act. Thus Sir Daniel keeps a watchful eye upon all I do. Good knight, my woman's reputation is easily defiled, never to make repair. Our sole safety lies in my unbending hostility toward you, so I pray you tolerate what slurs may vex you now, and think instead upon your coming reward."

Chris's jaw dropped open. She was behaving with exactly the same intense intimacy—the warm glance, the low voice, the soft caresses on the neck—that she had used with him. Chris had taken it to mean he had seduced her. Now it was clear that she had seduced him.

Sir Guy was sulky, despite her caress. "And your visits to the monastery? I would you visit there no more."

"How so? Are you jealous against the Abbot, my Lord?" she teased him.

"I say only, I would have you visit there no more," he said stubbornly.

"And yet my purpose was strong, for whoever knows the secret of La Roque commands Lord Oliver. He must do as he is asked to gain the secret."

"God's truth, Lady, yet you did not learn the secret," Sir Guy said. "Does the Abbot know it?"

"I did not see the Abbot," she said. "He was abroad."

"And the Magister claims to know not."

" 'Tis so, he claims. Yet I will ask the Abbot again, perhaps tomorrow."

There was a knock on the door, and a muffled male voice. They both turned to look. "That must be Sir Daniel," he said.

"Quick my Lord, to your secret place."

Sir Guy moved hastily toward the wall where they were hidden, pulled aside a tapestry, and then, as they watched in horror, he opened a door—and stepped into the narrow corridor alongside them. Sir Guy stared for a moment, and then he began to shout, "The prisoners! All escaped! Prisoners!"

This cry was taken up by the Lady Claire, who called out in the hallway.

In the passage, the Professor turned to them. "If we're separated, you go to the monastery. Find Brother Marcel. He has the key to the passage. Okay?"

Before any of them could answer, the soldiers came running into the passageway. Chris felt hands grab his arms, pull him roughly.

They were caught.

# 30:10:55

A solitary lute played in the great hall while servants finished setting out the tables. Lord Oliver and Sir Robert held the hands of their mistresses, danced as the dancing master clapped time, and smiled enthusiastically. After several steps, when Lord Oliver turned to face his partner, he found that her back was turned to him; Oliver swore.

"A trifle, my Lord," the dancing master said hastily, his smile unwavering. "As your Lordship recalls, it is forward-back, forward-back, turn, back, and turn, back. We missed a turn."

"I missed no turn," Oliver said.

"In deed, my Lord, you did not," Sir Robert said at once. "It was a phrase in the music which caused the confusion." He glared at the boy playing the lute.

"Very well, then." Oliver resumed his position, held out his hand to the girl. "What is it then?" he said. "Forward-back, forward-back, turn, back. . . ."

"Very good," the dancing master said, smiling and clapping the beat. "That's it, you have it now. . . ."

From the door, a voice: "My Lord."

The music stopped. Lord Oliver turned irritably, saw Sir Guy with guards, surrounding the Professor and several others. "What is it now?"

"My Lord, it appears the Magister has companions."

"Eh? What companions?"

Lord Oliver came forward. He saw the Hainauter, the foolish Irisher who could not ride, and a young woman, short and defiant-looking. "What companions are these?"

"My Lord, they claim they are the Magister's assistants."

"Assistants?" Oliver raised an eyebrow, looking at the group. "My dear Magister, when you said you had assistants, I did not realize they were here in the castle with you."

"I was not aware myself," the Professor said.

Lord Oliver snorted. "You cannot be assistants." He looked from one to the other. "You are too old by ten year. And you gave no sign you knew the Magister, earlier in the day. . . . You are not speaking sooth. None of you." He shook his head, turned to Sir Guy. "I do not believe them, and I will have the truth. But not now. Take them to the dungeon."

"My Lord, they were in the dungeon when they got free."

"They got free? How?" Immediately, he raised his hand to interrupt the reply. "What is our most secure place?"

Robert de Kere slipped forward and whispered.

"My tower chamber? Where I keep Mistress Alice?" Oliver began to laugh. "It is indeed secure. Yes, lock them there."

Sir Guy said, "I will see to it, my Lord."

"These 'assistants' will be surety to their master's good conduct." He smiled darkly. "I believe, Magister, you will yet learn to dance with me."

The three young people were dragged roughly away. Lord Oliver waved his hand, and the lutist and the dancing master departed with a silent bow. So did the women. Sir Robert lingered, but after a sharp glance from Oliver, he too left the room.

Now there were only servants, setting the tables. Otherwise, the room was silent.

"So, Magister, what game is this?"

"As God is my witness, they are my assistants, as I have told you from the start," the Professor said.

"Assistants? One is a knight."

"He owes me a boon, and so he serves me."

"Oh? What boon?"

"I saved his father's life."

"In deed?" Oliver walked around the Professor. "Saved it how?"

"With medicines."

"From what did he suffer?"

The Professor touched his ear and said, "My Lord Oliver, if you wish to assure yourself, bring back the knight Marek at once, and he will say to you what I say now, that I saved his father, who was ill with dropsy, with the herb arnica, and that this happened in Hampstead, a hamlet near to London, in the autumn of the year past. Call him back and ask him."

Oliver paused.

He stared at the Professor.

The moment was broken by a man in a costume streaked with white powder, who said from a far door, "My Lord."

Oliver whirled. *"What is it now?"*

"My Lord, a subtlety."

"A subtlety? Very well—but be quick."

"My Lord," the man said, bowing and simultaneously flicking his fingers. Two young boys raced forward with a tray on their shoulders.

"My Lord, the first subtlety—haslet."

The tray showed pale coils of intestines and an animal's large testicles and penis. Oliver walked around the tray, peering closely.

"The innards of the boar, brought back from the hunt," he said, nodding. "Quite convincing." He turned to the Professor. "You approve the work of my kitchen?"

"I do, my Lord. Your subtlety is both traditional and well executed. The testicles are particularly well made."

"Thank you, sir," the chef said, bowing. "They are heated sugar and prunes, if it please. And the intestines are strung fruit covered with a batter of egg and ale, and then honey."

"Good, good," Oliver said. "You will serve this before the second course?"

"I will, Lord Oliver."

"And what of the other subtlety?"

"Marchepane, my Lord, colored with dandelion and saffron." The chef bowed and gestured, and more boys came running with another platter. This held an enormous model of the fortress of Castelgard, its battlements five feet high, all done in pale yellow, matching the actual stones. The confection was accurate down to small details, and included tiny flags from the sugary battlements.

"*Elégant!* Well done!" Oliver cried. He clapped his hands with pleasure, delighted as a young child for the moment. "I am most pleased."

He turned to the Professor and gestured to the model. "You know the villain Arnaut lies fast upon our castle, and I must defend against him?"

Johnston nodded. "I do."

"How do you advise me to arrange my forces in Castelgard?"

"My Lord," Johnston said, "I would not defend Castelgard at all."

"Oh? Why say you that?" Oliver went to the nearest table, took a goblet, and poured wine.

"How many soldiers did you require to take it from the Gascons?" Johnston asked.

"Fifty or sixty, no more."

"Then you are answered."

"But we made no frontal attack. We used stealth. Craft."

"And the Archpriest will not?"

"He may try, but we shall be waiting. We shall be prepared for his attack."

"Perhaps," Johnston said, turning. "And perhaps not."

"So you *are* a cunning-man. . . ."

"No, my Lord: I do not see the future. I have no such abilities at all. I merely give you my advice as a man. And I say, the Archpriest will be no less stealthy than you."

Oliver frowned, drank in sullen silence for a while. Then he seemed to notice the chef, the boys holding the tray, all of them standing silent, and waved them away. As they departed, he said, "Take good care of that subtlety! I wish nothing to happen to it before the guests see it." In a few moments, they were alone again. He turned to Johnston, gestured to the tapestries. "Or to this castle."

"My Lord," Johnston said, "you have no need to defend this castle when you have another so much better."

"Eh? You speak of La Roque? But La Roque has a weakness. There is a passage that I cannot find."

"And how do you know the passage exists?"

"It must exist," Oliver said, "because old Laon was architect of La Roque. You know of Laon? No? He was the Abbot of the monastery before the present Abbot. That old bishop was crafty, and whenever he was called upon to give assistance rebuilding a town, or a castle, or a church, he left behind some secret known only to him. Every castle had an unknown passage, or an unknown weakness, which Laon could sell to an attacker, if need arose. Old Laon had a sharp eye for the interest of Mother Church—and a much sharper eye for himself."

"And yet," Johnston said, "if no one knows where this passage is, it might as well not exist. There are other considerations, my Lord. What is your present complement of soldiers here?"

"Two hundred and twenty men-at-arms, two hundred fifty bowsmen, and two hundred pikemen."

"Arnaut has twice as many," Johnston said. "Perhaps more."

"Think you so?"

"In deed he is no better than a common thief, but now he is a famous thief, for marching on Avignon, requiring the Pon-

tiff to dine with his men and then pay ten thousand livres to
leave the town intact."

"Sooth?" Lord Oliver said, looking troubled. "I have not
heard of this. Of course there are rumors that Arnaut *intends*
to march on Avignon, perhaps as soon as next month. And all
presume he will threaten the Pope. But he has not done so
yet." He frowned. "Has he?"

"You speak truth, my Lord," the Professor said promptly. "I
meant to say that the daring of his intended plans draws new
soldiers to his side every day. By now, he has a thousand in his
company. Perhaps two thousand."

Oliver snorted. "I am not afraid."

"I am sure you are not," Johnston said, "but this castle has a
shallow moat; a single drawbridge; a single gateway arch, no
deadfall, and a single portcullis. Your ramparts to the east are
low. You have space to store food and water for only a few
days. Your garrison is cramped in the small courtyards, and
your men not easily maneuverable."

Oliver said, "I tell you, my treasure is here, and I shall remain here with it."

"And my advice," Johnston said, "is to gather what you can
and depart. La Roque is built on a cliff, with sheer rock on
two sides. It has a deep moat on the third side, two gateway
doors, two portculli, two drawbridges. Even if invaders
manage to pass the outer gateway—"

*"I know the virtues of La Roque!"*

Johnston paused.

*"And I do not wish to hear your damnable instruction!"*

"As you will, Lord Oliver." And then Johnston said, "Ah."

"Ah? *Ah?*"

"My Lord," Johnston said, "I cannot counsel if you circumstance to me."

"Circumstance? I do not circumstance, Magister. I speak
plainly, holding nothing back."

"How many men have you garrisoned at La Roque?"

Oliver squirmed uncomfortably. "Three hundred."

"So. Your treasure is already at La Roque."

Lord Oliver squinted. He said nothing. He turned, walked

around Johnston, squinted again. Finally: "You are pressing me to go there by provoking my fears."

"I am not."

"You want me to move to La Roque because you know that castle has a weakness. You are the creature of Arnaut and you prepare the way for his assault."

"My Lord," Johnston said, "if La Roque is inferior, as you say, why have you placed your treasure there?"

Oliver snorted, again unhappy. "You are clever with words."

"My Lord, your own actions tell you which castle is superior."

"Very well. But Magister, if I go to La Roque, you go with me. And if another finds that secret entrance before you have told me of it, I will myself see that you die in a way that will make Edward's end"—he cackled at his pun—"appear a kindness."

"I take your meaning," Johnston said.

"Do you? Then see you take it to heart."

.

Chris Hughes stared out the window.

Sixty feet below him, the courtyard lay in shadow. Men and women in their finery drifted toward the lighted windows of the great hall. He heard the faint sounds of music. The festive scene made him feel even more morose, more isolated. The three of them were going to be killed—and there was nothing they could do about it.

They were locked in a small chamber, high in the central tower of the castle keep, overlooking the castle walls and the town beyond. This was a woman's room, with a spinning wheel and an altar off to one side, perfunctory signs of piety overwhelmed by the enormous bed with red plush coverings and fur trim in the center of the room. The door to the room was of solid oak, and fitted with a new lock. Sir Guy himself had locked the door, after placing one guard inside the room, sitting by the door, and two others outside.

They were taking no chances this time.

Marek sat on the bed, staring into space, lost in thought. Or perhaps he was listening; he had one hand cupped around his ear. Meanwhile, Kate paced restlessly, moving from one window to the next, inspecting the view from each. At the farthest window, she leaned way out, looking down, then walked to the window where Chris was standing and leaned out again.

"The view here is just the same," Chris said. Her restlessness annoyed him.

Then he saw she was reaching out to run her hand along the wall at the side of the window, feeling the stones and the mortar.

He stared at her, questioning.

"Maybe," she said, nodding. "Maybe."

Chris reached out and touched the wall. The masonry was nearly smooth, the wall curving and sheer. It was a straight drop to the courtyard below.

"Are you joking?" he said.

"No," she said. "I'm not."

He looked out again. In the courtyard, there were many others besides the courtiers. A group of squires talked and laughed as they cleaned the armor and groomed the horses of the knights. To the right, soldiers patrolled the parapet wall. Any of them could turn and look up if her movement caught their eye.

"You'll be seen."

"From this window, yes. Not from the other. Our only problem is him." She nodded toward the guard at the door. "Can you do anything to help?"

Sitting on the bed, Marek said, "I'll take care of it."

"What the hell is this?" Chris said, very annoyed. He spoke loudly. "You don't think I can do this myself?"

"No, I don't."

"Damn it, I'm sick of the way you treat me," Chris said. He was furious; looking around for something to fight with, he picked up the little stool by the spinning wheel and started toward Marek.

The guard saw it, said, *"Non, non, non"* quickly as he went toward Chris. He never saw Marek hit him from behind with a metal candlestick. The guard crumpled, and Marek caught him, eased him silently to the floor. Blood was pouring from the guard's head onto an Oriental carpet.

"Is he dead?" Chris said, staring at Marek.

"Who cares?" Marek said. "Just continue to talk quietly, so the ones outside hear our voices."

They looked over, but Kate had already gone out the window.

:

*It's just a free solo,* she told herself, as she clung to the tower wall, sixty feet in the air.

The wind pulled at her, rippling her clothes. She gripped the slight protrusions of the mortar with her fingertips. Sometimes the mortar crumbled away, and she had to grab, then grip again. But here and there, she found indentations in the mortar, large enough for her fingertips to fit in.

She'd flashed more difficult climbs. Any number of buildings at Yale were more difficult—although there, she'd always had chalk for her hands, and proper climbing shoes, and a safety rope. No safety here.

*It isn't far.*

She'd climbed out the west window because it was behind the guard, because it faced toward the town, and so she would be less likely to be seen from the courtyard below—and because it was the shortest distance to the next window, which stood at the end of the hallway that ran outside the chamber.

It isn't far, she told herself. Ten feet at most. Don't rush it. No hurry. Just one hand, then a foothold . . . another hand . . .

Almost there, she thought.

Almost there.

Then she touched the stone windowsill. She got her first firm handgrip. She pulled herself up one-handed, then peered cautiously down the corridor.

There were no guards.

The hallway was empty.

Using both hands now, Kate pulled up, flopped onto the

ledge, and slid over onto the floor. She was now standing in the hallway outside the locked door. Softly, she said, "I made it."

Marek said, "Guards?"

"No. But no key, either."

She inspected the door. It was thick, solid.

Marek said, "Hinges?"

"Yes. Outside." They were made of heavy wrought iron. She knew what he was asking her. "I can see the pins." If she could knock the pins out of the hinges, the door would be easy to break open. "But I need a hammer or something. There's nothing here I can use."

"Find something," Marek said softly.

She ran down the corridor.

.
.

"De Kere," Lord Oliver said as the knight with the scar came into the room. "The Magister counsels to remove to La Roque."

De Kere gave a judicious nod. "The risk would be grave, sire."

"And the risk to stay here?" Oliver said.

"If the Magister's advice is true and good, and without other intent, why did his assistants conceal their identity when first they came to your court? Such concealment is not the mark of honesty, my Lord. I would you be satisfied of their answer for this conduct, before I put faith in this new Magister and his advisements."

"Let us all be satisfied," Oliver said. "Bring the assistants to me now, and we shall ask them what you wish to know."

"My Lord." De Kere bowed, and left the room.

.
.

Kate came out of the stairwell and slipped into the crowd in the courtyard. She was thinking that she could use a carpenter's tool kit, or a blacksmith's hammer, or maybe some of the tools the farrier used to shoe horses. Over to the left, she saw the grooms and the horses, and she started to drift in that direction. In the excited throng, nobody paid her any attention. She slipped easily toward the east wall, and was beginning to consider how to distract the grooms, when directly ahead she saw a knight standing very still and staring at her.

Robert de Kere.

Their eyes met for a moment, and then she turned and ran. From behind her she heard de Kere shout for help, and the answering cries from soldiers all around. She pushed forward through the crowd, which was suddenly an impediment, hands clutching at her, plucking at her clothes. It was like a nightmare. To escape the crowd, she went through the nearest door, slamming it behind her.

She found herself in the kitchen.

The room was dreadfully hot, and more crowded than the courtyard. Huge iron cauldrons boiled on fires in the enormous fireplace. A dozen capons turned on a row of spits, the crank turned by a child. She paused, uncertain what to do, and then de Kere came through the door after her, snarled, *"You!"* and swung his sword.

She ducked, scrambled among the tables of food being prepared. The sword crashed down, sending platters flying. She scrambled, crouched low, beneath the tables. The cooks began to yell. She saw a giant model of the castle, made in some kind of pastry, and headed there. De Kere was right after her.

The cooks were shouting *"Non, Sir Robert, non!"* in a kind of chorus from all around the room, and some of the men were so distressed that they came forward to stop him.

De Kere swung again. She ducked, and the sword decapitated the castle battlements, raising a cloud of white powder. At this, the chefs gave a collective shriek of agony and fell on de Kere from all sides, shouting that this was Lord Oliver's favorite, that he had approved it, that Sir Robert must not do further damage. Robert rolled on the floor, swearing and trying to shake them off.

In the confusion, she ran back out the door again, into the afternoon light.

:

Off to the right she saw the curved wall of the chapel. The chapel was undergoing some restoration; there was a ladder going up the wall, and some perfunctory scaffolding on the roof, where tilers were making repairs.

She wanted to get away from the crowds, and the soldiers. She knew that on the far side of the chapel, a narrow passage ran between the chapel building and the outer wall of the castle tower. At least she would be out of the crowd if she went there. As she ran toward the passage, she heard de Kere behind her, shouting to the soldiers; he had gotten out of the kitchen. She ran hard, trying to gain some distance. She rounded the corner of the chapel. Looking back, she saw other soldiers running the other way around the chapel, intending to head her off at the far end of the passage.

Sir Robert barked more orders to the soldiers as he came around the corner after her—and then he stopped abruptly. The soldiers halted at his side, and everyone murmured in confusion.

They stared down a passage four feet wide between the castle and the chapel. The passage was empty. At the far end of the passage, other soldiers appeared, facing them.

The woman had disappeared.

∴

Kate was clinging ten feet up the chapel wall, the outline of her body concealed by the decorative border of the chapel window and thick vines of ivy. Even so, she was easily visible if anyone looked up. But the passage was dark, and no one did. She heard de Kere shout angrily, "Go to the other assistants, and dispatch them now!"

The soldiers hesitated. "But Sir Robert, they assist the Magister of Lord Oliver—"

"And Lord Oliver himself commands it. Kill them all!"

The soldiers ran off, into the castle.

De Kere swore. He was talking to a remaining soldier, but they were whispering, and her ear translator crackled and she couldn't make it out. In truth, she was surprised she had been able to hear as much as she had.

How had she been able to hear them? It seemed as if they were too far away to hear de Kere so clearly. And yet his voice was clear, almost amplified. Maybe the acoustics of the passage . . .

Glancing down, she saw that some soldiers hadn't left. They were just milling about. So she couldn't go back down. She decided to climb up onto the roof and wait until things were quieter. The roof of the chapel was still in sunlight: a plain peaked roof of tile, with small gaps where repairs were being made. The pitch was steep; she crouched at the gutter and said, "André."

A crackle. She thought she heard Marek's voice, but the static was bad.

"André, they're coming to kill you."

There was no answer, just more static.

"André?"

No answer.

Perhaps the walls around her were interfering with transmission; she might do better from the top of the roof. She began to climb the steep slope, easing around the tile repair sites. At each site, the mason had set up a small platform, with his mortar basin and stack of tiles. The chirp of birds made her pause. She saw there was actually a hole in the roof at these tiling sites, and—

A scraping sound made her look up. She saw a soldier come over the top of the roof. He paused, peering down at her.

Then a second soldier.

So that was why de Kere had been whispering: he'd seen her after all, on the wall, and had sent soldiers up the ladder on the opposite side.

She looked down and saw soldiers in the passage below. They were now staring up at her.

Now the first soldier swung his leg over the ridge of the roof and was starting to come down toward her.

There was only one thing she could do. The mason's hole was about two feet square. Through it she could see the bracing beneath the roof and, about ten feet below that, the stone arches of the chapel ceiling. There was a sort of wooden catwalk running over the arches.

Kate crawled through the hole, and dropped down to the ceiling below. She smelled the sour odor of dust and bird droppings. There were nests everywhere, along the flat walkways, in the corners and joists. She ducked as a few sparrows flew past her head, chittering. And suddenly, she was engulfed in a swirling tornado of shrieking birds and flying feathers. There were hundreds in here, she realized, and she had disturbed them. For a moment she could do nothing except put her arms over her face and stand quietly. The sounds lessened.

When she looked again, there were only a few flying birds. And the two soldiers were climbing down through holes in the roof to the ground below.

Quickly, she moved down the walkway to a far door, which probably led into the church. As she approached it, the door opened and a third soldier came through.

Three against one.

She backed away, moving along the walkway that went over the curves of the ceiling domes. But the other soldiers were moving toward her. They had taken their daggers out. She had no illusions about what they intended.

She backed away.

She remembered how she had hung beneath this ceiling, examining the many breaks and repairs that had been made over the centuries. Now she was standing above that same structure. The walkway clearly implied the curved arches themselves were weak. How weak? Would they support her weight? The men were moving steadily toward her.

She stepped out onto one of the domes gingerly, testing it. She put her full weight on it.

It held.

The soldiers were coming after her, but moving slowly. The birds suddenly were active again, shrieking and rising like a cloud. The soldiers covered their faces. The sparrows flew so close that their wings beat at her face. She moved backward again, her feet crunching on the thick layer of accumulated droppings.

She was now standing on a series of domes and pits, with

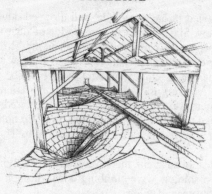

thicker stone ribs where the arches met in the center. She moved toward the ribs because she knew they would be structurally stronger, and walking on them, she made her way toward the far end of the chapel, where she saw a little door. This would probably take her to the interior of the church, perhaps coming down behind an altar.

One of the soldiers ran along the walkway and then stepped out on the bulge of a curving arch. He moved to block her progress. He held his knife in front of him.

Crouching, she gave a little feint, but the soldier simply stood his ground. A second soldier ran up to stand beside him. The third soldier was behind her. He also stepped out onto the dome.

She moved to her right, but the two men came directly toward her. The third was closing in behind.

The two men were just a few yards away from her when she heard a loud crack like a gunshot, and she looked down to see a jagged line open in the mortar between the stones. The soldiers scrambled backward, but the crack was already widening, sending branches out like a tree. The cracks went between their legs; they stared down in horror. Then the stones fell away beneath their feet, and they fell from view, screaming in terror.

She glanced back at the third man, who tripped and fell as he sprinted for the walkway. He landed with a *crack*, and Kate saw his frightened face as he lay there, feeling the stones beneath his body slowly give way, one after another. And then he disappeared, with a long cry of fear.

And suddenly, she was alone.

She was standing on the ceiling, with the birds shrieking around her. Too frightened to move, she just stood there, trying to slow her breathing. But she was okay.

She was okay.

Everything was okay.

She heard a single *crack*.

Then nothing. She waited.

Another *crack*. And this one she felt, directly beneath her feet. The stones were moving. Looking down, she saw the mortar cracking in several directions, streaking away from her. She quickly stepped to her left, heading for the safety of the ribline, but it was too late.

One stone fell, and her foot crashed through the hole. She fell to the level of her waist, then threw her body flat, flinging her hands wide, spreading the weight. She lay there for several seconds, gasping. She thought, *I told him it was bad construction.*

She waited, trying to figure out how to get out of this hole. She tried to wriggle her body—

*Crack.*

Directly in front of her, the mortar opened in a line, and several stones broke loose. And then she felt more give way beneath her; she knew in a moment of horrible certainty that she, too, was going to fall through.

:

In the plush red room in the tower, Chris was not sure what he had heard through his earpiece. It sounded like Kate had said, "They're coming to kill you." And then something else, which he didn't catch, before the static became constant.

Marek had opened the wooden chest near the little altar, and he rummaged through it hurriedly. "Come on, help!"

"What?" Chris said.

"Oliver keeps his mistress in this room," Marek said. "I'll bet he keeps a weapon here, too."

Chris went to a second chest, at the foot of the bed, and threw it open. This chest seemed to be filled with linens, dresses, silk garments. He flung them in the air as he searched; they fluttered to the floor around him.

He found no weapon.

Nothing.

He looked at Marek. He was standing amid a pile of dresses, shaking his head.

No weapon.

In the hallway outside, Chris heard running soldiers, coming toward them. And through the door, he heard the metallic *zing* as they drew their swords from their scabbards.

# 29:10:24

"I can offer you Coke, Diet Coke, Fanta or Sprite," Gordon said. They were standing by a dispensing machine in the hallway of the ITC labs.

"I'll take a Coke," Stern said.

The can clunked to the bottom of the machine. Stern took it, pulled the tab. Gordon got a Sprite. "It's important to stay hydrated in the desert," he said. "We have humidifiers in the building, but they don't work well enough."

They continued on down the corridor to the next doorway.

"I thought you might want to see this," Gordon said, taking Stern into another lab. "If only as a matter of historical interest. This was the lab where we first demonstrated the technology." He flicked on the lights.

The lab was a large and untidy room. The floor was

covered with gray antistatic tiles; the ceiling above was open, showing shielded lights and metal trays holding thick cables that ran down like umbilicus lines to computers on tables. On one table, there were two tiny cagelike devices, each about a foot high. They were about four feet apart on the table, and connected by a cable.

"This is Alice," Gordon said proudly, pointing to the first cage. "And this is Bob."

Stern knew that by long-standing convention, quantum transmission devices were labeled "Alice" and "Bob," or "A" and "B." He looked at the little cages. One held a child's plastic doll, a girl in a pioneer-style gingham dress.

"The very first transmission occurred here," Gordon said. "We successfully moved that doll between the cages. That was four years ago."

Stern picked up the doll. It was just a cheap figurine; he saw plastic seams running down the side of the face and body. The eyes closed and opened as he tipped it in his hand.

"You see," Gordon said, "our original intention was to perfect three-dimensional object transmission. Three-dimensional faxing. You may know there has been a lot of interest in that."

Stern nodded; he'd heard about the research work.

"Stanford had the earliest project," Gordon said. "And there was a lot of work in Silicon Valley. The idea was that in the last twenty years, all document transmission has become electronic—either fax or e-mail. You don't need to send paper physically anymore; you just send electronic signals. Many people felt that sooner or later, all objects would be sent the same way. You wouldn't have to ship furniture, for example, you could just transmit it between stations. That kind of thing."

"If you could do it," Stern said.

"Yes. And so long as we were working with simple objects, we could. We were encouraged. But, of course, it isn't sufficient to transmit between two stations connected by cables. We needed to transmit at a distance, over airwaves, so to speak. So we tried that. Here."

He crossed the room, and came to two more cages, some-what larger and more elaborate. They were beginning to re-semble the cages Stern had seen in the cave. These cages had no connecting cables between them.

"Alice and Bob, part two," Gordon said. "Or as we called them, Allie and Bobbie. This was our testbed for remote transmission."

"And?"

"Didn't work," Gordon said. "We transmitted from Allie but never got to Bob. Ever."

Stern nodded slowly. "Because the object from Allie went to another universe."

"Yes. Of course, we didn't know that right away," Gordon said. "I mean, that was the theoretical explanation, but who would suspect it was actually happening? It took us a hell of a long time to work it out. Finally, we built a homing machine —one that would go out, and come back automatically. The team called it 'Allie-Allie-in-come-free.' It's over here."

Another cage, still larger, perhaps three feet high, and rec-ognizably like the cages that were now used. The same three bars, the same laser arrangement.

"And?" Stern said.

"We verified that the object went out and back," Gordon said. "So we sent more elaborate objects. Pretty soon we suc-ceeded in sending a camera, and got back a picture."

"Yes?"

"It was a picture of the desert. Actually, this exact site. But before any buildings were here."

Stern nodded. "And you could date it?"

"Not immediately," Gordon said. "We kept sending the camera out, again and again, but all we got was the desert. Sometimes in rain, sometimes in snow, but always desert. Clearly, we were going out to different times—but what times? Dating the image was quite tricky. I mean, how would you use a camera to date an image of a landscape like that?"

Stern frowned. He saw the problem. Most old photographs were dated from the human artifacts in the image—a build-ing, or a car, or clothing, or ruins. But an uninhabited desert in New Mexico would hardly change appearance over thousands, even hundreds of thousands, of years.

Gordon smiled. "We turned the camera vertically, used a fish-eye lens, and shot the sky at night."

"Ah."

"Of course it doesn't always work—it has to be night, and the sky has to be clear of clouds—but if you have enough planets in your image, you can identify the sky quite exactly. To the year, the day and the hour. And that's how we began to develop our navigation technology."

"So the whole project changed. . . ."

"Yes. We knew what we had, of course. We weren't doing object transmission anymore—there wasn't any point in trying. We were doing transportation between universes."

"And when did you start to send people?"

"Not for some time."

Gordon led him around a wall of electronic equipment, into another part of the lab. And there, Stern saw huge hanging plastic sheets filled with water, like water beds turned on end. And in the center, a full-size machine cage, not as refined as the ones he had seen in the transit room, but clearly the same technology.

"This was our first real machine," Gordon said proudly.

"Wait a minute," Stern said. "Does this thing work?"

"Yes, of course."

"Does it work now?"

"It hasn't been used for some time," Gordon said. "But I imagine it does. Why?"

"So if I wanted to go back and help them," Stern said, "then I could—in this machine. Is that right?"

"Yes," Gordon said, nodding slowly. "You could go back in this machine, but—"

"Look, I think they're in trouble back there—or worse."

"Probably. Yes."

"And you're telling me we have a machine that works," Stern said, "right now."

Gordon sighed. "I'm afraid it's a little more complicated than that, David."

# 29:10:00

Kate fell in slow motion as the ceiling stones gave way. As she descended, her fingers closed on the ragged mortared edge, and with the practice of many years, she gripped it, and it held. She hung by one hand, looking down as the falling stones tumbled in a cloud of dust onto the floor of the chapel. She didn't see what had happened to the soldiers.

She raised her other hand, grabbing the stone edge. The other stones would break away any minute, she knew. The whole ceiling was crumbling. Structurally, the greatest strength was near the reinforced line of the groin, where the arches met. There, or at the side wall of the chapel, which was vertical stone.

She decided to try and get to the side wall.

The stone broke away; she dangled from her left hand. She crossed one hand over the other, reaching as far as she could manage, trying again to spread the weight of her body.

The stone in her left hand broke loose, falling to the floor. Again she swung in the air, and found another handhold. She was now only three feet from the side wall, and the stone was noticeably thicker as it swelled to meet the wall. The edge she was holding felt more stable.

She heard soldiers below, shouting and running into the chapel. It would not be long before they were shooting arrows at her.

She tried to swing her left leg up. The more she could distribute her weight, the better off she would be. She got the leg up; the ceiling held. Twisting her torso, she pulled her body up onto the shelf, then brought her second leg up. The first of the arrows whistled past her; others thunked against the stone, raising little white puffs. She was lying flat on top of the roof.

But she could not stay here. She rolled away from the edge, toward the groin line. As she did, more stones broke away and fell.

The soldiers stopped shouting. Maybe the falling stones had hit one of them, she thought. But no: she heard them running hastily out of the church. She heard men outside, shouting, and horses whinnying.

What was going on?

.
:
.

Inside the tower room, Chris heard the scrape of the key in the lock. Then the soldiers outside paused and shouted through the door—calling to the guard inside the room.

Meanwhile, Marek was searching like a madman. He was on his knees, looking under the bed. "Got it!" he cried. He scrambled to his feet, holding a broadsword and a long dagger. He tossed the dagger to Chris.

Outside, the soldiers were again shouting to the guard inside. Marek moved toward the door and gestured for Chris to step to the other side.

Chris pressed back flat against the wall by the door. He heard the voices of the men outside—many voices. His heart began to pound. He had been shocked by the way Marek killed the guard.

*They're coming to kill you.*

He heard the words repeated over and over in his head, with a sense of unreality. It didn't seem possible that armed men were coming to kill him.

In the comfort of the library, he had read accounts of past violent acts, murder and slaughter. He had read descriptions of streets slippery with blood, soldiers soaked in red from head to foot, women and children eviscerated despite their piteous pleas. But somehow, Chris had always assumed these stories were exaggerated, overstated. Within the university, it was the fashion to interpret documents ironically, to talk about the naïveté of narrative, the context of text, the privileging of power. . . . Such theoretical posturing turned history into a clever intellectual game. Chris was good at the game, but playing it, he had somehow lost track of a more straightforward reality—that the old texts recounted horrific stories and violent episodes that were all too often true. He had lost track of the fact that he was reading history.

Until now, when it was forcibly brought to his attention.

The key turned in the lock.

On the other side of the door, Marek's face was fixed in a snarl, his lips drawn back, showing teeth clenched. He was like an animal, Chris thought. Marek's body was taut as he gripped his sword, ready to swing. Ready to kill.

The door pushed open, momentarily blocking Chris's view. But he saw Marek swing high, and he heard a scream, and a huge gush of blood splashed onto the floor, and a body fell soon after.

The door banged against his body, stopping its full swing and pinning Chris behind it. On the other side a man slammed against it, then gasped as a sword splintered wood. Chris tried to get out from behind the door but another body fell, blocking his way.

He stepped over the body, and the door thunked flat against the wall as Marek swung at another attacker, and a third soldier staggered away with the impact and fell to the floor at Chris's feet. The soldier's torso was drenched in blood; blood gurgled out of his chest like a flowing spring. Chris bent down to take the sword still in the man's hand. As he pulled at the sword, the man gripped it tightly, grimacing at Chris. Abruptly, the soldier weakened and released the sword, so that Chris staggered back against the wall.

The man continued to stare at him from the floor. His face contorted in a grimace of fury—and then it froze.

Jesus, he thought, *he's dead*.

Suddenly, to his right, another soldier stepped into the room, his back to Chris as he fought Marek. Their swords clanged; they fought fiercely; but the man had not noticed Chris, and Chris raised his sword, which felt very heavy and unwieldy. He wondered if he could swing it, if he could actually kill the man whose back was turned to him. He lifted the sword, cocked his arm as if he were batting—*batting!*—and prepared to swing, when Marek cut the man's arm off at the shoulder.

The dismembered arm shot across the floor and thumped to rest against the wall, beneath the window. The man looked astonished for the instant before Marek cut his head off in a single swing, and the head tumbled through the air, banged against the door next to Chris, and fell onto his toes, face downward.

Hastily, he jerked his feet away. The head rolled, so the face was turned upward, and Chris saw the eyes blink and the mouth move, as if forming words. He backed away.

Chris looked away to the torso on the floor, still pumping blood from the stump of the neck. The blood flowed freely over the stone floor—gallons of blood, it seemed like. He looked at Marek, now sitting on the bed, gasping for breath, his face and doublet splattered with blood.

Marek looked up at him. "You all right?" he said.

Chris couldn't answer.

He couldn't say anything at all.

And then the bell in the village church began to ring.

:

Through the window, Chris saw flames licking up from two farmhouses at the far edge of the town, near the circling town wall. Men were running in the streets toward it.

"There's a fire," Chris said.

"I doubt it," Marek said, still sitting by the bed.

"No, there is," Chris said. "Look."

In the town, horsemen were galloping through the streets; they were dressed as merchants or traders, but they rode like fighters.

"This is a typical diversion," Marek said, "to start an attack."

"An attack?"

"The Archpriest is attacking Castelgard."

"So soon?"

"This is just an advance party, perhaps a hundred soldiers or so. They'll try to create confusion, disruption. The main body is probably still on the other side of the river. But the attack has begun."

Apparently others thought so, too. In the courtyard below, courtiers were streaming out of the great hall and hurrying toward the drawbridge, leaving the castle, the party abruptly ended. A company of armored knights galloped out, scattering the courtiers, thundered across the drawbridge, and raced down through the streets of the town.

Kate stuck her head in the door, panting. "Guys? Let's go. We have to find the Professor before it's too late."

# 28:57:32

There was pandemonium in the great hall. The musicians fled, the guests rushed out the doors, dogs barked and plates of food clattered to the floor. Knights were running to join the battle, shouting orders to their squires. From the high table, Lord Oliver came quickly down, grabbed the Professor by the arm, and said to Sir Guy, "We go to La Roque. See to the Lady Claire. And bring the assistants!"

Robert de Kere burst breathlessly into the room. "My Lord, the assistants are dead! Killed while trying to escape!"

"Escape? They tried to escape? Even if that risked their master's life? Come with me, Magister," Lord Oliver said darkly. Oliver led him to a side door that opened directly to the courtyard.

:

Kate scrambled down the circular staircase, with Marek and Chris close behind. At the second floor, they had to slow for a group descending ahead of them. Around the curve, Kate glimpsed ladies in waiting, and the red robes of an elderly, shuffling man. Behind her, Chris yelled, "What's the problem?" and Kate held up a warning hand. It was another minute before they burst through into the courtyard.

It was a chaotic scene. Knights on horseback whipped the throng of panicked revelers to force them aside. She heard the cries of the crowd, the whinny of horses, the shouts of soldiers on the battlements above. "This way," Kate said, and she led Marek and Chris forward, staying close to the castle wall, going around the chapel, then laterally into the outer courtyard, which they could see was equally crowded.

They saw Oliver on horseback, the Professor at his side and a company of armored knights. Oliver shouted something, and all moved forward toward the drawbridge.

Kate left Marek and Chris to chase them alone, and she just managed to catch sight of them at the end of the drawbridge. Oliver turned to the left, riding away from the town. Guards opened a door in the east wall, and he and his company rode through into the afternoon sunlight. The door was shut hastily behind them.

Marek caught up with her. "Where?" he said.

She pointed to the gate. Thirty knights guarded it. More stood on the wall above.

"We'll never get out that way," he said. Just behind them, a cluster of soldiers threw off brown tunics, revealing green-and-black surcoats; they began fighting their way into the castle. The drawbridge chains began to clank. "Come on."

They ran down the drawbridge, hearing the wood creak, feeling it begin to rise under their feet. The drawbridge was three feet in the air when they reached the far end and jumped, landing on the ground of the open field.

"Now what?" Chris said, picking himself up. He still carried his bloody sword in his hand.

"This way," Marek said, and he ran straight into the center of the town.

:

They headed toward the church, then away from the narrow main street, where intense fighting had already begun: Oliver's soldiers in maroon and gray, and Arnaut's in green and black. Marek led them to the left through the market, now deserted, the wares packed up and the merchants gone. They had to step quickly aside as a company of Arnaut's knights on horseback galloped past, heading toward the castle. One of them swung at Marek with his broadsword and shouted something as he passed. Marek watched them go, then went on.

Chris was looking for signs of murdered women and eviscerated babies, and he did not know whether to be disappointed or relieved that he saw none. In fact, he saw no women or children at all. "They've all run away or gone into hiding," Marek said. "There's been war for a long time here. People know what to do."

"Which way?" Kate said. She was in the front.

"Left, toward the main gate."

They turned left, going down a narrower street, and suddenly heard a shout behind them. They looked back, to see running soldiers coming toward them. Chris couldn't tell if the soldiers were chasing them or just running. But there was no point in waiting to find out.

Marek broke into a run; they all ran now, and after a while Chris glanced back to see the soldiers falling behind, and he felt a moment of odd pride; they were putting distance between them.

But Marek was taking no chances. Abruptly, he turned into a side street which had a strong and unpleasant odor. The shops here were all closed up, but narrow alleyways ran between them. Marek ran down one, which brought them to a fenced courtyard behind a shop. Within the courtyard stood huge wooden vats, and wooden racks beneath a shed. Here the stench was almost overpowering: a mixture of rotting flesh and feces.

It was a tannery.

"Quickly," Marek said, and they climbed over the fence, crouched down behind the reeking vats.

"Oof!" Kate said, holding her nose. "What is that smell?"

"They soak the skins in chicken shit," Chris whispered. "The nitrogen in the feces softens the leather."

"Great," she said.

"Dog shit, too."

"Great."

Chris looked back and saw more vats, and hides hanging on the racks. Here and there, stinking piles of cheesy yellow material lay heaped on the ground—fat scraped from the inside of the skins.

Kate said, "My eyes burn."

Chris pointed to the white crust on the vats around them. These were lime vats, a harsh alkali solution that removed all the hair and remaining flesh after the skins were scraped. And it was the lime fumes that burned their eyes.

Then his attention was drawn to the alleyway, where he heard running feet and the clatter of armor. Through the fence he saw Robert de Kere with seven soldiers. The soldiers were looking in every direction as they ran—searching for them.

Why? Chris wondered, peering around the vat. Why were they still being pursued? What was so important about them that de Kere would ignore an enemy attack and try instead to kill them?

Apparently the searchers liked the smell in the alley no better than Chris did, because soon de Kere barked an order and they all ran back up the alley, toward the street.

"What was that about?" Chris whispered finally.

Marek just shook his head.

And then they heard men shouting, and again they heard the soldiers running back down the street. Chris frowned. How could they have overheard? He looked at Marek, who seemed troubled, too. From outside the courtyard, they heard de Kere shout: *Ici! Ici!* Probably, de Kere had left a man behind. That must be it, Chris thought. Because he hadn't whispered loudly enough to be heard. Marek started forward, then hesitated. Already de Kere and his men were climbing over the fence—eight men altogether; they could not fight them all.

"André," Chris said, pointing to the vat. "It's lye."

Marek grinned. "Then let's do it," he said, and he leaned against the vat.

They all put their shoulders against the wood and, with effort, managed to push the vat over. Frothing alkali solution sloshed onto the ground and flowed toward the soldiers. The odor was acrid. The soldiers instantly recognized what it was—any contact with that liquid would burn flesh—and they scrambled back up the fence, getting their feet off the ground. The fence posts began to sizzle and hiss when the lye touched them. The fence wobbled with the weight of all the men; they shouted and scrambled back into the alley.

"Now," Marek said. He led them deeper into the tanning yard, up over a shed, and then out into another alley.

:

It was now late afternoon, and the light was beginning to fade; ahead they saw the burning farmhouses, which cast hard flickering shadows on the ground. Earlier, there had been attempts to put out the fires, but they were now abandoned; the thatch burned freely, crackling as burning strands rose into the air.

They were following a narrow path that ran among pigsties. The pigs snorted and squealed, distressed by the fires that burned nearby.

Marek skirted the fires, heading toward the south gate, where they had first come in. But even from a distance, they could see that the gate was the scene of heavy fighting; the entrance was nearly blocked by the bodies of dead horses; Arnaut's soldiers had to scramble over the corpses to reach the defenders inside, who fought bitterly with axes and swords.

Marek turned away, doubling back through the farm area.

"Where are we going?" Chris said.

"Not sure," Marek said. He was looking up at the curtain wall around the town. Soldiers ran along it, heading toward the south gate to join in the fight. "I want to get up on that wall."

"Up on the wall?"

"There." He pointed to a narrow, dark opening in the wall, with steps going up. They emerged on top of the town wall. From their high vantage point, they could see that more of the town was being engulfed in flames; fires were closer to the shops. Soon all Castelgard would be burning. Marek looked over the wall at the fields beyond. The ground was twenty feet below. There were some bushes about five feet high, which looked soft enough to break their impact. But it was getting hard to see.

"Stay loose," he said. "Keep your body relaxed."

"Loose?" Chris said.

But already Kate had swung her body over and was hanging from the wall. She released her grip, and fell the rest of the way, landing on her feet like a cat. She looked up at them and beckoned.

"It's pretty far down," Chris said. "I don't want to break a leg. . . ."

From the right, they heard shouts. Three soldiers ran along the wall, their swords raised.

"Then don't," Marek said, and jumped. Chris jumped after him in the twilight, landed on the ground, grunting and rolling. He got slowly to his feet. Nothing broken.

He was feeling relieved and rather pleased with himself, when the first of the arrows whined past his ear and thunked into the ground between his feet. Soldiers were shooting at them from the wall above. Marek grabbed his arm and ran to dense undergrowth ten yards away. They dropped down and waited.

Almost immediately, more arrows whistled overhead, but this time they came from outside the castle walls. In the growing darkness, Chris could barely make out soldiers in green-and-black surcoats on the hill below.

"Those're Arnaut's men!" Chris said. "Why are they shooting at *us*?"

Marek didn't answer; he was crawling away, his belly flat

to the ground. Kate crawled after him. An arrow hissed past Chris, so close that the shaft tore his doublet at the shoulder, and he felt a brief streak of pain.

He threw himself flat on the ground and followed them.

# 28:12:39

"There's good news and bad news," Diane Kramer said, walking into Doniger's office just before nine in the morning. Doniger was at his computer, pecking at the keyboard with one hand while he held a can of Coke in the other.

"Give me the bad news," Doniger said.

"Our injured people were taken to University Hospital. When they got there last night, guess who was on duty? The same doctor who treated Traub in Gallup. A woman named Tsosie."

"The same doctor works both hospitals?"

"Yes. She's mostly at UH, but she does two days a week at Gallup."

"Shit," Doniger said. "Is that legal?"

"Sure. Anyway, Dr. Tsosie went over our techs with a fine-tooth comb. She even put three of them through an MRI. She reserved the scanner specially, as soon as she heard it was an accident involving ITC."

"An MRI?" Doniger frowned. "That means she must have known that Traub was split."

"Yes," Kramer said. "Because apparently they put Traub through an MRI. So she was definitely looking for something. Physical defects. Body misalignments."

"Shit," Doniger said.

"She also made a big deal about her quest, getting everybody at the hospital huffy and paranoid, and she called that cop Wauneka in Gallup. It seems they're friends."

Doniger groaned. "I need this," he said, "like I need another asshole."

"Now you want the good news?"

"I'm ready."

"Wauneka calls the Albuquerque Police. The chief goes down to the hospital himself. Couple of reporters. Everybody sitting around waiting for the big news. They're expecting radioactive. They're expecting glow in the dark. Instead—big embarrassment. All the injuries are pretty minor. Mostly, it's flying glass. Even the shrapnel wounds are superficial; the metal's just embedded in the skin layer."

"Water shields must have slowed the fragments down," Doniger said.

"I think so, yes. But people are pretty disappointed. And then the final event—the MRI—the coup de grâce—is a bust three times running. None of our people has any transcription errors. Because, of course, they're just techs. Albuquerque chief is pissed. Hospital administrator is pissed. Reporters leave to cover a burning apartment building. Meanwhile some guy with kidney stones almost dies because they can't do an MRI, because Dr. Tsosie's tied up the machine. Suddenly, she's worried about her job. Wauneka's disgraced. They both run for cover."

"Perfect," Doniger said, pounding the table. He grinned. "Those dipshits deserve it."

"And to top it all off," Kramer said triumphantly, "the French reporter, Louise Delvert, has agreed to come tour our facility."

"Finally! When?"

"Next week. We'll give her the usual bullshit tour."

"This is starting to be an ultragood day," Doniger said. "You know, we might actually get this thing back in the bottle. Is that it?"

"The media people are coming at noon."

"That belongs under bad news," Doniger said.

"And Stern has found the old prototype machine. He wants

to go back. Gordon said absolutely not, but Stern wants you to confirm that he can't go."

Doniger paused. "I say let him go."

"Bob. . . ."

"Why shouldn't he go?" Doniger said.

"Because it's unsafe as hell. That machine has minimal shielding. It hasn't been used in years, and it's got a history of causing big transcription errors on the people who did use it. He might not even come back at all."

"I know that." Doniger waved his hand. "None of that's core."

"What's core?" she said, confused.

"Baretto."

"Baretto?"

"Do I hear an echo? Diane, *think*, for Christ's sake."

Kramer frowned, shook her head.

"Put it together. Baretto died in the first minute or two of the trip back. Isn't that right? Someone shot him full of arrows, right at the beginning of the trip."

"Yes. . . ."

"The first few minutes," Doniger said, "is the time when everybody is still standing around the machines, together, as a group. Right? So what reason do we have to think that Baretto got killed but nobody else?"

Kramer said nothing.

"What's reasonable is that whoever killed Baretto probably killed them all. Killed the whole bunch."

"Okay. . . ."

"That means they probably aren't coming back. The Professor isn't coming back. The whole group is gone. Now, it's unfortunate, but we can handle a group of missing people: a tragic lab accident where all the bodies were incinerated, or a plane crash, nobody would really be the wiser. . . ."

There was a pause.

"Except there's Stern," Kramer said. "He knows the whole story."

"That's right."

"So you want to send him back, too. Get rid of him as well. Clean sweep."

"Not at all," Doniger said promptly. "Hey, I'm opposed to it. But the guy's volunteering. He wants to help his friends. It'd be wrong for me to stand in the way."

"Bob," she said, "there are times when you are a real asshole."

Doniger suddenly started to laugh. He had a high-pitched, whooping, hysterical laugh, like a little kid. It was the way a lot of the scientists laughed, but it always reminded Kramer of a hyena.

"If you allow Stern to go back, I quit."

This made Doniger laugh even harder. Sitting in his chair, he threw back his head. It made her angry.

"I mean it, Bob."

He finally stopped giggling, wiped the tears from his eyes. "Diane, come on," he said. "I'm *kidding*. Of course Stern can't go back. Where's your sense of humor?"

Kramer turned to go. "I'll tell Stern that he can't go back," she said. "But you weren't kidding."

Doniger started laughing all over again. Hyena giggles filled the room. Kramer slammed the door angrily as she left.


# 27:27:22


For the last forty minutes, they had been scrambling up through the forest northeast of Castelgard. At last, they came to the top of the hill, the highest point in the area, and they could pause to catch their breath and look down.

"Oh my God," Kate said, staring.

They looked down on the river, and the monastery on the

opposite side. But their attention was drawn to the forbidding castle high above the monastery: the fortress of La Roque. It was enormous! In the deepening blue of evening, the castle glowed with light from a hundred windows and from torches along the battlements. But despite the glowing lights, the fortress was ominous. The outer walls were black above the still waters of the moat. Inside was another complete set of walls, with many round towers, and at the center of the complex, the actual castle, with its own great hall, and a dark rectangular tower, rising more than a hundred feet into the air.

Marek said to Kate, "Does it look like modern La Roque?"

"Not at all," she said, shaking her head. "This thing is gigantic. The modern castle has only one outer wall. This one has two: an additional ring wall that is no longer there."

"So far as I know," Marek said, "nobody ever captured it by force."

"You can see why," Chris said. "Look how it's sited."

On the east and south side, the fortress was built atop a limestone cliff, a sheer drop of five hundred feet to the Dordogne below. On the west, where the cliff was less vertical, the stone houses of the town climbed up toward the castle, but anyone following the road through the town would end up facing a broad moat and several drawbridges. On the north, the land sloped more gently away, but all the trees on the north had been cut down, leaving an exposed plain without cover—a suicidal approach for any army.

Marek pointed. "Look there," he said.

⋮

In the twilight, a party of soldiers approached the castle on a dirt road from the west. Two knights in the lead held torches, and by that light they could just barely discern Sir Oliver, Sir Guy, the Professor, and the rest of Oliver's knights bringing up the rear, in two columns. The figures were so far away that they really recognized them by body shape and posture. But Chris, at least, had no doubt what he was seeing.

He sighed as he watched the riders cross a drawbridge over a moat and pass through a large gatehouse with half-round twin towers—a so-called double-D gate, because the towers looked like twin D's when seen from above. Soldiers atop the towers watched the riders as they passed through.

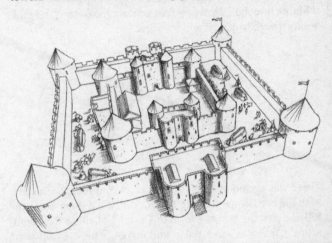

Beyond the gatehouse, the riders entered another enclosed courtyard. Here, many long wooden buildings had been erected. "That's where the troops are garrisoned," Kate said.

The party rode across this inner courtyard, crossed a second moat over a second drawbridge, passing through a second gatehouse with even larger twin towers: thirty feet high, and glowing with light from dozens of arrow slits.

Only then did they dismount, in the innermost court of the castle. The Professor was led by Oliver toward the great hall; they disappeared inside.

:

Kate said, "The Professor said that if we were separated, we should go to the monastery and find Brother Marcel, who has the key. I assume he meant the key to the secret passage."

Marek nodded. "And that's what we're going to do. It'll be dark soon. Then we can go."

Chris looked down the hill. In the gloom, he could see

small bands of soldiers in the fields, all the way down to the river's edge. They would have to make their way past all those soldiers. "You want to go to the monastery tonight?"

Marek nodded. "However dangerous it looks now," he said, "tomorrow morning, it will be worse."

# 26:12:01

There was no moon. The sky was black and filled with stars, with the occasional drifting cloud. Marek led them down the hill and past the burning town of Castelgard, into a dark landscape. Chris was surprised to find that once his eyes adjusted, he could actually see quite well by starlight. Probably because there was no air pollution, he thought. He remembered reading that in earlier centuries, people could see the planet Venus during the day as we can now see the moon. Of course, that had been impossible for hundreds of years.

He was also surprised by the utter silence of the night. The loudest sound they heard was their feet moving through the grass and past the scrubby bushes.

"We'll go to the path," Marek whispered. "Then down to the river."

Their progress was slow. Frequently, Marek paused, crouching down to listen for two or three minutes before moving on. Almost an hour passed before they came within sight of the dirt path that ran from the town to the river. It was a pale streak against the darker grass and foliage that surrounded it.

Here Marek paused. The silence around them was complete. He heard only the faint sound of the wind. Chris felt impatient to get started. After a full minute of waiting, he started to get up.

Marek pushed him down.

He held his finger to his lips.

Chris listened. It was more than wind, he realized. There was also the sound of men whispering. He strained to hear. There was a quiet cough, somewhere ahead. Then another cough, closer, on their side of the road.

Marek pointed, left and right. Chris saw a faint silver glint—armor in starlight—among the bushes opposite the path.

And he heard rustling closer by.

It was an ambush, soldiers waiting on both sides of the path.

Marek pointed back the way they had come. Quietly, they moved away from the path.

:

"Where now?" Chris whispered.

"We'll stay away from the path. Go east to the river. That way." Marek pointed, and they set out.

Chris felt on edge now, straining to hear the slightest sound. Their own footsteps were so loud, they masked any other sound. He understood now why Marek had stopped so often. It was the only way to be sure.

They went back two hundred yards from the path, then headed down to the river, moving between the fields of cleared land. Even though it was nearly black, Chris felt exposed. The fields were walled in low stone, so they had a slight cover. But he was still uneasy, and he gave a sigh of relief when they moved back into uncleared shrub land, darker in the night.

:

This silent, black world was entirely alien to him, yet he quickly adjusted to it. Danger lay in the tiniest movements, in sounds that were almost inaudible. Chris moved in a crouch, tense, testing each footstep before applying full weight, his head constantly turning left and right, left and right.

He felt like an animal, and he thought of the way Marek had bared his teeth before the attack in the room, like some kind of ape. He looked over at Kate and saw that she, too, was crouched and tense as she moved forward.

For some reason, he found himself thinking of the seminar room on the second floor of the Peabody, back at Yale, with the cream-colored walls and the polished dark-wood trim, and of the arguments among the graduate students sitting around the long table: whether processual archaeology was primarily historical or primarily archaeological, whether formalist criteria outweighed objectivist criteria, whether derivationist doctrine concealed normative commitment.

It was no wonder they argued. The issues were pure abstractions, consisting of nothing but thin air—and hot air. Their empty debates could never be resolved; the questions could never be answered. Yet there had been so much intensity, so much passion in those debates. Where had it come from? Who cared? He couldn't quite remember now why it had been so important.

The academic world seemed to be receding into the distance, vague and gray in memory, as he made his way down the dark hillside toward the river. Yet however frightened he was on this night, however tense and at risk of his life, it was entirely real in some way that was reassuring, even exhilarating, and—

He heard a twig snap, and he froze.

Marek and Kate froze, too.

They heard soft rustling in the brush to the left, and a low snort. They stayed motionless. Marek gripped his sword.

And the small dark shape of a wild pig snuffled past them.

"Should have killed it," Marek whispered. "I'm hungry."

They started to continue forward, but then Chris realized that they were not the ones who had frightened the pig. Because now they heard, unmistakably, the sound of many running feet. Rustling, crashing in the underbrush. Coming toward them.

:

Marek frowned.

He could see enough in the darkness to catch glimpses of metal armor now and again. There must be seven or eight soldiers, moving hastily east, then dropping down, hiding in the brush again, becoming silent.

What the hell was going on?

These soldiers had been back at the dirt path, waiting for them. Now the soldiers had moved east, and were waiting for them again.

How?

He looked at Kate, crouched beside him, but she just looked frightened.

Chris, also crouching, tapped Marek on the shoulder. Chris shook his head, then pointed deliberately to his own ear.

Marek nodded, listened. At first he heard nothing but the wind. Puzzled, he looked back at Chris, who made a distinct tapping motion against the side of his head, by his ear.

He was saying, Turn on your earpiece.

Marek tapped his ear.

After a brief crackle as the sound came on, he heard nothing. He shrugged at Chris, who held up his flat palms: Wait. Marek waited. Only after a few moments of quiet listening did he become aware of the soft, regular sound of a person breathing.

He looked at Kate and held his finger to his lips. She nodded. He looked at Chris. He nodded, too. They both understood. Make no noise at all.

Again, Marek listened intently. He still heard the sound of quiet breathing in his earpiece.

But it wasn't coming from any of them.

Someone else.

∴

Chris whispered, "André. This is too dangerous. Let's not cross the river tonight."

"Right," Marek whispered. "We'll go back to Castelgard and hide out for the night outside the walls."

"Okay. Good."

"Let's go."

In the darkness, they nodded to each other, then they deliberately tapped their ears, turning their earpieces off.

And they crouched down to wait.

In a few moments, they heard the soldiers start to move, once again running through the underbrush. This time, they were going up the hill—back toward Castelgard.

They waited another five or six minutes. And then they headed down the hill, away from Castelgard.

:

It was Chris who had put it all together. Climbing down the hillside in the night, he had brushed a mosquito away from his ear, and the movement had inadvertently turned his earpiece on; not long afterward, he had heard someone sneeze.

And none of them had sneezed.

A few moments later, they had come upon the pig, and by then he was hearing someone panting with exertion. While Kate and Marek, in the darkness beside him, were not moving at all.

That was when he realized for certain that someone else had an earpiece—and thinking it over now, he had a pretty good idea where it had come from. Gomez. Somebody must have taken it from Gomez's severed head. The only problem with that idea was—

Marek nudged him. Pointed ahead.

Kate gave the thumbs-up sign and grinned.

:

Broad and flat, the river rippled and gurgled in the night. The Dordogne was wide at this point; they could barely see the far shore, a line of dark trees and dense undergrowth. They saw no sign of movement. Looking upstream, Chris could just make out the dark outline of the mill bridge. He knew the mill would be closed up at night; millers could work only during daylight hours, because even a candle risked causing an explosion in the dusty air.

Marek touched Chris on the arm, then pointed toward the opposite bank. Chris shrugged; he saw nothing.

Marek pointed again.

Squinting, Chris could barely discern four wisps of pale smoke rising into the sky. But if they came from fires, why was there no light?

Following the riverbank, they moved upstream, and eventually came upon a boat tied to the shore. It thunked against rocks in the current. Marek looked toward the opposite shore. They were now some distance from the smoke.

He pointed to the boat. Did they want to risk it?

The alternative, Chris knew, was to swim the river. The night was chilly; he didn't want to get wet. He pointed to the boat and nodded.

Kate nodded.

They climbed aboard, and Marek rowed them quietly across the Dordogne.

:

Sitting next to Chris, Kate found herself thinking of their conversation while crossing the river a few days earlier. How many days had it been? It must be only two days ago, she realized. But it seemed like weeks to her.

She squinted at the far shore, looking for any movement. Their boat would be a dark shape on dark water against a dark hill, but they would still be visible if anyone was looking.

But apparently no one was. The shore was closer now, and then with a hiss the boat moved into the grass along the banks and crunched to a soft stop. They climbed out. They saw a narrow dirt path that followed the edge of the river. Marek held his fingers to his lips, and started down the path. He was going toward the smoke.

They followed cautiously.

A few minutes later, they had their answer. There were four fires, placed at intervals along the riverbank. The flames were surrounded by pieces of broken armor atop mounds of earth, so that only the smoke was visible.

But there were no soldiers.

Marek whispered. "Old trick. Fires give false position."

Kate wasn't quite sure what the "old trick" was meant to accomplish. Perhaps to indicate greater strength, greater numbers, than you really had. Marek led them past the row of untended fires, toward several others ranged farther along the riverbank. They were close to the water, hearing the gurgling of the river. As they came to the last fire, Marek abruptly spun on his heel and dropped to the ground. Kate and Chris dropped, too, and then they heard voices, singing a repetitive drinking song; the lyrics were something about "Ale makes a man slumber by fire, ale makes a man wallow in mire. . . ."

It went on interminably. Listening to the lyrics, she thought: This is "Ninety-nine Bottles of Beer on the Wall." And sure enough, as she raised her head to look, she saw half a dozen soldiers in green and black sitting around a fire, drinking and singing loudly. Perhaps they had been ordered to make enough noise to justify all the fires.

Marek pointed for them to go back, and when they had moved a distance away, he led them off to the left, away from the river. They left behind the cover of trees that lined the river, then were again slipping through open, cleared fields. She realized that these were the same fields where she had been that morning. And sure enough, now she could see on the left faint yellow lights in the upper windows of the monastery as some of the monks worked late. And the dark outlines of thatched farm huts, directly ahead.

Chris pointed toward the monastery. Why weren't they going there?

Marek made a pillow with his hands: Everybody sleeping.

Chris shrugged: So?

Marek pantomimed waking up, startled, alarmed. He seemed to mean that they would cause a commotion if they went in in the middle of the night.

Chris shrugged: So?

Marek wagged a finger: Not a good idea. He mouthed, *In the morning*.

Chris sighed.

Marek went past the farm huts, until he came to a burned-out farmhouse—four walls, and the black remains of timbers that had supported a thatched roof. He led them inside, through an open door that had a red streak across it. Kate could barely see it in the darkness.

Inside the hut was tall grass, and some pieces of broken crockery. Marek began rummaging through the grass, until he came up with two clay pots with cracked rims. They looked like chamber pots to Kate. Marek set them out carefully on one burned windowsill. She whispered, "Where do we sleep?"

Marek pointed to the ground.

"Why can't we go into the monastery?" she whispered, gesturing to the open sky above them. The night was cold. She was hungry. She wanted the comfort of an enclosed space.

"Not safe," Marek whispered. "We sleep here."

He lay on the ground and closed his eyes.

"Why isn't it safe?" she said.

"Because somebody has an earpiece. And they know where we're going."

Chris said, "I wanted to talk to you about—"

"Not now," Marek said without opening his eyes. "Go to sleep."

Kate lay down, and Chris lay beside her. She pushed her back against his. It was just for warmth. It was so damn cold.

In the distance, she heard the rumble of thunder.

:

Sometime after midnight it began to rain. She felt the heavy drops on her cheeks, and she got to her feet just as the downpour started. She looked around and saw a small wooden lean-to, partially burned but still standing. She crawled under it, sitting upright, again huddling together with Chris, who had joined her. Marek came over, lay down nearby, and immediately went back to sleep. She saw raindrops spatter his cheeks, but he was snoring.

# 26:12:01

Half a dozen hot-air balloons were rising above the mesas in the morning sun. It was now almost eleven o'clock. One of the balloons had a zigzag pattern, which reminded Stern of a Navajo sandpainting.

"I'm sorry," Gordon was saying. "But the answer is no. You can't go back in the prototype, David. It's just too dangerous."

"Why? I thought this was all so safe. Safer than a car. What's dangerous?"

"I told you we don't have transcription errors—the errors that occur during rebuilding," Gordon said. "But that's not precisely accurate."

"Ah."

"Ordinarily, it's true that we can't find any evidence of errors. But they probably occur during every trip. They're just too minor to detect. But like radiation exposure, transcription errors are cumulative. You can't see them after one trip, but after ten or twenty trips, the signs start to be visible. Maybe you have a small seam like a scar in your skin. A small streak in your cornea. Or maybe you begin to have noticeable symptoms, like diabetes, or circulatory problems. Once that happens, you can't go anymore. Because you can't afford to have the problems get worse. That means you've reached your trip limit."

"And that's happened?"

"Yes. To some lab animals. And to several people. The pioneers—the ones who used this prototype machine."

Stern hesitated. "Where are those people now?"

"Most of them are still here. Still working for us. But they don't travel anymore. They can't."

"Okay," Stern said, "but I'm only talking about one trip."

"And we haven't used or calibrated this machine for a long time," Gordon said. "It may be okay, and it may not be. Look: suppose I let you go back, and after you arrive in 1357, you discover you have errors so serious, you don't dare return. Because you couldn't risk more accumulation."

"You're saying I'd have to stay back there."

"Yes."

Stern said, "Has that ever happened to anybody?"

Gordon paused. "Possibly."

"You mean there's somebody back there now?"

"Possibly," Gordon said. "We're not sure."

"But this is very important to know," Stern said, suddenly excited. "You're telling me there might be somebody already back there who could help them."

"I don't know," Gordon said, "if this particular person would help."

"But shouldn't we tell them? Advise them?"

"There's no way to make contact with them."

"Actually," Stern said, "I think there is."

# 16:12:23

Shivering and cold, Chris awoke before dawn. The sky was pale gray, the ground covered by thin mist. He was sitting under the lean-to, his knees pulled up to his chin, his back against the wall. Kate sat beside him, still asleep. He shifted his body to look out, and winced with sudden pain. All his muscles were cramped and sore—his arms, his legs, his chest, everywhere. His neck hurt when he turned his head.

He was surprised to find the shoulder of his tunic stiff with dried blood. Apparently, the arrow the night before had cut him enough to cause bleeding. Chris moved his arm experimentally, sucking in his breath with pain, but he decided that he was all right.

He shivered in the morning damp. What he wanted now was a warm fire and something to eat. His stomach was growling. He hadn't eaten for more than twenty-four hours. And he was thirsty. Where were they going to find water? Could you drink water from the Dordogne? Or did they need to find a spring? And where were they going to find food?

He turned to ask Marek, but Marek wasn't there. He twisted to look around the farmhouse—sharp pain, lots of pain—but Marek was gone.

He had just begun to get to his feet when he heard the sound of approaching footsteps. Marek? No, he decided: he was hearing the footsteps of more than one person. And he heard the soft clink of chain mail.

The footsteps came close, then stopped. He held his breath. To the right, barely three feet from his head, a chain-mail gauntlet appeared through the open window and rested on the windowsill. The sleeve above the gauntlet was green, trimmed in black.

Arnaut's men.

*"Hic nemo habitavit nuper,"* a male voice said.

A reply came from the doorway. *"Et intellego quare. Specta, porta habet signum rubrum. Estne pestilentiae?"*

*"Pestilentia? Certo scisne? Abeamus!"*

The hand hastily withdrew, and the footsteps hurried away. His earpiece had translated none of it, because it was turned off. He had to rely on his Latin. What was *pestilentia*? Probably "plague." The soldiers had seen the mark on the door and had quickly moved away.

Jesus, he thought, was this a plague house? Is that why it had been burned down? Could you still catch the plague? He was wondering about this when to his horror a black rat scuttled out of the deep grass, and away through the door. Chris shivered. Kate awoke, and yawned. "What time is—"

He pressed his finger to her lips and shook his head.

He heard the men still moving away, their voices faint in the gray morning. Chris slid out from under the lean-to, crept to the window, and looked out cautiously.

He saw at least a dozen soldiers, all around them, wearing the green and black colors of Arnaut. The soldiers were methodically checking all the thatched cottages near the monastery walls. As Chris watched, he saw Marek walking toward the soldiers. Marek was hunched over, dragging one leg. He carried some greens in his hands. The soldiers stopped him. Marek bowed obsequiously. His whole body seemed small, weak-looking. He showed the soldiers what was in his hand. The soldiers laughed and shoved him aside. Marek walked on, still hunched and deferential.

:

Kate watched Marek walk past their burned-out farmhouse and disappear behind the monastery wall. He obviously wasn't going to come to them while the troops were still there.

Chris had crawled back under the lean-to, wincing. His shoulder seemed to be hurt; there was dried blood on the fabric. She helped him unbutton his doublet, and he screwed up his face and bit his lip. Gently, she pulled aside his loose-necked linen undershirt, and she saw that the entire left side of his chest was an ugly purple, with a yellowish black tinge at the edges. That must be where he had been hit by the lance.

Seeing the look on her face, he whispered, "Is it bad?"

"I think it's just a bruise. Maybe some cracked ribs."

"Hurts like hell."

She slid the shirt over his shoulder, exposing the arrow cut. It was a slanting two-inch tear across the skin surface, caked with dried blood.

"How is it?" he said, watching her face.

"Just a cut."

"Infected?"

"No, it looks clean."

She pulled the doublet down farther, saw more purple bruising on his back and his side, beneath his arm. His whole body was one big bruise. It must be incredibly painful. She was amazed that he wasn't complaining more. After all, this was the same guy who threw fits if he was served dried cèpe mushrooms instead of fresh ones in his morning omelette. Who could pout if he didn't like the choice of wine.

She started to button up his doublet for him. He said, "I can do that."

"I'll help you. . . ."

"I said, *I can do it.*"

She pulled away, held her palms up. "Okay. Okay."

"I have to get these arms moving, anyway," he said, wincing with each button. He did them all up by himself. But afterward, he sat back against the wall, eyes closed, sweating from the exertion and the pain.

"Chris. . . ."

He opened his eyes. "I'm fine. Really, don't worry about me. I'm perfectly fine."

And he meant it.

She almost felt as if she were sitting next to a stranger.

:

When Chris had seen his shoulder and chest—it was the purple color of dead meat—his own reaction had surprised him. The injury was severe. He expected to feel horrified, or frightened. But instead, he felt suddenly light, almost carefree. The pain might be making him gasp for breath, but the pain didn't matter. He just felt glad to be alive, and facing another day. His familiar complaints, his cavils and his uncertainties seemed suddenly irrelevant. In their place, he discovered that he had some source of boundless energy—an almost aggressive vitality that he could not recall ever experiencing before. He felt it flowing through his body, a kind of heat. The world around him seemed more vivid, more sensuous than he could remember before.

To Chris, the gray dawn took on a pristine beauty. The

cool, damp air bore a fragrance of wet grass and damp earth. The stones against his back supported him. Even his pain was useful because it burned away all unnecessary feeling. He felt stripped down, alert and ready for anything. This was a different world, with different rules.

And for the first time, he was in it.

Totally in it.

:

When the troops had gone, Marek returned. "Did you understand all that?" he said.

"What?"

"The soldiers are searching for three people from Castelgard: two men and a woman."

"Why?"

"Arnaut wants to talk to them."

"Isn't it nice to be popular," Chris said with a wry smile. "Everyone's after us."

Marek gave them each a handful of wet grass and leaves. "Field greens. That's breakfast. Eat up."

Chris chewed the plants noisily. "Delicious," he said. He meant it.

"The plant with the jagged leaves is feverfew. It'll help with the pain. The white stalk is willow. Reduce your swelling."

"Thanks," Chris said. "It's very good."

Marek was staring at him in disbelief. He said to Kate, "Is he okay?"

"Actually, I think he's fine."

"Good. Eat up, and then we'll go to the monastery. If we can get past the guards."

Kate pulled off her wig. "That won't be a problem," she said. "They're looking for two men and a woman. So: who's got the sharpest knife?"

:

Fortunately, her hair was already short; it took only a few minutes for Marek to cut away the longer strands and finish the job. While he worked, Chris said, "I've been thinking about last night."

"Obviously, somebody's got an earpiece," Marek said.

"Right," Chris said. "And I think I know where they got it."

"Gomez," Marek said.

Chris nodded. "That's my guess. You didn't take it from her?"

"No. I didn't think to."

"I'm sure another person could push it far enough into his own ear to hear it, even if it doesn't really fit him."

"Yes," Marek said. "But the question is, who? This is the fourteenth century. A pink lump that talks in little voices is witchcraft. It'd be terrifying to anyone who found it. Whoever picked it up would drop it like a hot potato—and then crush it immediately. Or run like mad."

"I know," Chris said. "That's why every time I think about it, I can see only one possible answer."

Marek nodded. "Those bastards didn't tell us."

"Tell us what?" Kate said.

"That there's somebody else back here. Somebody from the twentieth century."

"It's the only possible answer," Chris said.

"But who?" Kate said.

Chris had been thinking about that all morning. "De Kere," he said. "It's got to be de Kere."

Marek was shaking his head.

"Consider," Chris said. "He's only been here a year, right? Nobody knows where he came from, right? He's wormed his way in with Oliver, and he hates all of us, because he knows we might do it, too, right? He leads his soldiers away from the tannery, goes all the way up the street, *until we speak*— and then he's right back on us. I'm telling you, it has to be de Kere."

"There's only one problem," Marek said. "De Kere speaks flawless Occitan."

"Well, so do you."

"No. I speak like a clumsy foreigner. You two listen to the translations in the earpiece. I listen to what they actually say.

De Kere speaks like a native. He's completely fluent, and his accent exactly matches everybody else's. And Occitan is a dead language in the twentieth century. There's no way he could be from our century and speak like that. He's got to be a native."

"Maybe he's a linguist."

Marek was shaking his head. "It's not de Kere," he said. "It's Guy Malegant."

"Sir Guy?"

"No question," Marek said. "I've had my doubts about him ever since that time we were caught in the passage. Remember? We were almost perfectly silent in there—but he opens the door and catches us. He didn't even try to act surprised. He didn't draw his sword. Quite straightforward, shouting the alarm. Because he already knew we were there."

"But that's not how it happened. Sir Daniel came in," Chris said.

"Did he?" Marek said. "I don't remember him ever coming in."

"Actually," Kate said, "I think Chris might be right. It might be de Kere. Because I was in the alley between the chapel and the castle, pretty far up the chapel wall, and de Kere was telling the soldiers to kill you, and I remember I was too far away to hear them clearly, but I did."

Marek stared at her. "And then what happened?"

"Then de Kere whispered to a soldier. . . . And I couldn't hear what he said."

"Right. Because he didn't have an earpiece. If he had an earpiece, you would have heard everything, including whispers. But he didn't. It's Sir Guy. Who cut Gomez's head off? Sir Guy and his men. Who was most likely to go back to the body and retrieve the earpiece? Sir Guy. The other men were terrified of the flashing machine. Only Sir Guy was not afraid. Because he knew what it was. He's from our century."

"I don't think Guy was there," Chris said, "when the machine was flashing."

"But the clincher that it is Sir Guy," Marek said, "is that his

Occitan is terrible. He sounds like a New Yorker, speaking through his nose."

"Well, isn't he from Middlesex? And I don't think he's well-born. I get the impression he was knighted for bravery, not family."

"He wasn't a good-enough jouster to take you out with the first lance," Marek said. "He wasn't a good-enough swords-man to kill me hand-to-hand. I'm telling you. It's Guy de Malegant."

"Well," Chris said, "whoever it is, now they know we're going to the monastery."

"That's right," Marek said, stepping away from Kate and looking at her hair appraisingly. "So let's go."

Kate touched her hair cautiously. She said, "Should I be glad I don't have a mirror?"

Marek nodded. "Probably."

"Do I look like a guy?"

Chris and Marek exchanged glances. Chris said, "Kind of."

"Kind of?"

"Yes. You do. You look like a guy."

"Close enough, anyway," Marek said.

They got to their feet.

# 15:12:09

The heavy wooden door opened a crack. From the dark-ness inside, a shadowed face in a white cowl peered out at them. "God grant you growth and increase," the monk said solemnly.

"God grant you health and wisdom," Marek replied in Occitan.

"What is your business?"

"We come to see Brother Marcel."

The monk nodded, almost as if he had been expecting them. "Certes, you may enter," the monk said. "You are in good time, for he is still here." He opened the door a little wider, so they were able to pass through, one at a time.

They found themselves in a small stone anteroom, very dark. They smelled a fragrant odor of roses and oranges. From within the monastery itself, they heard the soft sound of chanting.

"You may leave your weapons there," the monk said, pointing to the corner of the room.

"Good brother, I fear we cannot," Marek said.

"You have nothing to fear here," he said. "Disarm, or depart."

Marek started to protest, then unbuckled his sword.

:

The monk glided ahead of them down a quiet hallway. The walls were bare stone. They turned a corner and went down another hallway. The monastery was very large, and mazelike.

This was a Cistercian monastery; the monks wore white robes of plain cloth. The austerity of the Cistercian order stood as a deliberate reproach to the more corrupt orders of Benedictines and Dominicans. Cistercian monks were expected to keep rigid discipline, in an atmosphere of severe asceticism. For centuries, the Cistercians did not permit any carved decoration on their plain buildings, nor any decorative illustrations to their manuscripts. Their diet consisted of vegetables, bread and water, with no meats or sauces. Cots were hard; rooms were bare and cold. Every aspect of their monastic life was determinedly Spartan. But, in fact, this quality of rigid discipline had—

*Thwock!*

Marek turned toward the sound. They were coming into a cloister—an open court within the monastery, surrounded by arched passages on three sides, intended as a place of reading and contemplation.

*Thwock!*

Now they heard laughter. Noisy shouts of men.

*Thwock! Thwock!*

As they came into the cloister, Marek saw that the fountain and garden in the center had been removed. The ground was bare, hard-packed dirt. Four men, sweating in linen smocks, were standing in the dirt, playing a kind of handball.

*Thwock!*

The ball rolled on the ground, and the men pushed and shoved each other, letting it roll. When it stopped, one man picked it up, cried, *"Tenez!"* and served the ball overhand, smacking it with his flat palm. The ball bounced off the side wall of the cloisters. The men yelled and jostled one another for position. Beneath the arches, monks and nobles shouted encouragement, clinking bags of gambling money in their hands.

There was a long wooden board attached to one wall, and every time a ball hit that board—making a loud *bonk!*—there were extra shouts of encouragement from the gamblers in the galleries.

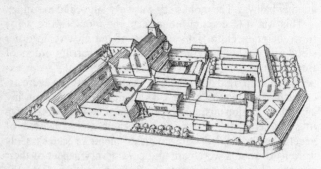

It took Marek a moment to realize what he was looking at: the earliest form of tennis.

*Tenez*—from the server's shout, meaning, "Receive it!"— was a new game, invented just twenty-five years earlier, and it had become the instant rage of the period. Racquets and nets would come centuries later; for now, the game was a variety of handball, played by all classes of society. Children played in the streets. Among the nobility, the game was so popular that it provoked a trend to build new monasteries—which were abandoned unfinished, once the cloisters had been constructed. Royal families worried that princes neglected their instruction as knights in favor of long hours on the tennis court, often playing by torchlight far into the night. Gambling was ubiquitous. King John II of France, now captive in England, had, over the years, spent a small fortune to pay his tennis debts. (King John was known as John the Good, but it was said that whatever John was good at, it was certainly not tennis.)

Marek said, "Do you play here often?"

"Exercise invigorates the body and sharpens the mind," the monk replied immediately. "We play in two cloisters here."

As they passed through the cloister, Marek noticed that several of the gamblers wore robes of green, trimmed in black. They were rough, grizzled men with the manner of bandits.

Then they left the cloister behind, and went up a flight of stairs. Marek said to the monk, "It appears the order makes welcome the men of Arnaut de Cervole."

"That is sooth," the monk said, "for they shall do us a boon and return the mill to us."

"Was it taken?" Marek asked.

"In a manner of speaking." The monk walked to the window, which overlooked the Dordogne, and the mill bridge, a quarter mile upstream.

"With their own hands, the monks of Sainte-Mère have built the mill, at the bidding of our revered architect, Brother Marcel. Marcel is much venerated in the monastery. As you know, he was architect for the former Abbot, Bishop Laon. So the mill that he designed, and we built, is the property of this monastery, as are its fees.

"Yet Sir Oliver demands a mill tax to himself, though he has no just cause for it, except that his army controls this territory. Therefore my Lord Abbot is well pleased that Arnaut should vow to return the mill to the monastery, and end the tax. And thus are we friendly to the men of Arnaut."

Chris listened to all this, thinking, My thesis! It was all exactly as his research had shown. Although some people still thought of the Middle Ages as a backward time, Chris knew it had actually been a period of intense technological development, and in that sense, not so different from our own. In fact, the industrial mechanization that became a characteristic feature of the West first began in the Middle Ages. The greatest source of power available at the time—water power—was aggressively developed, and employed to do ever more kinds of work: not only grinding grain but fulling cloth, blacksmithing, beer mashing, woodworking, mixing mortar and cement, papermaking, rope making, oil pressing, preparing dyes for cloth, and powering bellows to heat blast furnaces for steel. All over Europe, rivers were dammed, and dammed again half a mile downstream; mill boats were tethered beneath every bridge. In some places, cascades of mills, one after another, successively used the energy of flowing water.

Mills were generally operated as a monopoly, and they provided a major source of income—and of conflict. Lawsuits, murders and battles were the constant accompaniment of mill activity. And here was an example that showed—

"And yet," Marek was saying, "I see the mill is still in the hands of Lord Oliver, for his pennant flies from the towers and his archers man the battlements."

"Oliver holds the mill bridge," the monk said, "because the bridge is close to the road to La Roque, and whoever controls the mill controls the road. But Arnaut will soon take the mill from them."

"And return it to you."

"Indeed."

"And what will the monastery do for Arnaut in return?"

"We will bless him, of course," the monk said. And after a moment, he added, "And we will pay him handsomely, too."

:

They passed through a scriptorium, where monks sat in rows at their easels, silently copying manuscripts. But to Marek, it looked all wrong; instead of a meditative chant, their work was accompanied by the shouts and banging of the game in the cloister. And despite the old Cistercian proscription against illustration, many monks were painting illustrations in the corners and along the margins of manuscripts. The painters sat with an array of brushes and stone dishes of different colors. Some of the illustrations were brilliantly ornate.

"This way," the monk said, and led them down a staircase and into a small sunlit courtyard. To one side, Marek saw eight soldiers in the colors of Arnaut, standing in the sun. He noticed that they wore their swords.

The monk led them toward a small house at the edge of the courtyard, and then through a door. They heard the trickle of running water and saw a fountain with a large basin. They heard chanted prayers, in Latin. In the center of the room, two robed monks washed a naked, pale body lying on a table.

"Frater Marcellus," the monk whispered, giving a slight bow.

Marek stared. It took him a moment to realize what he was seeing.

Brother Marcel was dead.

# 14:52:07

Their reaction gave them away. The monk could clearly see that they had not known Marcel was dead. Frowning, he took Marek by the arm, and said, "Why are you here?"

"We had hoped to speak with Brother Marcel."

"He died last night."

"How did he die?" Marek said.

"We do not know. But as you can see, he was old."

"Our request of him was urgent," Marek said. "Perhaps if I could see his private effects—"

"He had no private effects."

"But surely some personal articles—"

"He lived very simply."

Marek said, "May I see his room?"

"I am sorry, that is not possible."

"But I would greatly appreciate it if—"

"Brother Marcel lived in the mill. His room has been there for many years."

"Ah." The mill was now under control of Oliver's troops. They could not go there, at least not at the moment.

"But perhaps I can help you. Tell me, what was your urgent request?" the monk asked. He spoke casually, but Marek was immediately cautious.

"It was a private matter," Marek said. "I cannot speak of it."

"There is nothing private here," the monk said. He was edging toward the door. Marek had the distinct feeling that he was going to raise an alarm.

"It was a request from Magister Edwardus."

"Magister Edwardus!" The monk's manner completely changed. "Why did you not say so? And what are you to Magister Edwardus?"

"Faith, we are his assistants."

"Certes?"

"In deed, it is so."

"Why did you not say it? Magister Edwardus is welcome here, for he was performing a service for the Abbot when he was taken by Oliver."

"Ah."

"Come with me now at once," he said. "The Abbot will wish to see you."

"But we have—"

"The Abbot will wish it. Come!"

:

Back in the sunlight, Marek noticed how many more soldiers in green and black were now in the monastery courtyards. And these soldiers were not lounging; they were watchful, battle-ready.

The Abbot's house was small, made of ornately carved wood, and located in a far corner of the monastery. They were led inside to a small wood-paneled anteroom, where an older monk, hunched and heavy as a toad, sat before a closed door.

"Is my Lord Abbot within?"

"Faith, he is advising a penitent now."

From the adjacent room, they heard a rhythmic creaking sound.

"How long will he keep her at her prayers?" the monk asked.

"It may be a goodly while," the toad said. "She is recidive. And her sins are oft repeated."

"I would you make known these worthy men to our Lord Abbot," the monk said, "for they bring news of Edwardus de Johnes."

"Be assured I shall tell him," the toad said in a bored tone. But Marek caught the gleam of sudden interest in the old man's eyes. Some meaning had registered.

"It is nigh on terce," the toad said, glancing up at the sun. "Will your guests dine on our simple fare?"

"Many thanks, but no, we shall—" Chris coughed. Kate poked Marek in the back. Marek said, "We shall, if it is not a great trouble."

"By the grace of God, you are welcome."

They were starting to leave for the dining room when a young monk ran breathlessly into the room. "My Lord Arnaut is coming! He will see the Abbot at once!"

The toad jumped to his feet and said to them, "Be you gone now." And he opened a side door.

:

Which was how they found themselves in a small, plain room adjacent to the Abbot's quarters. The squeaking of the bed stopped; they heard the low murmur of the toad, who was speaking urgently to the Abbot.

A moment later, another door opened and a woman came in, bare-legged, hastily adjusting her clothes, her face flushed. She was extremely beautiful. When she turned, Chris saw with astonishment that it was the Lady Claire.

She caught his look and said, "Why stare you thus?"

"Uh, my Lady . . ."

"Squire, your countenance is most unjust. How dare you judge me? I am a gentle woman, alone in a foreign part, with no one to champion me, to protect or guide me. Yet I must make my way to Bordeaux, eighty leagues distant, and thence to England if I am to claim my husband's lands. That is my duty as a widow, and in this time of war and tumult, I shall without hesitation do all that may be required to accomplish it."

Chris was thinking that hesitation was not a part of this woman's character. He was stunned by her boldness. On the other hand, Marek was looking at her with open admiration. He said smoothly, "Pray forgive him, Lady, for he is young and often thoughtless."

"Circumstances change. I had need of an introduction that only the Abbot could make for me. What persuasion is in my command, I use." The Lady Claire was hopping on one foot now, trying to keep her balance while pulling on her hose. She drew the hose tight, smoothed her dress, and then set her wimple on her head, tying it expertly beneath her chin, so only her face was exposed.

Within moments, she looked like a nun. Her manner became demure, her voice lower, softer.

"Now, by happenstance, you know what I had intended no person to know. In this, I am at your mercy, and I beg your silence."

"You shall have it," Marek said, "for your affairs are none of ours."

"You shall have my silence in return," she said. "For it is evident the Abbot does not wish your presence known to de Cervole. We shall all keep our secrets. Have I your word?"

"In sooth, yes, Lady," Marek said.

"Yes, Lady," Chris said.

"Yes, Lady," Kate said.

Hearing her voice, Claire frowned at Kate, then walked over to her. "Say you true?"

"Yes, Lady," Kate said, again.

Claire ran her hand over Kate's chest, feeling the breasts beneath the flattening cloth band. "You have cut your hair, damsel," she said. "You know that to pass as a man is punishable by death?" She glanced at Chris as she said this.

"We know it," Marek said.

"You must have great dedication to your Magister, to give up your sex."

"My Lady, I do."

"Then I pray most earnestly that you survive."

The door opened, and the toad gestured to them. "Worthies, come. My Lady, pray remain, the Abbot will do your bidding soon enough. But you worthies—come with me."

∴

Outside in the courtyard, Chris leaned close to Marek and whispered, "André. That woman is poison."

Marek was smiling. "I agree she has a certain spark. . . ."

"André. I'm telling you. You can't trust anything she says."

"Really? I thought she was remarkably straightforward," Marek said. "She wants protection. And she is right."

Chris stared. "Protection?"

"Yes. She wants a champion," Marek said, thoughtfully.

"A champion? What are you talking about? We have only—how many hours left?"

Marek looked at his wristband. "Eleven hours ten minutes."

"So: what are you talking about, a champion?"

"Oh. Just thinking," Marek said. He threw his arm over Chris's shoulder. "It's not important."

# 11:01:59

They were seated at a long table with many monks in a large hall, a steaming bowl of meat soup in front of them, and in the center of the table, platters piled high with vegetables, beef and roast capons. And no one moving a muscle, but all heads bowed in prayer, as the monks chanted.

> *Pater noster qui es in coelis*
> *Sanctivicetur nomen tuum*
> *Adveniat regnum tuum*
> *Fiat voluntas tua*

Kate kept sneaking looks at the food. The capons were steaming! They looked fat, and yellow juice flowed onto the plates. Then she noticed that the monks nearest her seemed puzzled by her silence. She should know this chant, it seemed.

Beside her, Marek was chanting loudly.

> *Panem nostrum quotidianum*
> *Da nobie hodie*
> *Et dimmitte nobis debita nostra*

She didn't understand Latin, and she couldn't join in, so she stayed silent until the final "Amen."

The monks all looked up, nodded to her. She braced herself: she had been fearing this moment. Because they would speak to her, and she wouldn't be able to answer back. What would she do?

She looked at Marek, who seemed perfectly relaxed. Of course he would be; he spoke the language.

A monk passed a platter of beef to her, saying nothing. In fact, the entire room was silent. The food was passed without a word; there was no sound at all except for the soft clink of plates and knives. They ate in silence!

She took the platter, nodding, and gave herself one large helping, then another, until she caught Marek's disapproving glance. She handed the platter to him.

From the corner of the room, a monk began to read a text in Latin, the words a kind of cadence in her ears, while she ate hungrily. She was famished! She could not remember when she had enjoyed a meal more. She glanced at Marek, who was eating with a quiet smile on his face. She turned to her soup, which was delicious, and after a moment, she glanced back at Marek.

He wasn't smiling anymore.

⋮

Marek had been keeping an eye on the entrances. There were three to this long rectangular room: one to his right, one to his left, and one directly opposite them, in the center of the room.

Moments before, he had seen a group of soldiers in green and black gathering near the doorway to the right. They peered in, as if interested in the meal, but remained outside.

Now he saw a second group of soldiers, standing in the doorway directly ahead. Kate looked at him, and he leaned very close to her ear and whispered, "Left door." The monks around them shot disapproving glances. Kate looked at Marek and gave a little nod, meaning she understood.

Where did the left-hand doorway lead? There were no soldiers at that door, and the room beyond was dark. Wherever it went, they would have to risk it. He caught Chris's eye and gave a small jerk with his thumb: time to get up.

Chris nodded almost imperceptibly. Marek pushed away his soup and started to get up, when a white-robed monk came up to him, leaned close, and whispered, "The Abbot will see you now."

:

The Abbot of Sainte-Mère was an energetic man in his early thirties, with the body of an athlete and the sharp eye of a merchant. His black robes were elegantly embroidered, his heavy necklace was gold, and the hand he extended to be kissed bore jewels on four fingers. He met them in a sunny courtyard and then walked side by side with Marek, while Chris and Kate trailed behind. There were green-and-black soldiers everywhere. The Abbot's manner was cheerful, but he had the habit of abruptly changing the subject, as if to catch his listener off guard.

"I am heartfelt sorry for these soldiers," the Abbot said, "but I fear intruders have entered the monastery grounds— some men of Oliver—and until we find them, we must be cautious. And my Lord Arnaut has graciously offered us his protection. You have eaten well?"

"By the grace of God and your own, very well, my Lord Abbot."

The Abbot smiled pleasantly. "I dislike flattery," he said. "And our order forbids it."

"I shall be mindful," Marek said.

The Abbot looked at the soldiers and sighed. "So many soldiers ruin the game."

"What game is that?"

"The game, the game," he said impatiently. "Yesterday morning we went hunting and returned haveless, with not so much as a roebuck to show. And the men of Cervole had not yet arrived. Now they are here—two thousand of them. What game they do not take, they frighten off. It will be months before the forests settle again. What news of Magister Edwardus? Tell me, for I am sore in need to have it."

Marek frowned. The Abbot did indeed appear tense, chafing to hear. But he seemed to be expecting specific information.

"My Lord Abbot, he is in La Roque."

"Oh? With Sir Oliver?"

"Yes, my Lord Abbot."

"Most unfortunate. Did he give you a message for me?" He must have seen Marek's puzzled look. "No?"

"My Lord Abbot, Edwardus gave me no message."

"Perhaps in code? Some trivial or mistaken turn of phrase?"

"I am sorry," Marek said.

"Not so sorry as I. And now he is in La Roque?"

"He is, my Lord Abbot."

"Sooth, I would not have it so," the Abbot said. "For I think La Roque cannot be taken."

"Yet if there is a secret passage to the inside . . . ," Marek said.

"Oh, the passage, the passage," the Abbot said, giving a wave of his hand. "It will be my undoing. It is all that I hear spoken. Every man wishes to know the passage—and Arnaut more than any of them. The Magister was assisting me, searching the old documents of Marcellus. Are you certain he said nothing to you?"

"He said we were to seek Brother Marcel."

The Abbot snorted. "Certes, this secret passage was the work of Laon's assistant and scribe, who was Brother Marcel. But for the last years, old Marcel was not well in spirit. That is why we let him live in the mill. All through the day, he muttered and mumbled to himself, and then of a sudden he would cry out that he saw demons and spirits, and his eyes rolled in his head, and his limbs thrashed wildly, until the visions passed." The Abbot shook his head. "The other monks venerated him, seeing his visions as proof of piety, and not of disorder, which in truth it was. But why did the Magister tell you to seek him out?"

"The Magister said Marcel had a key."

"A key?" the Abbot said. "A *key*?" He sounded very annoyed. "*Of course* he had a key, he had many keys, and they are all to be found in the mill, but we cannot—" He stumbled forward, then stared with a shocked expression at Marek.

All around the courtyard, men were shouting, pointing upward.

Marek said, "My Lord Abbot—"

The Abbot spat blood and collapsed into Marek's arms. Marek eased him to the ground. He felt the arrow in the Abbot's back even before he saw it. More arrows whistled down and thunked, quivering, in the grass beside them.

Marek looked up and saw maroon figures in the bell tower of the church, firing rapidly. An arrow ripped Marek's hat from his head; another tore through the sleeve of his tunic. Another arrow stuck deep in the Abbot's shoulder.

The next arrow struck Marek in the thigh. He felt searing red-hot pain streak down his leg, and he lost his balance, falling back on the ground. He tried to get up, but he was dizzy and his balance had deserted him. He fell back again as arrows whistled down all around him.

:

On the opposite side of the courtyard, Chris and Kate ran for cover through the rain of arrows. Kate yelled and stumbled, fell to the ground, an arrow sticking in her back. Then she scrambled up, and Chris saw it had torn through her tunic beneath her armpit but had not struck her. An arrow skinned his leg, tearing his hose. And then they reached the covered passageway, where they collapsed behind one of the arches, catching their breath. Arrows clattered off the stone walls and struck the stone arches all around them. Chris said, "You okay?"

She nodded, panting. "Where's Marek?"

Chris got to his feet, peered cautiously around the pillar. "Oh *no*," he said. And he started to run down the corridor.

:

Marek staggered to his feet, saw that the Abbot was still alive. "Forgive me," Marek said as he lifted the Abbot onto his shoulder and carried him away to the corner. The soldiers in the courtyard loosed answering volleys at the bell tower. Fewer arrows were coming down at them now.

Marek took the Abbot behind the arches of the covered passageway and placed him on his side on the ground. The

Abbot pulled the arrow out of his own shoulder and threw it aside. The effort left him gasping. "My back . . . back . . ."

Marek turned him over gently. The shaft in his back pulsed with each heartbeat. "My Lord, do you wish me to pull it?"

"No." The Abbot flung a desperate arm over Marek's neck, pulling him close. "Not yet . . . A priest . . . priest . . ." His eyes rolled. A priest was running toward them.

"He comes now, my Lord Abbot."

The Abbot appeared relieved by this, but he still held Marek in a strong grip. His voice was low, almost a whisper. "The key to La Roque . . ."

"Yes, my Lord?"

". . . room . . ."

Marek waited. "What room, my Lord? What room?"

"Arnaut . . . ," the Abbot said, shaking his head as if to clear it. "Arnaut will be angry . . . room . . ." And he released his grip. Marek pulled the arrow from his back and helped him to lie on the floor. "Every time, he would . . . make . . . told no one . . . so . . . Arnaut . . ." He closed his eyes.

The monk pushed between them, speaking quickly in Latin, removing the Abbot's slippers, placing a bottle of oil on the ground. He began to administer the last rites.

:

Leaning against one of the cloister pillars, Marek pulled the arrow out of his thigh. It had struck him glancingly, and was not as deep as he had thought; there was only an inch of blood on the shaft. He dropped the arrow to the ground just as Chris and Kate came up.

They looked at his leg, and at the arrow. He was bleeding. Kate pulled up her doublet and tore a strip from the bottom of her linen undershirt with her dagger. She tied it around Marek's thigh as an impromptu bandage.

Marek said, "It's not that bad."

"Then it won't hurt you to have it," she said. "Can you walk?"

"Of course I can walk," Marek said.

"You're pale."

"I'm fine," he said, and moved away from the pillar, looking into the courtyard.

Four soldiers lay on the ground, which was pincushioned with arrows. The other soldiers had departed; no one was shooting at the bell tower any longer: smoke billowed from the high windows. On the opposite side of the courtyard, they saw more smoke, thick and dark, coming from the area of the refectory. The whole monastery was starting to burn.

"We need to find that key," Marek said.

"But it's in his room."

"I'm not sure about that." Marek had remembered that one of the last things Elsie, the graphologist, had said to him back at the project site had to do with a key. And some word that she was puzzled by. He couldn't remember the details—he had been worried about the Professor at the time—but he remembered clearly enough that Elsie had been looking at one of the parchment sheets from the pile that had been found in the monastery. The same pile that had contained the Professor's note.

And Marek knew where to find those parchments.

:

They hurried down the corridor toward the church. Some of the stained-glass windows had been broken, and smoke issued out. From the interior, they heard men shouting, and a moment later a party of soldiers burst through the doors. Marek turned on his heel, leading them back the way they had come.

"What are we doing?" Chris said.

"Looking for the door."

"What door?"

Marek darted left, along a cloistered corridor, and then left again, through a very narrow opening that brought them into a tight space, a kind of storeroom area. It was lit by a torch. There was a wooden trapdoor in the floor; he flung it open, and they saw steps going down into darkness. He grabbed a torch, and they all went down the steps. Chris was last, closing the trapdoor behind him. He descended the stairs into a dank, dark chamber.

:

The torch sputtered in the cool air. By its flickering light, they saw huge casks, six feet in diameter, running along the wall. They were in a wine cellar.

"You know the soldiers will find this place soon enough," Marek said. He led them through several rooms of casks, moving without hesitation.

Following him, Kate said, "Do you know where you're going?"

"Don't you?" he said.

But she didn't; she and Chris stayed close behind Marek, wanting to be in the comforting circle of light from the torch. Now they were passing tombs, small indentations in the wall where bodies rested, their shrouds rotting away. Sometimes they saw the tops of skulls, with bits of hair still clinging; sometimes they saw feet, the bones partially exposed. They heard the faint squeak of rats in the darkness.

Kate shivered.

Marek continued on, until at last he stopped abruptly in a chamber that was nearly empty.

"Why are we stopping?" she said.

"Don't you know?" Marek said.

She looked around, then realized that she was in the same underground chamber she had crawled into several days before. There was the same sarcophagus of a knight, now with the lid on the coffin. Along another wall was a crude wooden table, where sheets of oilskin were stacked and manuscript bundles were tied with hemp. To one side was a low stone wall, on which stood a single manuscript bundle—and the glint of the lens from the Professor's eyeglasses.

"He must have lost it yesterday," Kate said. "The soldiers must have captured him down here."

"Probably." She watched as Marek started going through the bundled sheets, one after another. He quickly found the Professor's message, then turned back to the preceding sheet. He frowned, peering at it in the torchlight.

"What is it?" she said.

"It's a description," he said. "Of an underground river, and . . . here it is." He pointed to the side of the manuscript, where a notation in Latin had been scrawled.

"It says, 'Marcellus has the key.' " He pointed with his finger. "And then it says something about, uh, a door or opening, and large feet."

"Large feet?"

"Wait a minute," he said. "No, that's not it." What Elsie had said was coming back to him now. "It says, 'Feet of a giant.' A giant's feet."

"A giant's feet," she said, looking doubtfully at him. "Are you sure you have that right?"

"That's what it says."

"And what's this?" she said. Beneath his finger there were two words, one arranged above the other:

DESIDE
VIVIX

"I remember," Marek said. "Elsie said this was a new word for her, *vivix*. But she didn't say anything about *deside*. And that doesn't even look like Latin to me. And it's not Occitan, or old French."

With his dagger, he cut a corner from the parchment, then scratched the two words into the material, folded it, and slipped it into his pocket.

"But what does it mean?" Kate said.

Marek shook his head. "No idea at all."

"It was added in the margin," she said. "Maybe it doesn't mean anything. Maybe it's a doodle, or an accounting, or something like that."

"I doubt it."

"They must have doodled back then."

"I know, but this doesn't look like a doodle, Kate. This is a serious notation." He turned back to the manuscript, running his finger along the text. "Okay. Okay . . . It says here that *Transitus occultus incipit* . . . the passage starts . . . *propre ad capellam viridem, sive capellam mortis*—at the green chapel, also known as the chapel of death—and—"

"The green chapel?" she said in an odd voice.

Marek nodded. "That's right. But it doesn't say where the chapel is." He sighed. "If the passage really connects to the limestone caves, it could be anywhere."

"No, André," she said. "It's not."

"What do you mean?"

"I mean," she said, "that I know where the green chapel is."

⋮

Kate said, "It was marked on the survey charts for the Dordogne project—it's a ruin, just outside the project area. I remember wondering why it hadn't been included in the project, because it was so close. On the chart, it was marked *'chapelle verte morte,'* and I thought it meant the 'chapel of green death.' I remember, because it sounded like something out of Edgar Allan Poe."

"Do you remember where it is, exactly?"

"Not exactly, except that it's in the forest about a kilometer north of Bezenac."

"Then it's possible," Marek said. "A kilometer-long tunnel is possible."

From behind them, they heard the sound of soldiers coming down into the cellar.

"Time to go."

He led them to the left, into a corridor, where the staircase was located. When Kate had seen it before, it disappeared into a mound of earth. Now it ran straight up to a wooden trapdoor.

Marek climbed the stairs, put his shoulder to the door. It opened easily. They saw gray sky, and smoke.

Marek went through, and they followed after him.

⋮

They emerged in an orchard, the fruit trees in neat rows, the spring leaves a bright green. They ran ahead through the trees, eventually arriving at the monastery wall. It was twelve feet tall, too high to climb. But they climbed the trees, then dropped over the wall, landing outside. Directly ahead they saw a section of dense, uncleared forest. They ran toward it, once again entering the dark canopy of the trees.

# 09:57:02

In the ITC laboratory, David Stern stepped away from the prototype machine. He looked at the small taped-together electronic bundle that he had been assembling and testing for the last five hours.

"That's it," he said. "That'll send them a message."

It was now night in the lab; the glass windows were dark. He said, "What time is it, back there?"

Gordon counted on his fingers. "They arrived about eight in the morning. It's been twenty-seven hours elapsed time. So it's now eleven in the morning, the following day."

"Okay. That should be okay."

Stern had managed to build this electronic communications device, despite Gordon's two strong arguments that such a thing could not be done. Gordon said that you couldn't send a message back there because you didn't know where the machine would land. Statistically, the chances were overwhelming that the machine would land where the team wasn't. So they would never see a message. The second problem was that you had no way of knowing whether they had received the message or not.

But Stern had solved both those objections in an extremely simple way. His bundle contained an earpiece transmitter/ receiver, identical to the ones the team was already wearing, and two small tape recorders. The first tape recorder transmitted a message. The second recorded any incoming message to the earpiece transmitter. The whole contraption was, as Gordon admiringly termed it, a multiverse answering machine.

Stern recorded a message that said, "This is David. You have now been out for twenty-seven hours. Don't try to come back until thirty-two hours. Then we'll be ready for you at this end. Meanwhile, tell us if you're all right. Just speak and it'll be recorded. Good-bye for now. See you soon."

Stern listened to the message one final time, then said, "Okay, let's send it back."

Gordon pushed buttons on the control panel. The machine began to hum and was bathed in blue light.

:

Hours earlier, when he had begun working on this message machine, Stern's only concern was that his friends back there might not know they couldn't return. As a result, he could imagine them getting into a jam, perhaps being attacked from all sides, and calling for the machine at the last instant, assuming they could come home at once. So Stern thought they should be told that, for the moment, they couldn't come back.

That had been his original concern. But now there was a second, even greater concern. The air in the cave had been cleared for about sixteen hours now. Teams of workers were back inside, rebuilding the transit pad. The control booth had been continuously monitored for many hours.

And there had been no field bucks.

Which meant there had been no attempt to come back. And Stern had the feeling—of course, nobody would say anything outright, least of all Gordon—but he had the feeling that people in ITC thought that to go more than twenty hours without a field buck was a bad sign. He sensed that a large faction inside ITC believed the team was already dead.

So interest in Stern's machine was not so much about whether a message could be sent as whether one would be received. Because that would be evidence that the team was still alive.

Stern had rigged the machine with an antenna, and he had made a little ratchet device that turned the flexible antenna to different angles and repeated the outgoing message three times. So there would be three chances for the team to respond. After that, the entire machine would automatically return to the present, just as it had when they were using the camera.

"Here we go," Gordon said.

With flashes of laser light, the machine began to shrink into the floor.

.
.

It was an uncomfortable wait. Ten minutes later, the machine returned. Cold vapor whispered across the floor as Stern removed his electronic bundle, tore the tape away, and started to play back.

The outgoing message was played.

There was no response.

The outgoing message was played again.

Again, there was no response. The crackle of static, but nothing.

Gordon was staring at Stern, his face expressionless. Stern said, "There could be a lot of explanations. . . ."

"Of course there could, David."

The outgoing message was played a third time.

Stern held his breath.

More static crackling, and then, in the quiet of the laboratory, he heard Kate's voice say, "Did you guys just hear something?"

Marek: "What are you talking about?"

Chris: "Jeez, Kate, turn your earpiece off."

Kate: "But—"

Marek: "Turn it off."

More static. No more voices.

But the point was made.

"They're alive," Stern said.

"They certainly are," Gordon said. "Let's go see how they're doing at the transit pad."

:

Doniger was walking around in his office, mouthing the words to his speech, practicing his hand gestures, his turns. He had a reputation as a compelling, even charismatic speaker, but Kramer knew that it didn't come naturally. Rather, it was the result of long preparation, the moves, the phrasing, the gestures. Doniger left nothing to chance.

At one time, Kramer had been perplexed by this behavior: his endless, obsessive rehearsal for any public appearances seemed odd for a man who, in most situations, didn't give a damn how he came across to others. Eventually, she realized that Doniger enjoyed public speaking because it was so overtly manipulative. He was convinced he was smarter than anyone else, and a persuasive speech—"They'll never know what hit 'em"—was another way to prove it.

Now Doniger paced, using Kramer as an audience of one. "We are all ruled by the past, although no one understands it. No one recognizes the power of the past," he said, with a sweep of his hand.

"But if you think about it, the past has always been more important than the present. The present is like a coral island that sticks above the water, but is built upon millions of dead corals under the surface, that no one sees. In the same way, our everyday world is built upon millions and millions of events and decisions that occurred in the past. And what we add in the present is trivial.

"A teenager has breakfast, then goes to the store to buy the latest CD of a new band. The kid thinks he lives in a modern moment. But who has defined what a 'band' is? Who defined a 'store'? Who defined a 'teenager'? Or 'breakfast'? To say nothing of all the rest, the kid's entire social setting—family, school, clothing, transportation and government.

"None of this has been decided in the present. Most of it was decided hundreds of years ago. Five hundred years, a thousand years. This kid is sitting on top of a mountain that is the past. *And he never notices it.* He is *ruled* by what he never sees, never thinks about, doesn't know. It is a form of coercion that is accepted without question. This same kid is skeptical of other forms of control—parental restrictions, commercial messages, government laws. But the invisible rule of the past, which decides nearly everything in his life, goes unquestioned. This is real power. Power that can be taken, and used. For just as the present is ruled by the past, so is the future. That is why I say, the future belongs to the past. And the reason—"

Doniger broke off, annoyed. Kramer's cell phone was ringing, and she answered it. He paced back and forth, waiting. Trying one hand gesture, then another.

Finally, Kramer hung up the phone, looked at him. He said, "Yes? What is it?"

"That was Gordon. They're alive, Bob."

"Are they back yet?"

"No, but we got a recorded message of their voices. Three of them are alive for sure."

"A message? Who figured out how to do that?"

"Stern."

"Really? Maybe he's not as stupid as I thought. We should hire him." He paused. "So: are you telling me we'll get them back after all?"

"No. I'm not sure about that."

"What's the problem?"

"They're keeping their earpieces turned off."

"They are? But why? The earpiece batteries have plenty of power to go thirty-seven hours. There's no reason to keep them off." He stared. "Do you think? You think it's *him*? You think it's Deckard?"

"Maybe. Yes."

"How? It's been over a year. Deckard must be dead by now—remember the way he kept picking fights with everybody?"

"Well, *something* made them turn off their earpieces. . . ."

"I don't know," Doniger said. "Rob had too many transcription errors, and he was out of control. Hell, he was going to jail."

"Yes. For beating up some guy in a bar he'd never seen before," Kramer said. "The police report said Deckard hit him fifty-two times with a metal chair. The guy was in a coma for a year. And Rob was definitely going to jail. That's why he volunteered to go back one more time."

"If Deckard's still alive," Doniger said, "then they're still in trouble."

"Yes, Bob. They're still in plenty of trouble."

# 09:57:02

Back in the cool darkness of the forest, Marek drew a rough map in the dirt with a stick. "Right now, we're here, behind the monastery. The mill is over here, about a quarter mile from where we are. There's a checkpoint we have to get past."

"Uh-huh," Chris said.

"And then we have to get into the mill."

"Somehow," Chris said.

"Right. After that, we have the key. So we go to the green chapel. Which is where, Kate?"

She took the stick, and drew a square. "If this is La Roque, on top of the cliff, then there's a forest to the north. The road's about here. I think the chapel is not very far—maybe here."

"A mile? Two miles?"

"Say two miles."

Marek nodded.

"Well, that's all easy enough," Chris said, standing and wiping the dirt from his hands. "All we have to do is get past the armed checkpoint, into the fortified mill, then go to some chapel—and not get killed on the way. Let's get started."

:

Leaving the forest behind, they moved through a landscape of destruction. Flames leapt above the Monastery of Sainte-Mère, and clouds of smoke darkened the sun. Black ash covered the ground, fell on their faces and shoulders, and thickened the air. They tasted grit in their mouths. Across the river, they could just make out the dark outline of Castelgard, now a blackened, smoking ruin on the hillside.

Walking through this desolation, they saw no one else for a long time. They passed one farmhouse to the west of the monastery, where an elderly man lay on the ground, with two arrows in his chest. From inside, they heard the sound of a baby crying. Looking inside, they saw a woman, hacked to death, lying face down by the fire; and a young boy of six, staring at the sky, his innards sliced open. They did not see the baby, but the sounds seemed to be coming from a blanket in the corner.

Kate started toward it, but Marek held her back. "Don't."

They continued on.

:

The smoke drifted across an empty landscape, abandoned huts, untended fields. Aside from the farmhouse with its slaughtered inhabitants, they saw no one else.

"Where is everybody?" Chris said.

"They're all in the woods," Marek said. "They have huts there, and underground shelters. They know what to do."

"In the woods? How do they live?"

"By attacking any soldiers that pass by. That's why the knights kill anyone they find in the forest. They assume they're *godins*—brigands—and they know that the *godins* will return the favor, if they can."

"So that's what happened to us, when we first landed?"

"Yes," Marek said. "The antagonism between commoners and nobles is at its worst right now. Ordinary people are angry that they're forced to support this knightly class with their taxes and tithes, but when the time comes, the knights don't fulfill their part of the bargain. They can't win the battles to protect the country. The French king has been captured, which is very symbolic to the common folk. And now that the war between England and France has stopped, they see only too clearly that the knights are the cause of further destruction. Both Arnaut and Oliver fought for their respective kings at Poitiers. And now they both pillage the countryside to pay their troops. The people don't like it. So they form bands of *godins*, living in the forest, fighting back whenever they can."

"And this farmhouse?" Kate said. "How does that happen?"

Marek shrugged. "Maybe your father was killed in the forest by peasant bandits. Maybe your brother had too much to drink one night, wandered off, and was murdered and stripped naked by peasant bands. Maybe your wife and children were traveling from one castle to another and vanished without a trace. Eventually, you are ready to take out your anger and frustration on somebody. And eventually, you do."

"But—"

Marek fell silent, pointing ahead. Above a line of trees, a fluttering green-and-black banner moved quickly to the left, carried by a rider galloping on horseback.

Marek pointed to the right. They moved quietly upstream. And they came at last to the mill bridge, and the checkpoint.

:

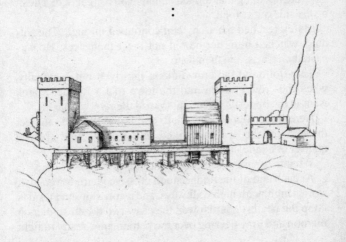

On the river bank, the mill bridge ended in a high stone wall
with an arched opening. A stone tollbooth stood on the other
side of the arch. The only road to La Roque ran through the
arch, which meant that Oliver's soldiers, who controlled the
bridge, also controlled the road.

Above the road, the limestone cliffs were high and sheer.
There was no alternative but to go through the arch. And
standing by the arch, talking with the soldiers by the toll-
house, was Robert de Kere.

Marek shook his head.

A stream of peasants, mostly women and children, some
carrying a few belongings, was walking up the road. They
were heading for the protection of the castle at La Roque.
De Kere talked to a guard, and glanced at the peasants from
time to time. He didn't seem to be paying much attention, but
they could never walk past him undetected.

Eventually, de Kere went back inside the fortified bridge.
Marek nudged the others, and they set out on the road,
moving slowly toward the checkpoint. Marek felt himself
start to sweat.

The guards were looking at peoples' belongings, and con-
fiscating anything that looked valuable, tossing it onto a heap
by the side of the road.

Marek reached the arch, then continued through. The soldiers watched him, but he did not meet their eyes. He was
past, then Chris, and then Kate.

They followed the crowd along the river, but eventually,
when the crowd turned into the town of La Roque, Marek
went in the opposite direction, toward the river's edge.

Here there was no one at all, and they were able to peer
through foliage at the fortified mill bridge, now about a
quarter of a mile downstream.

What they saw was not encouraging.

At each end of the bridge stood massive guard towers, two
stories high, with high walkways, and arrow slots on all sides.
Atop the nearest guard tower, they saw two dozen soldiers in
maroon and gray peering over the battlements, ready to fight.

There was an equal number of soldiers atop the far tower, where the pennant of Lord Oliver snapped in the breeze.

Between the two towers, the bridge consisted of two different-size buildings, connected by ramps. Four water wheels churned below, powered by the flowing stream, which was accelerated by a series of dams and watercourses.

"What do you think?" Marek said to Chris. This structure was, after all, Chris's particular interest. He'd been studying it for two years. "Can we get in?"

Chris shook his head. "Not a chance. Soldiers everywhere. There's no way in."

"What is the building nearest us?" Marek said, indicating a two-story structure of wood.

"That's got to be a flour mill," Chris said. "Probably with the grinding wheels on the upper floor. The flour goes down a chute to bins on the bottom floor, where it's easier to sack the flour and carry it out."

"How many people work there?"

"Probably two or three. But right now"—he pointed to the troops—"maybe none at all."

"Okay. The other building?"

Marek pointed to the second building, connected by a short ramp to the first. This building was longer and lower. "Not sure," Chris said. "It might be for metalwork, a pulper for paper, or a pounder for beer mash, or even a woodworking mill."

"You mean with saws?"

"Yes. They have water-powered saws at this time. If that's what it is."

"But you can't be sure?"

"Not just by looking, no."

Kate said, "I'm sorry, why are we even bothering to talk about this? Just look at it: there's no way we can ever get in."

"We have to get in," Marek said. "To look at Brother Marcel's cell, to get the key that is there."

"But how, André? How do we get in?"

Marek stared silently at the bridge for a long time. Finally, he said, "We swim."

Chris shook his head. "No way." The bridge pylons in the water were sheer, the stones green and slippery with algae. "We'd never climb there."

"Who said anything about climbing?" Marek said.

# 09:27:33

Chris gasped as he felt the chill of the river. Marek was already pushing away from the shore, drifting downstream with the current. Kate was right behind him, moving to the right, trying to align herself in the center of the stream. Chris plunged after them, glancing nervously toward the shore.

So far, the soldiers hadn't seen them. The gurgle of the river was loud in his ears, the only sound he heard. He turned away, looking forward, toward the approaching bridge. He felt his body tense. He knew he had only one chance—if he missed, the current would sweep him downstream, and it was unlikely that he would ever make his way back up again without being captured.

So this was it.

One chance.

A series of small stone walls had been built out from the sides of the river to accelerate the water, and he moved forward more rapidly now. Directly ahead was a watercourse slide, just before the wheels. They were in the shadow of the bridge. Everything was happening fast. The river was white water, a rushing roar. He could hear the creak of the wooden wheels as he came closer.

Marek reached the first wheel; he grabbed hold of the spokes, swung around, stepped onto a paddle and rose upward, carried by the wheel, then was lost from view.

He made it look easy.

Now Kate had reached the second wheel, near the center of the bridge. Agile, she easily caught the rising spoke, but in the next moment she almost lost her grip, struggling to hold on. She finally swung up onto a paddle, crouching low.

Chris slid down the angled watercourse, grunting as his body bounced over the rocks. The water around him boiled like rapids, the current carrying him swiftly toward the spinning water wheel.

Now it was his turn.

The wheel was close.

Chris reached out for the nearest spoke as it broke water, and grabbed—cold and slippery—hand slid on algae—splinters cut his fingers—losing his grip—he grabbed with his other hand—desperate—the spoke was rising into the air—he couldn't hold it—let go, fell back in the water— grabbed for the next spoke as it came up—missed it—*missed it*—and then was swept relentlessly onward, back into the sunlight, going downstream.

He'd missed!

*Damn.*

The current pushed him onward. Away from the bridge, away from the others.

He was on his own.

# 09:25:12

Kate got one knee on the paddle of the water wheel and felt herself lifted clear of the water. Then her other knee, and she crouched down, feeling her body rise into the air. She looked back over her shoulder in time to see Chris heading down-stream, his head bobbing in the sunlight. And then she was carried up and over, and into the mill.

:

She dropped to the ground, crouching in darkness. The wooden boards beneath her feet sagged, and she smelled an odor of rotting damp. She was in a small chamber, with the wheel behind her and a rotating set of wooden-tooth gears creaking noisily to her right. Those gears meshed with a ver-tical spindle, making the vertical shaft turn. The shaft disap-peared up into the ceiling. She felt water splatter on her as she paused, listening. But she could hear nothing but the sound of water and the creaking of the wood.

A low door stood directly ahead. She gripped her dagger and slowly pushed the door open.

:

Grain hissed down a wooden chute from the ceiling above and emptied into a square wooden bin beside her on the floor. Sacks of grain were piled high in the corner. The air was hazy with yellow dust. Dust covered all the walls, the surfaces and the ladder in the corner of the room that led up to the second floor. She remembered that Chris had once said that this dust was explosive, that a flame would blow the building apart. And indeed, she saw no candles in the room, no candle-holders on the walls. No sort of fire.

Cautiously, she crept toward the ladder. Only when she reached it did she see two men lying among the sacks, snoring loudly, empty wine bottles at their feet. But neither gave any sign of awakening.

She began to climb the ladder.

She passed a rotating granite wheel turning noisily against another below. The grain came down a sort of funnel and en-tered a hole in the center of the upper wheel. Then ground grain came out the sides, spilling through a hole to the floor below.

In the corner of the room, she saw Marek, crouched over

the body of a soldier lying on the ground. He held his finger to his lips and pointed to a door on the right. Kate heard voices: the soldiers in the gatehouse. Quietly, Marek raised the ladder and slid it over to block the door shut.

Together, they removed the soldier's broadsword, his bow, and his quiver of arrows. The dead body was heavy; it was surprisingly difficult to strip the weapons. It seemed to take a long time. She looked at the man's face—he had a two-day growth of beard, and a canker sore on his lip. His eyes were brown, staring.

She jumped back with fright when the man suddenly raised his hand toward her. Then she realized she'd caught her damp sleeve on his bracelet. She pulled it free. The hand dropped back with a thunk.

Marek took the man's broadsword. He gave the bow and arrows to her.

Several white monk's habits hung in a row on pegs on the wall. Marek slipped one on, gave a second one to her.

Now he pointed to the left, toward the ramp leading to the second building. Two soldiers in maroon and gray stood on the ramp, blocking their way.

Marek looked around, found a heavy stick used for stirring grain, and handed it to her. He saw more bottles of wine in the corner. He took two, opened the door, and said something in Occitan, waving the bottles at the soldiers. They hurried over. Marek pushed Kate to the side of the door and said one word: "Hard."

The first soldier came in, followed immediately by the second. She swung the stick at his head and hit him so hard she was sure she had broken his skull. But she hadn't; the man fell, but immediately started to get up again. She hit him two more times, and then he fell flat on his face and didn't move. Meanwhile, Marek had broken the wine bottle over the other soldier's head, and he was now kicking him repeatedly in the stomach. The man struggled, raising his arms to protect himself, until she brought the stick down on his head. Then he stopped moving.

Marek nodded, slipped the broadsword under his robes,

and started across the ramp, head slightly bowed, like a monk. Kate followed behind.

She did not dare to look at the soldiers on the guard towers. She had concealed the quiver under her robes, but she had to carry the bow outside, in plain view. She didn't know if anybody had noticed her or not. They came to the next building, and Marek paused at the door. They listened, but heard nothing except a loud repetitive banging and the rush of the river below.

Marek opened the door.

.
.

Chris coughed and sputtered, bobbing in the river. The current was slower now, but he was already a hundred yards downstream from the mill. On both sides of the river, Arnaut's men were standing around, obviously waiting for the order to attack the bridge. A large number of horses stood nearby, held by pages.

The sun reflected brightly off the surface of the water into the faces of Arnaut's men. He saw them squinting, and turning their backs to the river. The glare was probably why they hadn't seen him, Chris realized.

Without splashing or raising his arms, he made his way to the north bank of the Dordogne and slipped among overhanging rushes at the water's edge. Here no one would see him. He could catch his breath for a moment. And he had to be on this side of the river—the French side—if he hoped to rejoin André and Kate.

That is, assuming they made it out of the mill alive. Chris didn't know what the chances of that were. The mill was crawling with soldiers.

And then he remembered that Marek still had the ceramic. If Marek died, or disappeared, they'd never get back home. But they'd probably never get back anyway, he thought.

Something thumped the back of his head. He turned to see a dead rat, bloated with gas, floating in the water. The moment of revulsion spurred him to get out of the river. There were no soldiers right where he was now; they were standing in the shade of an oak grove, a dozen yards downstream. He climbed out of the water and sank down in the undergrowth. He felt the sun on his body, warming him. He heard the soldiers laughing and joking. He knew he should move to a more secluded place. Where he was now, lying among low bushes on the shore, anyone walking along the riverside trail would easily see him. But as he felt warmer, he also felt overcome with exhaustion. His eyes were heavy, his limbs weary, and despite his sense of danger, he told himself, he would close his eyes just for a few moments.

Just for a few moments.

:

Inside the mill, the noise was deafening. Kate winced as she stepped onto the second-floor landing and looked down on the room below. Running the length of the building, twin rows of trip-hammers clanged down on blacksmith's anvils, making a continuous banging that reverberated off the stone walls.

Beside each anvil was a tub of water and a brazier with glowing coals. This was clearly a forge, where steel was annealed by alternately heating, pounding and cooling in water; the wheels provided the pounding force.

But now, the trip-hammers were banging down unattended as seven or eight uniformed soldiers in maroon and gray methodically searched every corner of the room, looking beneath the rotating cylinders and under the banging hammers, feeling the walls for secret compartments in the stone, and rummaging through the chests of tools.

She had no doubt what they were looking for: Brother Marcel's key.

Marek turned to her and signaled that they should go down the stairs and toward a side door, now standing ajar. This was the only door in the side wall; it had no lock, and it was almost certainly Marcel's room.

And clearly, it had already been searched.

For some reason, this didn't bother Marek, who went down intently. At the foot of the stairs, they made their way past the banging trip-hammers and slipped inside Marcel's room.

Marek shook his head.

This was indeed a monk's cell, very small, and strikingly bare: just a narrow cot, a basin of water and a chamber pot. By the bed stood a tiny table with a candle. That was all. Two of Marcel's white robes hung on a peg inside the door.

Nothing else.

It was clear from a glance that there were no keys in this room. And even if there had been, the soldiers would already have found them.

Nevertheless, to Kate's surprise, Marek got down on his hands and knees and began to search methodically under the bed.

:

Marek was remembering what the Abbot had said just before he was killed.

The Abbot didn't know the location of the passage, and he desperately wanted to find out, so he could provide it to Arnaut. The Abbot had encouraged the Professor to search through old documents—which made sense, if Marcel was so demented that he could no longer tell anybody what he had done.

The Professor had found a document that mentioned a key, and he seemed to think this was a discovery of importance. But the Abbot had been impatient: "Of course there is a key. Marcel has many keys. . . ."

So the Abbot already knew about the existence of a key. He knew where the key was. But he still couldn't use it.

Why not?

Kate tapped Marek on the shoulder. He looked over, to see she had pushed aside the white robes. On the back of the door he saw three carved designs, in some Roman pattern. The designs had a formal, even decorative quality that seemed distinctly unmedieval.

And then he realized that these weren't designs at all. They were explanatory diagrams.

They were keys.

:

The diagram that held his attention was the third one, on the far right side. It looked like this:

The diagram had been carved in the wood of the door many years before. Undoubtedly, the soldiers had already seen it. But if they were still searching, then they hadn't understood what it meant.

But Marek understood.

Kate was staring at him, and she mouthed, *Staircase?*

Marek pointed to the image. He mouthed, *Map.*

Because now at last it was all clear to him.

VIVIX wasn't found in the dictionary, because it wasn't a word. It was a series of numerals: V, IV and IX. And these numerals had specific directions attached to them, as indicated by the text in the parchment: DESIDE. Which was also not a word, but rather stood for DExtra, SInistra, DExtra. Or in Latin: "right, left, right."

Therefore, the key was this: once inside the green chapel, you walked five paces to the right, four paces to the left and nine paces to the right.

And that would bring you to the secret passage.

He grinned at Kate.

What everybody was looking for, they had at last found. They had found the key to La Roque.

# 09:10:23

Now all they had to do was get out of the mill alive, Kate thought. Marek went to the door, peered cautiously out at the soldiers in the main room. She came up alongside him.

She counted nine soldiers. Plus de Kere. That made ten altogether.

Ten against two.

The soldiers seemed less preoccupied with their search than before. Many of them were looking at one another over the pounding trip-hammers, and shrugging, as if to say, Aren't we finished? What's the point?

Clearly, it would be impossible for Kate and Marek to leave without detection.

Marek pointed at the stairs to the upper ramp. "You go straight to the stairs and out of here," he said. "I'll cover you. Later, we'll regroup downstream on the north bank. Okay?"

Kate looked at the soldiers. "It's ten against one. I'll stay," she said.

"No. One of us has to make it out of here. I can handle this. You go." He reached in his pocket. "And take this with you." He held out the ceramic to her.

She felt a chill. "Why, André?"

*"Take it."*

And they moved out into the room. Kate headed toward the stairs, returning as she had come. Marek moved across the room, toward the far windows, overlooking the river.

Kate was halfway up the stairs when she heard a shout. All around the room, soldiers were running toward Marek, who had thrown back his monk's cowl and was already battling one.

Kate didn't hesitate. Taking her quiver from beneath her robes, she notched the first arrow, and drew her bow. She remembered Marek's words: *If you want to kill a man . . .* She had thought it was laughable at the time.

A soldier was shouting, pointing at her. She shot him; the arrow struck his neck at the shoulder. The man staggered back into a brazier, screaming as he fell into glowing coals. A second soldier near him was backing away, looking for cover, when Kate shot him full in the chest. He sagged to the ground, dead.

Eight left.

Marek was battling three at one time, including de Kere. Swords clanged as the men dodged among the pounding triphammers and leapt over spinning cams. Marek had already killed one soldier, who lay behind him.

Seven left.

But then she saw the soldier get to his feet; his death had been a pretense, and now he moved forward cautiously, intending to attack Marek from behind. Kate notched another arrow, shot him. The man tumbled down, clutching his thigh; he was only wounded; Kate shot him in the head as he lay on the wood.

She was reaching for another arrow when she saw that de Kere had broken away from the fight with Marek and was now running up the stairs toward her with surprising speed.

Kate fumbled for another arrow, notched it, and shot at de Kere. But she was hasty and missed. Now de Kere was coming fast.

Kate dropped her bow and arrow and ran outside.

•

She ran along the ramp to the mill, looking down at the water. Everywhere, she could see river stones beneath the hissing white water: it was too shallow for her to jump. She'd have to go back down the way she had come up. Behind her, de Kere was shouting something. On the guard tower ahead, a group of archers drew their bows.

By the time the first arrows were flying, she had reached

the door to the flour mill. De Kere was by then running backward, screaming at the archers, shaking his fist in the air. Arrows thunked down all around him.

In the upper mill room, troops were crashing against the door, which was blocked by the ladder. She knew the ladder wouldn't hold for long. She went to the hole in the floor and swung down into the room beneath. With all the commotion, the drunken soldiers were waking up, staggering bleary-eyed to their feet. But with so much yellow dust in the air, it was hard to see them very well.

That was what gave her the idea: all the dust in the air.

She reached into her pouch and brought out one of the red cubes. It said "60" on it. She pulled the tab, and tossed it in a corner of the room.

She started counting silently backward in her mind.

Fifty-nine. Fifty-eight.

De Kere was now on the floor directly above her, but he hesitated to come down, unsure if she was armed. She heard many voices and footsteps up above; the soldiers from the guardhouse had broken through. There must be a dozen men up there. Maybe more.

Out of the corner of her eye, she saw one of the drunken soldiers by the sacks lunge forward and grab at her. She kicked hard between his legs and he fell whimpering, curling on the ground.

Fifty-two. Fifty-one.

She crouched down, and moved into the small side room where she first arrived. The water wheel was creaking, spraying water. She shut the low door, but it had no latch or lock. Anyone could come in.

Fifty. Forty-nine.

She looked down. The opening in the floor, where the wheel continued its rotation downward, was wide enough to allow her to pass through. Now all she had to do was grab one of the passing paddles and ride the wheel down until she was low enough to drop safely into the shallow water.

But as she faced the water wheel, trying to time her move, she realized it was easier said than done. The wheel seemed to be turning very fast, the paddles blurring past her. She felt the water spatter her face, blurring her vision. How much time was left? Thirty seconds? Twenty? Staring at the wheel, she'd lost track. But she knew she couldn't wait. If Chris was right, the entire mill would explode any second now. Kate reached forward, grabbed a passing paddle—started to fall with it—chickened out—released it—reached again—chickened out—and then pulled back, took a breath, steadied herself, got ready again.

She heard the thump of men jumping down from the upper floor, one after another, into the adjacent room. She had no time left.

She had to go.

She took a deep breath, grabbed the next paddle with both hands, pressing her body against the wheel. She slipped through the opening—and emerged into sunlight—she had made it!—until suddenly she was yanked away from the wheel, and found herself hanging in midair.

She looked up.

Robert de Kere held her arm in a steel grip. Reaching down through the opening, he had caught her at the last moment as she descended. And now he was holding her, dangling her in the air. Inches away, the wheel continued to turn. She tried to twist free of de Kere's grip. His face was grim, determined as he watched her.

She struggled.

He held tight.

Then she saw something change in his eyes—some instant of uncertainty—and the soggy wooden floor began to give way beneath him. Their combined weight was too much for the old wood planking, which for years had been soaked by water from the wheel. The planks now bent slowly downward. One plank broke soundlessly, and de Kere's knee went through, but still he held her fast.

How much time? she thought. With her free hand, she pounded on de Kere's wrist, trying to make him release her.

How much time?

De Kere was like a bulldog, hanging on, never letting go.

Another plank in the floor broke, and he lurched sideways. If another broke, he would fall through alongside her.

And he didn't care. He would hang on to the end.

*How much time?*

With her free hand, she grabbed a passing paddle and used the force of the wheel to drag her body downward against de Kere's restraining grip. Her arms burned with the tension, but it worked—the boards cracked—de Kere was falling through—he released her—and she fell the final few feet toward boiling white water around the wheel.

And then there was a flash of yellow light, and the wooden building above her vanished in a hot roar. She glimpsed boards flying in all directions, and then she upended and plunged head first into the icy water. She saw stars, briefly, and then she lost consciousness beneath the churning water.

# 09:04:01

Chris was awakened by the shouts of soldiers. He looked up, to see soldiers running across the mill bridge in great confusion. He saw a monk in a white robe climb out a window from the larger building, then he realized it was Marek, hacking at someone inside with his sword. Marek slid down on vines until he was low enough to risk jumping, then dropped into the river. Chris didn't see Marek come to the surface.

He was still watching when the flour mill exploded in a blast of light and flying timbers. Soldiers, thrown into the air by the force of the explosion, tumbled like dolls from the battlements. As the smoke and dust cleared, he saw that the flour mill was gone—all that remained were a few wooden timbers, now burning. Dead soldiers floated in the river below, which was thick with boards from the shattered mill.

He still didn't see Marek anywhere, and he didn't see Kate, either. A white monk's robe drifted past him, carried by the current, and he had the sudden sick feeling that she was dead.

If so, then he was alone. Risking communication, he tapped his earpiece and said softly, "Kate. André."

There was no response.

"Kate, are you there? André?"

He heard nothing in his earpiece, not even static.

He saw a man's body floating face down in the river, and it looked like Marek. Was it? Yes, Chris was sure: dark-haired, big, strong, wearing a linen undershirt. Chris groaned. Soldiers farther up the bank were shouting; he turned to see how close they were. When he looked back at the river again, the body had floated away.

Chris dropped back down behind the bushes and tried to figure out what to do next.

∶

Kate broke the surface, lying on her back. She floated helplessly downstream with the current. All around her, beams of jagged wood were smashing down into the water like missiles. The pain in her neck was so severe it made her gasp for breath, and with each breath, electric shocks streaked down her arms and legs. She couldn't move her body at all, and she thought she was paralyzed, until she slowly realized that she could move the very tips of her fingers, and her toes. The pain began to withdraw, moving up her limbs, localizing now in her neck, where it was very severe. But she could breathe a little better, and she could move all her limbs. She did it again: yes, she could move her limbs.

So she wasn't paralyzed. Was her neck broken? She tried a small movement, turning ever so slightly to the left, then to the right. It was painful as hell, but it seemed okay. She drifted. Something thick was dripping into her eye, making it hard to see. She wiped it away, saw blood on her fingertips. It must be coming from somewhere on her head. Her forehead burned. She touched it with the flat of her hand. Her palm was bright red with blood.

She drifted downstream, still on her back. The pain was still so strong, she didn't feel confident to roll over and swim. For the moment, she drifted. She wondered why the soldiers hadn't seen her.

Then she heard shouts from the shore, and realized that they had.

·
·

Chris peered over the bushes just in time to see Kate floating on her back downstream. She was injured; the whole left side of her face was covered in blood, flowing from her scalp. And she wasn't moving much. She might be paralyzed.

For a moment, their eyes met. She smiled slightly. He knew if he revealed himself now he would be captured, but he didn't hesitate. Now that Marek was gone, he had nothing to lose; they might as well stay together to the end. He splashed into the water, wading out to her. Only then did he realize his mistake.

He was within bowshot of the archers still on the remaining bridge tower, and they began firing at him, arrows hissing into the water.

Almost immediately, a knight in full armor splashed out on horseback into the river from Arnaut's side. The knight wore his helmet, and it was impossible to see his face, but he evidently feared nothing, for he placed his body and horse in a position to block the archers. His horse sank deeper as it came forward, and it was eventually swimming, the knight waist-deep in the water when he hauled Kate across his saddle like a wet sack and then grabbed Chris by the arm, saying, *"Allons!"* as he turned back to shore.

·
·

Kate slid off the saddle and onto the ground. The knight barked an order, and a man carrying a flag with diagonal red-and-white stripes came running up. He examined Kate's head injury, cleaned it and stanched the bleeding, then bandaged it with linen.

Meanwhile, the knight dismounted, unlaced his helm, and removed it. He was a tall and powerful man, extraordinarily handsome and dashing, with dark wavy hair, dark eyes, a full, sensuous mouth, and a twinkle in his eyes that suggested amusement at the foolish ways of the world. His complexion was dark, and he looked Spanish.

When Kate had been bandaged the knight smiled, showing perfect white teeth. "If you will do me the great honor to accompany me." He led them back toward the monastery and its church. At the side door to the church stood a group of soldiers, and another on horseback, carrying the green-and-black banner of Arnaut de Cervole.

As they walked toward the church, every soldier they passed along the way bowed to the knight, saying, "My Lord . . . My Lord . . ."

Following, Chris nudged Kate. "That's *him*."

"Who?"

"Arnaut."

"That knight? You're kidding."

"Look how the soldiers behave."

"Arnaut saved our lives," Kate said.

Chris was aware of the irony. In twentieth-century historical accounts of this time, Sir Oliver was portrayed as something close to a soldier-saint, while de Cervole was a black figure, "one of the great evildoers of his age," in the words of one historian. Yet apparently the truth was just the opposite of the histories. Oliver was a despicable rogue, and Cervole a dashing exemplar of chivalry—to whom they now owed their lives.

Kate said, "What about André?"

Chris shook his head.

"Are you sure?"

"I think so. I think I saw him in the river."

Kate said nothing.

Outside the church of Sainte-Mère were long rows of men, standing with their hands bound behind their backs, waiting to go inside. They were mostly soldiers of Oliver in maroon and gray, with a few peasants in rough garb. Chris guessed there were forty or fifty men in all. As they went past, the men stared sullenly at them. Some of them were wounded; they all seemed weary.

One man, a soldier in maroon, said sarcastically to another, "There goes the bastard lord of Narbonne. He does the work too dirty even for Arnaut."

Chris was still trying to understand this when the handsome knight whirled. "Say you so?" he cried, and he grabbed a fistful of the man's hair, jerked his head up, and with his other hand slashed his throat with a dagger. Blood gushed down the man's chest. The man remained standing for a moment, making a kind of rasping sound.

"You have made your last insult," the handsome knight said. He stood, smiling at the man, watching as the blood flowed, grinning as the man's eyes widened in horror. Still the man remained standing. To Chris, he seemed to stand forever, but it must have been thirty or forty seconds. The handsome knight just watched silently, never moving, the smile never leaving his face.

Finally the man fell to his knees, head bowed, as if in prayer. The knight calmly put his foot under the man's chin and kicked him so he fell backward. He continued to watch the man's death gasps, which continued for another minute or so. At last he died.

The handsome knight bent over, wiped his blade on the man's hose, and wiped his bloody shoe on his jerkin. Then he nodded to Chris and Kate.

And they entered the church of Sainte-Mère.

:

The interior was hazy with smoke. The ground floor was a large open space; there would be no benches or pews for another two hundred years. They stood at the back, with the handsome knight, who seemed content to wait. Off to one side, they saw several soldiers in a tight, whispering knot.

A solitary knight in armor was down on his knees in the center of the church, praying.

Chris turned back to look at the other knights. They seemed to be in the middle of some intense dispute; their whispers were furious. But he could not imagine what it was about.

While they waited, Chris felt something drip on his shoulder. Looking up, he saw a man hanging directly above him, twisting slowly on a rope. Urine dribbled down his leg. Chris stepped away from the wall and saw half a dozen bodies, hands tied behind their backs, hanging from ropes tied to the second-floor balustrade. Three wore the red surcoat of Oliver. Two others had peasant garb, and the last wore the white habit of a monk. Two more men sat on the floor, watching silently as more ropes were tied above; they were passive, apparently resigned to their fate.

In the center of the room, the man in armor crossed himself and got to his feet. The handsome knight said, "My Lord Arnaut, here are the assistants."

"Eh? What do you say? Assistants?"

The knight turned. Arnaut de Cervole was about thirty-five years old and wiry, with a narrow, unpleasant, cunning face. He had a facial tic that made his nose twitch and gave him the appearance of a sniffing rat. His armor was streaked with blood. He looked at them with bored, lazy eyes. "You say they are assistants, Raimondo?"

"Yes, my Lord. The assistants of Magister Edwardus."

"Ah." Arnaut walked around them. "Why are they wet?"

"We pulled them from the river, my Lord," Raimondo said. "They were in the mill and escaped at the last minute."

"Oh so?" Arnaut was bored no longer. His eyes gleamed with interest. "I pray you tell me, how did you destroy the mill?"

Chris cleared his throat and said, "My Lord, we did not."

"Oh?" Arnaut frowned. He looked at the other knight. "What speech is this? He is incomprehensible."

"My Lord, they are Irishers, or perhaps Hebrideans."

"Oh? Then they are not English. That is something in their

favor." He circled them, then stared at their faces. "Do you understand me?"

Chris said, "Yea, my Lord." That seemed to be understood.

"Are you English?"

"No, my Lord."

"Faith, you do not appear it. You look too mild and unwarlike." He looked at Kate. "He is as fresh as a young girl. And this one . . ." He squeezed Chris's biceps. "He is a clerk or a scribe. Certes he is not English." Arnaut shook his head, his nose twitching.

"Because the English are savages," he said loudly, his voice echoing in the smoky church. "You agree?"

"We do, my Lord," Chris said.

"The English know no way of life except endless dissatisfaction and interminable strife. They are always murdering their own kings; it is their savage custom. Our Norman brethren conquered them and tried to teach them civilized ways, but of course they failed. Saxon blood is too deeply barbaric. The English delight in destruction, death and torture. Not content to fight among themselves on their wretched chilly island, they bring their armies here, to this peaceful and prosperous land, and wreak havoc on a simple people. You agree?"

Kate nodded, gave a bow.

"As you should," Arnaut said. "Their cruelty is unsurpassed. You know their old king? The second Edward? You know how they chose to assassinate him, with a red-hot poker? And that, to a king! Little wonder they treat our countryside with even greater savagery."

He strode back and forth. Then turned again to them.

"And the man who next took power, Hugh Despenser. According to the English custom, in due course he too must be killed. You know how? He was tied to a ladder in a public square, and his privates were cut off his body and burned in front of his face. And that was *before* he was beheaded! Eh? *Charmant*."

Again he looked at them for agreement. Again, they nodded.

"And now the latest king, Edward III, has learned the lesson of his forebears—that he must perpetually lead a war, or risk death at the hands of his own subjects. Thus he and his dastard son, the Prince of Wales, bring their barbarian ways to France, a country that knew not savage war until they came to our soil with their *chevauchées*, murdered our commoners, raped our women, slaughtered our animals, ruined our crops, destroyed our cities and ended our trade. For what? So that bloodthirsty English spirits may be occupied abroad. So that they can steal fortunes from a more honorable land. So that every English Lady can serve her guests from French plates. So that they can claim to be honorable knights, when they do nothing more valiant than hack children to death."

Arnaut paused in his tirade and looked back and forth between their faces, his eyes restless, suspicious. "And that is why," he said, "I cannot understand why you have joined the side of the English swine, Oliver."

Chris said quickly, "Not true, my Lord."

"I am not patient. Say sooth: you aid Oliver, for your Magister is in his employ."

"No, my Lord. The Magister is taken against his will."

"Against . . . his . . ." Arnaut threw up his hands in disgust. "Who can tell me what this drowned rascal says?"

The handsome knight approached them. "My English is good," he said. To Chris: *"Spek ayain."* Speak again.

Chris paused, thinking, then said, "Magister Edwardus . . ."

"Yes. . . ."

". . . is prisoner."

*"Priz-un-ner?"* The handsome knight frowned, puzzled. *"Pris-ouner?"*

Chris had the feeling that the knight's English was not as good as he thought. He decided to try his Latin again, poor and archaic as it was. *"Est in carcere—captus—heri captus est de coenobio sanctae Mariae."* He hoped that meant "He was captured from Sainte-Mère yestermorn."

The knight raised his eyebrows. *"Invite?"* Against his will?

"Sooth, my Lord."

The knight said to Arnaut, "They say Magister Edwardus was taken from the monastery yesterday against his will and is now Oliver's prisoner."

Arnaut turned quickly, peered closely at their faces. In a low, threatening voice: *"Sed vos non capti estis. Nonne?"* Yet you were not taken?

Chris paused again. "Uh, we . . ."

*"Oui?"*

"No, no, my Lord," Chris said hastily. "Uh, *non.* We escaped. Uh, *ef— effugi—i—imus. Effugimus."* Was that the right word? He was sweating with tension.

Apparently it was good enough, because the handsome knight nodded. "They say they escaped."

Arnaut snapped, "Escaped? From where?"

Chris: *"Ex Castelgard heri. . . ."*

"You escaped from Castelgard yesterday?"

*"Etiam, mi domine."* Yes, my Lord.

Arnaut stared at him, said nothing for a long time. On the second-floor balcony, the men had ropes put around their necks and then were pushed over. The fall did not break their necks, and so they hung there, making gargling sounds and writhing as they slowly died.

Arnaut looked up at them as if annoyed to be interrupted by their death gasps. "A few ropes remain," he said. He looked back at them. "I will have the truth from you."

Chris said, "I tell you sooth, my Lord."

Arnaut spun on his heel. "Did you speak to the monk Marcel before he died?"

"Marcel?" Chris did his best to appear confused. "Marcel, my Lord?"

"Yes, yes. Marcel. *Cognovistine fratrem Marcellum?"* Do you know Brother Marcel?

"No, my Lord."

*"Transitum ad Roccam cognitum habesne?"* For this Chris didn't need to wait for the translation: The passage to La Roque, you know it?

"The passage . . . *transitum . . ."* Chris shrugged again,

feigning lack of knowledge. "Passage? . . . To La Roque? No, my Lord."

Arnaut looked frankly unbelieving. "It seems you know nothing at all." He peered closely at them, his nose twitching, giving the impression that he was smelling them. "I doubt you. In fact, you are liars."

He turned to the handsome knight. "Hang one, so the other talks."

"Which one, my Lord?"

"Him," Arnaut said, pointing to Chris. He looked at Kate, pinched her cheek, then caressed her. "Because this fair boy touches my heart. I will entertain him in my tent tonight. I would not waste him before."

"Very well, my Lord." The handsome knight barked an order, and from the second floor, men began to string another rope. Other men grabbed Chris's wrists and tied them swiftly behind his back.

Chris thought, Jesus, they're going to do it. He looked at Kate, whose eyes were wide with horror. The men started to drag Chris off.

"My Lord," came a voice from the side of the church. "If you please." The knot of waiting soldiers opened, and the Lady Claire emerged.

:

Claire said softly, "My Lord, I beg you, a word in private."

"Eh? Of course, as you wish." Arnaut walked over to her, and she whispered in his ear. He paused, shrugged. She whispered again, more intently.

After a moment, he said, "Eh? What will that serve?"

More whispering. Chris could not hear any of it.

Arnaut said, "Good Lady, I have already decided."

Still more whispering.

Finally, shaking his head, Arnaut came back to them. "The Lady seeks safe passage from me to Bordeaux. She says that she knows you, and that you are honest men." He paused. "She says that I should release you."

Claire said, "Only if it please you, my Lord. For it is well known the English are indiscriminate in killing, while the French are not. The French show the mercy that comes of intelligence and breeding."

"This is so," he said. "It is true that we French are civilized men. And if these two know nothing of Brother Marcel and the passage, then I have no further use of them. And so I say, give them horses and food and send them on their way. I would be in the good graces of your Magister Edwardus, and so I commend myself to him, and wish God grant you safe journey to join him at his side. And so depart."

Lady Claire bowed.

Chris and Kate bowed.

The handsome knight cut Chris's bonds and led them back outside. Chris and Kate were so stunned by this reversal that they said nothing at all as they walked back toward the river. Chris was feeling wobbly and lightheaded. Kate kept rubbing her face, as if she were trying to wake up.

Finally, the knight said, "You owe your lives to a clever lady."

Chris said, "Certes. . . ."

The handsome knight smiled thinly.

"God smiles upon you," he said.

He didn't sound happy about it.

:

The scene at the river was entirely transformed. Arnaut's men had taken the mill bridge, which now flew the green-and-black banner from the battlements. Both sides of the river were occupied by Arnaut's mounted knights. And now a river of men and matériel marched up the road toward La Roque, raising clouds of dust. There were men with horse-drawn wagons laden with supplies, carts of chattering women, ragtag children, and other wagons loaded with enormous wooden beams—disassembled giant catapults, to fling stones and burning pitch over the castle walls.

The knight had found a pair of horses for them—two ragged nags, bearing marks of the plow collar. Leading the animals, he guided them past the toll checkpoint.

A sudden commotion on the river made Chris look back. He saw a dozen men knee-deep in the water, struggling with a breech-loading cannon, cast of iron, with a wooden block as a mount. Chris stared, fascinated. No cannon this early had survived, or even been described.

Everyone knew primitive artillery had been used at this time; archaeologists had dug up cannonballs from the site of the Battle of Poitiers. But historians believed that cannon were rare, and primarily for show—a matter of prestige. But as Chris watched the men struggling in the river to lift the cylinder and hoist it back on a cart, it was clear to him that such effort would never be wasted on a purely symbolic device. The cannon was heavy; it slowed the progress of the entire army, which surely wanted to reach the walls of La Roque by nightfall; there was no reason why the cannon could not be brought up later. The present effort could only mean the cannon would be important in the attack.

But in what way? He wondered. The walls of La Roque were ten feet thick. A cannonball would never penetrate them.

The handsome knight gave a brief salute and said, "God bring you grace and safety."

"God bless you and grant you increase," Chris replied, and then the knight slapped the horses on their rumps, and they were riding off, toward La Roque.

•

As they rode, Kate told him about what they had found in Marcel's room, and about the green chapel.

"Do you know where this chapel is?" Chris said.

"Yes. I saw it on one of the survey maps. It's about half a mile east of La Roque. There's a path through the forest that takes you there."

Chris sighed. "So we know where the passage is," he said, "but André had the ceramic, and now he's dead, which means we can't ever leave, anyway."

"No," she said. "I have the ceramic."

"You do?"

"André gave it to me, on the bridge. I think he knew he'd

never get out alive. He could have run and saved himself. But he didn't. He stayed and saved me instead."

She started to cry softly.

Chris rode in silence, saying nothing. He remembered how Marek's intensity had always amused the other graduate students—"Can you imagine? He really believes this chivalry shit!"—and how they had assumed his behavior was some kind of weird posturing. A role he was playing, an affectation. Because in the late twentieth century, you couldn't seriously ask other people to think that you believed in honor and truth, and the purity of the body, the defense of women, the sanctity of true love, and all the rest of it.

But apparently, André really had believed it.

:

They moved through a nightmare landscape. The sun was weak and pale in the dust and smoke. Here there were vineyards, but all the vines were burned, leaving gnarled gnome stumps, with smoke rising into the air. The orchards, too, were black and desolate, skeletal trees. Everything had been burned.

All around them, they heard the pitiful cries of wounded soldiers. Many retreating soldiers had fallen beside the road itself. Some were still breathing; others were gray with death.

Chris had paused to take weapons from one of the dead men, when a nearby soldier raised his hand and cried pitifully, *"Secors, secors!"* Chris went over to him. He had an arrow embedded deep in his abdomen, and another in his chest. The soldier was in his early twenties, and he seemed to know he was dying. As he lay on his back, he looked pleadingly at Chris, saying words Chris couldn't understand. Finally, the soldier began to point to his mouth, saying, *"Aquam. Da mihi aquam."* He was thirsty; he wanted water. Chris shrugged helplessly. He had no water. The man looked angry, winced, closed his eyes, turned away. Chris moved off. Later, when they passed men crying for help, he continued on without stopping. There was nothing he could do.

They could see La Roque in the distance, standing high

and impregnable atop the Dordogne cliffs. And they would reach the fortress in less than an hour.

:

In a dark corner of the church of Sainte-Mère, the handsome knight helped André Marek to his feet. He said, "Your friends have departed."

Marek coughed, and grabbed the knight's arm to steady himself as a wave of pain shot up his leg. The handsome knight smiled. He had captured Marek just after the explosion at the mill.

When Marek had climbed out the mill window, by sheer luck he fell into a small pool so deep that he did not hurt himself. And when he came to the surface again, he found he was still beneath the bridge. The pool produced a swirling eddy, so the current hadn't taken him downstream.

Marek had stripped off his monk's habit and thrown it downstream when the flour mill exploded, timbers and bodies flying in all directions. A soldier splashed into the water near him, his body turning in the eddy. Marek started to scramble up onto the bank—and a handsome knight put a sword point at his throat and beckoned for him to come forward. Marek was still wearing the maroon and gray colors of Oliver, and he began to babble in Occitan, pleading innocence, begging for mercy.

The knight said simply, "Be silent. I saw you." He had seen Marek climb out the window, and discard his monk's garb. He took Marek to the church, where he found Claire and Arnaut. The Archpriest was in a sullen and dangerous mood, but Claire seemed to have some ability to influence him, if only by contradiction. It was Claire who had ordered Marek to sit silently in the darkness when Chris and Kate came in. "If Arnaut can set you against the other two, he may yet spare you and your friends. If you are three united before him, he will in rage kill you all." Claire had stage-managed the subsequent events. And all had turned out reasonably well.

So far.

Now Arnaut eyed him skeptically. "So: your friends know the location of this passage?"

"They do," Marek said. "I swear it."

"On your word, I have spared their lives," Arnaut said. "Yours, and the word of this Lady, who vouches for you." He gave a small nod to the Lady Claire, who allowed a faint smile to cross her lips.

"My Lord, you are wise," Claire said, "for to hang one man may loosen the tongue of his friend who watches. But as often, it may harden his resolve, so that the friend takes his secret to the grave. And this secret is so important that I would your Lordship have it for certain in his grasp."

"Then we will follow those two, and see where they lead." He nodded to Marek. "Raimondo, see to this poor man's mount. And provide him as escort two of your best *chevaliers*, as you follow behind."

The handsome knight bowed. "My Lord, if it please you, I will accompany him myself."

"Do so," Arnaut said, "for there may yet be some mischief here." And he gave the knight a significant look.

Meanwhile, Lady Claire had gone up to Marek and was pressing his hand warmly in both of hers. He felt something cool in her fingers, and realized it was a tiny dagger, barely four inches long. He said, "My Lady, I am greatly in your debt."

"Then see you repay this debt, knight," she said, looking into his eyes.

"I shall, as God is my witness." He slipped the dagger under his robes.

"And I will pray to God for you, knight," she said. She leaned over to kiss his cheek chastely. As she did, she whispered, "Your escort is Raimondo of Narbonne. He likes to cut throats. When he knows the secret, have a care he does not cut yours, and those of your friends, as well." She stepped away, smiling.

Marek said, "Lady, you are too kind. I shall take your kind wishes to heart."

"Good knight, God speed you safe and true."

"Lady, you are always in my thoughts."

"Good sir knight, I would wish—"

"Enough, enough," Arnaut said in a disgusted voice. He turned to Raimondo. "Go now, Raimondo, for this surfeit of sentiment makes my stomach heave."

"My Lord." The handsome knight bowed. He led Marek to the door and out into the sunlight.

# 07:34:49

"I'll tell you what the goddamn problem is," Robert Doniger said, glaring at the visitors. "The problem is to bring the past alive. To make it real."

There were two young men and a young woman, all slouching on the couch in his office. They were dressed entirely in black, wearing those pinch-shoulder jackets that looked like they'd shrunk in the wash. The men had long hair and the woman had a buzz cut. These were the media people that Kramer had hired. But Doniger noticed that today Kramer was sitting opposite them, subtly divorcing herself from them. He wondered if she had already seen their material.

It made Doniger irritable. He didn't like media people anyway. And this was his second meeting with the breed today. He'd had the PR dipshits in the morning, now *these* dipshits.

"The problem," he said, "is that I have thirty executives coming to hear my presentation tomorrow. The title of my presentation is 'The Promise of the Past,' and I have no compelling visuals to show them."

"Got it," one of the young men said crisply. "That was

exactly our starting point here, Mr. Doniger. The client wants to bring the past alive. That's what we set out to do. With Ms. Kramer's help, we asked your own observers to generate sample videos for us. And we believe this material will have the compelling quality—"

"Let's see it," Doniger said.

"Yes, sir. Perhaps if we lowered the lights—"

"Leave the lights as they are."

"Yes, Mr. Doniger." The video screen on the wall came up blue as it glowed to life. While they were waiting for the image, the young man said, "The reason we like this first one is because it is a famous historical event that lasts only two minutes from start to finish. As you know, many historical events occurred very slowly, especially to modern sensibilities. This one was quick. Unfortunately, it occurred on a somewhat rainy day."

The screen showed a gray, gloomy image, overhanging clouds. The camera panned to show some sort of gathering, shot over the heads of a large crowd. A tall man was climbing up onto a plain, unpainted wood platform.

"What's this? A hanging?"

"No," the media kid said. "That's Abraham Lincoln, about to deliver the Gettysburg Address."

"It is? Jesus, he looks like hell. He looks like a corpse. His clothes are all wrinkled. His arms stick out of his sleeves."

"Yes, sir, but—"

"And is that his voice? It's *squeaky*."

"Yes, Mr. Doniger, no one's ever heard Lincoln's voice before, but that is his actual—"

"Are you out of your fucking minds?"

"No, Mr. Doniger—"

"Oh, for Christ's sake, I can't use this," Doniger said. "No one wants Abraham Lincoln to sound like Betty Boop. What else have you got?"

"It's right here, Mr. Doniger." Unruffled, the young man changed the tapes, saying, "For the second video, we adopted a different premise. We wanted a good action sequence, but again, a famous event that everybody would know. So this is Christmas Day, 1778, on the Delaware River, where—"

"I can't see shit," Doniger said.

"Yes, I'm afraid it *is* a bit dark. It's a night crossing. But we thought George Washington crossing the Delaware would be a good—"

"George Washington? Where is George Washington?"

"He's right there," the kid said, pointing to the screen.

"Where?"

"There."

"He's that guy huddled in the back of the boat?"

"That's correct, and—"

"No, no, no," Doniger said. "He has to be standing in the bow, like a general."

"I know that's the way the paintings portray him, but it's not what actually happened. Here you see the real George Washington as he actually crossed the—"

"He looks seasick," Doniger said. "You want me to show a video of George Washington looking seasick?"

"But this is reality."

"Fuck reality," Doniger said, throwing one of their video-tapes across the room. "What's the *matter* with you people? I don't care about reality. I want something intriguing, some-thing sexy. You're showing me a walking corpse and a drowned rat."

"Well, we can go back to the drawing board—"

"My talk is tomorrow," Doniger said. "I have three major executives coming here. And I have already told them they would see something very special." He threw up his hands. "Jesus Christ."

Kramer cleared her throat. "What about using stills?"

"Stills?"

"Yes, Bob. You could take single frames from these videos, and that might be quite effective," Kramer said.

"Uh-huh, yes, that would work," the media woman said, head bobbing.

Doniger said, "Lincoln would still look wrinkled."

"We'll take the wrinkles out with Photoshop."

Doniger considered that. "Maybe," he said finally.

"Anyway," Kramer said, "you don't want to show them too much. Less is more."

"All right," Doniger said. "Make the stills up, and show them to me in an hour."

The media people filed out. Doniger was alone with Kramer. He went behind his desk, shuffled through his presentation. Then he said, "Do you think it should be 'The Promise of the Past,' or 'The Future of the Past'?"

"'The Promise of the Past,'" Kramer said. "Definitely 'The Promise.'"

# 07:34:49

Accompanied by two knights, Marek rode in the dust of the baggage carts, moving toward the head of the column. He could not see Chris or Kate yet, but his little group was moving swiftly. He would catch up to them soon.

He looked at the knights on either side of him. Raimondo on his left, erect, in full armor, with his thin smile. On his right, a grizzled warrior in armor, clearly tough and competent. Neither man paid him much attention, so secure were they in their control over him. Especially since his hands were bound together by ropes, with a six-inch gap between the wrists.

He rode along, coughing in the dust. Eventually he managed to slip his small dagger from beneath his coat, and palm it beneath his hand as he gripped the wooden pommel of the saddle in front of him. He tried to position the knife so the gentle movement of the horse up and down would slowly fray the rope at his wrists. But this was easier said than done; the knife seemed to be always in the wrong position, and his bonds were not cut. Marek glanced at his wristband counter; it read 07:31:02. There were still more than seven hours left before the batteries ran out.

Soon they had left the riverside trail behind and started to climb the twisting road up through the village of La Roque. The village was built into the cliffs above the river, the houses almost entirely of stone, giving the town a unified, somber appearance, especially now, when every door and window was boarded shut in anticipation of war.

Now they moved among the lead companies of Arnaut's soldiers, more knights in armor, each with their retinues following. Men and horses climbed the steep cobbled streets, horses snorting, baggage carts slipping as they went up. These knights in the lead had a sense of urgency; many of the carts carried pieces of disassembled siege engines. Evidently, they planned to begin the siege before nightfall.

They were still within the town when Marek caught sight of Chris and Kate, riding side by side on sagging mounts. They were perhaps a hundred yards ahead, alternately visible and hidden as the road twisted up. Raimondo put his hand on Marek's arm. "We approach no closer."

In the dust ahead, a banner flapped too near a horse's face. The horse reared, whinnying; a cart turned over, spilling cannonballs, which began to roll down the hill. This was the moment of confusion Marek had been waiting for, and he acted on it. He spurred his horse, which refused to go. Then he saw the grizzled knight had deftly grabbed the reins.

"My friend," Raimondo said calmly, riding beside him. "Do not make me kill you. At least, not yet." He nodded to Marek's hands. "And put that foolish little blade away, before you hurt yourself."

Marek felt his cheeks burn. But he did as he was told; he put the small dagger back beneath his robes. They rode on in silence.

From behind the stone houses, they heard the cry of a bird, repeated twice. Raimondo's head snapped around when he heard it; so did his companion's on the other side. Evidently it was not a bird.

The men listened, and soon there was an answering cry from farther up the hill. Raimondo rested his hand on his sword, but did nothing else.

"What is it?" Marek said.

"No wise your affair."

And they said nothing else.

The soldiers were busy and no one paid them any attention, especially since their saddles had Arnaut's colors of green and black. Eventually, they arrived at the top of the cliff and came out into an open field with the castle on their right. The forest was close by on their left, and the broad, sloping, grassy plain was to the north.

With Arnaut's soldiers all around them, Marek did not particularly think about the fact that they were passing some fifty yards from the outer moat and the gatehouses of the castle entrance. Chris and Kate were still about a hundred yards ahead, up the column.

The attack came with stunning swiftness. Five mounted knights charged from the woods to their left, shouting battle cries and swinging their swords over their heads. They ran right for Marek and the others. It was an ambush.

With a howl, Raimondo and the grizzled knight drew their swords to fight. The horses wheeled; blades clanged. Arnaut himself galloped up and joined the fray, fighting furiously. Marek was momentarily ignored.

Looking up the column, he saw that another group had attacked Kate and Chris. Marek glimpsed the black plume of Sir Guy, and then the horsemen had surrounded the two. Marek spurred his mount and began galloping up the line.

Ahead, he saw one knight grab Chris by his coat and try to pull him from his horse; another grabbed the reins of Kate's horse, which whinnied and turned. Another knight had taken Chris's reins, but he kicked his horse so that it reared; the knight let go, but Chris was suddenly covered in blood, and he cried out in shock. Chris lost control of his horse, which whinnied and galloped away into the woods while he slid sideways in the saddle, hanging on weakly. In a moment, he had vanished among the trees.

Kate was still trying to pull her reins free from the knight who held them. All around them was pandemonium; Arnaut's men shouting and circling, running for their weapons, jabbing at the attacking knights with their pikes. One stabbed at the knight holding her horse, and the knight dropped the reins. Marek, though unarmed, charged into the middle of the fight, separating Kate from her attacker. She cried, "André!" but he said to her, "Go! *Go!*" and then Marek cried, *"Malegant!"* and Sir Guy turned to face him.

Marek immediately rode his own horse away from the fray, galloping directly toward La Roque. The other knights wheeled and broke free of the soldiers, thundering across the open field after Marek. Down the line, Marek saw Raimondo and Arnaut fighting in a great cloud of dust.

Kate kicked her horse, spurring him toward the woods to the north. Looking behind her as she rode, she saw Marek ride over the drawbridge of La Roque, into the castle, and out of sight. The pursuing riders followed him. Then the heavy grill of the portcullis gate came rumbling down. And the drawbridge raised up.

Marek was gone. Chris was gone. Either or both of them might be dead. But one thing was clear. She was the only one still free.

It was up to her now.

# 07:24:33

Surrounded on all sides by soldiers, she spent the next half hour threading her way through Arnaut's baggage train of horses and carts, trying to reach the northern woods. Arnaut's men were setting up a vast tented camp at the edge of the woods, facing the great grassy plain that sloped up to the castle.

Men shouted to her to come and help them, but she could only wave in what she hoped was a manly greeting, and keep moving. At length she reached the edge of the forest, and followed it until she saw the narrow trail leading into darkness and isolation. Here she paused a few moments to let the horse rest, and to let her own pounding heart slow down, before she went into the woods.

Back on the plain, the trebuchets were being swiftly assembled by groups of engineers. The trebuchets looked ungainly—oversized slingshots with heavy wooden beams

bracing the armature for the firing paddle, which was winched back by stout hemp ropes, then released to snap upward, flinging its payload over the castle walls. The entire contraption appeared to weigh five hundred pounds, but the men constructed it swiftly, working in quick coordination, then going on to the next engine. But at least she understood now how, in some instances, a church or a castle could be built in a couple of years. The workers were so skilled, so self-effacing, they hardly needed direction.

She turned the horse away and entered the dense woods north of the castle.

:

The path was a narrow track through the forest, which rapidly grew dark as she went deeper. It felt spooky to be alone here; she heard the hooting of owls and the distant cries of strange birds. She passed one tree with a dozen ravens sitting on branches. She counted them, wondering if it was an omen, and what it might portend.

Riding slowly through the forest, she had the sense of slipping backward in time, of taking on more primitive ways of thought. The trees closed over her; the ground was as dark as evening. She had a sense of confinement, of oppression.

After twenty minutes, she was relieved to come into a clearing with tall grass in sunlight. She saw a break in the trees on the far side, where the path resumed. She was riding through the clearing when she saw a castle off to her left. She didn't remember any sort of structure from her charts, but it was here nevertheless. The castle was small—almost a manor house—and whitewashed, so that it shone brightly in the sun. It had four small turrets and a blue slate roof. At first glance, it looked cheerful, but then she noticed all the windows were barred; part of the slate roof had fallen in, leaving a ragged hole; the outbuildings were crumbling and in disrepair. This clearing had once been a mown field in front of the castle, now grown wild from neglect. She had a strong sense of stagnation and decay.

She shivered and spurred the horse on. She noticed that the grass ahead had recently been trampled down—by the footprints of another horse, moving in the same direction as she. As she looked, she saw the long blades of grass slowly rising upward, returning to their original position.

Someone had been here very recently. Perhaps only a few minutes before. Cautiously, she proceeded toward the far end of the clearing.

Darkness closed around her again as she slipped back into the forest. The trail ahead was becoming muddy, and she could see distinct hoofprints going forward.

From time to time, she paused and listened intently. But

she heard nothing at all up ahead. Either the rider was far in front of her or he was very quiet. Once or twice, she thought she heard the sound of a horse, but she couldn't be sure.

It was probably her imagination.

She pushed on, toward the green chapel. To what had been called, on her maps, *la chapelle verte morte*. The chapel of green death.

:

In the darkness of the forest, she came upon a figure leaning wearily against a fallen tree. He was a wizened old man, wearing a hood and carrying a woodsman's ax. As she rode by, he said, "I beg you, good master, I beg you." His voice was thin, rasping. "Give me some small thing to eat, for I am poor, and have no food."

Kate did not think she had any food, but then she remembered the knight had given them a small bundle, tied behind her saddle. She reached back, found a crust of bread and a piece of dried beef. It didn't look appetizing, particularly since it now smelled strongly of horse sweat. She held the food out to him.

Eagerly, the man came forward, reached a bony hand for the food—but instead he grabbed her outstretched arm at the wrist with a surprisingly strong grip and, with a swift yank, tried to pull her from the horse. He cackled with delight, a nasty sound; as he struggled with her, his hood fell back, and she saw that he was younger than she had thought. Now, three other men ran forward from the shadows on both sides of the path, and she realized that they were *godins*, the peasant bandits. Kate was still in the saddle, but clearly not for long. She kicked the horse, but it was tired and unresponsive. The older man continued tugging at her arm, all the while muttering, "Foolish boy! You silly boy!"

Not knowing what else to do, she screamed for help, screaming at the top of her lungs, and this seemed to startle the men, so that they paused for a moment before resuming their attack. But then they heard the sound of a galloping horse coming toward them, and the roar of a warrior's battle cry, and the *godins* looked at one another and scattered. All except the wizened man, who refused to release Kate and now threatened her with his ax, which he raised in his other hand.

But in that moment an apparition, a bloodred knight on horseback, came crashing down the trail, his horse snorting, flinging clops of mud, the knight himself so fierce and bloody that the last man ran for his life, plunging into the darkness of the forest.

Chris reined up and circled around her. She felt a huge wave of relief flood through her; she had been badly frightened. Chris was smiling, clearly pleased with himself.

"Are you all right, ma'am?" he said.

"Are *you*?" Kate asked, amazed. Chris was literally drenched in blood; it had dried all over his face and body, and when he smiled, it cracked at the sides of his mouth, revealing the pink skin beneath. He looked as if he had fallen in a vat of red.

"I'm fine," Chris said. "Somebody hacked the horse next to me, cut an artery or something. I was soaked in a second. Blood is *hot*, did you know that?"

Kate was still staring at him, amazed to see anyone who looked like that making jokes, and then he took her horse's reins and led her quickly away. "I think," Chris said, "we won't wait for them to regroup. Didn't your mother tell you not to talk to strangers, Kate? Especially when you meet them in the woods?"

"Actually, I thought you were supposed to give them food and they helped you."

"Only in fairy tales," he said. "In the real world, if you stop to help the poor man in the woods, he and his friends steal your horse and kill you. That's why nobody does it."

Chris was still grinning, and he seemed so confident and amused, and she had the feeling that she had never noticed, never been aware, that he was quite an attractive man, that he had a certain genuine appeal. But of course, she thought, he had saved her life. She was just grateful.

"What were you doing, anyway?" she said.

He laughed. "Trying to catch up to you. I thought you were way ahead of me."

:

The path divided. The main path appeared to go off to the right, beginning a slow descent. A much narrower track went to the left, on flat ground. But it seemed much less used.

"What do you think?" Kate said.

"Take the main road," Chris said. He led the way forward, and Kate was quite happy to follow him. The forest around them grew more lush, the ground ferns six feet high, like huge elephant ears, obscuring her view ahead. She heard a distant roar of water. The land began to slope downward more sharply, and she couldn't see her footing because of the ferns. They both dismounted and tied their horses loosely to a tree. They proceeded on foot.

The land sloped steeply downward now, and the path turned into a muddy track. Chris slipped, grasping at branches and shrubs to break his slide. She watched as he slipped and slid, and then with a yell, he was gone.

She waited. "Chris?"

No answer.

She tapped her earpiece. "Chris?"

Nothing.

She was not sure what to do, whether to go forward or retrace her steps backward. She decided to follow him, but cautiously, now that she knew how slippery the path was, and what had happened to him. Yet after only a few careful steps, her feet shot out from beneath her, and she was sliding helplessly in the mud, banging against tree trunks, getting the wind knocked out of her.

The terrain grew steeper. Kate fell backward in the mud and slid down on her backside, trying to use her feet to push off tree trunks as they rushed up. Branches scratched her face, tore at her hands as she reached for them. She didn't seem able to stop her headlong rush down.

And all the time, the terrain grew steeper. Now the trees ahead were thinning, she could see light between the trunks, and she heard the rush of water. She was sliding down a path that ran parallel to a small stream. The trees thinned more, and she saw that the forest ended abruptly about twenty yards ahead. The rushing sound of water grew louder.

And then she realized why the forest ended.

It was the edge of a cliff.

And beyond was a waterfall. Directly ahead.

Terrified, Kate rolled over on her stomach, dug her fingers like claws into the mud, but to no avail. She still continued to slide. She couldn't stop. She rolled onto her back, still sliding down a chute of mud, helpless to do anything but watch the end coming, and then she shot out of the forest and was flying in the air, hardly daring to look down.

:

Almost immediately, she smashed down into foliage, clutched at it, and held. She swung up and down. She was in the branches of a large tree, hanging out over the cliff. The waterfall was directly below her. It wasn't as large as she had thought. Maybe ten, fifteen feet high. There was a pool at the base. She couldn't tell how deep it was.

She tried to climb back along the branches of the tree, but her hands were slippery from the mud. She kept slipping, twisting on the branch. Eventually, she was hanging beneath, clutching it with hands and legs like a sloth as she tried to work her way backward. She went another five feet, then realized she would never make it.

She fell.

She struck another branch, four feet lower. She hung there a moment, gripping the branch with slippery, muddy hands. Then she fell again, struck a lower branch.

Now she was just a few feet above the waterfall as it curved, roaring, over the lip of the cliff. The branches of the tree were wet from mist. She looked at the churning pool of water at the base. She couldn't see the bottom; she couldn't be sure how deep it was.

Hanging precariously from the branch, she thought:

Where the hell is Chris? But in the next moment, she lost her grip and fell the rest of the way.

∴

The water was an icy shock, bubbling, opaque, roiling furiously around her. She tumbled, disoriented, kicked to the surface, banged against rocks on the bottom. Finally, she came up beneath the waterfall, which pounded on her head with incredible force. She couldn't breathe. She ducked down again, swam ahead, and came out a few yards downstream. The water in the pool was calmer, though still chillingly cold.

She climbed out and sat on a rock. She saw that the churning water had washed all the mud from her clothes, from her body. She felt somehow new—and very glad to be alive.

Catching her breath, she looked around.

She was in a narrow little vale, the afternoon light misty from the waterfall. The valley was lush and wet, the grass was wet, the trees and rocks covered in moss. Directly ahead, a stone path led to a small chapel.

The chapel was wet, too, its surfaces covered with a kind of slimy mold, which streaked the walls and dripped from the edge of the roof. The mold was bright green.

The green chapel.

She also saw broken suits of armor heaped untidily beside the chapel door, old breastplates rusting in the pale sun and dented helmets lying on their sides; also swords and axes casually thrown all around.

Kate looked for Chris but didn't see him. Evidently, he hadn't fallen all the way, as she had. Probably he was now making his way down by another path. She thought she would wait for him; she had been happy to see him earlier, and missed him now. But she didn't see Chris anywhere. And aside from the waterfall, she heard no sound at all in the little valley, not even birds. It was ominously silent.

And yet she did not feel alone. She had the strong sense of something else here—a *presence* in the valley.

And then she heard a growling sound from inside the chapel: a guttural, animal sound.

She stood, and moved cautiously along the stone path toward the weapons. She picked up a sword and gripped the handle in both hands, even though she felt foolish; the sword was heavy, and she knew she had neither the strength nor the skill to use it. She was now close to the chapel door, and she smelled a strong odor of decay from inside. The growling came again.

And suddenly, an armored knight stepped forward, blocking the doorway. He was a huge man, nearly seven feet tall, and his armor was smeared with green mold. He wore a heavy helmet, so she could not see his face. He carried a heavy double-bladed ax, like an executioner's.

The ax swung back and forth as the knight advanced toward her.

:

Instinctively, she backed away, her eyes on the ax. Her first thought was to run, but the knight had jumped out at her quickly; she suspected he might be able to catch her. Anyway, she didn't want to turn her back on him. But she couldn't attack; he seemed to be twice her size. He never spoke; she heard only grunting and snarling from inside the helmet—animal sounds, demented sounds. He must be insane, she thought.

The knight came quickly closer, forcing her to act. She swung her sword with all her strength; he raised his ax to block and metal clanged against metal; her sword vibrated so strongly, she nearly lost her grip. She swung again, low, trying to cut his legs, but he easily blocked again, and with a quick twist of his ax, the blade flew out of her hands, landing on the grass beyond.

She turned and ran. Snarling, the knight raced forward and grabbed a fistful of her short hair. He dragged her, screaming, around to the side of the chapel. Her scalp burned; ahead, she saw a curved block of wood on the ground, showing the marks of many deep cuts. She knew what it was: a beheading block.

She was powerless to oppose him. The knight pushed her down roughly, forcing her neck onto the block. He stood with his foot in the middle of her back, to hold her in position. She flailed her arms helplessly.

She saw a shadow move across the grass as he raised his ax into the air.


# 06:40:27


The telephone rang insistently, loudly. David Stern yawned, flicked on the bedside lamp, picked up the receiver. "Hello," he said, his voice groggy.

"David, it's John Gordon. You'd better come down to the transit room."

Stern fumbled for his glasses, looked at his watch. It was 6:20 a.m. He had slept for three hours.

"There's a decision to make," Gordon said. "I'll be up to get you in five minutes."

"Okay," Stern said, and hung up. He got out of bed and opened the blinds at the window; bright sunlight shone in, so bright that it made him squint. He headed for the bathroom to take a shower.

He was in one of three rooms that ITC maintained in their laboratory building for researchers who had to work through the night. It was equipped like a hotel room, even down to the little bottles of shampoo and moisturizing cream by the sink. Stern shaved and dressed, then stepped out into the hallway. He didn't see Gordon anywhere, but he heard voices from the far end of the corridor. He walked down the hall, looking through the glass doors into the various labs. They were all deserted at this hour.

But at the end of the corridor, he found a lab with its door open. A workman with a yellow tape was measuring the height and width of the doorway. Inside, four technicians were all standing around a large table, looking down at it. On the table was a large scale model built of pale wood, showing the fortress of La Roque and the surrounding area. The men were murmuring to one another, and one was tentatively lifting the edge of the table. It seemed they were trying to figure out how to move it.

"Doniger says he has to have it," the technician said, "as an exhibit after the presentation."

"I don't see how we get it out of the room," another said. "How'd they get it in?"

"They built it in place."

"It'll just make it," said the man at the door, snapping his tape measure shut.

Curious, Stern walked into the room, looked more closely at the model. It showed the castle, recognizable and accurate, in the center of a much larger complex. Beyond the castle was a ring of foliage, and outside that a complex of blocky buildings and a network of roads. Yet none of that existed. In medieval times, the castle had stood alone on a plain.

Stern said, "What model is this?"

"La Roque," a technician said.

"But this model isn't accurate."

"Oh yes," the technician said, "it's entirely accurate. At least according to the latest architectural drawings they've given us."

"What architectural drawings?" Stern said.

At that, the technicians fell silent, worried looks on their faces. Now Stern saw there were other scale models: of Castelgard, and of the Monastery of Sainte-Mère. He saw large drawings on the walls. It was like an architect's office, he thought.

At that moment, Gordon stuck his head in the door. "David? Let's go."

∴

He walked down the corridor with Gordon. Looking over his shoulder, he saw the technicians had turned the model on end and were carrying it through the door.

"What's that all about?" Stern said.

"Site-development study," Gordon said. "We do them for every project site. The idea is to define the immediate environment around the historical monument, so that the site itself is preserved for tourists and scholars. They study view lines, things like that."

"But why is that any of your business?" Stern said.

"It's absolutely our business," Gordon said. "We're going to spend millions before a site is fully restored. And we don't want it junked up with a shopping mall and a bunch of high-rise hotels. So we try to do larger site planning, see if we can get the local government to set guidelines." He looked at Stern. "Frankly, I never thought it was particularly interesting."

"And what about the transit room? What's going on there?"

"I'll show you."

∴

The rubber floor of the transit site had been cleared of debris and cleaned. In the places where acid had eaten through the rubber, the flooring was being replaced by workmen on their hands and knees. Two of the glass shields were in place, and one was being inspected closely by a man wearing thick goggles and carrying an odd hooded light. But Stern was looking upward as the next big glass panels were swung in on overhead cranes from the second transit site, still being built.

"It's lucky we had that other transit site under construction," Gordon said to him. "Otherwise, it'd take us a week to get these glass panels down here. But panels were already here. All we have to do is move them over. Very lucky."

Stern still stared upward. He hadn't realized how large the shielding panels were. Suspended above him, the curved glass panels were easily ten feet high and fifteen feet wide, and almost two feet deep. They were carried in padded slings toward special mounting brackets in the floor below. "But," Gordon said, "we have no spares. We just have one full set."

"So?"

Gordon walked over to one of the glass panels, already standing in place. "Basically, you can think of these things as big glass hip flasks," Gordon said. "They're curved containers that fill from a hole at the top. And once we fill them with water, they're very heavy. About five tons each. The curve actually improves the strength. But it's the strength I'm worried about."

"Why?" Stern said.

"Come closer." Gordon ran his fingers over the surface of the glass. "See these little pits? These little grayish spots? They're small, so you'd never notice them unless you looked carefully. But they're flaws that weren't there before. I think the explosion blew tiny drops of hydrofluoric acid into the other room."

"And now the glass has been etched."

"Yes. Slightly. But if these pits have weakened the glass, then the shields may crack when they are filled with water and the glass is put under pressure. Or worse, the entire glass shield may shatter."

"And if it does?"

"Then we won't have full shielding around the site," Gordon said, looking directly at Stern. "In which case, we can't safely bring your friends back. They'd risk too many transcription errors."

Stern frowned. "Do you have a way to test the panels? See if they'll hold up?"

"Not really, no. We could stress-test one, if we were willing to risk breaking it, but since we have no spare panels, I won't do that. Instead, I'm doing a microscopic polarization visual inspect." He pointed to the technician in the corner, wearing goggles, going over the glass. "That test can pick up preexisting stress lines—which always exist in glass—and give us a rough idea of whether they'll break. And he's got a digital camera that is feeding the data points directly into the computer."

"You going to do a computer simulation?" Stern said.

"It'll be very crude," Gordon said. "Probably not worth doing, it's so crude. But I'll do it anyway."

"So what's the decision?"

"When to fill the panels."

"I don't understand."

"If we fill them now, and they hold up, then everything is probably fine. But you can't be sure. Because one of the tanks may have a weakness that will break only after a period of pressure. So that's an argument to fill all the tanks at the last minute."

"How fast can you fill them?"

"Pretty fast. We have a fire hose down here. But to minimize stress, you probably want to fill them slowly. In which case, it would take almost two hours to fill all nine shields."

"But don't you get field bucks starting two hours before?"

"Yes—if the control room is working right. But the control room equipment has been shut down for ten hours. Acid fumes have gotten up there. It may have affected the electronics. We don't know if it is working properly or not."

"I understand now," Stern said. "And each of the tanks is different."

"Right. Each one is different."

It was, Stern thought, a classic real-world scientific problem. Weighing risks, weighing uncertainties. Most people never understood that the majority of scientific problems took this form. Acid rain, global warming, environmental cleanup, cancer risks—these complex questions were always a balancing act, a judgment call. How good was the research data? How trustworthy were the scientists who had done the work? How reliable was the computer simulation? How significant were the future projections? These questions arose again and again. Certainly the media never bothered with the complexities, since they made bad headlines. As a result, people thought science was cut and dried, in a way that it never was. Even the most established concepts—like the idea that germs cause disease—were not as thoroughly proven as people believed.

And in this particular instance, a case directly involving the safety of his friends, Stern was faced with layers of uncertainty. It was uncertain whether the tanks were safe. It was uncertain whether the control room would give adequate warning. It was uncertain whether they should fill the tanks slowly now, or quickly later. They were going to have to make a judgment call. And lives depended on that call.

Gordon was staring at him. Waiting.

"Are any of the tanks unpitted?" Stern said.

"Yes. Four."

"Then let's fill those tanks now," Stern said. "And wait for the polarization analysis and the computer sim before filling the others."

Gordon nodded slowly. "Exactly what I think," he said.

Stern said, "What's your best guess? Are the other tanks okay, or not?"

"My best guess," Gordon said, "is that they are. But we'll know more in a couple of hours."

# 06:40:22

"Good Sir André, I pray you come this way," Guy de Malegant said with a gracious bow and a wave of his hand.

Marek tried to conceal his astonishment. When he had galloped into La Roque, he fully expected that Guy and his men would kill him at once. Instead, they were treating him deferentially, almost as an honored guest. He was now deep in the castle, in the innermost court, where he saw the great hall, already lit inside.

Malegant led him past the great hall and into a peculiar stone structure to the right. This building had windows fitted not only with wooden shutters but with windowpanes made of translucent pig bladders. There were candles in the windows, but they were outside the pig bladders, instead of inside the room itself.

He knew why even before he stepped into the building, which consisted of a single large room. Against the walls, gray fist-size cloth sacks stood heaped high on raised wooden platforms above the floor. In one corner, iron shot was piled in dark pyramids. The room had a distinctive smell—a sharp, dry odor—and Marek knew exactly where he was.

The arsenal.

Malegant said, "Well, Magister, we found one assistant to help you."

"I thank you for that." In the center of the room, Professor Edward Johnston sat cross-legged on the floor. Two stone basins containing mixtures of powder were set to one side. He held a third basin between his knees, and with a stone mortar, he was grinding a gray powder with a steady, circular motion. Johnston did not stop when he saw Marek. He did not register surprise at all.

"Hello, André," he said.

"Hello, Professor."

Still grinding: "You all right?"

"Yes, I'm okay. Hurt my leg a little." In fact, Marek's leg was throbbing, but the wound was clean; the river had washed it thoroughly, and he expected it to heal in a few days.

The Professor continued to grind, patiently, ceaselessly. "That's good, André," he said in the same calm voice. "Where are the others?"

"I don't know about Chris," Marek said. He was thinking of how Chris had been covered with blood. "But Kate is okay, and she is going to find the—"

"That's fine," the Professor said quietly, his eyes flicking up to Sir Guy. Changing the subject, he nodded to the bowl. "You know what I'm doing, of course?"

"Incorporating," Marek said. "Is the stuff any good?"

"It's not bad, all things considered. It's willow charcoal,

which is ideal. The sulfur's fairly pure, and the nitrate's organic."

"Guano?"

"That's right."

"So, it's about what you'd expect," Marek said. One of the first things Marek had studied was the technology of gunpowder, a substance that first became widely employed in Europe in the fourteenth century. Gunpowder was one of those inventions, like the mill wheel or the automobile, that could not be identified with any particular person or place. The original recipe—one part charcoal, one part sulfur, six parts saltpeter—had come from China. But the details of how it had arrived in Europe were in dispute, as were the earliest uses of gunpowder, when it was employed less as an explosive than as an incendiary. Gunpowder was originally used in weapons when *firearms* meant "arms that make use of fire," and not the modern meaning of explosive projectile devices such as rifles and cannon.

This was because the earliest gunpowders were not very explosive, because the chemistry of the powder was not understood, and because the art hadn't been developed yet. Gunpowder exploded when charcoal and sulfur burned extremely rapidly, the combustion enabled by a rich source of oxygen—namely nitrate salts, later called saltpeter. The most common source of nitrates was bat droppings from caves. In the early years, this guano was not refined at all, simply added to the mixture.

But the great discovery of the fourteenth century was that gunpowder exploded better when it was ground extremely fine. This process was called "incorporation," and if properly done, it yielded gunpowder with the consistency of talcum powder. What happened during the endless hours of grinding was that small particles of saltpeter and sulfur were forced into microscopic pores in the charcoal. That was why certain woods, like willow, were preferred; their charcoal was more porous.

Marek said, "I don't see a sieve. Are you going to corn it?"

"No." Johnston smiled. "Corning's not discovered yet, remember?"

Corning was the process of adding water to the gunpowder mixture, making a paste that was then dried. Corned powder was much more powerful than dry-mixed powder. Chemically, what happened was that the water partially dissolved the saltpeter, allowing it to coat the inside of the charcoal micropores, and in the process, it carried the insoluble sulfur particles inside, too. The resulting powder was not only more powerful but also more stable and long-lasting. But Johnston was right; corning was only discovered around 1400— roughly forty years from now.

"Should I take over?" Marek said. Incorporating was a lengthy process; sometimes the grinding went on for six or eight hours.

"No. I'm finished now." The Professor got to his feet, then said to Sir Guy, "Tell my Lord Oliver that we are ready for his demonstration."

"Of Greek Fire?"

"Not precisely," Johnston said.

∴

In the late afternoon sun, Lord Oliver paced impatiently along the massive wall of the outer perimeter. The battlement was more than fifteen feet wide here, dwarfing the row of cannon nearby. Sir Guy was with him, as well as a sullen Robert de Kere; they all looked up expectantly when they saw the Professor. "Well? Are you at last prepared, Magister?"

"My Lord, I am," the Professor said, walking with two of his bowls, one under each arm. Marek carried a third bowl, in which the fine gray powder had been mixed with a thick oil that smelled strongly of resin. Johnston had told him not to touch this mixture on any account, and he needed no reminding. It was a disagreeable, reeking goo. He also carried a bowl of sand.

"Greek Fire? Is it Greek Fire?"

"No, my Lord. Better. The fire of Athenaios of Naukratis, which is called 'automatic fire.' "

"Is that so?" Lord Oliver said. His eyes narrowed. "Show me."

Beyond the cannon was the broad eastern plain, where the trebuchets were being assembled in a line. They were just out of shot range, two hundred yards away. Johnston set his bowls on the ground between the first two cannon. The first cannon he loaded with a sack from the armory. He then placed a thick metal arrow with metal vanes into the cannon. "This is your powder, and your arrow."

Turning to the second cannon, he carefully poured his finely ground gunpowder into a sack, which he stuffed into the cannon mouth. Then he said, "André, the sand, please." Marek came forward and set the basin of sand at the Professor's feet.

"What is that sand for?" Oliver asked.

"A precaution, my Lord, against error." Johnston picked up a second metal arrow, handling it gingerly, holding it only at each end and gently inserting it into the cannon. The tip of the arrow was grooved, the grooves filled with thick brown acrid paste.

"This is my powder, and my arrow."

The gunner handed the Professor a thin stick of wood, glowing red at one end. Johnston touched the first cannon.

There was a modest explosion: a puff of black smoke, and the arrow flew onto the field, landing a hundred yards short of the nearest trebuchet.

"Now my powder, and my arrow."

The Professor touched the second cannon.

There was a loud explosion and a blast of dense smoke. The arrow landed alongside a trebuchet, missing it by ten feet. It lay in the grass.

Oliver snorted. "Is that all? You will forgive me if I have—"

Just then, the arrow burst into a circle of fire, spitting blobs of flame in all directions. The trebuchet immediately caught fire, and men on the field ran forward, carrying the horses' water bags to put it out.

"I see . . . ," Lord Oliver said.

But water seemed to spread the fire, not quench it. With

each new dousing, the flames leapt higher. The men stepped back, confused. In the end, they watched helplessly as the tre-buchet burned before them. In a few moments, it was a mass of charred, smoking timbers.

"By God, Edward and Saint George," Oliver said.

Johnston gave a small bow, smiled.

"You have twice the range and an arrow that alights itself—how?"

"The powder is ground fine and so explodes more fiercely. The arrows are filled with oil, sulfur and quicklime, mixed with tow. Touching any water makes them catch fire—here it's the dampness of the grass. That is why I have a basin of sand, should the slightest bit of the mixture be upon my fin-gers and start to burn from the moisture of my hands. It is a most delicate weapon, my Lord, and delicate to handle."

He turned to the third basin, near Marek.

"Now, my Lord," Johnston said, picking up a wooden stick, "I pray you observe what follows." He dipped the stick into the third bowl, coating the tip with the oily, foul-smelling mixture. He held the stick in the air. "As you see, there is no change. And there shall be no change for hours, or days, until . . ." With the theatricality of a magician, he splashed the stick with a small cup of water.

The stick made a hissing sound, began to smoke, and then burst into flames as the Professor held it. The flame was a hot-orange color.

"Ah," Oliver said, sighing with pleasure. "I must have a quantity of this. How many men do you require to grind and make your substance?"

"My Lord, twenty will do. Fifty is better."

"You shall have fifty, or more as you will," Oliver said, rub-bing his hands. "How quickly can you make it?"

"The preparation is not lengthy, my Lord," Johnston said, "but it cannot be done in haste, for it is dangerous work. And once made, the substance is a hazard within your castle, for Arnaut is certain to attack you with flaming devices."

Oliver snorted. "I care nothing for that, Magister. Make it now, and I shall put it to use this very night."

:

Back in the arsenal, Marek watched as Johnston arranged the soldiers in rows of ten, with a grinding bowl in front of each man. Johnston walked down the rows, pausing now and again to give instructions. The soldiers were grumbling about what they called "kitchen work," but Johnston told them that these were, in his words, the herbs of war.

It was several minutes later when the Professor came over to sit in the corner with him. Watching the soldiers work, Marek said, "Did Doniger give you that speech, about how we can't change history?"

"Yes. Why?"

"It seems like we're giving Oliver a lot of help to defend his castle against Arnaut. Those arrows are going to force Arnaut to push his siege engines back—too far back to be effective. No siege engines, no assault on the fortress. And Arnaut won't play a waiting game. His men want quick scores—all the free companies do. If they can't take a castle right away, they move on."

"Yes, that's true. . . ."

"But according to history, this castle falls to Arnaut."

"Yes," Johnston said. "But not because of a siege. Because a traitor lets Arnaut's men in."

"I've been thinking about that, too," Marek said. "It doesn't make sense. There are too many gates in this castle to open. How could a traitor possibly do it? I don't think he could."

Johnston smiled. "You think we might be helping Oliver keep his castle, and so we're changing history."

"Well. I'm just wondering."

Marek was thinking that whether or not a castle fell was actually a very significant event, in terms of the future. The history of the Hundred Years War could be seen as a series of key sieges and captures. For instance, a few years from now, brigands would capture the town of Moins, at the mouth of the Seine. In itself, a minor conquest—but it would give them control of the Seine, allowing them to capture castles all the way back to Paris itself. Then there was the matter of who lived and who died. Because more often than not, when a castle fell, its inhabitants were massacred. There were several hundred people inside La Roque. If they all survived, their thousands of descendants could easily make a different future.

"We may never know," Johnston said. "How many hours have we got left?"

Marek looked at his bracelet. The counter said 05:50:29. He bit his lip. He had forgotten that the clock was ticking. When he had last looked, there were almost nine hours; there had seemed to be plenty of time. Six hours didn't sound quite so good.

"Not quite six hours," Marek said.

"And Kate has the marker?"

"Yes."

"And where is she?"

"She went to find the passage." Marek was thinking that it was now late afternoon; if she found the passage, she could easily make her way inside the castle in two or three hours.

"Where did she go to find the passage?"

"The green chapel."

Johnston sighed. "Is that where Marcel's key said that it was?"

"Yes."

"And she went alone?"

"Yes."

Johnston shook his head. "No one goes there."

"Why?"

"Supposedly, the green chapel is guarded by an insane knight. They say his true love died there and that he lost his mind with grief. He's imprisoned his wife's sister in a nearby castle, and now he kills anybody who comes near the castle, or the chapel."

"Do you think all that's true?" Marek said.

Johnston shrugged. "No one knows," he said. "Because no one has ever come back alive."

# 05:19:55

Her eyes squeezed tightly shut, Kate waited for the ax to fall. The knight above her was snorting and grunting, his breath coming faster, more and more excited before he delivered the killing blow—

Then he was silent.

She felt the foot in the middle of her back twist.

He was looking around.

The ax thunked down on the block, inches from her face. But he was resting it, leaning on it while he looked at something behind him. He started grunting again, and now he sounded angry.

Kate tried to see what he was looking at, but the flat blade of the ax blocked her view.

She heard footsteps behind her.

There was someone else here.

The ax was raised again, but now the foot came off her back. Hastily, she rolled off the block and turned to see Chris standing a few yards away, holding the sword that she had dropped.

"Chris!"

Chris smiled through clenched teeth. She could see he was terrified. He kept his eyes on the green knight. With a growl, the knight spun, his ax hissing as he swung it. Chris held up his sword to parry. Sparks flew from clanging metal. The men circled each other. The knight swung again, and Chris ducked, stumbled backward, and got hastily to his feet again as the ax thunked into the grass. Kate fumbled in her pouch and found the gas cylinder. This foreign object from another time seemed absurdly small and light now, but it was all they had.

"Chris!"

Standing behind the green knight, she held up the cylinder, so he could see it. He nodded vaguely, continuing to dodge and back away. She saw he was tiring fast, losing ground, the green knight advancing on him.

Kate had no choice: she ran forward, leapt into the air, and landed on the green knight's back. He grunted in surprise at the weight. She clung to him, brought the canister around to the front of his helmet, and fired gas through the slit. The knight coughed and shivered. She squeezed again, and the knight began to stagger. She dropped back to the ground.

She said, "Do it!"

Chris was on one knee, gasping. The green knight was still on his feet, but weaving. Chris came slowly forward and stabbed the sword into the knight's side, between the armor plates. He gave a roar of fury and fell onto his back.

Chris was on him immediately, cutting the laces of his helmet, kicking it away with his foot. She glimpsed tangled hair, matted beard, and wild eyes as he swung the sword down, and severed the knight's head.

∶

It didn't work.

The blade came down, crunched into bone, and stuck there, only partway through his neck. The knight was still alive, looking at Chris in fury, his mouth moving.

Chris tried to pull the sword out, but it was caught in the knight's throat. As he struggled, the knight's left hand came up and grabbed his shoulder. The knight was immensely strong—demonically strong—and pulled him down until his face was inches away. His eyes were bloodshot. His teeth were cracked and rotten. Lice crawled in his beard, among bits of discolored food. He stank of decay.

Chris was revolted. He felt his hot, reeking breath. Struggling, he managed to put his foot on the knight's face, and he stood up, forcing himself free of the grip. The sword came free in the same moment, and he lifted it to swing down.

But the knight's eyes rolled upward and his jaw went slack. He was already dead. Flies began to buzz over his face.

Chris collapsed, sitting on the wet ground, trying to catch his breath. Revulsion swept over him like a wave, and he started to shiver uncontrollably. He hugged himself, trying to stop it. His teeth were chattering.

Kate put her hand on his shoulder. She said, "My hero." He hardly heard her. He didn't say anything. But eventually he stopped shivering and got to his feet again.

"I was glad to see you," she said.

He nodded and smiled. "I took the easy way down."

Chris had managed to stop his slide in the mud. He had spent many difficult minutes working his way back up the slope, and then he took the other path down. It turned out to be an easy walk to the base of the waterfall, where he found Kate about to be beheaded.

"You know the rest," he said. He got to his feet, leaned on the sword. He looked up at the sky. It was starting to get dark. "How much time do you think is left?"

"I don't know. Four, five hours."

"Then we better get started."

:

The ceiling of the green chapel had fallen in at several places, and the interior was in ruins. There was a small altar, Gothic frames around broken windows, pools of stagnant water on the floor. It was hard to see that this chapel had once been a jewel, its doorways and arches elaborately carved. Now slimy mold dripped from the carvings, which were eroded beyond recognition.

A black snake slithered away as Chris went down spiral stairs to the crypts below ground. Kate followed more slowly. Here it was darker, the only light coming from cracks in the floor above. There was the constant sound of dripping water. In the center of the room they saw a single intact sarcophagus, carved of black stone, and the broken fragments of several others. The intact sarcophagus had a knight in armor carved on the lid. Kate peered at the knight's face, but the stone had been eroded by the omnipresent mold, and the features were gone.

"What was the key again?" Chris said. "Something about the giant's feet?"

"That's right, so many paces from the giant's feet. Or gigantic feet."

"From the giant's feet," Chris repeated. He pointed to the sarcophagus, where the feet of the carved knight were two rounded stumps. "Do you suppose it means these feet?"

Kate frowned. "Not exactly giant."

"No. . . ."

"Let's try it," she said. She stood at the foot of the sarcophagus, turned right, and went five paces. Then she turned left, and went four paces. She turned right again, and took three paces before she came up against the wall.

"Guess not," Chris said.

They both turned away and began to search in earnest. Almost immediately, Kate made an encouraging discovery: half a dozen torches, stacked in a corner, where they would stay dry. The torches were crudely made, but serviceable enough.

"The passage has to be here somewhere," she said. "It has to be."

Chris didn't answer. They searched in silence for the next half hour, wiping mold off the walls and floor, looking at the corroded carvings, trying to decide if one or another might represent a giant's feet.

Finally, Chris said, "Did the thing say the feet were *inside* the chapel, or *at* the chapel?"

"I don't know," Kate said. "André read it to me. He translated the text."

"Because maybe we should be looking outside."

"The torches were in here."

"True."

Chris turned, frustrated, looking.

"If Marcel made a key that took off from a landmark," Kate said, "he wouldn't use a coffin or sarcophagus, because that could be moved. He would use something fixed. Something on the walls."

"Or the floor."

"Yes, or the floor."

She was standing by the far wall, which had a little niche cut into the stone. At first she thought these were little altars, but they were too small, and she saw bits of wax; evidently, they had been made to hold a candle. She saw several of these candle niches in the walls of the crypt. The inner surfaces of this niche were beautifully carved, she noticed, with a symmetrical design of bird's wings going up each side. And the carving had not been touched, perhaps because the heat of the candles had suppressed the growth of mold.

She thought, Symmetrical.

Excited, she went quickly to the next candle niche. The carvings depicted two leafy vines. The next niche: two hands clasped in prayer. She went all around the room in this way, checking each one.

None had feet.

Chris was sweeping his toe in big arcs across the floor, scraping away the mold from the underlying stone. He was muttering, "Big feet, big feet."

She looked over at Chris and said, "I feel really stupid."

"Why?"

She pointed to the doorway behind him—the doorway that they had passed through when they first came down the stairs. The doorway that had once been elaborately carved but was now eroded.

It was possible to see, even now, what the original design of the carving had been. On both left and right, the doorway had been carved into a series of lumps. Five lumps, with the largest at the top of the door and the smallest at the bottom. The large lump had a sort of flat indentation on its surface, leaving no doubt what all the lumps were meant to represent.

Five toes, on either side of the door.

"Oh my God," Chris said. "It's the whole damned door."

She nodded. "Giant feet."

"Why would they do that?"

She shrugged. "Sometimes they put hideous and demonic images at entrances and exits. To symbolize the flight or banishment of evil spirits."

They went quickly to the door, and then Kate paced off five steps, then four, then nine. She was now facing a rusty iron ring mounted on the wall. They were both excited by this discovery, but when they tugged at it, the ring broke loose in their hands, crumbling in red fragments.

"We must have done something wrong."

"Pace it again."

She went back and tried smaller steps. Right, left, right again. She was now facing a different section of wall. But it was just wall, featureless stone. She sighed.

"I don't know, Chris," she said. "We must be doing something wrong. But I don't know what." Discouraged, she put her hand out, leaned against the wall.

"Maybe the paces are still too large," Chris said.

"Or too small."

Chris went over, stood next to her by the wall. "Come on, we'll figure it out."

"Do you think?"

"Yeah, I do."

They stepped away from the wall and had started back to the doorway when they heard a low rumbling sound behind them. A large stone in the floor, right where they had been standing, had now slid away. They saw stone steps leading downward. They heard the distant rush of a river. The opening gaped black and ominous.

"Bingo," he said.

# 03:10:12

In the windowless control room above the transit pad, Gordon and Stern stared at the monitor screen. It showed an image of five panels, representing the five glass containers that had been etched. As they watched, small white dots appeared on the panels.

"That's the position of the etch points," Gordon said.

Each point was accompanied by a cluster of numbers, but they were too small to read.

"That's the size and depth of each etching," Gordon said.

Stern said nothing. The simulation continued. The panels began to fill with water, represented by a rising horizontal blue line. Superimposed on each panel were two large numbers: the total weight of the water and the pressure per square inch on the glass surface, at the bottom of each panel, where the pressure was greatest.

Even though the simulation was highly stylized, Stern found himself holding his breath. The waterline went higher, and higher.

One tank began to leak: a flashing red spot.

"One leaking," Gordon said.

A second tank began to leak, and as the water continued to rise, a jagged lightning streak crossed the panel, and it vanished from the screen.

"One shattered."

Stern was shaking his head. "How rough do you think this simulation is?"

"Pretty fast and dirty."

On the screen, a second tank shattered. The final two filled to the top without incident.

"So," Gordon said. "The computer's telling us three out of five panels can't be filled."

"If you believe it. Do you?"

"Personally, I don't," Gordon said. "The input data's just not good enough, and the computer is making all kinds of stress assumptions that are pretty hypothetical. But I think we better fill those tanks at the last minute."

Stern said, "It's too bad there isn't a way to strengthen the tanks."

Gordon looked up quickly. "Like what?" he said. "You have an idea?"

"I don't know. Maybe we could fill the etchings with plastic, or some kind of putty. Or maybe we could—"

Gordon was shaking his head. "Whatever you do, it has to be uniform. You'd have to cover the entire surface of the tank evenly. *Perfectly* evenly."

"I can't see any way to do that," Stern said.

"Not in three hours," Gordon said. "And that's what we have left."

Stern sat down in a chair, frowning. For some reason, he was thinking of racing cars. A succession of images flashed through his mind. Ferraris. Steve McQueen. Formula One. The Michelin Man with his rubber tube body. The yellow Shell sign. Big truck tires, hissing in rain. B. F. Goodrich.

He thought, I don't even like cars. Back in New Haven, he owned an ancient VW Bug. Clearly, his racing mind was trying to avoid an unpleasant reality—something he didn't want to face up to.

The risk.

"So we just fill the panels at the last minute, and pray?" Stern said.

"Exactly," Gordon said. "That's exactly what we do. It's a little hairy. But I think it'll work."

"And the alternative?" Stern said.

Gordon shook his head. "Block their return. Don't let your

friends come back. Get brand new glass panels down here, panels that don't have imperfections, and set up again."

"And that takes how long?"

"Two weeks."

"No," Stern said. "We can't do that. We have to go for it."

"That's right," Gordon said. "We do."

# 02:55:14

Marek and Johnston climbed the circular stairs. At the top, they met de Kere, who was looking smugly satisfied. They stood once more on the wide battlements of La Roque. Oliver was there, pacing, red-faced and angry.

"Do you smell it?" he cried, pointing off toward the field, where Arnaut's troops continued to mass.

It was now early evening; the sun was down, and Marek guessed it must be about six o'clock. But in the fading light, they saw that Arnaut's forces now had a full dozen trebuchets assembled and set out in staggered rows on the field below. After the example of the first incendiary arrow, they had moved their engines farther apart, so that any fire would not spread beyond one engine.

Beyond the trebuchets, there was a staging area, with troops huddled around smoking fires. And at the very rear, the hundreds of tents of the soldiers nestled back against the dark line of the forest.

It looked, Marek thought, perfectly ordinary. The start of a siege. He couldn't imagine what Oliver was upset about.

A distinct burning odor drifted toward them from the smoking fires. It reminded Marek of the smell that roofers made. And with good reason: it was the same substance. "I do, my Lord," Johnston said. "It is pitch."

Johnston's blank expression conveyed that he, too, did not know why Oliver was so upset. It was standard practice in siege warfare to lob burning pitch over the castle walls.

"Yes, yes," Oliver said, "it is pitch. Of course it is pitch. But that is not *all*. Do you not smell it? They are *mixing something* with the pitch."

Marek sniffed the air, thinking Oliver was almost certainly right. When burning, pure pitch had a tendency to go out. Thus pitch was usually combined with other substances— oil, tow or sulfur—to make a more robustly burning mixture.

"Yes, my Lord," Johnston said. "I smell it."

"And what is it?" Oliver said in an accusing tone.

"*Ceraunia*, I believe."

"Also called the 'thunderbolt stone'?"

"Yes, my Lord."

"And do we also employ this thunderbolt stone?"

"No, my Lord—" Johnston began.

"Ah! I thought as much."

Oliver was now nodding to de Kere, as if their suspicions were confirmed. Clearly, de Kere was behind all this.

"My Lord," Johnston said, "we have no need of the thunderbolt stone. We have better stone. We use pure *sulfure*."

"But *sulfure* is not the same." Another glance at de Kere.

"My Lord, it is. The thunderbolt stone is *pyrite kerdonienne*. When ground fine, it makes *sulfure*."

Oliver snorted. He paced. He glowered.

"And how," he said finally, "does Arnaut come to have this thunderbolt stone?"

"I cannot say," Johnston said, "but the thunderbolt stone is well known to soldiers. It is even mentioned in Pliny."

"You evade me with tricks, Magister. I speak not of Pliny. I speak of Arnaut. The man is an illiterate pig. He knows nothing of *ceraunia*, or the thunderbolt stone."

"My Lord—"

"*Unless he is aided*," Oliver said darkly. "Where are your assistants now?"

"My assistants?"

"Come, come, Magister, evade me no further."

"One is here," Johnston said, gesturing to Marek. "I am given that the second is dead, and I have no word of the third."

"And I believe," Oliver said, "that you know very well where they are. They are both working in the camp of Arnaut, even as we speak. That is how he comes to possess this arcane stone."

Marek listened to this with a growing sense of unease. Oliver had never seemed mentally stable, even in better times. Now, faced with impending attack, he was becoming openly paranoid—goaded by de Kere. Oliver seemed unpredictable, and dangerous.

"My Lord—" Johnston began.

"And further, I believe what I suspected from the first! You are the creature of Arnaut, for you have passed three days in Sainte-Mère, and the Abbot is the creature of Arnaut."

"My Lord, if you will hear—"

"*I will not!* You shall hear. I believe you work against me, that you, or your assistants, know the secret entrance to my castle, despite all your protestations, and that you plan to escape at the earliest moment—perhaps even tonight, under cover of Arnaut's attack."

Marek was carefully expressionless. That was, of course, exactly what they intended, if Kate ever found the entrance to the passage.

"Aha!" Oliver said, pointing at Marek. "You see? His jaw clenches. He knows what I say is true."

Marek started to speak, but Johnston put a restraining hand on his arm. The Professor said nothing himself, just shook his head.

"What? Will you stop his confession?"

"No, my Lord, for your surmises are not true."

Oliver glowered, paced. "Then bring me the weapons I bade you make earlier."

"My Lord, they are not ready."

"Ha!" Another nod to de Kere.

"My Lord, the grinding of the powder takes many hours."

"In many hours, it will be too late."

"My Lord, it will be in good time."

"You lie, you lie, you *lie!*" Oliver spun, stamped his foot, stared off at the siege engines. "Look to the plain. See how they make ready. Now answer me, Magister. *Where is he?*"

There was a pause. "Where is who, my Lord?"

"Arnaut! *Where is Arnaut?* His troops mass for attack. He always leads them. But now he is not there. Where is he?"

"My Lord, I cannot say. . . ."

"The witch of Eltham is there—see her, standing by the engines? You see? She watches us. The damnable woman."

Marek turned quickly to look. Claire was indeed down among the soldiers, walking with Sir Daniel at her side. Marek felt his heart beat faster, just to see her, though he was not sure why she would walk so near the siege lines. She was looking up at the walls. And suddenly she stopped abruptly. And he thought, with a kind of certainty, that she had seen him. He had an almost irresistible impulse to wave, but of course he did not. Not with Oliver snorting and puffing beside him. But he thought, I'm going to miss her when I go back.

"The Lady Claire," Oliver growled, "is a spy of Arnaut and was so from the beginning. She let his men into Castelgard. All arranged, no doubt, with that scheming Abbot. But where is the villain himself? Where is the pig Arnaut? Nowhere to be seen."

There was an awkward silence. Oliver smiled grimly.

"My Lord," Johnston began, "I understand your concer—"

"You do not!" He stamped his foot and glared at them. Then, "Both of you. Come with me."

:

The surface of the water was black and oily, and even looking down from thirty feet above, it stank. They were standing beside a circular pit, located deep in the bowels of the castle. All around them, the walls were dark and damp, barely illuminated by flickering torches.

At Oliver's signal, a soldier beside the pit started to crank an iron winch. Clattering, a thick chain began to rise from the depths of the water.

"They call this Milady's Bath," Oliver said. "It was made by François le Gros, who had a taste for these things. They say Henri de Renaud was kept here for ten years before he died. They threw live rats down to him, which he killed and ate raw. For ten years."

The water rippled, and a heavy metal cage broke the surface and began to rise, dripping, into the air. The bars were black and filthy. The stench was overpowering.

Watching it rise, Oliver said, "In Castelgard I promised you, Magister, that if you deceived me, I would kill you. You shall bathe in Milady's Bath."

He looked at them intently, his eyes wild.

"Confess now."

"My Lord, there is nothing to confess."

"Then you have nothing to fear. But hear this, Magister. If I discover that you, or your assistants, know the entrance to this castle, I shall lock you away in this place, from which you will never escape, never in your life, and I will leave you here, in darkness, to starve and rot forever."

Holding a torch in the corner, Robert de Kere allowed himself a smile.

# 02:22:13

The steps led steeply downward, into darkness. Kate went first, holding the torch. Chris followed. They went through a narrow passage, almost a tunnel, that seemed to be man-made, and then came out into a much larger chamber. This was a natural cave. Somewhere high up and off to the left, they saw the pale glimmer of natural light; there had to be a cave entrance up there.

The ground before them still sloped down. Ahead, she saw a large pool of black water and heard the rush of a river. The interior smelled strongly of a sweet-sour odor, like urine. She scrambled over the boulders until she reached the black pool. There was a little sandy margin around the edge of the water.

And in the sand, she saw a footprint.

Several footprints.

"Not recent," Chris said.

"Where's the path?" she said. Her voice echoed. Then she saw it, off to the left, a protruding section of rock wall that had been artificially cut back, making an indentation that allowed you to skirt around the pool and to pass by.

She started forward.

Caves didn't bother her. She'd been in several in Colorado and New Mexico with her rock-climbing friends. Kate followed the path, seeing footprints here and there, and pale streaks in the rock that might have been scratches from weapons.

"You know," she said, "this cave can't be all that long if people used it to carry water to the castle during a siege."

"But they didn't," Chris said. "The castle has another supply of water. They would have been bringing food, or other supplies."

"Even so. How far could they go?"

"In the fourteenth century," Chris said, "peasants didn't think anything about walking twenty miles a day, and sometimes more. Even pilgrims walked twelve or fifteen miles in a day, and those groups included women and old people."

"Oh," she said.

"This passage could be ten miles," he said. And then he added, "But I hope it's not."

Once past the protruding rock, they saw a cut passage leading away from the dark lake. The passage was about five feet high and three feet wide. But at the edge of the dark pool, a wooden boat was tied up. A small boat, like a rowboat. It thunked softly against the rocks.

Kate turned. "What do you think? Walk, or take the boat?"

"Take the boat," Chris said.

They climbed in. There were oars. She held the torch and he rowed, and they moved surprisingly fast, because there was a current. They were on the underground river.

:

Kate was worried about the time. She guessed they might have only two hours left. That meant they had to get to the castle, reunite with the Professor and Marek, and get themselves into an open space so they could call the machine—all within two hours.

She was glad for the current, for the speed with which they glided deeper into the cavern. The torch in her hand hissed and crackled. Then they heard a rustling sound, like papers ruffled in the wind. The sound grew louder. They heard a squeaking, like mice.

It was coming from somewhere deeper in the cave.

She looked at Chris questioningly.

"It's evening," Chris said, and then she began to see them—just a few at first, and then a hazy cloud, then a torrent of bats flying out of the cave, a brown river in the air above their boat. She felt a breeze from hundreds of flapping wings.

The bats continued for several minutes, and then it was silent again, except for the crackle of the torch.

They glided onward, down the dark river.

:

Her torch sputtered, and began to go out. She quickly lit one of the others that Chris had carried from the chapel. He had brought four torches, and now they had three left. Would three more torches see them to the surface again? What would they do if the final torch went out and they still had farther—perhaps miles—to go? Would they crawl forward in darkness, feeling their way along, perhaps for days? Would they ever make it, or would they die here, in darkness?

"Stop it," Chris said.

"Stop what?"

"Thinking about it."

"Thinking about what?"

Chris smiled at her. "We're doing okay. We'll make it."

She didn't ask him how he knew. But she was comforted by what he said, even though it was just bluster.

They had been passing through a twisting passageway, very low, but now the cave opened out into a huge chamber, a full-blown cave, with stalactites hanging down from the roof, in some places reaching to the ground, and even into the water. Everywhere the flickering light of the torch faded into blackness. She did, however, see a footpath along one dark shore. Apparently there was a path running the entire length of the cave.

The river was narrower, and moved faster, threading its way among the stalactites. It reminded her of a Louisiana swamp, except it was all underground. Anyway, they were making good time; she began to feel more confident. At this rate, they would cover even ten miles in a few minutes. They might make the two-hour deadline after all. In fact, they might make it easily.

The accident happened so fast, she hardly realized what had occurred. Chris said, "Kate!" and she turned in time to see a stalactite just by her ear, and her head struck the stone hard, and her torch hit it as well—and the burning cloth tip shook free from the stick it was tied to, and in a kind of ghastly slow motion, she watched it fall from her torch onto the surface of the water, joining its reflection. It sputtered, hissed and went out.

They were in total blackness.

She gasped.

She had never been in such darkness before. There was absolutely no light at all. She heard the dripping of the water, felt the slight cold breeze, the hugeness of the space around her. The boat was still moving; they were banging against stalactites, seemingly at random. She heard a grunt, the boat rocked wildly, and she heard a loud splash from the stern.

"Chris?"

She fought panic.

"Chris?" she said. "Chris, what do we do now?"

Her voice echoed.

# 01:33:00

It was now early night, the sky deepening from blue to black, the stars appearing in greater numbers. Lord Oliver, his threats and boasts finished for the moment, had gone with de Kere into the great hall to dine. From the hall, they heard shouts and carousing; Oliver's knights were drinking before the battle.

Marek walked with Johnston back to the arsenal. He glanced at his counter. It said 01:32:14. The Professor didn't ask him how much time was left, and Marek didn't volunteer. That was when he heard a whooshing sound. Men on the ramparts yelled as a huge fiery mass arced over the walls, tumbling in the air, and descended toward them in the inner courtyard.

"It's starting," the Professor said calmly.

Twenty yards away from them, the fire smashed onto the ground. Marek saw that it was a dead horse, the legs protruding stiffly from the flames. He smelled burning hair and flesh. The fat popped and sputtered.

"Jesus," Marek said.

"Dead for a long time," Johnston said, pointing to the stiff legs. "They like to fling old carcasses over the walls. We'll see worse than that before the night is over."

Soldiers ran with water to put the fire out. Johnston went back into the powder room. The fifty men were still there, grinding the powder. One of them was mixing a large, wide basin of resin and quicklime, producing a quantity of the brown goo.

Marek watched them work, and he heard another *whoosh* from outside. Something heavy thunked on the roof; all the candles in the windows shook. He heard men shouting, running onto the roof.

The Professor sighed. "They hit it on the second try," he said. "This is just what I was afraid of."

"What?"

"Arnaut knows there is an armory, and he knows roughly where it is—you can see it if you climb the hill. Arnaut knows this room will be full of powder. If he can hit it with an incendiary, he knows he'll cause great damage."

"It'll explode," Marek said, looking around at the stacked bags of powder. Although most medieval powder wouldn't explode, they had already demonstrated that Oliver's would detonate a cannon.

"Yes, it will explode," Johnston said. "And many people inside the castle will die; there will be confusion, and a huge fire left burning in the center courtyard. That means men will have to come off the walls to fight the fire. And if you take men off the walls during a siege . . ."

"Arnaut will scale."

"Immediately, yes."

Marek said, "But can Arnaut really get an incendiary into this room? These stone walls must be two feet thick."

"He won't go through the walls. The roof."

"But how . . ."

"He has cannon," the Professor said. "And iron balls. He will heat his cannonballs red-hot, then fire them over the walls, hoping to hit this arsenal. A fifty-pound ball will tear right through the roof and come down inside. When that happens, we don't want to be here." He gave a wry smile. "Where the hell is Kate?"

# 01:22:12

She was lost in infinite darkness. It was a nightmare, she thought, as she crouched in the boat, feeling it drift in the current and bump from stalactite to stalactite. Despite the cool air, she had begun to sweat. Her heart was pounding. Her breathing was shallow; she felt like she couldn't get a full breath.

She was terrified. She shifted her weight, and the boat rocked alarmingly. She put both hands out to steady it. She said, "Chris?"

She heard a splashing from far off in the darkness. Like someone swimming.

"Chris?"

From a great distance: "Yeah."

"Where are you?"

"I fell off."

He sounded so far away. Wherever Chris was, she was drifting farther and farther from him every minute. She was alone. She had to get light. Somehow, she had to get light. She began to crawl back toward the stern of the boat, groping with her hands, hoping her fingers would close on a wooden pole that meant one of the remaining torches. The boat rocked again.

*Shit.*

She paused, waiting for it to steady beneath her.

Where were the damn torches? She thought they were in the center of the boat. But she didn't feel them anywhere. She felt the oars. She felt the planking. But she didn't feel torches.

Had they fallen off the boat with Chris?

Get light. She had to get light.

She fumbled at her waist for her pouch, managed to get it open by feel, but then could not tell what was in there. There were pills . . . the canister . . . her fingers closed over a cube, like a sugar cube. It was one of the red cubes! She took it out and put it between her teeth.

Then she took her dagger and cut the sleeve of her tunic, tearing off a section about a foot long. She wrapped this cloth around the red cube and pulled the string.

She waited.

Nothing happened.

Maybe the cube had gotten soaked when she went in the river at the mill. The cubes were supposed to be waterproof, but she'd been in the river a long time. Or maybe this one was just defective. She ought to try another one. She had one more. She had started to reach into her pouch again, when the cloth in her hand burst into flame.

"Yow!" she cried. Her hand was burning. She hadn't thought this through very well. But she refused to drop it; gritting her teeth, she held it high above her head, and immediately she saw the torches to her right, pushed up against the side of the boat. She grabbed one torch, held it against the burning rag, and the torch caught fire. She dropped the rag in the river and plunged her hand under the water.

Her hand really hurt. She looked at it closely; the skin was red, but otherwise did not appear too bad. She ignored the pain. She'd deal with it later.

She swung the torch. She was surrounded by pale white stalactites hanging down into the river. It was like being in the half-open mouth of some gigantic fish, moving between its teeth. The boat banged from one to another.

"Chris?"

Far away: "Yeah."

"Can you see my light?"

"Yeah."

She grabbed a stalactite with her hand, feeling the slippery, chalky texture. She managed to stop the boat. But she couldn't row back to Chris, because she had to hold the torch.

"Can you get to where I am?"

"Yeah."

She heard him splashing somewhere in the darkness behind.

:

Once he was back in the boat, soaked but smiling, she let go of the stalactite and they began moving again with the current. They spent several more minutes in the stalactite forest, and then they came out into an open chamber again. The current moved faster. From somewhere ahead, they heard a roaring sound. It sounded like a waterfall.

But then she saw something that made her heart leap. It was a large stone block by the side of the river. The block was worn around the sides from rope chafing. It had clearly been used to tie up boats.

"Chris. . . ."

"I see it."

She saw what looked like a worn path beyond the block, but she couldn't be sure. Chris rowed to the side, and they tied up the boat and got out. There was a definite path, leading to a tunnel with smooth, artificially cut walls. They started down the tunnel. She held the torch in front of her.

She caught her breath.

"Chris? There's a step."

"What?"

"A step. Cut in the rock. About fifty feet ahead." She moved faster. They both moved faster. "In fact," she said, raising the torch higher, "there's more than a step. There's a whole staircase."

By the flickering torchlight, they saw more than a dozen steps, rising at a steep angle upward, without a railing, until they ended in a stone ceiling—a trapdoor fitted with an iron handle.

She handed Chris the torch, then scrambled up the stairs. She pulled at the ring, but nothing happened. She pushed at it, putting her shoulder into it.

She managed to raise the stone an inch.

She saw yellow light, so bright that it made her squint. She heard the roar of a nearby fire, and the laughter of men's voices. Then she couldn't hold the weight any longer, and the stone came back down again.

Chris was already coming up the stairs toward her. "Earpieces on," he said, tapping his ear.

"You think?"

"We have to risk it."

She tapped her ear, heard the crackle. She heard Chris's breathing, amplified as he stood beside her on the narrow ledge.

She said, "I'll go first." She reached into her pocket, took out the marker, and gave it to him. He frowned. She said, "Just in case. We don't know what's on the other side."

"Okay." Chris set the torch down, then leaned his shoulder against the trapdoor. The stone crunched, moved upward. She scrambled through the opening, then helped him quietly swing the door all the way open and lay it on the floor.

They had made it.

They were inside La Roque.

# 01:13:52

Robert Doniger spun, holding the microphone in his hand. "Ask yourself," he said to the empty, darkened auditorium. "What is the dominant mode of experience at the end of the twentieth century? How do people see things, and how do they expect to see things? The answer is simple. In every field, from business to politics to marketing to education, the dominant mode has become entertainment."

Across from the narrow stage, three padded booths had

been set up, all in a row. Each booth contained a desk and chair, a notepad, and a glass of water. Each booth was open at the front, so that a person in the booth could see only Doniger, and not the people in the other booths.

This was the way Doniger gave his presentations. It was a trick he had learned from old psychological studies of peer pressure. Each person knew there were people in the other booths, but he couldn't see or hear them. And it put tremendous pressure on the listeners. Because they had to worry what the other people were going to do. They had to worry if the other people were going to invest.

He walked back and forth across the stage. "Today, everybody expects to be entertained, and they expect to be entertained all the time. Business meetings must be snappy, with bullet lists and animated graphics, so executives aren't bored. Malls and stores must be engaging, so they amuse as well as sell us. Politicians must have pleasing video personalities and tell us only what we want to hear. Schools must be careful not to bore young minds that expect the speed and complexity of television. Students must be amused—everyone must be amused, or they will switch: switch brands, switch channels, switch parties, switch loyalties. This is the intellectual reality of Western society at the end of the century.

"In other centuries, human beings wanted to be saved, or improved, or freed, or educated. But in our century, they want to be entertained. The great fear is not of disease or death, but of boredom. A sense of time on our hands, a sense of nothing to do. A sense that we are not amused.

"But where will this mania for entertainment end? What will people do when they get tired of television? When they get tired of movies? We already know the answer—they go into participatory activities: sports, theme parks, amusement rides, roller coasters. Structured fun, planned thrills. And what will they do when they tire of theme parks and planned thrills? Sooner or later, the artifice becomes too noticeable. They begin to realize that an amusement park is really a kind of jail, in which you pay to be an inmate.

"This artifice will drive them to seek authenticity. *Authenticity* will be the buzzword of the twenty-first century. And what is authentic? Anything that is not devised and structured to make a profit. Anything that is not controlled by corporations. Anything that exists for its own sake, that assumes its own shape. But of course, nothing in the modern world is allowed to assume its own shape. The modern world is the corporate equivalent of a formal garden, where everything is planted and arranged for effect. Where nothing is untouched, where nothing is authentic.

"Where, then, will people turn for the rare and desirable experience of authenticity? They will turn to the past.

"The past is unarguably authentic. The past is a world that already existed before Disney and Murdoch and Nissan and Sony and IBM and all the other shapers of the present day. The past was here before they were. The past rose and fell without their intrusion and molding and selling. The past is real. It's authentic. *And this will make the past unbelievably attractive.* That's why I say that the future is the past. The past is the only real alternative to— Yes? Diane, what is it?" He turned as she walked into the room.

"There's a problem in the transit room. It seems the explosion damaged the remaining water shields. Gordon's run a computer simulation that shows three shields breaking when they're filled with water."

"Diane, this is a goddamn no-brainer," Doniger said, tugging at his tie. "Are you telling me they may come back unshielded?"

"Yes."

"Well, we can't risk that."

"It's not that simple. . . ."

"Yes, it is," Doniger said. "We can't take the risk. I'd rather they didn't come back at all than to have them come back seriously damaged."

"But—"

"But what? If Gordon has this computer projection, why is he going forward?"

"He doesn't believe the projection. He says it's quick and dirty, and he thinks the transit will go fine."

"We can't risk it," Doniger said, shaking his head. "They can't come back without shields. Period."

She paused, bit her lip. "Bob, I think the—"

"Hey," he said. "We got short-term-memory loss here? You were the one who wouldn't let Stern go back, because of the risk of transcription errors. Now you want to let the whole goddamn bunch come back unshielded? No, Diane."

"Okay," she said, obviously reluctant. "I'll go and talk to—"

"No. No talk. Kill it. Pull the power plug if you have to. But don't let those people come back. I'm right about this, and you know it."

:

In the control room, Gordon said, "He said *what*?"

"They can't come back. Absolutely not. Bob was firm."

"But they have to come back," David Stern said. "You have to let them."

"No, I don't," Kramer said.

"But—"

"John," Kramer said, turning to Gordon. "Has he seen Wellsey? Have you shown him Wellsey?"

"Who's Wellsey?"

"Wellsey's a cat," Gordon said.

"Wellsey's split," Kramer said to Stern. "He was one of the first test animals that we sent back. Before we knew that you had to use water shields in a transit. And he's very badly split."

"Split?"

Kramer turned to Gordon. "Haven't you told him anything?"

"Of course I told him," Gordon said. He said to Stern, "Split means he had very severe transcription errors." He turned back to Kramer. "But that happened years ago, Diane, back when we also had problems with the computers as well—"

"Show him," Kramer said. "And then see if he's still so

eager to bring his friends back. But the point of the conversation is, Bob's made his decision on this, and the answer is no. If we don't have secure shields, nobody can come back. Under any circumstances."

At the consoles, one of the technicians said, "We've got a field buck."

⋮

They crowded around the monitor, looking at the undulating wave and the tiny ripples in the surface.

"How long before they come back?" Stern said.

"Judging from this signal, about an hour."

"Can you tell how many?" Gordon said.

"Not yet, but . . . it's more than one. Maybe four, or five."

"That's all of them," Gordon said. "They must have gotten the Professor, and they're all coming home. They've done what we asked them to do, and they're coming back."

He turned to Kramer.

"Sorry," she said. "If there're no shields, nobody comes back. That's final."

# 01:01:52

Crouched beside the trapdoor, Kate got slowly to her feet. She was standing in a narrow space, no more than four feet wide, with high stone walls on either side. Firelight was coming in from an opening to her left. By its yellow light, she saw a door directly ahead of her. Behind her was a set of stairs, going steeply upward to the top of the chamber, some thirty feet above.

But where was she?

Chris peered over the edge of the trapdoor, and pointed to the firelight. He whispered, "I think we know why they never found the door to this passage."

"Why?"

"It's behind the fireplace."

"Behind the fireplace?" she whispered. And then she realized he was right. This narrow space was one of the secret passages of La Roque: behind the fireplace of the great hall.

Kate moved forward cautiously, past the wall to her left—and found herself staring out from the back wall of the fireplace in the great hall. The fireplace was nine feet high. Through the leaping flames, she saw Oliver's high table, where his knights were sitting and eating, their backs to her. She could not be more than fifteen feet from them.

She whispered, "You're right. It's behind the fireplace."

She looked back to Chris, then beckoned him to come forward. She was about to continue to the door directly ahead when Sir Guy glanced back at the fire as he tossed a chicken wing into the flames. He turned back to the table, resumed eating.

She thought, *Get out of here*.

But it was too late. Guy's shoulders twitched; he was already turning back again. He saw her clearly, his eyes met hers, and he shouted, "My Lord!" He pushed back from the table and drew his sword.

Kate ran to the door, tugged at it, but it was locked, or stuck shut. She couldn't open it. She turned back to the narrow stairs behind her. She saw Sir Guy standing on the other side of the flames, hesitating. He looked at her again, and plunged through the fire toward her. She saw Chris coming through the trapdoor and said, "Down!" He ducked down as she scrambled up the stairs.

Sir Guy swung at her feet, narrowly missing her, his sword clanging off the stone. He cursed her, then looked down at the opening to the passage below. Apparently he didn't see Chris, because immediately afterward she heard him coming up the stairs behind her.

She had no weapon; she had nothing.

She ran.

∶

At the top of the stairs, thirty feet above the ground, was a narrow platform, and when she reached it, she felt a thicket of cobwebs clinging to her face. She brushed them away impatiently. The platform could not have been more than two feet square. It was precarious, but she was a climber and it didn't bother her.

But it bothered Sir Guy. He was moving very slowly up the stairs toward her, pressing his shoulder against the wall, keeping as far from the edge of the stairs as he could, clutching at tiny handholds in the mortar of the wall. He had a desperate look and he was breathing hard. So, the valiant knight was afraid of heights. But not afraid enough to stop, she saw. If anything, his discomfort seemed to make him angrier. He glared at her with murderous intent.

The platform faced a rectangular wooden door, fitted with a round view hole the size of a quarter. The stairs had clearly been built to lead to this hole, allowing an observer to look down on the great hall and see everything that occurred there. Kate pushed at the door, leaning her weight against it, but instead of opening, the entire rectangle fell through, dropping onto the floor of the great hall below, and she half-fell through after it.

She was inside the great hall.

She was up high, among the heavy wooden beams of the open ceiling. She looked down at the tables thirty feet below her. Directly ahead was the enormous central rafter, running the length of the hall. This beam was crisscrossed with horizontal rafters every five feet, which ran out to the walls on both sides. All the rafters were elaborately carved, and crossbraced at intervals.

Without hesitation, Kate stepped out onto the central beam. Everyone below was looking up; they gasped when they saw her, pointed upward. She heard Oliver cry loudly, "Saint George and damnation! The assistant! We are betrayed! The Magister!"

He pounded the table, and stood, glaring up at her.

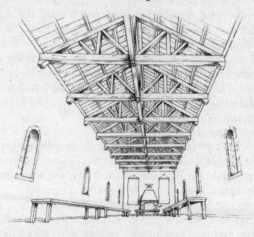

She said, "Chris. Find the Professor."

She heard a crackle. "—kay."

"Did you hear me? Chris."

Just a static crackle.

Kate moved quickly down the center rafter. Despite the height above the floor, she felt perfectly comfortable. The beam was a foot wide. Nothing to it. Hearing another gasp from the people below, she glanced back and saw Sir Guy step out on the center beam. He seemed frightened, but the presence of an audience emboldened him. Either that or he was unwilling to show fear at so public a moment. Guy took a hesitant step, found his balance, and came directly for her, moving rapidly. He swung the sword loosely in his hand. He reached the first vertical brace, took a breath, and, holding on to the upright post, maneuvered his body around it. He continued on down the center beam.

Kate backed away, realizing that this center beam was too wide, too easy for him. She walked laterally along a horizontal rafter, heading toward the side wall. This horizontal rafter was only six inches wide; he would have trouble. She clambered around a difficult cross-braced section, then continued on.

Only then did she realize her mistake.

Generally, open medieval ceilings had a structural detail where they met the wall—another brace, a decorative beam, some sort of rafter that she could move along. But this ceiling reflected the French style: the beam ran straight into the side wall, where it fitted into a notch some four feet below the line of the roof. There was no wall detail at all. She remembered now that she had stood in the ruins of La Roque and had seen those notches. What was she thinking of?

She was trapped on the beam.

She couldn't go farther out, because the beam ended at the wall. She couldn't go back to the center, because Guy was there, waiting for her. And she couldn't go to the next parallel rafter, because it was five feet away, very far to jump.

Not impossible, but far. Especially without a safety.

Looking back, she saw Sir Guy coming out along the beam toward her, balancing cautiously, swinging his sword lightly in his hand. He smiled grimly as he came forward. He knew he had caught her.

She had no choice now. She looked at the next beam, five feet away. She had to do it. The problem was to get enough height. She had to jump up if she hoped to make it across.

Guy was working his way around the cross-beam bracing. He was only seconds away from her now. She crouched on the beam, took a breath, tensed her muscles—and kicked hard with her legs, sending her body flying out into open space.

:

Chris came up through the stone trapdoor. He looked through the fire and saw that everybody in the room was staring up at the ceiling. He knew Kate was up there, but there was nothing he could do for her. He went directly to the side door and tried to open it. When it didn't budge, he slammed his full weight against it, felt it give an inch. He shoved again; the door creaked, then swung wide.

He stepped out into the inner courtyard of La Roque. Soldiers were running everywhere. A fire had broken out in one of the hoardings, the wooden galleries that ran along the top of the walls. Something was burning like a bonfire in the

center of the courtyard itself. Amid the chaos, no one paid
any attention to him.

He said, "André. Are you there?"

A static crackle. Nothing.

And then: "Yes." It was André's voice.

"André? Where are you?"

"With the Professor."

"Where?" Chris said.

"The arsenal."

"Where is that?"

# 00:59:20

There were two dozen animals in cages in the laboratory
storeroom, mostly cats, but also some guinea pigs and mice.
The room smelled of fur and feces. Gordon led him down the
aisle, saying, "We keep the split ones isolated from the
others. We have to."

Stern saw three cages along the back wall. The bars of
these cages were thick. Gordon led him to one, where he saw
a small, curled-up bundle of fur. It was a sleeping cat, a Per-
sian, pale gray in color.

"This is Wellsey," Gordon said, nodding.

The cat seemed entirely normal. It breathed slowly, gently,
as it slept. He could see half the face above the curve of the
fur. The paws were dark. Stern leaned closer, but Gordon put
his hand on his chest. "Not too close," he said.

Gordon reached for a stick, ran it along the bars of the cage.

The cat's eye opened. Not slowly and lazily—it opened
wide, instantly alert. The cat did not move, did not stretch.
Only the eye moved.

Gordon ran the stick along the bars a second time.

With a furious hiss, the cat flung itself against the bars, mouth wide, teeth bared. It banged against the bars, stepped back, and attacked again—and again, relentlessly, without pause, hissing, snarling.

Stern stared in horror.

The animal's face was hideously distorted. One side appeared normal, but the other side was distinctly lower, the eye, the nostril, everything lower, with a line down the center of the face, dividing the halves. That's why they called it "split," he thought.

But worse was the far side of the face, which he didn't see at first, with the cat lunging and banging against the bars, but now he could see that back on the side of the head, behind the distorted ear, there was a third eye, smaller and only partially formed. And beneath that eye was a patch of nose flesh, and then a protruding bit of jaw that stuck out like a tumor from the side of the face. A curve of white teeth poked out from the fur, though there was no mouth.

Transcription errors. He now understood what that meant.

The cat banged again and again; its face was starting to bleed with the repeated impacts. Gordon said, "He'll do that until we leave."

"Then we better leave," Stern said.

They walked back in silence for a while. Then Gordon said, "It's not just what you can see. There are mental changes, too. That was the first noticeable change, in the person who was split."

"This is the person you were telling me about? The one who stayed back?"

"Yes," Gordon said. "Deckard. Rob Deckard. He was one of our marines. Long before we saw physical changes in his body, there were mental changes. But we only understood later that transcription errors were the cause."

"What kind of mental changes?"

"Originally, Rob was a cheerful guy, very good athlete, extremely gifted with languages. He would sit around having a beer with somebody foreign, and by the end of the beer he'd have started to pick up the language. You know, a phrase here, a sentence there. He'd just start speaking. Always with a perfect accent. After a few weeks, he could speak like a native. The marines spotted it first, and had sent him to one of their language schools. But as time went by, and Rob accumulated more damage, he wasn't so cheerful anymore. He turned mean," Gordon said. "Really mean."

"Yes?"

"He beat the hell out of the gate guard here, because the guard took too long checking his ID. And he practically killed a guy in an Albuquerque bar. That was when we started to realize that Deckard had permanent damage to his brain, and it wasn't going to get better, that if anything, it would get worse."

:

Back in the control room, they found Kramer hunched over the monitor, staring at the screen, which showed the field fluctuations. They were coming more strongly now. And the technicians were saying that at least three were coming back, and maybe four or five. From her expression, it was clear Kramer was torn; she wanted to see them all come back.

"I still think the computer is wrong, and the panels will hold," Gordon said. "We certainly can fill the tanks now and see if they hold."

Kramer nodded. "Yes, we can do that. But even if they fill without breaking, we can't be certain they won't blow out later, in the middle of the transit. And that would be a disaster."

Stern shifted in his seat. He felt suddenly uneasy. Something was nagging at him, tickling the back of his mind. When Kramer said "blow out," he once more saw automobiles in his mind—the same succession of images, all over again. Car races. Huge truck tires. Michelin Man. A big nail in the road, and a tire driving over it.

*Blowout.*

The water tanks would blow out. The tires would blow out. What was it about blowouts?

"To pull this off," Kramer said, "we somehow need to strengthen the tanks."

"Yes, but we've been over that," Gordon said. "There's just no way to do it."

Stern sighed. "How much time left?"

The technician said, "Fifty-one minutes, and counting."

# 00:54:00

To Kate's astonishment, she heard applause from the floor below. She had made the jump; she swung back and forth, dangling beneath the beam. And down on the floor, they were applauding, as if this were a circus act.

She quickly kicked her legs up and clambered onto the beam.

On the rafter behind her, Guy Malegant was hurrying back to the centerline beam. He clearly intended to try to block her return from her present rafter.

She ran down the beam, back to the center of the ceiling. She was more agile than Guy, and she arrived at the wide central rafter well before he did. She had a moment to collect herself, to decide what to do.

What *was* she going to do?

She was standing in the middle of the open roof, holding on to a thick vertical strut, about twice the diameter of a telephone pole. The strut had supporting braces that angled out diagonally on both sides, starting midway up the shaft and then connecting to the roof. These braces were so low that if Sir Guy intended to get to her, he would have to crouch down as he made his way around the strut.

Kate crouched down now, seeing what it felt like to move around under the brace. It was awkward, and it would be slow.

She got to her feet again. As she did so, her hand brushed her dagger. She'd forgotten she had it. She drew it out now, held it in front of her.

Guy saw her, and laughed. His laughter was picked up by the watching crowd on the floor below. Guy shouted something down to them, which made them laugh all the harder.

She watched him come toward her, and she backed away. She was allowing him room to move around the vertical strut. She tried to look terrified—it wasn't difficult—and she cowered, her knife trembling in her hand.

It's all going to be timing, she thought.

Sir Guy paused on the far side of the strut, watching her for a moment. Then he crouched down and started to make his way around the strut. His hand was wrapped around the wood, the sword in his right hand temporarily pressed against the strut.

She ran forward and stabbed his hand with the dagger, pinning it to the strut. Then she swung around to the opposite side of the strut and kicked his feet off the central beam. Guy fell into space, dangling from his pinned hand. He clenched his teeth but didn't make a sound. Jesus, these guys were tough!

Still clutching his sword, he tried to get back up on the beam. But by then she had swung back to her original position, on the other side of the beam. His eyes met hers.

He knew what she was going to do.

"Rot in hell," he snarled.

"You first," she said.

She pulled her dagger free from the wood. Guy fell silently to the ground below, his body growing smaller. Halfway down, he struck a pole from which a banner hung; his body caught on the wrought-iron point, and for a moment he hung there; then the pole snapped and he slammed onto a table, sending crockery flying. The guests jumped back. Guy lay among the broken crockery. He didn't move.

Oliver was pointing up at Kate and shouting, "Kill him! Kill him!" The cry was taken up around the room. Archers ran for weapons.

Oliver did not wait; in a fury, he stomped out of the hall, taking several soldiers with him.

She heard maids in waiting, young children, everyone, chanting, "Kill him!" and she sprinted along the center beam, going for the wall at the far end of the great hall. Arrows whooshed past her, thunked into the wood. But they were too late; she could see that there was a second door in the other wall, matching the first, and she hit it hard, knocking it open, and crawled out of the hall, into darkness.

It was a very tight space. She banged her head against the ceiling, and she realized that this was the north end of the great hall, which meant it was freestanding and did not abut the castle wall. Therefore . . .

She pushed upward, at the roof. A section gave way. She stepped out onto the roof, and from there she climbed easily up onto the ramparts of the inner wall.

From here, she could see the siege was fully under way. Volleys of fiery arrows hissed overhead in smooth arcs, then descended to the courtyard below. Archers on the battlements returned the fire. Cannon on the battlements were being loaded with metal arrows, with de Kere striding back and forth, barking instructions. De Kere didn't notice her.

She turned away, pressed her ear and said, "Chris?"

De Kere spun, his hand clapped over his ear. Suddenly he was turning, looking everywhere, along the length of the battlements and down into the courtyard.

*It was de Kere.*

And then de Kere saw her. He recognized her immediately.

Kate ran.

.
.

Chris said, "Kate? I'm down here." Flaming arrows were slashing down all over the courtyard. He waved to her up on the wall, but he was not sure she could see him in the darkness.

She said, "It's—" but the rest was lost in static. By then he had turned away, watching Oliver and four soldiers cross the courtyard, and go into a square building that he assumed was the arsenal.

Chris at once began to follow, when a flaming ball landed at his feet, bounced, and rolled to a stop. Through the flames he could see that it was a human head, eyes open, lips drawn back. The flesh burned, the fat popping. A passing soldier kicked it away like a soccer ball.

One of the arrows raining down on the courtyard brushed past his shoulder and left behind a streak of flame on his sleeve. He could smell the pitch and feel the heat on his arm and face. Chris threw himself onto the ground, but the fire did not go out. It seemed to be smoldering; the heat became worse. He got to his knees and, using his dagger, cut his doublet open. He shrugged out of the burning coat and threw it aside. The back of his hand was still aflame, from tiny drops of pitch. He rubbed his hand in the dust of the courtyard.

The fire at last went out.

Standing again, he said, "André? I'm coming." But there was no answer. Alarmed, he jumped to his feet, just in time to see Oliver emerge from the arsenal, leading the Professor and Marek away, heading to a far door in the castle wall. The soldiers pushed them forward at swordpoint. Chris didn't like the look of it. He had the uneasy sense that Oliver was going to kill them.

"Kate."

"Yes, Chris."

"I see them."

"Where?"

"Going into that corner door."

He started to follow, realized he needed a weapon. Just a few feet away, a burning arrow struck a soldier in the back, knocking him face down on the ground. Chris bent over, took the man's sword, then stood again and turned to go.

*"Chris."*

A man's voice, in his earpiece. An unfamiliar voice that he didn't recognize. Chris looked around, but saw only running soldiers, flaming arrows whizzing through the air, a burning courtyard.

*"Chris."* The voice was soft. "Over here."

Through the flames he saw a dark figure standing motionless as a statue, staring at him across the courtyard. This dark figure ignored the fighting that swirled around him. He stared fixedly at Chris. It was Robert de Kere.

"Chris. Do you know what I want?" de Kere said.

Chris didn't answer him. Nervously, he hefted the sword in his hand, feeling the weight. De Kere just watched him. He chuckled softly. "Are you going to fight me, Chris?"

And then de Kere started walking toward him.

Chris took a breath, not certain whether to stay or run. And suddenly a door behind the great hall burst open and a knight came out, in full armor except for his helmet, bellowing, "For God and the Archpriest Arnaut!" He recognized the handsome knight, Raimondo. Dozens of soldiers in green and black were pouring out into the courtyard, engaging Oliver's troops in a pitched battle.

De Kere was still stalking him, but now he paused, uncertain about this new development. Suddenly Arnaut grabbed Chris by the throat, holding his sword high. Arnaut pulled him close, shouting, "Oliver! Where is *Oliver*!"

Chris pointed to the far door.

"Show me!"

He went with Arnaut across the courtyard, through the door. Following stairs spiraling downward, they came to a series of underground chambers. They were large and gloomy, with high curved ceilings.

Arnaut pushed ahead, panting, red-faced with fury. Chris hurried to keep up with him. They passed through a second chamber, empty like the first. But now Chris heard voices up ahead. One of them sounded like the Professor's.

# 00:36:02

On the control room monitors, the computer-generated undulating field had begun to show spikes. Biting her lip, Kramer watched the spikes grow in higher and wider. She drummed her fingers on the table. Finally, she said, "Okay. Let's fill the tanks at least. Let's see how they do."

"Good," Gordon said, looking relieved. He picked up the radio, began to give orders to the technicians down in the transit room.

On the video monitors, Stern watched as heavy hoses were dragged over to the first of the empty shield tanks. Men climbed up ladders and adjusted the nozzles. "I think this is best," Gordon said. "At least we'll—"

Stern jumped to his feet. "No," he said. "Don't do it."

"What?"

"Don't fill the tanks."

Kramer stared at him. "Why? What can—"

"Don't do it!" Stern said. He was shouting in the small control room. On the screen, technicians were holding water nozzles above the fill aperture. "Tell them to stop! No water whatever in the tank! Not a drop!"

Gordon gave an order on the radio. The technicians looked up in surprise, but they stopped their work, lowered the hoses back to the floor.

"David," Gordon said gently. "I think we have to—"

"No," Stern said. "We don't fill the tanks."

"Why not?"

"Because it'll screw up the glue."

"The glue?"

"Yes," he said. "I know how to strengthen the tanks."

Kramer said, "You do? How?"

Gordon turned to the technicians. "How much time?"

"Thirty-five minutes."

He turned back to Stern. "There's just thirty-five minutes, David. There isn't time to do anything now."

"Yes there is," Stern said. "There's still enough time. If we go like hell."

# 00:33:09

Kate came into the central courtyard of La Roque, to the place where she had last seen Chris. But Chris was gone.

"Chris?"

She heard no answer in her earpiece.

And he had the ceramic, she thought.

All around her in the courtyard lay burning bodies. She ran from one to the next, looking to see if one of them was Chris.

She saw Raimondo, who gave her a little nod and a wave— and then he shuddered. For a moment she thought it was the heat waves from the flames, but then she saw Raimondo turn, bleeding from his side. There was a man standing behind him, hacking repeatedly with his sword, cutting Raimondo at the arm, shoulder, torso, leg. Every cut was deep enough to wound, but not to kill. Raimondo staggered backward, bleeding freely. The man advanced, still hacking. Raimondo fell to his knees. The man stood over Raimondo, cutting again and again. Raimondo fell backward, and now the man was slashing Raimondo's face, cutting diagonally across lips and nose, sending bits of flesh flying. The attacker's face was hidden by flames, but she heard him say, "Bastard, bastard,

bastard," with each blow. She realized he was speaking English. And then she knew who the man was.

The attacker was de Kere.

:

Chris followed Arnaut deeper into the dungeon. They heard voices echoing somewhere up ahead. Arnaut moved more cautiously now, staying closer to the walls. At last they could see into the next chamber, which was dominated by a large pit in the ground. Above the pit, a heavy metal cage hung from a chain. The Professor was standing inside the bars, his face expressionless as the cage was lowered by two soldiers who turned a winch crank. Marek had been pushed against the far wall, his hands tied. Two soldiers stood near him.

Lord Oliver stood at the edge of the pit, smiling as the cage descended. He drank from a gold cup, wiped his chin. "I made you my promise, Magister," he said, "and I will keep it." To the soldiers at the winch he said, "Slower, slower."

Staring at Oliver, Arnaut growled like an angry dog, and drew his sword. He turned back to Chris and whispered, "I shall take Oliver. You may have the others."

Chris thought: The others? There were four soldiers in the room. But he had no time to protest, for with a scream of fury, Arnaut was running forward, shouting, "Oliverrrrr!"

Lord Oliver turned, still holding his goblet. With a sneer of disdain, he said, "So. The pig approaches." He threw his cup aside and drew his sword. In a moment the battle was joined.

Chris was now running toward the soldiers at the winch, not quite sure what he would do; the soldiers beside Marek had raised their swords. Oliver and Arnaut fought bitterly, swords clanging, cursing each other between blows.

Everything was happening fast now. Marek tripped one of the soldiers near him, and stabbed him with a knife so small Chris couldn't see it. The other soldier turned back to face Marek, and Marek kicked him hard, so that he staggered back against the winch, knocking the men away.

Unattended, the winch began to clank down more rapidly. There was a ratchet mechanism of some kind, so it turned noisily, but it was clearly moving faster than before. Chris saw the Professor's cage descend below ground level, disappearing into the pit.

By then Chris had reached the first of the soldiers, whose back was to him. The man started to turn and Chris swung, badly wounding him. He swung again; the man fell.

Now there were only two soldiers. Marek, his wrists still tied, was backing away from one, ducking the hissing blade. The second soldier stood by the winch. He had his sword out and was ready to fight. Chris swung; the man parried easily. Then Marek, backing in a circle, banged against the soldier, who turned momentarily. Marek shouted, "Now!" and Chris stabbed with the sword. The man collapsed.

The winch was still turning. Chris grabbed it, then jumped away as the fourth soldier's sword came down with a clang. The cage sank lower. Chris backed away. Marek was holding his bound wrists out to Chris; but Chris was not sure he could control the sword. Marek was shouting, "Do it!" so Chris swung; the rope snapped; and then the fourth soldier was on him. The soldier fought with the fury of a man trapped; Chris was cut on the forearm as he backed away. He realized he was in trouble, when suddenly his attacker looked down in horror, the bloody point of a sword protruding from his abdomen. The soldier toppled, and Chris saw Marek holding the blade.

Chris ran for the winch. He grabbed the crank and managed to stop the descent. Now he could see that the cage was deep in the oily water; the Professor's head was barely above the surface. Another turn of the crank and he would have been submerged.

Marek came over, and together they began to crank the cage back up. Chris said, "How much time is left?"

Marek looked at his counter. "Twenty-six minutes."

Meanwhile, Arnaut and Oliver fought on; they were now in a dark corner of the dungeon, and Chris could see the sparks from their clashing swords.

The cage rose dripping into the air. The Professor smiled at Chris. "I thought you'd be in time," he said.

The black bars of the cage were slippery in Chris's hands

as he swung the cage overhead, away from the pit. Slime and black water dripped onto the dirt floor of the dungeon, leaving little pools. Chris went back to the winch; he and Marek cranked the cage down, lowering it to the floor. The Professor was soaked, but he seemed relieved to be on solid ground again. Chris went back to open the cage, but he saw that it was locked. There was a heavy iron padlock the size of a man's fist.

"Where's the key?" Chris said, turning to Marek.

"I don't know," Marek said. "I was on the ground when they put him in, I didn't see what happened."

"Professor?"

Johnston shook his head. "I'm not sure. I was looking *there*." He nodded toward the pit.

Marek clanged his sword against the lock. Sparks flew, but the padlock was solid; the sword only scratched it. "That's never going to work," Chris said. "We need the damn key, André."

André turned and looked around the dungeon. Chris said, "How much time is left?"

"Twenty-five minutes."

Shaking his head, Chris went to the nearest dead soldier, and began searching the body.

## 00:21:52

In the control room, Stern watched as the technicians dipped the pale rubber membrane into a bucket of adhesive, and then placed it, still dripping, inside the mouth of the glass shield. Then they attached a compressed-air hose and the rubber began to expand. For a moment, it was possible to see that it was a weather balloon, but then it expanded still further, the rubber spreading and thinning, becoming translucent, assuming the curving shape of the glass shield until it had reached every corner of the container. Then the technicians capped it, clicked a stopwatch, and waited while the adhesive hardened.

Stern said, "How much time?"

"Twenty-one minutes to go." Gordon pointed to the balloons. "It's homely, but it works."

Stern shook his head. "It was staring me in the face, for the last hour."

"What was?"

"Blowouts," he said. "I kept thinking, what are we trying to avoid here? And the answer is, blowouts. Just like a car, when the tires blow out. I kept thinking of car blowouts. And it seemed odd, because blowouts are so rare now. New cars hardly ever have them. Because the new tires have an inner membrane that's self-sealing." He sighed. "I kept wondering why this rare thing was on my mind, and then I realized that was the whole point: there was a way to make a membrane here, too."

"This is not self-sealing," Kramer said.

"No," Gordon said, "but it'll add thickness to the glass and spread the stress."

"Right," Stern said.

The technicians had put balloons in all the tanks, and capped them. Now they were waiting for the glue to harden. Gordon glanced at his watch. "Three more minutes."

"And then how long for each tank?"

"Six minutes. But we can do two tanks at a time."

Kramer sighed. "Eighteen minutes. Cutting it close."

"We'll make it," Gordon said. "We can always pump the water faster."

"Won't that stress the tanks more?"

"Yes. But we can do it, if we have to."

Kramer looked back at the monitor, where the field was undulating. But the peaks were clearer now. She said, "Why are the field bucks changing?"

"They're not," Gordon said without looking back.

"Yes," she said. "They are. The spikes are getting smaller."

"Smaller?"

Gordon came over to look. He frowned as he stared at the screen. There were four peaks, then three, then two. Then four again, briefly. "Remember, what you're seeing is really a probability function," he said. "Field amplitudes reflect the probability that the event will take place."

"In English?"

Gordon stared at the screen. "Something must have gone wrong back there. And whatever it is, it's changed the probability that they will return."

# 00:15:02

Chris was sweating. He grunted as he flopped the soldier's inert body onto its back, and resumed his search. He'd spent frantic minutes going through the maroon-and-gray uniforms of two of the dead soldiers, trying to find the key. The surcoats were long, and underneath that, the soldiers wore quilted shirts; all in all, a lot of cloth. Not that the key could be easily concealed; Chris knew that the cage padlock would require a key several inches long, and made of iron.

But Chris didn't find it. Not on the first soldier, and not on the second. Swearing, he got to his feet.

Across the dungeon, Arnaut was still fighting with Oliver; the clang of their swords continued ceaselessly, a steady metallic rhythm. Marek was walking along the walls, holding a torch, searching the dark corners of the dungeon. But he didn't seem to be having success, either.

Chris could almost hear the clock ticking in his head. He

looked around, wondering where a key could be hidden. Unfortunately, he realized, it could be almost anywhere: hanging on a wall, or tucked into the base of a torch holder. He went over to the winch and looked around the mechanism. And there he found it—a large iron key, at the foot of the winch. "Got it!"

Marek looked up, glanced at his wrist counter as Chris hurried over to the cage to insert the key. The key went right in, but it wouldn't turn. At first he thought the mechanism was stuck, but after thirty agonizing seconds of effort, he was forced to conclude that this was not the key, after all. Feeling helpless and angry, he flung the key to the ground. He turned to the Professor, locked behind the bars.

"I'm sorry," Chris said. "I'm really sorry."

As always, the Professor was unruffled. "I've been thinking, Chris," he said, "about exactly what happened."

"Uh-huh . . ."

"And I think Oliver had it," the Professor said. "He locked me in himself. I think he kept the key."

"Oliver?"

Across the room, Oliver continued to fight, although he was now obviously losing. Arnaut was a better swordsman, and Oliver was drunk and winded. Smiling grimly, Arnaut drove Oliver back with measured blows to the edge of the pit. There Oliver, gasping and sweating, leaned on the railing, too exhausted to continue.

Arnaut gently put the point of his sword to Oliver's neck. "Mercy," Oliver said, panting. "I beg mercy." But it was clear that he did not expect it. Arnaut slowly pressed harder with the sword. Oliver coughed.

"My Lord Arnaut," Marek said, stepping forward. "We need the key to the cage."

"Eh? Key? To the cage?"

Gasping, Oliver smiled. "I know where it lies."

Arnaut jabbed with the sword. "Tell us."

Oliver shook his head. "Never."

"If you tell us," Arnaut said, "I shall spare your life."

At this, Oliver glanced up sharply. "Certes?"

"I am no treacherous, two-faced Englishman," Arnaut said. "Give us the key, and I swear as a true gentle of France that I shall not kill you."

Panting, Oliver stared at Arnaut for several seconds. Finally he stood once again and said, "Very well." He threw away his sword, reached under his robe, and brought out a heavy iron key. Marek took it.

Oliver turned back to Arnaut. "So: I have done my part. Are you a man of your word?"

"In deed," Arnaut said, "I shall not kill you . . ." He moved forward swiftly, and clasped Oliver's knees. "I shall bathe you."

And he flipped Oliver bodily over the rail, into the pit. Oliver landed with a splash in the black water below; he came up sputtering. Cursing, he swam to the side of the pit and reached toward the rocks to get a handhold. But the rocks that lined the pit were dark with slime. Oliver's hands slipped off. He could get no purchase. He treaded water, slapping ineffectually at the surface. He looked up at Arnaut, and swore.

Arnaut said, "Do you swim well?"

"Very well, you son of a French pig."

"Good," Arnaut said. "Then your bath will take some time."

And he turned away from the pit. With a nod to Chris and Marek, he said, "I am in your debt. May God grant you mercy all your days." And then he ran quickly away to rejoin the battle. They heard his footsteps fading.

Marek unlocked the padlock, and the cage door creaked open. The Professor stepped out. He said, "Time?"

"Eleven minutes," Marek said.

They hurried out of the dungeon. Marek was hobbling, but he managed to move quickly. Behind them, they heard Oliver splashing in the water.

"Arnaut!" Oliver cried, his voice echoing from the dark stone walls. *"Arnaut!"*

# 00:09:04

The big screens at the far end of the control room showed the technicians filling the shields with water. The shields were holding up fine. But nobody in the control room was looking at the shields. Instead, they stared silently at the console monitor, watching the undulations of the shimmering, computer-generated field. During the last ten minutes, the peaks had become steadily lower, until now they had nearly vanished; when they appeared at all, they were just occasional ripples in the surface.

Still, they watched.

For a moment, the ripples seemed to grow stronger, more definite. "Is something happening?" Kramer said hopefully.

Gordon shook his head. "I don't think so. I think that's just random fluctuations."

"I thought it might be getting stronger," Kramer said.

But Stern could see it wasn't true. Gordon was right; the change was just random. The ripples on the screen remained intermittent, unstable.

"Whatever the problem is back there," Gordon said, "they still have it."

# 00:05:30

Through the flames that leapt up in the central courtyard of La Roque, Kate saw the Professor and the others come out of a far doorway. She ran to join them. They all seemed to be okay. The Professor nodded to her. They were all moving fast.

Kate said to Chris, "Do you have the ceramic?"

"Yes. I have it." He brought it out of his pocket, turned it to press the button.

"There's not enough space."

"There's space . . . ," Chris said.

"No. You need two meters on all sides, remember?"

They were surrounded by fire. "You won't find that anywhere in this courtyard," Marek said.

"That's right," the Professor said. "We have to go to the next courtyard."

Kate looked ahead. The gatehouse leading to the outer courtyard was forty yards away. But within the gatehouse, the portcullis was up. In fact, it didn't look as if the gate was guarded at all; the soldiers had all abandoned it, to fight the intruders.

"How much time?"

"Five minutes."

"Okay," the Professor said. "Let's get moving."

:

They moved at a trot through the fiery courtyard, sidestepping flames and battling soldiers. The Professor and Kate were in the lead. Marek, wincing with the pain in his leg, followed behind. And Chris, worried about Marek, brought up the rear.

Kate reached the first gate. There were no guards at all. They ran through the gate, passing beneath the spikes of the raised portcullis. They entered the middle courtyard. "Oh no," Kate said.

All of Oliver's soldiers were garrisoned in the middle court, and there seemed to be hundreds of knights and pages running back and forth, shouting to the men on the battlements, carrying weapons and provisions.

"No room here," the Professor said. "We'll have to go through the next gate. Outside the castle."

"Outside?" Kate said. "We'll never even get across this courtyard."

Marek came hobbling up, panting. He took one look at the courtyard and said, "Hoarding."

"Yes," the Professor said, nodding. He pointed up at the walls. "The hoarding."

The hoarding was the enclosed wooden passageway built along the outside rim of the walls. It was a covered fighting platform that enabled soldiers to shoot down at attacking troops. They might be able to move along the hoarding and make their way to the far side of the courtyard, and the far gatehouse.

Marek said, "Where's Chris?"

They looked back into the central courtyard.

They didn't see him anywhere.

⋮

Chris had been following Marek, thinking that perhaps he would have to carry Marek and wondering whether he could, when suddenly he was shoved to one side, slammed bodily against a wall. He heard a voice behind him say in perfect English, "Not you, pal. You stay here." And he felt the point of a sword jabbed in his back.

He turned to see Robert de Kere standing in front of him, holding his sword. De Kere grabbed him roughly by the collar, shoved him against another wall. Chris saw with alarm that they were just outside the arsenal. With the courtyard in flames, this was not the place to be.

De Kere didn't seem to care. He smiled. "In fact," he said, "none of you bastards are going anywhere."

"Why is that?" Chris said, keeping his eye on the sword.

"Because you have their marker, pal."

"No I don't."

"I can hear your transmissions, remember?" De Kere held out his hand. "Come on, give it to me."

He grabbed Chris again, and shoved him through the door. Chris stumbled into the arsenal. It was empty now, the soldiers having fled. All around him were stacked bags of gunpowder. The basins where the soldiers had been grinding still lay on the floor.

"Your fucking Professor," de Kere said, seeing the bowls. "Think you know so much. Give it to me."

Chris fumbled under his doublet, reaching for his pouch.

De Kere snapped his fingers impatiently. "Come on, come on, hurry up."

"Just a minute," Chris said.

"You guys are all the same," de Kere said. "Just like Doniger. You know what Doniger said? Don't worry, Rob, we're making new technology that will fix you up. It's always new technology that will fix you up. But he didn't make any new technology. He never intended to. He was just lying, the way he always does. My goddamn face." He touched the scar that ran down the center. "It hurts all the time. Something about the bones. It *aches*. And my insides are screwed up. Hurts."

De Kere held out his palm irritably. "Come on. You keep this up, and I'll kill you now."

Chris felt his fingers close around the canister. How far away would the gas work? Not at the distance of a sword. But there was no alternative.

Chris took a deep breath, and sprayed the gas. De Kere coughed, more irritated than surprised, and stepped forward. "You asshole," he said. "You think that's a bright idea? Real tricky. Tricky boy."

He poked at Chris with the sword, jabbing him backward. Chris backed up.

"For that, I'm going to cut you open and let you watch your guts spill out." And he swung upward, but Chris dodged it easily, and he thought, It's had some effect. He sprayed again, closer to de Kere's face, then ducked as the sword swung and struck the floor, knocking over one of the basins.

De Kere wobbled, but he was still on his feet. Chris sprayed a third time, and de Kere somehow remained standing. He swung, the blade hissing; Chris dodged it, but the blade sliced his arm above the right elbow. Blood dripped from the wound, spattering on the floor. The canister fell from his hand.

De Kere grinned. "Tricks don't work here," he said. "This is the real thing. Real sword. Watch it happen, pal."

He prepared to swing again. He was still unsteady, but growing stronger quickly. Chris ducked as the blade whined over his head and slashed into the stacked bags of powder. The air was filled with gray particles. Chris stepped back again, and this time felt his foot against a basin on the floor. He started to kick it aside, then noticed its weight beneath his foot. It wasn't one of the powder basins, it was a heavy paste. And it had a harsh smell. He recognized it immediately: it was the smell of quicklime.

Which meant the basin at his feet was filled with automatic fire.

Quickly, Chris bent over and lifted the basin in his hands.

De Kere paused.

He knew what it was.

Chris took the moment of hesitation and threw the basin directly at de Kere's face. It struck him in the chest, the brown paste spattering his face and arms and body.

De Kere snarled.

Chris needed water. Where was there water? He looked around, desperate, but he already knew the answer: there was no water in this room. He was backed into a corner now. De Kere smiled. "No water?" he said. "Too bad, tricky boy." He held his sword horizontally in front of him, and moved forward. Chris felt the stone against his back, and knew that he was finished. At least the others might get away.

He watched de Kere approach, slowly, confidently. He could smell de Kere's breath; he was close enough to spit on him.

*Spit on him.*

In the instant that he thought it, Chris spat on de Kere—not in the face, but in the chest. De Kere snorted, disgusted: the kid couldn't even spit. Wherever spittle touched the paste, it began to smoke and sputter.

De Kere looked down, horrified.

Chris spat again. And again.

The hissing was louder. There were the first sparks. In a moment, de Kere would burst into flames. Frantic, de Kere brushed at the paste with his fingers, but only spread it; now it was sizzling and crackling on his fingertips, from the moisture of his skin.

"Watch it happen, pal," Chris said.

He ran for the door. Behind him, he heard a *whump!* as de Kere burst into flame. Chris glanced back to see that the knight's entire upper body was engulfed in fire. De Kere was staring at him through the flames.

Then Chris ran. As hard and as fast as he could, he ran. Away from the arsenal.

:

At the middle gate, the others saw him running toward them. He was waving his hands. They didn't understand why. They stood in the center of the gate, waiting for him to catch up.

He was shouting, "Go, go!" and gesturing for them to move around the corner. Marek looked back, and saw flames begin to leap up through the windows of the arsenal.

"Move!" he said. He pushed the others through the gate and into the next courtyard.

Chris came running through the gate and Marek grabbed his arm, pulling him to cover, just as the arsenal exploded. A great sphere of flame rose about the wall; the entire courtyard was bathed in fiery light. Soldiers and tents and horses were knocked flat by the shock wave. There was smoke and confusion everywhere.

"Forget the hoarding," the Professor said. "Let's go." And

they ran straight across the courtyard. They could see the final gatehouse directly ahead.

# 00:02:22

In the control room, there were screams and cheers. Kramer was jumping up and down. Gordon was pounding Stern on the back. The monitor was showing field fluctuations again. Intense and powerful.

"They're coming home!" Kramer yelled.

Stern looked at the video screens, which showed the tanks in the room below. The technicians had already filled several shields with water, and the shields were holding. The remaining tanks were still being filled, though the water level was nearing the top.

"How much time?" he said.

"Two minutes twenty."

"How long to fill the tanks?"

"Two minutes ten."

Stern bit his lip. "We going to make it?"

"You bet your ass we are," Gordon said.

Stern turned back to the field fluctuations. They were growing stronger and clearer, the false colors shimmering on the spikes. The unstable mountain peak was now stable, protruding above the surface, taking form. "How many are coming back?" he said. But he already knew the answer, because the mountain peak was dividing into separate ridges.

"Three," the technician said. "Looks like three coming back."

# 00:01:44

The outermost gatehouse was closed: the heavy grill of the portcullis was down and the drawbridge had been raised. Five guards now lay sprawled on the ground, and Marek was raising the portcullis just enough so they could pass beneath it. But the drawbridge was still shut fast.

"How do we get it open?" Chris said.

Marek was looking at the chains, which ran into the gatehouse itself. "Up there," he said, pointing above. There was a winch mechanism on the second floor.

"You stay here," Marek said. "I'll do it."

"Come right back," Kate said.

"Don't worry. I will."

Hobbling up a spiral staircase, Marek came into a small stone room, narrow and bare, and dominated by the iron winch that raised the drawbridge. Here he saw an elderly man, white-haired, shaking with fear as he held an iron bar in the links of the chain. This iron bar was keeping the drawbridge closed. Marek shoved the old man aside and pulled the bar free. The chain rattled; the drawbridge began to lower. Marek watched it go down. He looked at his counter, and was startled to see that it said 00:01:19.

"André." He heard Chris in his earpiece. "Come on."

"I'm on my way."

Marek turned to go. Then he heard running feet, and realized that there were soldiers on the roof of the guardhouse, coming down to see why the drawbridge was being lowered.

If he left the room now, they would immediately stop the drawbridge from lowering any farther.

Marek knew what this meant. He had to stay longer.

⋮

On the ground floor below, Chris watched the drawbridge as it lowered, chains clanking. Through the opening, he could see dark sky and stars. Chris said, "André, come on."

"There's soldiers."

"So?"

"I have to guard the chain."

"What do you mean?" Chris said.

Marek didn't answer. Chris heard a grunt, and a scream of pain. Marek was up there, fighting. Chris watched the drawbridge continue to descend. He looked at the Professor. But the Professor's face was expressionless.

⋮

Standing by the staircase leading down from the roof, Marek held his sword high. He killed the first soldier as he came out. He killed the second one, too, kicking the bodies as they fell, keeping the floor clear. The other soldiers on the stairs paused in confusion, and he heard muttering and consternation.

The drawbridge chain still rattled. The drawbridge continued down.

"André. Come on."

Marek glanced at his counter. It said 00:01:04. Just a little more than a minute, now. Looking out the window, he saw the others had not waited until the drawbridge was entirely down; they ran to the descending edge, and jumped out onto the field beyond the castle. Now he could hardly see them in the darkness.

"André." It was Chris again. "André."

Another soldier came down the stairs, and Marek swung his sword, which clanged against the winch, spitting sparks. The man hastily backed up, shouting and pushing the others.

"André, run for it," Chris said. "You have time."

Marek knew that was true. He could just make it. If he left now, the men couldn't raise the drawbridge before he had run across it and was out on the plain with the others. He knew they were out there, waiting for him. His friends. Waiting to go back.

As he turned to go down the stairs, his glance fell on the old man, still cowering in the corner. Marek wondered what it must be like to live your entire life in this world. To live and love, constantly on the edge, with disease and starvation and death and killing. To be alive in this world.

"André. Are you coming?"

"There's no time," Marek said.

"André."

He looked out on the plain and saw successive flashes of light. They were calling the machines. Getting ready to go.

:

The machines were there. They were all standing on their platforms. Cold vapor was drifting from the bases, curling across the dark grass.

Kate said, "André, come on."

There was a short silence. Then: "I'm not leaving," Marek said. "I'm staying here."

"André. You're not thinking right."

"Yes, I am."

She said, "Are you serious?"

Kate looked at the Professor. He just nodded slowly.

"All his life, he's wanted this."

Chris put the ceramic marker in the slot at his feet.

:

Marek watched from the window of the gatehouse.

"Hey, André." It was Chris.

"See you, Chris."

"Take care of yourself."

"André." It was Kate. "I don't know what to say."

"Good-bye, Kate."

Then he heard the Professor say: "Good-bye, André."

"Good-bye," Marek said.

Through his earpiece, he heard a recorded voice say, "Stand still—eyes open—deep breath—hold it. . . . *Now!*"

On the plain, he saw a brilliant flash of blue light. Then there was another, and another, diminishing in intensity, until there was nothing more.

Doniger strode back and forth across the darkened stage. In the auditorium, the three corporate executives sat silently, watching him.

"Sooner or later," he said, "the artifice of entertainment—constant, ceaseless entertainment—will drive people to seek authenticity. *Authenticity* will be the buzzword of the twenty-first century. And what is authentic? Anything that is not controlled by corporations. Anything that is not devised and structured to make a profit. Anything that exists for its own sake, that assumes its own shape. And what is the most authentic of all? The past.

"The past is a world that already existed before Disney and Murdoch and British Telecom and Nissan and Sony and IBM and all the other shapers of the present. The past was here before they were. The past rose and fell without their intrusion and molding. The past is real. It's authentic. *And this will make the past unbelievably attractive.* Because the past is the only alternative to the corporate present.

"What will people do? They are already doing it. The fastest-growing segment of travel today is cultural tourism. People who want to visit not other places, but other times. People who want to immerse themselves in medieval walled cities, in vast Buddhist temples, Mayan pyramid cities, Egyptian necropolises. People who want to walk and be in the world of the past. The vanished world.

"And they don't want it to be fake. They don't want it to be made pretty, or cleaned up. They want it to be authentic. Who will guarantee that authenticity? Who will become the brand name of the past? ITC.

"I am about to show you," he said, "our plans for cultural tourism sites around the world. I will concentrate on one in France, but we have many others, as well. In every case, we turn over the site to the government of that country. But we own the surrounding territory, which means we will own the hotels and restaurants and shops, the entire apparatus of tourism. To say nothing of the books and films and guides and costumes and toys and all the rest. Tourists will spend ten dollars to get into the site. But they'll spend five hundred dollars in living expenses outside it. All that will be controlled by us." He smiled. "To make sure that it is executed tastefully, of course."

A graph came up behind him.

"We estimate that each site will generate in excess of two billion dollars a year, including merchandising. We estimate that total company revenues will exceed one hundred billion dollars annually by the second decade of the coming century. That is one reason for making your commitment to us.

"The other reason is more important. Under the guise of tourism, we are in effect building an intellectual brand name. Such brand names now exist for software, for example. But none exist for history. And yet history is the most powerful intellectual tool society possesses. Let us be clear. History is not a dispassionate record of dead events. Nor is it a playground for scholars to indulge their trivial disputes.

"The purpose of history is to explain the present—to say why the world around us is the way it is. History tells us what is important in our world, and how it came to be. It tells us why the things we value are the things we should value. And it tells us what is to be ignored, or discarded. That is true power—profound power. The power to define a whole society.

"The future lies in the past—in whoever controls the past. Such control has never before been possible. Now, it is. We at ITC want to assist our clients in the shaping of the world in which we all live and work and consume. And in doing so, I believe we will have your full and wholehearted support."

There was no applause, just stunned silence. That was the way it always was. It took them a while to realize what he was saying. "Thanks for your attention," Doniger said, and strode off the stage.

:

"This better be good," Doniger said. "I don't like to cut a session like that short."

"It's important," Gordon said. They were walking down the corridor, toward the machine room.

"They're back?"

"Yes. We got the shields working, and three of them are back."

"When?"

"About fifteen minutes ago."

"And?"

"They've been through a lot. One of them is pretty badly injured and will need hospitalization. The other two are okay."

"So? What's the problem?"

They went through a door.

"They want to know," Gordon said, "why they weren't told ITC's plans."

"Because it's none of their business," Doniger said.

"They risked their lives—"

"They volunteered."

"But they—"

"Oh, fuck them," Doniger said. "What is all this sudden concern? Who cares? They're a bunch of *historians*—they're all going to be out of a job, anyway, unless they work for me."

Gordon didn't answer. He was looking over Doniger's shoulder. Doniger slowly turned.

Johnston was standing there, and the girl, who now had her hair hacked short, and one of the men. They were dirty, ragged and covered in blood. They were standing by a video monitor, which showed the auditorium. The executives were now leaving the auditorium, the stage empty. But they must have heard the speech, or at least part of it.

"Well," Doniger said, suddenly smiling, "I'm very glad you are back."

"So are we," Johnston said. But he didn't smile.

No one spoke.

They just stared at him.

"Oh, fuck you people," he said. He turned to Gordon. "Why did you bring me here? Because the historians are upset? This is the future, whether they like it or not. I don't have time for this shit. I have a company to run."

But Gordon was holding a small gas cylinder in his hand. "There have been some discussions, Bob," he said. "We think someone more moderate should run the company now."

There was a hiss. Doniger smelled a sharp odor, like ether.

He awoke, hearing a loud humming, and what sounded like the scream of rending metal. He was inside the machine. He saw all of them staring at him from behind the shields. He knew not to step out, not once it had started. He said loudly, "This isn't going to work," and then the violet flash of laser light blinded him. The flashes came quickly now. He saw the transit room rise up around him as he shrank—then the hissing foam as he descended toward it—then the final shriek in his ears, and he closed his eyes, waiting for the impact.

Blackness.

He heard the chirp of birds, and he opened his eyes. The first thing he did was look up at the sky. It was clear. So it wasn't Vesuvius. He was in a primeval forest with huge trees. So it wasn't Tokyo. The twittering of the birds was pleasant, the air warm. It wasn't Tunguska.

Where the hell was he?

The machine rested at a slight angle; the forest ground sloped downward to the left. He saw light between the tree trunks, some distance away. He got out of the machine and walked down the slope. Somewhere in the distance, he heard the slow beat of a solitary drum.

He came to a break in the trees and looked down over a fortified town. It was partially obscured by the smoke of many fires, but he recognized it at once. Oh hell, he thought, it's just Castelgard. What was the big deal, forcing him to come here?

It was Gordon, of course, who was behind it. That bullshit line about how the academics were disappointed. It was Gordon. The son of a bitch had been running the technology, and now he thought he could run the company, as well. Gordon had sent him back, thinking he couldn't return.

But Doniger could return, and he would. He wasn't worried, because he carried a ceramic with him at all times. He kept it in a slot in the heel of his shoe. He pulled the shoe off, and looked at the slot. Yes, the white ceramic was there. But it was pushed deep in the slot, and it seemed to be stuck there. When he shook the shoe, it didn't drop out. He tried a twig, poking in the slot, but the twig bent.

Next he tried to pull the heel off the shoe, but he couldn't get enough leverage; the heel stayed on. What he needed was a metal tool of some kind, a wedge or a chisel. He could find one in the town, he felt sure.

He put the shoe back on, stripped off his jacket and tie, and walked down the slope. Looking at the town, he noticed some odd details. He was just above the east gate in the town wall, but the gate was wide open. And there were no soldiers along the walls. That was odd. Whatever year this was, it was obviously a time of peace—there were those times, between English invasions. But still, he'd have thought the gate would always be guarded. He looked at the fields and saw no one tending them. They seemed neglected, with large clumps of weeds.

What the hell? he thought.

He passed through the gate and walked into the town. He saw that the gate was unguarded because the soldier on guard lay dead on his back. Doniger leaned over to look at him. There were bright streaks of blood coming from around his eyes. He must have been struck on the head, he thought.

He turned to the town itself. The smoke, he now saw, was issuing from little pots that had been placed everywhere—on the ground, on walls, or on fence posts. And the town seemed to be deserted, empty in the bright, sunny day. He walked to the market, but nobody was there. He heard the sound of monks chanting; they were coming toward him. And he heard the drum.

He felt a chill.

A dozen monks, all dressed in black, rounded the corner in

a kind of procession, chanting. Half of them were stripped to the waist, lashing themselves with leather whips studded with bits of metal. Their shoulders and backs were bleeding freely.

Flagellants.

That was what they were, flagellants. Doniger gave a low moan and backed away from the monks, who continued past him in stately fashion, ignoring him. He continued to step away, farther and farther, until his back touched something wooden.

He turned and saw a wooden horse cart, but there was no horse. He saw bundles of cloth piled high on the cart. Then he saw a child's foot protruding from one of the bundles. A woman's arm from another. The buzzing of flies was very loud. A cloud of flies, swarming over the bodies.

Doniger began to shiver.

The arm had odd blackish lumps on it.

The Black Death.

He knew now what year it was. It was 1348. The year the plague first struck Castelgard and killed a third of the population. And he knew how it spread—by the bites of fleas, by touch and by air. Just breathing the air could kill you. He knew that it could kill swiftly, that people just fell over in the street. One minute you were perfectly fine. Then the coughing began, the headache. An hour later you were dead.

He had been very close to the soldier by the gate. He had been close to the man's face.

Very close.

Doniger slumped down against a wall, feeling the numbness of terror creep over him.

As he sat there, he began to cough.

# EPILOGUE

Rain slashed across the gray English landscape. The windshield wipers snicked back and forth. In the driver's seat, Edward Johnston leaned forward and squinted as he tried to see through the rain. Outside were low, dark green hills, demarcated by dark hedges, and everything blurred by the rain. The last farm had been a couple of miles back.

Johnston said, "Elsie, are you sure this is the road?"

"Absolutely," Elsie Kastner said, the map open on her lap. She traced the route with her finger. "Four miles beyond Cheatham Cross to Bishop's Vale, and one mile later, it should be up there, on the right."

She pointed to a sloping hill with scattered oak trees.

"I don't see anything," Chris said, from the back seat.

Kate said, "Is the air conditioner on? I'm hot." She was seven months pregnant, and always hot.

"Yes, it's on," Johnston said.

"All the way?"

Chris patted her knee reassuringly.

Johnston drove slowly, looking for a mileage marker at the side of the road. The rain diminished. They could see better. And then Elsie said, "There!"

On the top of the hill was a dark rectangle, with crumbling walls.

"That's it?"

"That's Eltham Castle," she said. "What's left of it."

Johnston pulled the car over to the side of the road, and cut the ignition. Elsie read from her guidebook. "First built on this site by John d'Elthaim in the eleventh century, with several later additions. Notably the ruined keep from the twelfth century, and a chapel in the English Gothic style, from the fourteenth. Unrelated to Eltham Castle in London, which is from a later period."

The rain lessened, now just scattered drops in the wind. Johnston opened the car door and got out, shrugging on his raincoat. Elsie got out on the passenger side, her documents encased in plastic. Chris ran around the car to open the door for Kate, and helped her out. They climbed over a low stone wall, and began climbing up toward the castle.

The ruin was more substantial than it had seemed from the road; high stone walls, dark with rain. There were no ceilings; the rooms were open to the sky. No one spoke as they walked through the ruins. They saw no signs, no antiquities markers, nothing at all to indicate what this place had been, or even its name. Finally Kate said, "Where is it?"

"The chapel? Over there."

Walking around a high wall, they saw the chapel, surprisingly complete, its roof rebuilt at some time in the past. The windows were merely open arches in the stone, without glass. There was no door.

Inside the chapel, the wind blew through cracks and windows. Water dripped from the ceiling. Johnston took out a large flashlight, and shone it on the walls.

Chris said, "How did you find out about this place, Elsie?"

"In the documents, of course," she said. "In the Troyes archives, there was a reference to a wealthy English brigand named Andrew d'Eltham who had paid a visit to the Monastery of Sainte-Mère in his later years. He brought his entire family from England, including his wife and grown sons. That started me searching."

"Here," Johnston said, shining his light on the floor.

They all walked over to see.

Broken tree branches and a layer of damp leaves covered the floor. Johnston was down on his hands and knees, brushing them away to expose weathered burial stones that had been set in the floor. Chris sucked in his breath when he saw the first one. It was a woman, dressed demurely in long robes, lying on her back. The carving was unmistakably the Lady Claire. Unlike many carvings, Claire was depicted with her eyes open, staring frankly at the viewer.

"Still beautiful," Kate said, standing with her back arched, her hand pressed into her side.

"Yes," Johnston said. "Still beautiful."

Now the second stone was cleared away. Lying next to Claire, they saw André Marek. He, too, had his eyes open. Marek looked older, and he had a crease on the side of his face that might have been from age, or might have been a scar.

Elsie said, "According to the documents, Andrew escorted Lady Claire back to England from France, and then married her. He didn't care about the rumors that Claire had murdered her previous husband. By all accounts he was deeply in love with his wife. They had five sons, and were inseparable all their lives.

"In his old age," Elsie said, "the old *routier* settled down to a quiet life, and doted on his grandchildren. Andrew's dying words were 'I have chosen a good life.' He was buried in the family chapel in Eltham, in June 1382."

"Thirteen eighty-two," Chris said. "He was fifty-four."

Johnston was cleaning the rest of the stone. They saw Marek's shield: a prancing English lion on a field of French lilies. Above the shield were words in French.

Elsie said, "His family motto, echoing Richard Lionheart, appeared above the coat of arms: *Mes compaingnons cui j'amoie et cui j'aim, . . . Me di, chanson.*" She paused. " 'Companions whom I loved, and still do love, . . . Tell them, my song.' "

They stared at André for a long time.

Johnston touched the stone contours of Marek's face with his fingertips. "Well," he said finally, "at least we know what happened."

"Do you think he was happy?" Chris said.

"Yes," Johnston said. But he was thinking that however much Marek loved it, it could never be his world. Not really. He must have always felt a foreigner there, a person separated from his surroundings, because he had come from somewhere else.

The wind whined. A few leaves blew, scraping across the floor. The air was damp and cold. They stood silently.

"I wonder if he thought of us," Chris said, looking at the stone face. "I wonder if he ever missed us."

"Of course he did," the Professor said. "Don't you miss him?"

Chris nodded. Kate sniffled, and blew her nose.

"I do," Johnston said.

They went back outside. They walked down the hill to the car. By now the rain had entirely stopped, but the clouds remained dark and heavy, hanging low over the distant hills.

# ACKNOWLEDGMENTS

Our understanding of the medieval period has changed dramatically in the last fifty years. Although one occasionally still hears a self-important scientist speak of the Dark Ages, modern views have long since overthrown such simplicities. An age that was once thought to be static, brutal and benighted is now understood as dynamic and swiftly changing: an age where knowledge was sought and valued; where great universities were born, and learning fostered; where technology was enthusiastically advanced; where social relations were in flux; where trade was international; where the general level of violence was often less deadly than it is today. As for the old reputation of medieval times as a dark time of parochialism, religious prejudice and mass slaughter, the record of the twentieth century must lead any thoughtful observer to conclude that we are in no way superior.

In fact, the conception of a brutal medieval period was an invention of the Renaissance, whose proponents were at pains to emphasize a new spirit, even at the expense of the facts. If a benighted medieval world has proven a durable misconception, it may be because it confirms a cherished contemporary belief—that our species always moves forward to ever better and more enlightened ways of life. This belief is utter fantasy, but it dies hard. It is especially difficult for modern people to conceive that our modern, scientific age might not be an improvement over the prescientific period.

A word about time travel. While it is true that quantum teleportation has been demonstrated in laboratories around the world, the practical application of such phenomena lies in the future. The ideas presented in this book were stimulated by the speculations of David Deutsch, Kip Thorne, Paul Nahin and Charles Bennett, among others. What appears here may amuse them, but they would not take it seriously. This is a novel: time travel rests firmly in the realm of fantasy.

But the representation of the medieval world has a more substantial basis, and for it I am indebted to the work of many scholars, some of whom are identified in the bibliography that follows. Errors are mine, not theirs.

I'm grateful as well to Catherine Kanner for the illustrations, and to Brant Gordon for the computer-generated architectural renderings.

Finally, my particular thanks to historian Bart Vranken for his invaluable insights, and for his companionship while tramping through little-known and neglected ruins of the Périgord.

# BIBLIOGRAPHY

Allmand, Christopher. *The Hundred Years War: England and France at War c. 1300–c. 1450*. Cambridge, Eng.: Cambridge University Press, 1988.

Anonymous. *Lancelot of the Lake*. Trans. Corin Corley. Oxford: Oxford University Press, 1989.

Artz, Frederick B. *The Mind of the Middle Ages: An Historical Survey, A.D. 200–1500*. Chicago: University of Chicago Press, 1980.

Ayton, Andrew. *Knights and Warhorses: Military Service and the English Aristocracy under Edward III*. Woodbridge, Eng.: Boydell Press, 1994.

Barber, Richard. *Edward, Prince of Wales and Aquitaine*. Woodbridge, Eng.: Boydell Press, 1996.

———, ed. and trans. *The Life and Campaigns of the Black Prince*. London: Folio Society, 1979.

———, and Juliet Barker. *Tournaments*. Woodbridge, Eng.: Boydell Press, 1989.

Bentley, James. *Fort Towns of France: The Bastides of the Dordogne and Aquitaine*. London: Tauris Parke, 1994.

Berry, Duc de. *The Très Riches Heures of Jean, Duke of Berry*. Ed. Jean Longnon. New York: Millard Meiss, 1969.

Black, Maggie. *The Medieval Cookbook*. British Museum Press, 1992.

Blair, Claude. *European and American Arms, c. 1100–1850*. B. T. Batsford, 1962.

Bloch, Marc. *Feudal Society*. Trans. L. A. Mayon. Chicago: University of Chicago Press, 1961.

Bradbury, Jim. *The Medieval Siege*. Woodbridge, Eng.: Boydell Press, 1997.

Burne, Alfred H. *The Crécy War*. Wordsworth edns, 1999.

Cantor, Norman F. *Inventing the Middle Ages*. Lutterworth, 1992. One of the finest intellectual histories ever written. Informative about medievalists and the period.

Chrétien de Troyes. *Cliges*. Yale University Press, 1998.

Chrétien de Troyes. *Lancelot: The Knight of the Cart*. Yale University Press, 1997.

Christine de Pizan. *The Book of the Duke of True Lovers*. Trans. Thelma S. Fenster. New York: Persea Books, 1992.

Contamine, Philippe. *War in the Middle Ages.* Trans. Michael Jones. Oxford: Blackwell, 1986.

Cosman, Madeleine P. *Fabulous Feasts: Medieval Cookery and Ceremony.* New York: George Braziller, 1995.

Curry, Anne, and Michael Hughes, eds. *Arms, Armies and Fortifications in the Hundred Years War.* Woodbridge, Eng.: Boydell Press, 1994. See particularly the chapters by Vale and Hardy.

Delbruck, Hans. *Medieval Warfare.* Trans. Walter J. Renfroe, Jr. Lincoln: University of Nebraska Press, 1991.

Duby, Georges, ed. *A History of Private Life, Vol. II: Revelations of the Medieval World.* Trans. Arnold Goldhammer. Cambridge, Mass.: Harvard University Press, 1988.

———. *France in the Middle Ages: 987–1460.* Oxford, Eng.: Blackwell, 1991.

Ferguson, Niall, ed. *Virtual History: Alternatives and Counterfactuals.* London: Papermac, 1988.

Ffoulkes, Charles. *The Armourer and His Craft: From the XIth to the XVth Century.* 1912. Reprint, London, Dover Publications, 1989.

Froissart, Jean. *Chronicles of England, France and Spain.* Trans. Thomas Johnes. London, William Smith, 1848.

———. *Froissart: Chronicles.* Trans. Geoffrey Brereton. London: Penguin, 1978. A readable translation in a single volume.

———. *Froissarts Cronycles.* Trans. Lord Berniers. Oxford, Eng.: Blackwell, 1927.

Geoffroi de Charny. *The Book of Chivalry of Geoffroi de Charny.* Trans. Richard W. Kaeuper and Elspeth Kennedy. Philadelphia: University of Pennsylvania Press, 1996.

Gies, Francis and Joseph. *Cathedral, Forge and Waterwheel: Technology and Invention in the Middle Ages.* New York: HarperCollins, 1994.

Gillmeister, Heiner. *Tennis: A Cultural History.* Leicester University Press, 1998.

Gimpel, Jean. *The Medieval Machine: The Industrial Revolution of the Middle Ages.* London: Pimlico, 1992.

Goetz, Hans-Werner. *Life in the Middle Ages.* Trans. Albert Wimmer. Notre Dame, Ind.: University of Notre Dame Press, 1993.

Goodrich, Michael E. *Violence and Miracle in the Fourteenth Century.* Chicago: University of Chicago Press, 1996.

Henisch, Bridget Ann. *Fast and Feast: Food in Medieval Society.* University Park: Pennsylvania State University Press, 1976.

Hilton, R. H. *English and French Towns in Feudal Society.* Cambridge, Eng.: Cambridge University Press, 1992.

Horn, Walter, and Ernest Born. *The Plan of St. Gall.* 3 vols. Berkeley: University of California Press, 1979.

Houston, Mary G. *Medieval Costume in England and France: The 13th, 14th and 15th Centuries.* London: Dover, 1996.

Huizinga, Johan. *The Autumn of the Middle Ages.* Trans. Rodney J. Payton and Ulrich Mammitzsch. Chicago: University of Chicago Press, 1996.

Huppert, George. *After the Black Death: A Social History of Early Modern Europe.* Bloomington: Indiana University Press, 1998.

Hyland, Ann. *The Medieval Warhorse.* Conshohocken, Pa.: Combined Books, 1994.

Johnson, Eric A., and Eric H. Monkkonen. *The Civilization of Crime: Violence in Town and Country since the Middle Ages.* Urbana: University of Illinois Press, 1996.

Kaeuper, Richard W. *War, Justice and Public Order: England and France in the Later Middle Ages.* Oxford: Oxford University Press, 1988.

Keen, Maurice. *Chivalry.* Yale University Press, 1986.

La Sale, Antoine de. *Le Petit Jehan de Saintre.* Trans. Irvine Gray. 1931. Reprint, Westport, Conn.: Hyperion, 1978.

La Tour Landry, Geoffrey de. *The Book of the Knight of La Tour Landry.* Ed. G. S. Taylor. London: John Hamilton, n.d.

LaBarge, Margaret Wade. *Gascony: England's First Colony, 1204–1453.* London: Hamish Hamilton, 1980.

Lambert, Joseph B. *Traces of the Past: Unraveling the Secrets of Archaeology Through Chemistry.* Reading, Mass.: Addison-Wesley, 1997.

Lodge, Eleanor C. *Gascony under English Rule.* Assoc. Faculty Press, 1971.

McFarlane, K. B. *The Nobility of Later Medieval England.* Oxford: Oxford University Press, 1973.

McKisack, May. *The Fourteenth Century, 1307–1399.* New York: Oxford University Press, 1991.

Mesqui, Jean. *Châteaux, Forts et Fortifications en France.* Paris: Flammarion Press, 1997.

Muir, Lynette R. *Literature and Society in Medieval France.* London, Macmillan, 1985.

Murrin, Michael. *History and Warfare in Renaissance Epic.* Chicago: University of Chicago Press, 1995.

Oman, C.W.C. *The Art of War in the Middle Ages.* Ithaca, N.Y.: Cornell University Press, 1960.

Origo, Iris. *The Merchant of Prato.* New York: Penguin, 1992.

Orser, Charles E., Jr., and Brian M. Fagan. *Historical Archaeology.* New York: HarperCollins, 1995.

Ottaway, Patrick. *Archaeology in British Towns.* Routledge, 1992.

Partington, J. R. *A History of Greek Fire and Gunpowder.* Baltimore: Johns Hopkins University Press, 1998. See especially the excellent introduction by Bert S. Hall.

Paterson, Linda M. *The World of the Troubadours: Medieval Occitan Society c. 1000–c. 1300.* Cambridge, Eng.: Cambridge University Press, 1995.

Perroy, Edouard. *The Hundred Years War.* Trans. W. B. Wells. Eyre & Spottiswoode, 1951.

Pirenne, Henri. *Medieval Cities: Their Origins and the Revival of Trade.* Princeton: Princeton University Press, 1969.